Helen and Brenda

Also by C.D. Payne

Youth in Revolt: The Journals of Nick Twisp

Revolting Youth: The Further Journals of Nick Twisp

Young and Revolting: The Continental
Journals of Nick Twisp

Revoltingly Young: The Journals of
Nick Twisp's Younger Brother

Son of Youth in Revolt: The Journals
of Scott Twisp

Invisibly Yours

Cheeky Swimsuits of 1957

Cut to the Twisp

Civic Beauties

Frisco Pigeon Mambo

Queen of America

Helen and Brenda

Two complete novels:

Helen of Pepper Pike
Brenda the Great

C.D. Payne

To: Marcel Nekvinda, Jan Pazdirek,
Vanda Ohnisková, Tamara Vánová, and
everyone at JOTA of Brno

Special thanks to my agent Winifred Golden and to Till Hack
for his editorial assistance.

"We must be prepared to begin life many times afresh."
– Gabrielle Dalzant

Helen of Pepper Pike

WINTER

January 1 – New Year's Day and we've got the weather to prove it. Sleet now and snow forecast for tonight. Horrifying result from tentative contact with bathroom scale. Gain of six pounds as zero restraint was demonstrated during the holidays. Many cookies and several fruitcakes were consumed. Eggnog was imbibed freely. Also a two-pound box of chocolates (mixed soft centers) was mysteriously devoured. No one to blame but myself as I had taken pains to conceal it in the pantry behind the canned soups (which my kids wouldn't touch with a barge pole).

Am now resolved to eat more sensibly this year. Cutting back on meat, dairy, fat, desserts, pastries, chocolate, and booze–all the food groups that make life worth living. Read an article that we are living in an era of artificial plenty compared to our primitive ancestors. Hence our tendency to overstuff ourselves–evilly abetted by our modern stretchy fabrics.

Need more exercise too, but Ohio winters are not conducive to healthy, invigorating walks. One wants to huddle inside and hike only to the refrigerator.

Harkness (husband) and Kyle (son) watching yet another bowl game. It sounded like the TV jocks announced it as the Bedwetter Bowl, but I may have misheard.

January 2 – Life back to normal. Harkness went to his office, Kyle drove back to Purdue, and I took down the Christmas tree. It now lies at the curb with its tinsel bits blowing forlornly in the wind.

Shopped only for healthy foods at the market. Expected to save a bundle, but have you priced tofu lately? And fish these days is priced like they're harvesting it out of some millionaire's koi pond.

Made an experimental beef stroganoff for dinner with vegetarian ground "meat" and non-fat, non-dairy sour cream. Served it over brown rice instead of noodles.

Harkness said it looked like the "discharge from a sick beast" and tasted worse. Rather hurtful, but then Harkness has always prided himself on being Brutally Frank. He once told me that he would have preferred to marry his previous fiancee, but she broke off their engagement (I wonder why). Over the past 27 years he's also found fault with every aspect of my behavior, taste in clothes, grammar, appearance, personality, spending, etc. He's a tax attorney, so perhaps being B.F. is an asset in his profession.

January 3 – Looked at my high school yearbook again today. I do this to reinforce my commitment to skipping desserts. I need to enlarge that photo of me leading the cheers for the homecoming game to poster size and paste it to my refrigerator–all framed in menacing razor wire.

I also have moved my cheerleader's uniform (yes, I still have it) from the back of my closet to front and center.

I see no reason why I shouldn't get down to a sensible size 7. A mere 15 pounds gone should do the trick.

Scary thought: In 22 months I'll be 60. Where did all those years go? And how come they went by so fast?

January 5 – A chilly morning since the furnace wouldn't ignite. Harkness gave the thermostat a couple of swats and told me to call a repair man. A fellow identified as "Devon" on his tan uniform showed up around 10:30. Handsome guy. Could have been George Clooney's fortyish cousin. Informed me very soberly that my furnace board would have to be replaced. I told him to do whatever he thought best. Later, when heat had been restored, I served him a cup of coffee with the two top buttons of my blouse unbuttoned.

Devon wrote out his invoice, drank half the coffee, accepted my personal check, and departed. Don't know what I would have done if he had grabbed me. I suspect my reaction would not have involved loud screaming. Not my usual conduct around strange men. Feeling rather embarrassed now. I blame it all on an overexposure at an impressionable age to *Lady Chatterley's Lover*.

January 6 – Went to the hairdresser today. Rafael's been agitating to add some red to my hair color, but I told him to stick to my usual "rat fur" brown. He was horrified when I told him I hadn't used any makeup for over a month. (I didn't mention yesterday's hasty lipstick application for that disinterested furnace man.) Rafael insisted makeup was a necessity "to age 110." He said I was still a "lovely woman" who should do "everything possible" to look her best. Nice to hear, but then he's a guy who depends on flattering his clients for tips. And he's never met my husband. I could walk around made up like Liz Taylor in "Cleopatra" and I doubt Harkness would even notice.

Thank God I never smoked like my friend Gabby. She smoked for 40 years (she supposedly quit last year), and has skin like a coal miner.

Gabby's in real estate sales, so she has to slather on the cosmetics with a trowel. From ten feet away in a dim room she still looks fairly decent. She has a pretty name (Gabrielle), but her parents should have figured it was going to get shortened into some abomination. She's a total chatterbox, so in her case the nickname fits.

I have one of those dreary names (Helen) that can't be truncated without giving offence. Named after my mother's whiny grandmother, who drove everyone nuts for 86 years then took forever to die after she got cancer. My grandmother was reputed to be a doll, but she died before I was born (car wreck). Uncle Tommy was driving drunk and killed his own mother. Gave him yet another reason to imbibe.

My last name (courtesy of Harkness) is Spall, as in your concrete has a problem.

January 8 – Harkness surprised me by getting amorous last night. He does that about as often as he trims his nose hair. These days his erections are about as firm as my breasts. Still, we managed to get it on after a fashion. It's nice to be desired by a man, even if it is only Harkness. I used to worry that he was getting some on the side, but then I realized that in his world sex has been replaced by golf. I'm not sure what replaced it for me. Maybe nothing.

January 11 – A new low in Monica cuisine. Some sort of vegan casserole involving lentils, cabbage, and diced okra. Healthy I suppose, but everyone stared at it in horror. Harkness took one bite, then left to have dinner at the country club. I whipped up a quick salad; Casta microwaved a frozen pizza.

Monica's been living here rent-free ever since she got her masters in film two years ago. All I ask is that she run the vacuum once in a while and make dinner one night a week. She'll be 25 in a few months. No job, no boyfriend, no social life to speak of, and forever bickering with her sister. I keep dropping hints that a person wishing to pursue a career in film might want to consider living in Los Angeles instead of a leafy suburb (Pepper Pike) of Cleveland. But she claims the field is "too competitive" out there. Very true, except in California they do make movies, whereas in Cleveland they make auto parts and toxic chemicals.

As a favor to me Gabby once hired Monica to shoot a video of one of her listings. The lighting was so somber and the camera angles so strange, Gabby said it made that lovely Shaker Heights home look like the setting for a horror movie. I don't know why my children turned out so creative. I've always been extremely practical, and Harkness has never had a creative impulse in his life.

January 17 – Found another dent in the Beast (my minivan). Casta denied she hit anything, but I know it had to be her. She just got her license (she's 16), and drives like she does everything else–with crazed abandon. She was the worst baby in the world and went straight down-hill from there. Strictly an accident and very nearly dealt with. On more than a few occasions I've wondered why I canceled that appointment. I was slightly worried at the time that she might not be Harkness's child, but now she manifests all of his most irksome traits, including a fierce need to be Brutally Frank about my perceived shortcomings.

First she suggested a snowplow had hit it, but I pointed out we haven't had any plowable snow for weeks. Then she said I probably dented the door myself by "absent-mindedly" closing it with my "massive butt." If I ever said anything like that to my mother, I'd have been slapped silly on the spot. My butt, allowing for its temporary post-holiday augmentation, is still within the normal range for a woman of my age and height. Casta, of course, has practically no butt. Picture a slim nine-year-old boy with perky breasts and way too much eyeliner–that's my teenage daughter.

January 19 – Dropped a hint at breakfast that the Beast may have to be replaced soon. Harkness sighed and said this was not a good time to buy another car. Very predictable response. If everyone waited for Harkness to decide to buy, the economy would have ground to a halt long ago. I pointed out I wasn't asking for a new car. Harkness grunted, "That goes without saying."

My husband thinks only idiot spendthrifts buy new cars off the lot. He prefers to buy three-year-old used cars, thus saving "a fortune in depre-ciation." I often think car magazines should offer special subscriptions for tightwads like Harkness. They could mail out their magazines with a three-year delay.

"I'm done with minivans," I pointed out. "I am not a soccer mom."

A rude chortle from Casta.

She is such a clone of her father. I don't think I had any genetic input into that child at all.

"Kyle's quarterly tuition payment is due at the end of the month," harrumphed Harkness.

A junior at Purdue, our son is allegedly studying electrical engineer-ing, but from his grades I've deduced he's majoring in partying with a minor in applied sexology. Like Monica, he insisted on going to an ex-pensive, out-of-state college. Thankfully, Casta's grades are so crummy she'll be lucky to get into Cleveland State. I sometimes find myself hop-ing she'll finish high school, then run off with one of her lowlife, tat-tooed boyfriends. I've already informed her (and Monica) that I will NOT be providing childcare for later generations. I expect any future grandkids to show up well-scrubbed and neatly dressed for Thanksgiving dinner, but that's the only meal I'll be providing. If my kids can't cope with their progeny, I say let the little bastards be adopted by some prosperous couple in China. Or India, that works for me too.

January 20 – Astounding but true: Monica just left for a job interview. Not getting my hopes up though. I can't quite imagine anyone hiring my elder daughter to do anything. She did a little babysitting in high school, but calls for that tapered off after she nearly drowned a neighbor baby in the bathtub. The paramedics were able to revive him, and I understand he's making decent grades now in school. Her explanation after the hysterics died down: "The soap made him slippery and he wiggled too much."

January 23 – Awakened at 5:27 a.m. by the sound of our handyman Sam plowing the driveway. Nearly a foot of snow from this storm and more forecast for later in the week. Harkness was able to get to his office, but I'm staying put. School got canceled–always a dreaded development. Just the three of us stuck here on our five snow-bound acres like something out of *Dr. Zhivago*. Could be fun for some families, but just makes me feel guilty for how poorly we all get along. Too much accumulated acrimony for festive popcorn-popping around the fire.

After a tense lunch Casta lit up a cigarette right in front of me. I know nothing I say could make her stop, but I gave it a shot. I said holding a cigarette these days is like waving a sign reading: "Look at me! I'm stupid!" I said cigarettes make you look old before your time, drain thousands from your wallet, and kill half the fools who get hooked on them.

Casta smiled her smug smile and puffed away.

Someone please remind me why I had children. Was it just for the daily dose of industrial-strength heartache?

January 31 – Had lunch today with my 92-year-old mother. I offered to take her out, but she said the dining hall was fine. Bland and tasteless as always. For that boring cuisine and her little room she's paying over $4,000 a month.

Her first husband (my father) died before I was born. He was a bridge inspector who slipped, hence my lifelong fear of heights. Ernie, my sweetheart of a stepfather, showed up when I was nine and departed when I was in college. Years later I asked him why he tolerated my mother's acid tongue for as long he did. His reply: "I mostly tuned her out. And I loved her buttermilk biscuits."

These days Mom thinks I'm her sister Maddy. Works for me, because she always got along better with her sister than she did with me. She went to Maddy's funeral with us last summer, but I guess the news didn't stick. I was complaining to her about Casta when she said, "What are you talking about, Maddy? You never had any children. I'm the one who had to put up with that impossible daughter. You should have just admitted you were a lesbian."

Well, that was a shockeroo. I felt since I was the substitute Maddy I should defend her honor.

"What are *you* talking about, Lorraine?" I demanded. "I was happily married to Phil for over 50 years!"

My late uncle Phil Tishby was the one successful creative person in the family. He wrote the insides of greeting cards. He remembered everything he ever wrote and always had the perfect poem to recite for any occasion.

"I'm not turning over that ugly rock!" exclaimed my dotty mother.

"What's that supposed to mean?"

"Oh, Maddy dear, let those sleeping dogs lie. Let the dead remain buried."

I didn't alert Mom that she had spinach on her chin just to observe her look of embarrassment when we got back to her room and she checked herself in the mirror. Score another small victory for her "impossible daughter."

"What do you hear from your daughter these days?" I inquired as I was leaving.

"Not much, Maddy dear. Sometimes I don't even know why I bothered. Children are so ungrateful."

More proof that my tribe is not cut out for motherhood.

When Harkness returned from his office, I asked him if my aunt Maddy ever impressed him as being gay.

"You mean that big gal married to that weird poet?"

"She wasn't that big. Just pleasingly plump."

"I didn't think about her at all. She could never have been a client because her income was too small."

I'm always freshly appalled when I peek too far into my husband's mind.

February 2 – I'm stupefied. Monica got the job. She's starts work tomorrow in the office of a self-storage warehouse. The pay is $9.75 a hour plus a tiny commission for each storage unit she rents out. For this we forked over $300,000+ for six years of college. But I'm trying to be supportive. Kids have it tough in the job market these days, and I suppose they have to start somewhere. At least it may put a stop to some of the pilferage from my purse.

Not that I should talk. I'm a college grad (Oberlin), but haven't had a paying job for nearly three decades. As it was, I never made much over $7 an hour. I was installing mini-blinds for a living when I met Harkness and got swept away by his legalistic charm.

I majored in English. That reminds me: I should read a book one of these days.

February 4 – Got a thick envelope in the mail today. It contained the keys to Aunt Maddy's house. I was supposed to go to her lawyer's office to pick them up, but I never felt quite motivated to do that. I suppose I'll have to deal with it now. I now own an old house in Euclid, Ohio (about 15 miles north). Only a block from Lake Erie, but not the greatest neighborhood these days. Also prone to heavy accumulations of snow from storms off the lake. As I recall, Uncle Phil had his first heart attack shoveling out his driveway back in the pre-snowblower era. I suppose I'll have to clear out all their stuff and put it on the market. Harkness, I know, won't lift a finger to help and will expect all the proceeds to go into our joint account.

Rather surprised by Aunt Maddy's bequest. I'd only seen her a handful of times in the past 20 years. She left her modest bank balance to a women's health clinic in Cleveland, but I got the house.

Sudden thought: Now that Monica's employed, I could try sticking her in Maddy's house. Hell, I might even be able to extract some rent from her.

Not likely, but it may be worth a shot.

February 9 – Amazing but true: Monica likes her job. This week she's been sending out the monthly bills. She says Phyllis, the manager, is easygoing and pleased so far with her performance. Phyllis lives in a mobile home right on the premises and gets to experience the self-storage lifestyle 24/7. The only part of her job Monica doesn't like is kicking out homeless people who try to live in their storage units.

"We have to emphasize that $65 a month doesn't give them the privilege to live-in with their stuff," she said.

"How do they come up with the $65 a month?" I asked.

"Some don't, Mom. Then we have to auction off their goods. It's really sad. Some of our impoverished renters even have advanced degrees."

Let me guess, in film-making?

February 14 – Valentine's Day. Not celebrated here. Harkness says it's a holiday concocted by commercial interests to sell cards, candy, flowers, lingerie, overpriced restaurant meals, and condoms. The last time he laid that speech on me I pointed out that it could also cook up some business for divorce lawyers. This doesn't worry Harkness; he knows I'm not going anywhere.

None of Casta's lowlife beaus gave her as much as a card. My daughter's moderately alluring in your cheesy jailbait sort of way, but I can't see her warming anyone's heart. Just as well. Romance as a lifestyle may be overrated.

Monica called to say she was going out "with friends" after work and would be home late. Since it was her night to cook dinner, I'm making

Harkness take me out for an overpriced restaurant meal whether he wants to or not.

February 17 – Gabby finally talked me into driving up to Euclid to check out Aunt Maddy's house. It's well beyond her usual sales territory, but she tagged along for moral and professional support. Maddy's street has some cute 1920s homes (modest mock Tudors and faux Cotswold cottages, etc.), but my aunt's house was by far the most boring on the block. Just your stark two-story box with a plain gable roof. It was graced originally by a big front porch, but that got yanked off in the 1960s when they slapped on the aluminum siding and fake stone.

"Low maintenance exterior, that's a plus," said Gabby as we exited the Beast. "And the original slate roof still looks good. Not bad for 80-some years of Ohio lakefront weather."

"Does this style house have a name?" I asked. "I mean, besides eyesore."

"It's a Dutch colonial, Helen. A very common house style around here."

"Yeah, way too common."

The front door opened straight into the living room. The house was just as my aunt had left it when the ambulance took her away. Smelled a bit musty now from being shut up so long. Chilly too; the heat was turned on just enough to keep the pipes from freezing.

"Well, would you look at that," exclaimed Gabby, contemplating the wallpaper. "I feel like an aphid on a twig."

Acres of cabbage roses rioted across the living and dining room walls. We're talking BIG roses; each jumbo blossom measured nearly two feet across.

"Aunt Maddy wasn't shy with her wallpaper," I said. "If it didn't knock the wind out of visitors, she wouldn't have it."

"I've seen worse," said Gabby.

"You're kidding?"

"Nope. This isn't a pattern I'd choose, but it's clean, in good condition, and was professionally applied."

"You mean I should leave it?"

"No, dear. It has to go. Otherwise, we'll have to restrict our marketing to the vision-impaired."

"Can I paint over it?"

"Some people do, Helen, but it's really best to strip down to the bare walls."

The kitchen had been remodeled in the 1970s, the ugliest decade on record. Funky dark cabinets, orange Formica counters, and dingy Harvest Gold appliances. Fairly tidy, but cleaned by an old lady who was no longer seeing the grime. Yellow sunflowers blazed forth from the wallpaper.

"Kind of a disaster zone, huh?" I said.

"I've seen worse."

"You sell houses in Shaker Heights, Gabby. When did you ever see a kitchen this bad?"

"There are depressing houses everywhere these days, Helen. You wouldn't believe what I walk into on beautiful streets in prestige neighborhoods."

Upstairs were three bedrooms and the house's single bath. All fully wallpapered to fatigue the eye and harass the spirit. The vintage linoleum appeared designed to camouflage vomit.

"I like that they never painted the oak woodwork," commented Gabby. "And you still have the original linen closet in the hall."

"Yeah, and stocked with the original threadbare towels. You think I could sell it for enough to buy a decent car?"

"We'll see. Let's go back to my office and run some comps."

The comps proved pretty discouraging, plus we discovered there were three foreclosures for sale on that block. Nothing appeared to be moving. Over the past six months, only a handful of houses in the neighborhood had sold.

"Should I burn it down for the insurance money?" I asked Gabby.

"No, dear. A little elbow grease will make a world of difference. I'm sure there's a buyer out there somewhere who will love it."

Like everyone in sales, Gabby only gets through her days by being mindlessly optimistic.

February 18 – Harkness said at breakfast he wasn't interested in spending his weekends stripping wallpaper. Nor was he inclined to pay to hire our handyman for that task.

"I'm not going to get much for that house," I pointed out. "If I bust my ass fixing it up, I intend to keep all the proceeds."

Harkness put down his paper and gave me his severest look.

"OK," he said at last.

"Monica here is my witness. You're agreeing that anything I get from my aunt's estate I can keep for myself?"

"Jesus, I suppose. Just don't bug me to help you. As I recall, your aunt and uncle were a couple of packrats. That house must be jammed to the rafters with useless junk."

"Yeah, I could open my own thrift store. Want to help sort stuff, Monica?"

"Sorry, Mom. I'm busy this weekend."

"Doing what?" I asked.

"I'm an adult now," she replied. "I don't have to report to you on my activities."

"I'm just taking a friendly interest, Monica. I'm not trying to pry into your private life."

Actually I was, but as usual I wasn't getting anywhere.

February 19 – Spent a gray and gloomy Sunday poking through my aunt's house. The whole job is kind of overwhelming. Where does a person start? I decided I couldn't tackle any redecorating until I had cleared out some of the clutter. So I opened a giant garbage bag and started going through stuff. Kind of diverting, if you enjoy snooping through other people's lives.

One upstairs bedroom was Uncle Phil's office, apparently untouched since he died over a decade ago. It appears he saved a sample of every greeting card he ever wrote. Four big filing cabinets filled with cards, some dating back to the early 1950s. A lifetime of work, but what am I supposed to do with it? Who would want it? Are there museums devoted to cards? Are there greeting card collectors who would go nuts over this trove?

Intriguing find in his closet: a big black fireproof safe. Rather ancient-looking with ornate gold-painted trim. God knows how they got that monster up the stairs. A search of the dusty oak desk produced no hint to the combination of the lock. It could be loaded with stacks of $100 bills (I wish), or it could contain tax records from 1957 and a lock of his grandmother's hair (more likely).

Another bedroom served as Aunt Maddy's crafts studio. She was big on needlepoint, knitting, crochet, macrame, Lucite-carving, gem-polishing, quilting, rug-hooking, embroidery, origami, weaving, wood-burning, decoupage, and painting ceramic figurines. It just goes to show how much free time a person has if they don't have children driving them insane.

February 22 – Got a call from Kyle, our slacker engineering student. He and his Purdue buddies are planning a spring-break excursion to New Orleans. To be done on the cheap by driving there nonstop and cramming the whole drunken lot of them into one motel room. He figures he can do the entire ten days in the Big Easy for a mere $500, which he was hoping to extort from us. I told him to talk to his dad, but I for one was dubious.

"I figured it out, Mom," he explained. "It's actually cheaper for me to go to Louisiana than to stay here in Lafayette."

"Why not come here instead, Kyle? It's way closer and we wouldn't charge you a cent for room and board. You could socialize with your loving parents instead of getting arrested for being drunk and disorderly on Basin Street."

"No one goes to Cleveland for spring break, Mom. I'm only asking for $500."

"Good luck prying that out of your father."

"I was hoping you could help me out, Mom. I hear you inherited a house."

So I gave him another lecture on the Economic Realities of Modern Life, but I doubt it did much good.

February 24 – I have to keep making progress on Maddy's house or I know I'll get paralyzed by the entire ordeal. I talked to Maddy's lawyer; he doesn't have the combination to Uncle Phil's safe. He suggested I call a locksmith. As if Harkness wants to foot the bill for that. I know he resents my paying the Euclid utility bills from our household account. The whole thing is one massive ongoing pain.

Met a neighbor from across the street: a chatty older gal named Peach. She said my aunt and uncle were a wonderful asset to the neighborhood. I took that as a hint not to sell their house to riffraff.

Meanwhile, Casta informs me that her sister has a new boyfriend. Apparently, Monica met him through her job. He's a wannabe screen-writer/director who lives in his car on the frigid streets of Cleveland. You wouldn't think a fellow in that state of impoverishment would be doing much dating. Where does he take her? To the soup kitchen at the Salva-tion Army? Do they stay for the sermon? Needless to say, I haven't heard boo about him from Monica.

I'm keeping Harkness totally in the dark on that subject and have instructed Casta to do the same. As usual, I had to threaten her with dire consequences to extract her grudging "OK."

February 25 – Made over $300 in cash so far. I put this ad on Craigslist: "Estate crafters sale in Euclid. Tons of yarn, thread, looms, ceramics—you name it. Clearing all out cheap. Cash only. Plus, an amazing find for greet-ing card collectors!"

So far, no one's shown up jonesing for cards. But several dozen eager buyers have put a big dent in Aunt Maddy's mountain of crafts supplies. A few forked over actual dollars for her finished handicrafts. Also had three inquiries about the stained-glass lamp on the dining-room side-board. I'm assuming it's just a Tiffany knockoff, but no way am I selling it for $25 (the highest offer so far). I may be new at this estate-liquidating game, but I didn't just fall off the turnip cart.

February 26 – Spent the night here in Euclid. I wasn't warming up to crawling into Maddy's big walnut bed in the master bedroom, so I camped on the daybed in the craft room. Got up early and took a long walk along the lakeshore. Not too windy and a bit sunny at times. Lake Erie is rather scenic these days since it is no longer a giant festering cesspool of pollu-tion. You still don't want to eat too much of the fish though.

Had breakfast in a little place where the owners were Czech by way of

Hungary. It's nice being able to walk to stores and local businesses. Everything in Pepper Pike is so spread out, since the minimum lot size there is one acre. You have to drive your car to get to anything, and you only see your neighbors to wave to them as they cruise by on their riding mowers. (Golf and lawn-mowing are the two big non-winter activities in our town.)

Just got a distress call from Harkness wanting to know "our policy on sleep-overs." I said I didn't have a problem with them as long as the other mothers gave their permission.

"I don't think mothers are involved here," he replied. "There's a rusty heap leaking oil on my driveway. Casta says I should ask Monica about it."

"Well, did you?"

"She's not up yet. And I haven't had my breakfast. You know you always make pancakes on Sunday morning."

"The recipe's right on the box, Harkness. Or, you can try something new. For example, I just had a delicious omelet that I purchased in a local restaurant."

Prolonged and predictable grumbling. I told Harkness to be nice to whomever emerged with Monica from her bedroom, then rang off with a cheery "good luck!"

Got the story on Aunt Maddy's wallpaper fixation. A friendly old gal named Grace invited me over for coffee. She's lived next door to my aunt for over 40 years. She said my aunt hated painted walls.

"Like you're living in some institution," said Grace. "Too plain and impersonal according to Maddy."

"But why the giant cabbage roses?" I asked.

"Oh, that was something of a mistake. Your aunt had striped wallpaper downstairs before, but she decided the stripes made her look fat."

"She *was* a bit on the heavy side," I pointed out.

"All the more reason to go for something slimming. So Maddy looked through all her paperhanger's pattern books, but didn't find anything she liked. She had her heart set on something flowery, except mostly what they offer these days are those tiny little repeats. Too boring for your aunt. Finally, her paperhanger found that cabbage rose paper on closeout, but all he could show her was a photo of it, not a sample. She told him to buy every roll. Then when she saw them, she didn't feel like she could inconvenience everyone by sending them back. You know how nice and accommodating Maddy was. She never wanted to make trouble for anyone."

"How did my uncle react?"

"I don't think Phil was too thrilled, but he didn't complain. Home decorating was Maddy's department and he didn't interfere."

"Did Maddy ever say anything about that big safe upstairs?"

"Only that she resented how much closet space it hogged. All of our houses have such meager closet space."

"I can't find the combination to it. Do you have any idea what's in it?"

"Sorry, dear, not a clue. Your aunt may have known, but she never mentioned it to me. As far as I know, she never opened it."

February 27 – According to Harkness, Monica's new young man is a "scruffy and obnoxious fat moron." He said he appeared to be at least 30, had no manners, "ate like a pig," and told Harkness that lawyers were "useless parasites on American society."

"Were you nice to him?" I asked.

"I was as civil to the beast as could be expected under the circumstances. After he shoveled down a monstrous breakfast, I told him to remove his dripping hulk from my driveway."

"What's his name?"

"I saw no reason to remember his name, Helen, since I never expect to see the lout again. He really was the lowest of the low. Your daughters have such abysmal standards. I'm sure they didn't get it from my side of the family."

Not very complimentary to me, nor to Harkness if you follow his reasoning to its logical conclusion.

Harkness continued his rant, "We can't have Monica dragging these degenerates home and having sex under our roof. It sets a bad example for Casta."

"I wouldn't worry about that, dear. Casta's having more sex than all the rest of us put together."

Another shock to my husband; I sometimes wonder what planet he's living on.

Casta reported the fellow's name was Igor or possibly Roland. She added that like all of Monica's boyfriends, he was a Major Creep. She said his car was stacked to the roof with a smelly jumble of "clothes, papers, books, and junk."

"The dude drives a rolling slum, Mom. And my sister's getting undressed and letting him touch her."

"You needn't be so graphic, Casta."

"If I knew she was that desperate, I'd have volunteered one of my friends on the football team to give her a mercy fuck."

"That will do, Casta. I won't have that language in my home."

"I'm not touching anything that Monica comes in contact with. That girl is diseased!"

February 28 – Cornered Monica before she left for work. I said I was sorry I didn't get to meet her new fellow on Sunday.

"Roland's not sorry he missed you. I've told him all about you."

"What's that supposed to mean?"

"He knows you're a prude and wouldn't approve. Daddy was horrible to him. We only came here because we couldn't afford a motel."

"Does he live in his car?"

"That's none of your business. Roland is a Major Talent. Like all geniuses he has to struggle for recognition."

"Why don't you invite him here for dinner some evening, Monica? I'd love to meet him."

"You just want to see if he's as awful as Daddy says."

As usual, my daughter could read me like a book.

"I'm sure he's a nice young man, dear. Naturally, I take an interest in who you're seeing."

"I have to go, Mother. I don't want to be late for work."

More bad news. The locksmith I called wasn't encouraging about Uncle Phil's safe. He said that brand of safes was designed to resist drilling, sledging, explosive attacks, and burning with a torch. He said it was equipped with a first-rate anti-manipulation lock with a punch-resistant hardened spindle.

"There aren't many of those old puppies around," he said. "Your uncle obviously knew his safes."

"Can you get it open?"

"Sorry, lady. If I were you, I'd track down the combination. It's usually noted down somewhere on the premises. Otherwise, you'd better find yourself a safecracker."

"Where do I find one of those?"

"Try the state prison."

February 29 – In honor of Leap Year, I just mailed $500 to Kyle for his spring break trip. I sent him a money order so Harkness wouldn't find out. It cleaned out all but $8 of my proceeds from last weekend's estate sale. I know I'm an Indulgent Mother, but Kyle is the only one of my children who possesses any personal charm. I feel this is a quality that should be rewarded. Of course, I'm aware that many sociopaths can be charming, but I've seen my son tear up during sad movies and he was inconsolable once when his bunny died. I believe he has a conscience. Casta, on the other hand, I'm not so sure about.

Watched some Youtube demonstration videos on wallpaper stripping, then went out and bought the recommended tools. Also stocked up on frozen dinners to tide my family over while I'm away assaulting Aunt Maddy's walls. Packed my suitcase and left a farewell note on the dining room table. I also noted the address in case any of them cares to show up and help.

HELEN AND BRENDA

March 1 – A sunny day and almost springlike. Noticed some crocuses poking up by the back stoop. Neglected back yard looking like Berlin circa 1945. Gabby suggested I spruce it up to add some eye appeal. I am so not cut out for this kind of work.

I set Aunt Maddy's kitchen timer to one hour and started searching for that damn safe combination. I gave myself a time limit because hunting for something that I'm not even sure exists is the world's most irksome task. I tried to be as thorough as possible, even pulling out all the desk and bureau drawers to check their undersides. Vastly relieved when the bell rang and I could walk the three blocks to a local bakery for my promised reward of a coffee and sweet roll. Lingered longer than I should have over the Euclid newspaper and my third refill.

Not sure if I'm inherently lazy or just unmotivated. I suppose most people would say I've had a pretty easy life. I lashed myself with those sentiments as I dragged a stepladder up from the basement and started rolling the perforating tool over a dining room wall. This is a little plastic pod with pointy wheels that score the paper as you move it in circles. Kind of tiring to the arm, but I told myself that it might be a good workout for firming the bust. After scoring a large patch, I rollered on the releasing liquid that dissolves the wallpaper paste. You let this soak for a bit, then go at the paper with your large scraper. I was horrified to discover that lurking under the cabbage roses were the original girth-enhancing stripes. I've got multiple layers of wallpaper to remove!

This news was so discouraging I had to sit down and watch a game show on Maddy's vintage TV. Meanwhile my released paper dried out and reattached itself even more firmly to the wall.

Later, I resolved the issue of that possible Tiffany stained-glass lamp. While moving the stepladder, I accidentally snagged the lamp cord. Tremendous crash as it shattered against the floor. Preferring now to believe I wrecked a $39 knockoff and not a $75,000 heirloom.

No call from Harkness, nor did I call him.

I find I am not minding this vacation from my marriage.

March 2 – Got a text from Casta. Hard to decipher as usual (2 mny abbrvs), but I think she was complaining that if I was going to force them to eat artificial food, I should at least buy frozen pizzas. My one-word reply: "Noted." Fired up my iPad and detected an open WiFi network labeled "Peach Pit." I'm assuming it's from my friendly neighbor across the street. I logged on, collected my usual junk email, and Googled "wallpaper removing machine." No such luck. No brilliant inventor has yet automated this repellent job.

I can envision some sort of laser-powered device. You point it at your wall, pull the trigger, and the wallpaper flies off neatly in one big sheet.

HELEN AND BRENDA

While eating my cornflakes, I idly typed in a name and found the Facebook page for Deke M. Brennan. This was the fellow I once suspected might be the father of Casta. Not very likely, since we always used a condom. He listed his status as divorced and his location as Medina (a suburb of Akron). Looked a bit craggier in his photo, but not that different. Of course, it might not be a current photo. Couldn't help but wonder if some doting female helped him pick out those trendy eyeglasses.

Deke was my one digression from marital fidelity. He was the newly divorced father of a preschool playmate of Kyle's. We used to arrange play dates for our sons, then graduated to motel play dates for ourselves. Unnerving, but extremely intense. I lived for those Thursday afternoons. When I found out I was pregnant, I told myself he was on the rebound and it would never work out. So I broke it off. He called me a few times after that, but I discouraged any further contact. Very distraught my entire pregnancy. Plus, I felt guilty for cheating on Deke with my husband. Perhaps that's why Casta turned out to be such a problem child.

I Googled the distance from Euclid to Medina: 46 miles. In less than an hour, I could be knocking on Deke's door.

If I were deranged.

March 3 – No call from Harkness. He's either punishing me for abandoning him or hasn't yet noticed my absence.

Still searching for that elusive combination (aren't we all?). Now looking through the books on Uncle Phil's office shelves. He was quite the reader. Lots of poetry by Ogden Nash, James Whitcomb Riley, Edward Lear, Dorothy Parker, etc. Perhaps they helped inspire his greeting-card verse. To my surprise Uncle Phil also had a dozen or so novels by Gloria Anne Lenore. Lots of my friends back in junior high were big fans of her books. I brought one home from the library once, and my mother pitched a giant fit. She said no daughter of hers was going to read such trash. Rather strange, because they were innocuous romances aimed toward teenage girls. As I recall a couple of them got made into movies back in the 1960s. Probably not read much these days because their wholesome attitudes would be off-putting to modern teens. Very dated plots too (no sex, just tender yearning). Casta, I'm sure, would gag after one page.

Lost a whole morning to *This Savannah Moon* by Gloria Anne Lenore. I sat there getting teary-eyed while rows of intact cabbage roses loomed above me in silent reproach. My escape to 1950s Savannah was interrupted by a phone call from Perla, Harkness's officious secretary. She reminded me we were expected at his brother's house tonight for dinner. I told her to tell Harkness I would meet him there.

A dilemma: I hadn't brought anything nice to wear. I could stay here and scrape wallpaper or go to the mall and shop for a dress. Another test of my character!

After we bought our house in Pepper Pike, Harkness's brother Eliot felt compelled to buy one in Rocky River (about 20 miles west of us). He's a CPA and at six-four is the tallest Spall of all (towering one inch above my husband). Both are lanky and balding like all male Spalls.

Eliot welcomed Harkness with his standard greeting: "Hark, who goes there?"

Everyone in Harkness's family calls him Hark. At his office he is known as H.K. I'm one of the few people who addresses him by his actual name.

"Is that a new dress?" inquired Bodana, Eliot's ever-glamorous second wife.

"Rather newish," I admitted.

"And such delightful shoes too!" she exclaimed. "Frightfully expensive?"

"On sale for a song," I lied.

A knowing smile from Bodana. She had not escaped from privation in Russia by her looks alone.

Apparently, I'm on the outs with my husband. He was cold and distant to me all through Bodana's excellent dinner. Or I should say, he was colder and more distant than usual. Even at his friendliest, Harkness never exactly radiates warmth. It takes an expert to tell when Harkness is giving you the cold shoulder.

I don't think he was thrilled by my new outfit either.

March 4 – Another sunny Sunday in Euclid. The TV is predicting a high of 65. Got to love that global warming. No more dawdling! I am turning over a new leaf. Today's agenda is non-stop score, roller, and scrape.

Finished *This Savannah Moon*. Not great literature, I suppose, but Ms. Lenore sure knows how to push a reader's buttons. Her prose is tremendously paralyzing to the will; I felt compelled to sit there until I finished the book. And it's really unfair that Uncle Phil's library offers such an extensive selection of her works. It's like Aunt Maddy's wall decor is battling for supremacy with her husband's taste in books. And Uncle Phil is so winning that contest.

Got a call in the late afternoon from Harkness. He asked me if I was done painting all the rooms yet. Somehow the twit imagined that I had finished stripping all the wallpaper. I told him I was making "steady progress," but had encountered "multiple layers dating back to the early years of the previous century."

Harkness sighed and asked me when I thought I might be finished.

"Hard to say, dear. It's a big job. Anything new with the kids?"

"That beast slept over again last night. I'm thinking of serving Monica with a three-day eviction notice."

"You can't do that to your own daughter."

"She's an employed adult, Helen. It's time for the chick to leave the nest."

"I want to meet this guy. Tell Monica to invite him to dinner this week. I'll come home and cook dinner."

Another sigh. "This is getting intolerable, Helen."

"We have to be nice to him, Harkness. Girls have been known to marry fellows just because their parents dislike him."

My mother, for example, always referred to Harkness when I was dating him as that "tall toad."

"I'm tired of frozen meals," Harkness complained.

"I know, darling. Arrange things with Monica, and I'll make you all a nice dinner."

March 5 – So pleasant yesterday, but woke up to sleet this morning. Typical Ohio weather. Found myself studying Deke's Facebook photo again at breakfast. Too bad he only shares his posts with his 79 Facebook friends. What has that guy got to hide? When I knew him, he owned a small travel agency. Now he lists his job as "corporate relocation facilitator." Didn't know such an occupation existed. Were I to join Facebook, I could send Deke a message. Saying what exactly?

I am such a Gloria Anne Lenore zombie. Very much against my will I found myself lurching up the stairs and grasping another novel (*The Summer of Romola*). I then fixed myself a cup of tea and settled on the sofa with my book. The thermostat was turned up to a comfy 75 (which I'm never allowed to do at home). By page three all guilt had been anaesthetized and I was basking in the warm Monterey, California sun with that promising young equestrian Romola Swandor.

Invited my elderly neighbors Peach and Grace over for lunch. Grace is one of five sisters all named after Christian virtues: Grace, Hope, Faith, Charity, and Duty. Peach's maiden name was Peach Sarah Herbert, which her parents customarily shortened to Peach S. Herbert. They were confectionary inclined, having met at an ice cream social.

Peach noticed that the sideboard was missing its lamp. Not wanting to 'fess up to being a klutz, I lied and said I had taken it home to Pepper Pike.

"You really should have that lamp appraised," said Grace.

"I doubt it's valuable," I replied. "My aunt mostly shopped at Sears and K-Mart."

"She didn't buy that lamp, Helen. It belonged to Phil's grandmother."

"Well, perhaps she bought it at Sears."

"According to Phil, his grandmother was a portrait painter. She traded a painting for it with a glass craftsman who worked at a studio in New York City. Phil's whole family—those Tishbys–were very talented, you know."

All the blood rushed from my brain, and I nearly gagged on my tuna-fish sandwich.

Peach smiled and gazed around at my dining-room walls.

"Not making much progress on the wallpaper are we, dear?"

March 6 – Had a hearty cry last night over that lamp and Romola's unrequited love for Riley, her handsome but impecunious horse trainer. I could have sold that lamp, donated the house as-is to some charity, bought the fanciest car on the lot, and never had to strip another square inch of wallpaper. Instead, I may be stuck here in Euclid for the rest of my life.

Can't flagellate myself any more. Have to go buy groceries. Giving a dinner party tonight in Pepper Pike for Monica and her new beau.

March 7 – Got serviced by Harkness this a.m. Rather abrupt, as he ALWAYS gets to the office on time. My lovelife appears to lie at the farthest end of the romantic spectrum from virginal Romola's. But perhaps after nearly 30 years of marriage, she too would be having brisk two-minute intercourse with Riley.

Speaking of grand passions, I wasn't too impressed with Roland, Monica's not-so-young car-dwelling genius. One of your loping, roly-poly types with Strong Opinions and a major case of narcissism run amok. Very sloppy eater too. By the end of dinner he was wearing a representative sample of my cookery on his not-too-clean-to-begin-with shirt.

Roland reports he is currently revising his 900-page screenplay on the 1966 race riots in the Hough neighborhood of Cleveland. Works out to roughly a ten-hour movie. Funding, he concedes, might be a problem. His backup plan is to spark another riot, film it on the sly, then weave in his own narrative employing non-actors from the streets.

Monica was enthusiastic, but Harkness sat there beaming bolts of hatred. Made for a very tense meal. Then, when I was loading the dishwasher, Monica took me aside to berate me over Casta.

"Do you realize, Mother, that while you're up in Euclid, my sister is running around totally unsupervised?"

"Running around doing what?" I asked.

"God knows! She's hardly ever here!"

"As I recall, Monica, you weren't big on being supervised when you were her age either."

"I always acted responsibly, Mother. Casta is out of control."

"I have to get Aunt Maddy's house on the market, Monica. If you hear of any concrete transgressions by Casta, please do keep me informed."

Returned to peaceful Euclid and had lunch in their sleepy downtown. I do like this little burg. Everything you need is just a short stroll away. Noticed the Polka Hall of Fame as I walked home with another Gloria

Anne Lenore novel I scored in a thrift store. Ohio, I've discovered, is lousy with halls of fame. I'm surprised no one's started a Mafia Hall of Fame here. Not many people know this, but quite a few of those casino pioneers who put Las Vegas on the map were from the Cleveland mob. We're a tribe that likes to celebrate our heroes.

Exciting find: my new book (still with its original dust jacket) is a first edition. Not bad for a fifty-cent investment.

March 8 – Choice of stripping wallpaper or visiting my mother. A tough decision, but familial duty won by a nose. This time I tried telling her that I was Helen, not her sister.

"Don't be ridiculous, Maddy," she sneered. "You're an old woman. Anyone can see that–even if you do dye your hair. My daughter is young!"

"If I'm Maddy, then where's Phil?"

"You really are losing it, Maddy. Phil died years ago. Remember, you sprinkled his ashes in Lake Erie and he blew right back into your face. In my day, we buried people in the ground where they belonged."

A glutton for punishment, I asked Mother if she remembered Aunt Maddy's dining room lamp.

"A bit gaudy for my tastes, but that's Phil's ancestors for you."

"Was it by any chance a Tiffany lamp?"

"Of course, it is! It's the only thing of value in that entire house!"

A gray fog of depression settled into my bones.

"How about that big old safe upstairs? I asked. "Do you know what's in it?"

Startled glance from my mother.

"Maddy, I told you to call a junk man and have that hunk of useless metal carted away."

"Why should I do that?"

"I told you. Because it's better to let sleeping dogs lie."

March 9 – Progress, of sorts, at last. Bodana, my energetic Russian sister-in-law, showed up to light a fire under me. Even dressed for wall-stripping, she still ranks as glamorous. Blond and voluptuous with those tremendous Slavic cheekbones. I know Harkness is jealous of his brother for lapping him so crushingly in the arm candy department. Fortunately for me, Harkness doesn't envy the financial hit Eliot took to unsplice from Pam, his redundant first wife. Since I rate Bodana a BIG improvement in every department over the prior Mrs. Spall, I have chosen not to regard her as a home wrecker.

Two walls in the dining room have now been freed from three layers of wallpaper, revealing an ancient paint I'm calling Bile Duct Excretion Brown. Truly the world's most hideous color. Combine that wall treatment with our cloudly lakeside weather and you have an environment in which wrist-slashing starts to seem like a viable alternative.

My mood wasn't improved after I swore Bodana to secrecy and spilled the beans about my recent lamp disaster.

"How badly was it broken?" she inquired, scraping away.

"One side was totally caved in," I admitted.

"And you threw it in the garbage?"

"I did, yes."

"Ah, Helen, you should have called me. Maybe I think that the shade could have been re-fabricated. And the metal base?"

"Also tossed."

"It was damaged?"

"Uh, I didn't really notice."

"Even without the shade, the base was worth probably several thousand dollars."

"Oh."

Bodana flashed me a look that said, "Had you been born like me in Russia you would still be there starving on three kopeks a day."

Waiting for the Friday evening traffic to die down and then I'm heading back to Pepper Pike. Got a call from Monica begging me to let her stay here tonight with Roland. So I'm clearing out and leaving her a key under the mat on the back stoop.

Hard as it is for me to understand her fascination with Roland's mind, I really don't get her attraction to his body.

March 10 – I was immersed in the exotic milieu of San Francisco's Chinatown, circa 1943 (courtesy of Gloria Anne Lenore), when Casta shuffled out from her bedroom. The clock on the wall oven read 11:47 a.m.

"Oh, you're here," she said. "I thought you and Daddy were separated."

"No, and I was here Thursday night if you'd bothered to show up for dinner."

"You couldn't pay me to eat with Monica's repulsive creep. The guy is such a cheese wipe."

"Have you been going to school?"

"Of course."

She poured chocolate milk on her sugary cereal, then slurped up a big spoonful like she was three years old. Once upon a time, I'd have found that endearing.

"You might as well be the second to the last to know," she chewed. "I've come out as a lesbian."

"That will be a grave disappointment to your numerous boyfriends."

"I'm serious, Mom. I've had it with guys. You can kiss your grandkids goodbye."

"Many lesbian couples have children through artificial insemination," I pointed out.

"You're not taking this serious, Mom. I'm like totally attracted to chicks."

"And I'm totally supportive of your decision. Girls could only be an improvement over the class of fellows you've been going out with. Shall I inform your father of your news?"

Casta made a face and flounced out with her bowl.

She's been messing with my head since she was one day old, but that was a new ploy for her. I often wonder if she works them out in advance or just wings it when the mood strikes her.

As a baby she always did her BMs in two parts. She'd wait until I put on a fresh diaper, then let fly with her stinky reserves–smiling smugly as I cursed her perversity.

March 11 – Just because I've now joined Facebook, it doesn't necessarily follow that I intend to poke anyone out of the blue with some creepy stalker message. Were I a heroine in a Gloria Anne Lenore novel, however, it goes without saying that I would do exactly that.

I made Sunday morning pancakes for Harkness, then restocked the freezer with easy microwaveable meals. It's the least I can do for my loving family. Went through my accumulated mail and found no thank-you note from Kyle for the money order. No call either. Fortunately, I've long since given up being disappointed by my family.

March 12 – Returned to Euclid this morning and found this note on the kitchen table:

Mom,

Thanks for letting us stay here. You're getting low on groceries. Hope you don't mind, but Roland opened that safe upstairs. Just some old papers inside.

See you later,

Monica

Ran upstairs, but was disappointed to find the safe was again locked up tight. The twit had reclosed it. Called Monica's office and had to wait forever on hold. At last, Monica picked up and I asked her how Roland got the safe open.

"I told you he was a genius, Mother. Roland's family owns a chain of pawn shops. He knows all about safes."

"If his family's well off, why is he living in his car?"

"He's estranged from them. They don't respect his repudiation of materialism. Or his artistic vision."

"Right. Could he open the safe again?"

"Of course. But I'm not sure he has enough gas to get to Euclid."

"Well, tell him I'll give him $100 to open the safe."

Roland showed up 45 minutes later. He was eating glazed donuts out of a greasy sack.

"I understand you need some safe-cracking," he said, licking his pudgy fingers.

"I do," I admitted. "I'd offer you some coffee, but someone cleaned out my pantry."

Roland simultaneously belched and farted as we trooped up the stairs. He flung himself down in front of the safe and licked his fingers again.

"Safes are like pianos, Mrs. Spall. They function best when they are used often. This is a fine little box, but it's been neglected. Over time your delicate lubricating oils start to wick away. Parts no longer mesh smoothly. Cams click instead of glide, revealing their secrets to sensitive fingers."

He positioned a dingy ear right next to the safe and began rotating the dial. On his second try, the handle clicked down and the door swung open.

"Voila!" said Roland, grabbing a fresh donut from his sack. "I understand you are offering some modest remuneration for this feat."

"You've earned $100 so far. I'll give you another twenty if you can note down the combination for me."

"No problemo, señora."

Citing his "appalling handwriting," Roland sat down at Uncle Phil's old Underwood and typed out the combination. I counted out six $20 bills and sent him on his way. Rather creepy being alone in the house with that fellow. I do hope he won't be contributing any grandchildren to our family tree.

No cash or valuables in the safe. Just a great stack of yellowing papers. Mostly old contracts, but also many years' worth of royalty statements. Contracts and statements in the name of Gloria Anne Lenore.

Kind of peculiar, as my mother would say.

Mystified by this development, I decided I needed to find out more about Ms. Lenore. The brief Wikipedia article was word-for-word almost the same as the bio information on her dust jackets. Vague generalities about her "immense popularity" with readers, but no specifics about her birth, education, marital status, residence, etc. No author photo either. After the Wikipedia listing of her novels, someone had added this paragraph:

> Very little is known about this former best-selling author of young adult novels. Some have speculated that Gloria Anne Lenore may have been the pen name of some other highly regarded novelist known for their more serious works of fiction. There is no record of Gloria Anne

Lenore ever having given a reading or made a public appearance in the United States. [Citation needed]

I found a few of her books listed for sale on-line, but they were only available used. It appears her novels are out of print. She was mentioned on several obscure fan blogs, and at imdb.com for her three movies, but that was it. Gloria Anne Lenore is, alas, the (mostly) forgotten mystery woman of teen fiction.

So why are all her business papers residing in my late uncle's safe?

March 13 – Mother was surprised to see me so soon after my last visit.

"I hope you're not planning on moving here, Maddy. I'm not ready for prolonged sisterly togetherness. Nor do I need any more of your crocheted novelties."

"I got Phil's safe open, Lorraine. So tell me about Gloria Anne Lenore."

"Never heard of her."

"Then why were you so adamant that I not open the safe? You know who she is. So why are her papers in Phil's safe?"

"Oh, you mean that dreary authoress? Why didn't you say so? Need I remind you, Maddy, she's the gal you bought that ugly house from. As I recall, the safe came with the house."

"We bought the house in 1961, Lorraine. There are documents in the safe dated as late as 1983. You'll have to do better than that."

My mother squirmed in her recliner. "There's really nothing to tell, Maddy. Your so-called husband was friends with that no-talent scribbler. He advised her on business matters. Which may be another reason why she has sunk into well-deserved obscurity."

"Did you ever meet her?"

"Lord, no. I had bigger fish to fry."

"Do you know where she is today?"

"Probably in some cemetery. Or whisking up someone's nose."

"Is that all you know about her?"

"I'm amazed I remembered that much. I'm four years older than you are, Maddy. I can't even recall what I had for breakfast."

I had no better luck phoning New York. Her original publisher had merged with another firm, then got bought by some foreign conglomerate. Nobody there knew anything about her. Her literary agent had died in 1997, and the agency no longer existed.

I used Uncle Phil's ancient mechanical adding machine to total up the figures on Ms. Lenore's papers. She had earned a bit over $3.8 million from book royalties and movie sales. A nice chunk of change, as Harkness would say.

A long trail leading to a dead end. And I wasn't getting any wallpaper scraped either.

HELEN AND BRENDA

March 14 – Finished *Farewell to Chinatown* and started *Songs along the River*. This one's about a girl who gets a summer job on the last showboat plying the Mississippi River. Pure escapism, but–let's face it–I have a lot on my plate to escape from. I very much like the thought that I'm reading her novels in the same room where Gloria Anne Lenore once sat and chatted with my relatives. One mystery: why aren't any of her books in Uncle Phil's collection signed? Wouldn't he have asked her to sign at least a few if they were such great pals?

March 15 – I hate snow in March. Doesn't winter realize we have already moved on? I shoveled five inches off my sidewalk, then helped Grace next door clear off hers. She's still fairly spry for an old gal. As a thank you, she invited me to have lunch with her and Peach at the local senior center.

I hesitated. Stepping into a senior center I ranked as one of those major rites of passage–like getting your first bra and losing your virginity. I wasn't sure I was ready. Hell, I hadn't even joined the A.A.R.P.

Grace talked me into it. A nourishing hot meal with beverage of your choice for only 85 cents. And she was offering to pick up the tab. We drove the dozen blocks in the Beast. Grace said they often walk there when the weather is better.

Your institutional room crowded with white-haired oldsters. All races and nationalities. I was by far the youngest, but nobody carded me for being an impostor. Stuffed cabbage, mashed potatoes, and salad. Not bad, and the cherry crisp was excellent. All through lunch–like the groupie I had become–I bent my companions' ears about Gloria Anne Lenore.

Grace said she remembered the name and recalled how excited Maddy would be when one of her books came out.

"Did you ever meet her?" I asked.

"No, but I remember this lady who used to visit them sometimes. She always arrived in a cab. That was kind of unusual back then."

"Oh, I remember that gal," said Peach. "She always carried this dainty little briefcase."

"What did she look like?" I asked.

"Very elegant lady," replied Grace. "You never saw her without her gloves and hat. Had the veil and everything. Quite a sophisticated look. Extremely thin–a bit on the bony side. My husband used to comment on that. He said a fellow could get a nasty bruise fooling around with a girl that skinny. My Gergo was Hungarian on both sides and not too enlightened by today's standards."

"What did he do?"

"He was an electrician at the welder plant for 42 years. He worked with Peach's husband Marv."

Still a big employer in town, it was one of the few factories in the area that hadn't been packed off to China or Mexico.

"When was the last time you saw her visit?" I asked.

"Gosh, a long time ago, Helen. Probably back in the 1980s. I didn't spy on my neighbors, but I'd notice people coming and going."

"Did you ever read any of her books?"

"Nah, I didn't have much time for reading."

"Me neither," said Peach. "Not enough hours in the day."

"I can lend you some if you like."

"Aren't you sweet," replied Grace. "But these old eyes of mine aren't much good for reading."

"I'd rather work crosswords," said Peach. "Books put me right to sleep."

March 16 – Another week nearly over, and I'm still mired in wallpaper paralysis. All I do is read teen fiction and wallow in guilt. Hey, why can't Gabby dredge up some eager house-buyer who loves cabbage roses, the bigger the better? I'm sure there's such a person out there somewhere.

Meanwhile, I have composed a friendly message to Deke, but have yet to work up the nerve to send it. What exactly do I want from that man? I fear my overexposure to Gloria Anne Lenore has stimulated long-dormant romantic impulses. Yes, her willowy 17-year-old heroines have little trouble attracting earnest and attractive suitors, but how many fellows wish to hook up with married 58-year-old matrons? This, I fear, could constitute an even smaller pool than your potential cabbage-rose fanatics.

I could always go older. I noticed several gents at the senior center checking me out. But would a swain in his 80s, however ardent, be a step up from Harkness?

Probably not.

March 17 – Looked too ratty even for me to stand, so I got my hair done. Confessed to Rafael all about my new Gloria Anne Lenore fixation. He thought it over and asked me if I had considered my uncle as the possible author of those novels. I replied I had, but rejected him for several reasons. First, the novels read very much like they were written by a woman–a woman who was completely in tune with the teenage feminine heart.

"I don't know," said Rafael, "sometimes those guys can fool you. What was that chick book everyone was reading a few years back that people were amazed was written by a dude?"

I drew a blank. "I have no idea."

"You know, Helen. It was written by some guy named Sheep, or Mutton, or . . ."

"You mean *She's Come Undone* by Wally Lamb?"

"That's the one. You read that, didn't you?"

"Uh, I intended to. Oprah sure loved it. But consider this: Gloria Anne Lenore earned nearly $4 million from her writing. My aunt and uncle lived in a modest little house in blue-collar Euclid. They were pinching pennies their whole lives."

"He could have just been cheap. You always hear about people dying in some crummy rented room despite having a fortune in the bank."

"Well, my uncle didn't, because their estate was quite modest. Just the house and a few thousand in the bank."

"Too bad, Helen. I could use more rich clients. I bet if you inherited a pile, I could talk you into a splashier hair color. Something with a bit more pizzazz."

"I have to keep this shade of brown, Rafael. It totally matches the wall color I unearthed in my aunt's dining room."

March 18 – Drove down early to Pepper Pike to make Harkness his Sunday pancakes and see if my family was still alive. No one noticed my freshened hair color and stylish cut. Monica, looking exultant, was packing her stuff in boxes. She's moving out. It seems she and Roland have rented a little duplex just down the block from her job.

"Your salary is enough to cover the rent?" I asked.

"Well, Roland will be paying half."

"I thought he was penniless."

"He got an early installment on his inheritance from his grandmother."

"You sure you want to do this, dear? You just met the fellow."

"It's my life, Mother. Please don't interfere."

"Sorry. Do you need any help moving?"

"We can manage. Roland's buying a van. We'll need it for our movie."

"Don't tell me you intend to start that race riot."

"That project's on hold. We're going to make a feature on location at the self-storage lot. Phyllis is all for it. Roland and I are writing it now. He'll direct and I'll be DP."

"A disabled person?"

"No, Mom. Director of photography."

"Isn't it expensive to make a movie?"

"Not these days. We'll be shooting in high-def video. For about $5,000 you can get a camera, lenses, filters, sound recorder, mixer, microphones, tripod, dolly, and lights–everything you need to be M.G.M. on the cheap."

"What will you do for actors?"

"No problem. I've met a ton of them storing their stuff with us."

"Well, it sounds very exciting, dear."

"We've already got the title: 'Store Rage'."

"Oh, dear. I hope it won't be full of violence and gore."

"Well, Roland's favorite director is Quentin Tarantino. You have to go a bit extreme to get your first film noticed. And Roland's a master at creating horrifyingly realistic wounds."

That news didn't surprise me.

After Harkness left to play golf (chilly drizzle doesn't phase him), I waited around to check in with my younger daughter. Casta woke to this world a little before noon. She shuffled into the kitchen wearing a size triple-XXX Cleveland Browns jersey and a bit of a black eye.

"What happened to you?" I asked.

She winced and turned away. "I got beat up by my pimp."

Why me, God?

I played along: "Are you outcall or do you stand on a street corner somewhere?"

"We work in a big hotel out by the airport."

"And your clients are?"

"Bored businessmen and mafioso jetting in to do hits."

I wet a finger with my tongue and rubbed it under her eye.

"Good news, Casta. Your bruise appears to be self-inflicted, possibly with purple eye shadow."

"Daddy thinks you're having an affair. That's why you're never home."

I doubt he suspected that, but you never know.

"Are you telling the truth, Casta? Or lying as usual?"

"He says no one can take that long to strip off a little wallpaper."

March 19 – Woke up at 2:00 a.m. with an ugly thought. A few days after opening my uncle's safe, Roland suddenly gets an early legacy from his granny. Or did he?

It must have been quite a windfall if he can now pay rent, buy a van, start his own movie studio, and keep himself in donuts.

Call me paranoid, but I'm smelling a rat here.

After breakfast, I called Monica at work to inquire if she had been in the room when Roland opened the safe. She was instantly on the defensive.

"Why do you want to know that, Mother?"

"Just wondering."

"I was downstairs, but he called me right away. Roland's not a thief. There was nothing in that safe except those papers. He didn't touch a thing."

"Right. Did you by any chance see the check from his grandmother?"

"He put it straight into the bank. But I trust him."

"Right. Well, how's the move going?"

"I have to go, Mother. Phyllis doesn't like me to receive personal calls at work."

"Right, OK. Talk to you soon."

Since I don't know what was in the safe, I have no way of proving that Roland took anything. If he did swipe cash or valuables, he was able to remove them from the house without Monica noticing. The lug may have committed the perfect crime. Not to mention eating all my groceries and lightening my purse by another $120.

I can only pray Monica is employing extremely rigorous birth control.

No wonder I spend all my time reading Gloria Anne Lenore novels. Her stories are remarkably free of people like Roland (or Harkness, for that matter).

March 20 – Been mulling over Casta's comments on my husband's state of mind. Probably just her way of stirring up trouble, but you never know. I've decided to regard it as an unsubstantiated rumor.

Got so annoyed by the topic, I finally clicked "send" on my message to Deke. Five minutes later I got a two-word reply.

No, it wasn't "drop dead."

He wrote: "Lunch tomorrow?"

I replied, "Sure. Noonish," and added my Euclid address.

Rather unnerving that he's so eager to see me.

The bad news is I have just 24 hours to lose 15 pounds.

SPRING

March 21 – First day of spring, although you wouldn't know it from the gray skies. Spent the morning trying to decide what to wear and how much makeup to slather on. Too little and one looks like an earth mother or indifferent slattern. Too much, however, just screams desperation. Tried for that elusive middle ground.

Kind of nervous-making as Deke interpreted "noonish" to mean 12:52. Arrived in an older rusty Mustang. Apologized for being late and gave me something of a hug, though distracted by my living-room wallpaper. Updated him on my home redecorating woes on the short drive to the restaurant.

I ordered the chicken paprikash, he went for the roast duck. We clicked wine glasses and said the usual inanities about the other person "not having changed a bit." I do think it's unfair that guys can pile on 16 years and still look presentable, while time wreaks such havoc with my sex.

Deke was surprised to hear I was still with Harkness.

"Why's that?" I asked.

"Well, Mok, you didn't have much good to say about him way back when."

I'd forgotten he used to call me that. It stood for Mother of Kyle. I called him Foj for Father of Jamie.

"Sorry. I hate women who complain endlessly about their husbands. Harkness is, uh, still hanging in there."

"Let me guess. He's not doing a thing to help you fix up that house."

"Well, he's busy with his job."

"Is he still advising rich people how to avoid paying their taxes?"

"Something like that. So tell me about your job."

Deke said the arrival of the Internet caused his travel agency to "dry up and blow away." After that he got into corporate relocations.

"I get enough referrals to pay the bills, but it's been a struggle. It's hard to start a new career at my age."

"And how's Jamie doing?"

"Uh, OK. He tried a semester of college, but it wasn't for him. He's working in a muffler shop now."

"Does he like it?"

"He likes the money. When swapping mufflers starts to pale, I expect he'll try something else."

I told him about my kids, then jumped the track and started in on my current obsession. Deke listened politely as I rattled on.

"It's strange that she hid from view all those years," he commented. "Most writers are always out there begging for attention."

"It's very odd, Deke. And she was so much better than your usual run-of-the-mill genre writer."

"Have you considered that perhaps your aunt Maddy wrote those books?"

"Not really. Her husband was the writer. She was big on crafts."

"Even writers need hobbies."

"But why would she keep it a secret?"

"I don't know. Perhaps she didn't want to show up her old man."

"In that case, what happened to the $3.8 million?"

"How thoroughly have you searched that house?"

"Why would they hide cash when they had a secure safe to stash it in?"

"I don't know, Mok. That safe might have been a decoy. They sound like quite an eccentric couple."

"My whole family is weird," I admitted.

Eventually, I got around to asking Deke if he was seeing anyone.

"I got a wake-up call last year, Mok. I had a PSA test that was off the charts. So I opted to have my prostate removed. I've pretty much hung up my spurs on that activity."

"That's awful, Deke. I'm so sorry."

"Well, I got my share," he winked. "It's a small sacrifice to make if the alternative is being dressed in a blue suit for casket photos. There's a lot to life besides rubbing knees with some cutie."

"You shouldn't give up, Deke. Many women . . . probably most women our age, are fine with, uh, companionship."

God, that came out sounding lame.

Deke smiled and said, "Well, perhaps it will happen. Who knows?"

He insisted on paying the check. Some awkwardness when we returned to my house. I gave him the tour, then he asked to see a photo of my "younger daughter." I fished one out of my wallet; he put on his stylish glasses and studied it for some time.

"Casta Spall, that's a pretty feeble pun, Mok."

"It was entirely unintentional, I assure you. Casta was the name of my grandmother who died before I was born. It's Latin for pure, pious, and modest. So inappropriate for my daughter."

"Well, she's a cute kid," he said, handing back the photo.

"Cute, but diabolical."

He didn't have a current photo of Jamie to show me. More awkwardness as he was leaving. Another quick hug and he was out the door. I watched his car drive slowly up the street in a squall of seasonally inappropriate snow flurries.

I turned up the heat, made myself a cup of tea, and picked up my second-to-the-last Gloria Anne Lenore novel. Nowhere in that text, I knew, would I encounter the word "prostate."

March 22 – Got an email from Deke thanking me for lunch yesterday. Attached was a 1970s high-school photo of his sister Sarah. She looked enough like Casta to be her twin.

March 23 – Passed a restless night. I never told Deke I was pregnant, but I suppose Kyle could have blabbed to Jamie about it. As I recall, he wasn't very enthusiastic about getting a baby sister. Keep reminding myself that one photo does not constitute a proof of paternity. Trying to remember how careful we were with those damn condoms. I suspect we might have been a bit lackadaisical at times because I thought I was past the age of conception.

Kind of a mind-bender. All these years I kept thinking how much Casta took after Harkness.

I suspect if Harkness found out he wouldn't take it very well. What would I do if he kicked me out? I'm sure I'm even less employable than Monica.

Worrying thought: You never know when Casta might need some medical test that would reveal all.

Something of a disaster. And all I got for my trouble were two perfunctory hugs.

Another paranoid thought: Was Deke really sick or did he invent that story of prostate cancer because he was repulsed by the prospect of sleeping with me? Did my makeup signal desperation to him? Is that how guys his age are letting girls down easy these days?

March 24 – Still no sign of spring. Drove home to Pepper Pike to wave the wifely flag. Grilled Harkness a nice steak for dinner and smothered it in his favorite mushroom wine sauce. Then at lights out I practically raped him. As usual I fantasized that I was Andie MacDowell just returning with Hugh Grant from another wedding. (God, I loved that movie.) One does require some mental distraction when making it with Harkness.

"Darling, I've missed you," I lied when the act was terminated.

"Missed you too," he sniffed, rolling over and immediately losing consciousness.

I used to feel a little self-conscious finishing with my hand, but Harkness never wakes up. It's like his prostate turns off all the lights in his brain two seconds after it's done its thing.

March 25 – Figured out why I always get a headache Sunday mornings. It's those damn pancakes I eat with Harkness.

Monica and Roland just hauled off the last of her stuff in his new van. My daughter has left home, possibly for good. Neither had much to say to me, the harridan mother. That van may not have been brand new, but it was certainly a shiny late model that must have cost at least ten grand. "Granny" was certainly generous. New magnetic signs on the doors read: Pacalac Productions. When that slimy slug is ripping your guts out emerging into this world, you never imagine that some day she'll be leaving home with a portly safecracker named Roland Pacalac.

March 26 – What would we do without the Internet? I found four obscure Gloria Anne Lenore novels at Abebooks.com. Three reasonably priced, but one greedhead wanted $38 for a lousy paperback. I cursed him soundly as I added it to my cart. Anyway, the joke's on him because I wouldn't have blinked if he'd asked $100.

Searching through boxes in Maddy's basement, I felt something brush against my bare ankle. I turned around and was staring at the world's biggest rat. I screamed, dropped the box, ran up the steps, and slammed the door. Within an hour the exterminator had arrived, done his thing in the basement, and was giving me his report.

"I set six traps. He may be wise to traps so I also spread around the sticky paper. If you hear some thrashing around, give me a call. You got a floor drain down there with no grate. That's probably how he got in. I found a bowling ball and put it over it, if that's OK with you?"

"Fine. It's not my bowling ball."

"Good. Were you by any chance a cheerleader?"

A very startling question.

"I was. Several millennia ago."

"I thought so. You're Helen Manders."

"I used to be. Do I know you?"

He was about my age, with all his hair and a nice build. His trim blue uniform nicely accented his eyes.

"Probably not. I was in the class behind you. I'm Joe Ducowski."

A long-dormant synapse in my brain snapped to attention.

"God, Joe Ducowski. I remember you. You're Joe the Toe."

"Yeah."

"You muffed that kick."

"Yeah, that was me. Shanked it pretty bad."

"You drilled it straight into Mary Ann Morganstern, the head majorette."

"Yeah."

"You knocked out her six front teeth."

"Well, technically the football did that. I was about 15 yards away."

"God, I've never seen so much blood, including the three times I gave birth."

"Yeah, it was pretty bad. Wow, Helen Manders is now a client of mine. You were the goddess of all goddesses."

"Not hardly, Joe."

"Weren't you the homecoming queen?"

"Possibly."

"And head cheerleader and editor of the school newspaper. You interviewed me after that football game."

"Did I really? I don't remember."

"You were very nice to me. I appreciated that. Jesus, Helen Manders–right here in Euclid, with a rat in her basement. It's a small world."

"A very small world, Joe."

March 27 – More snow flurries. Can't they drain Lake Erie and send all that snow-inducing water to parched Arizona?

Deke called to ask if I'd uncovered any of Gloria Anne Lenore's lost millions. I told him about my encounter with the scary rat. He commiserated, then expressed a desire to meet my younger daughter. I asked him in what context we could contrive to do that.

"I've been giving it some thought, Mok. You could bring her by your house and introduce me as a neighbor helping you strip wallpaper."

"Not going to work, Deke. My daughter has a mind like a Soviet agent. She'd immediately suspect something was up between us."

"Well that might not be so bad."

"Not for you maybe."

"I'd like to see her once before I croak, Mok."

"You're not even 60, Deke."

"Our warranties have long since expired, Mok. Lots of us won't be seeing 70."

"All right. I'll give it some thought. There might be some way to do it."

"I'd appreciate that, Mok."

"Probably not after you meet her."

March 28 – Called Joe back to deal with the death screams from my basement. Took him ten minutes to do the job and to cart out the remains. An hour later we were reclining in Aunt Maddy's big walnut bed and basking in a warm post-coital glow.

"God, I've actually slept with Helen Manders," he sighed. "I can die happy now."

"Brought together by a rat, Joe. Is that romantic or what?"

By staying as horizontal as possible, I was able to minimize the appearance of sag (and its heinous cousin flab).

I asked Joe to tell me about himself. He said his entire life was defined by that one kick.

"I was very dedicated as a kid, Helen. I spent years practicing. I was going to ride my golden foot all the way into the NFL and on to the Hall of Fame in Canton. Even as a junior, I had lots of interest from college recruiters."

"So you muffed one kick, Joe. Was that such a big deal?"

"It was for me. It wrecked my confidence. Kicking is about 51 percent mental. So instead of going to college on an athletic scholarship, I went to Vietnam."

"How was that, Joe?"

"About the same as for the guys in Iraq and Afghanistan. We went to the jungle to watch our buddies die. They go to the desert or the mountains. We were there to hold the line against the Commies. So I bought a DVD player last month. Guess where it was made."

"Uh, Vietnam."

"You got it, Helen."

"The bullshit never changes, Joe. So are you married?"

"Yeah, 31 years this June. How about you?"

"Pretty much the same story."

"Gary Matuski claimed he nailed you. Any truth to that?"

"Not hardly, Joe. I went out with that jerk one time. He had the worst B.O. on the planet. And a personality to match."

"Any interest in taking another shot at the goal line? My offense seems to be regrouping."

"Why not, Joe? Anything to keep from stripping wallpaper."

I was amazed a fellow his age was able to recover so quickly. Harkness usually requires at least three weeks.

Later, when I was kissing Joe good-bye, I told him I didn't want to break up his marriage. He said that was good, because he didn't want to "mess up" mine either.

March 29 – Actual sunshine is attempting to penetrate the omnipresent cloud cover. If there is such a thing as free will, why am I living in northeastern Ohio? Why cannot I compel my hand to roll the little scoring tool over my aunt's repellent wallpaper? Why am I stalled in redecorating hell?

Took a long walk with my neighbor Grace along the lakefront. She guessed that I was in the throes of some inner conflict that blocked me from acting.

"Why don't you want to finish the house, Helen?"

"But I do! I hate being stuck in limbo like this."

"Some part of you must like things the way they are."

"Well, I sort of enjoy being on my own. I like spending the afternoon reading instead of fixing dinner for my family. I like walking to places in Euclid. I like hanging out with you. I like the lake on nice days."

"All fine reasons, Helen, to leave that wallpaper be."

"But I can't go on like this forever."

"Why not?"

"I have responsibilities, Grace. I'm feeling guilty for deserting my family. My husband is eating microwaved dinners every night. He's an attorney. They expect better treatment than that."

"Is he that fellow in the beat-up Mustang?"

So I spilled the beans about Deke. While I was at it, I confessed to my recent infidelity with Joe the Toe. Grace listened with her usual solicitude, then commented, "Well, I'm glad it was a rat and not termites. I was a little concerned when I saw that truck. Not that I spy on my neighbors."

Grace generously offered to advance me the money to hire pros to strip the wallpaper and repaint. She said I could pay her back when I sold the house.

I replied I wouldn't dream of taking her money, but she pointed out that it was just sitting in the bank earning 0.09 percent interest. She added that I could pay her a little interest on the loan if I wished.

I told her I would think about it.

Since we were in the neighborhood, we stopped in at the senior center for their 85-cent meatloaf lunch. Decent, but we both agreed ours were better. Grace puts a little spicy sausage in hers. My secret is crushed pita chips in place of breadcrumbs.

March 30 – Thinking seriously of taking Grace up on her offer. But accepting a loan from an old lady–could that be construed as elder abuse?

Rifled some more through the junk in the basement. Aunt Maddy

must have gone all out on the Christmas decorating. And got pretty festive at Halloween too. Kind of strange for a gal with no kids or grandchildren. I did find a big box of old family photos. Most of the people unknown to me, but quite a few shots of my mother, her sister, and their
parents. You can tell by leafing through the albums that my mother was
the pretty sister and Maddy was the nice one. No photos of a young Uncle
Phil though.

Three Gloria Anne Lenore novels arrived in the mail today–rescuing
me from acute G.A.L. withdrawal. Don't know what I'll do when I've read
them all. Probably have to go on methadone to preserve my sanity.

March 31 – Spent my Saturday restoring the Pepper Pike house to a
semblance of order and cleanliness. While I was folding laundry, Casta
showed up to lord it over me that she and her father had dined the night
before at Monica's new place. No invitation had been extended to the
shrewish mother.

"So how was it?" I asked, feigning indifference.

"Monica lives in such a slum! I was sure we were going to get mugged
walking from the car to her front door. They got the first floor of this old
house that was divided. They have the original living room, kitchen, and
dining room, which they're using as a bedroom. Daddy averted his eyes
every time he had to walk through there. They're doing it hippie style on
a mattress on the floor. Someone else lives upstairs; we heard them
clopping around. Probably cooking up a fresh batch of meth. And guess
where the bathroom is!"

"Where?"

"In the funky dark freezing basement! They have to troop down the
stairs every time they need to pee!"

"How was dinner?"

"Horrible, as usual. Very gloppy and gross. Daddy found a pubic hair
in his salad. One of these days Monica's going to poison someone. I only
hope it's Roland and not me."

"I'm surprised your father accepted her invitation."

"Ghoulish curiosity, Mom. That's the only reason either of us agreed
to go. You guys so failed with your first-born, I hope you realize that."

"Monica has a master's degree from a prestigious college and is doing
what she finds interesting. That's not so bad."

"She's shacking with a fat creep and working a menial job for pea-
nuts."

"All the more reason, Casta, that you should start paying attention in
school. Your last report card was a disgrace. How are you going to make
a living?"

"I'm leaving those details to my pimp."

"That isn't funny, Casta. If you exhibited a better attitude, I might consider taking you shopping tomorrow for spring clothes."

That perked her up.

"I'm by far your nicest kid, Mom. I'm the one success story you can point to with pride."

"We'll make a day of it. Just the two of us. We'll have lunch someplace nice."

"Don't let Daddy give you a spending limit. I'm in desperate need of everything."

April 1 – More gray drizzle, which may be why God invented shopping malls. While Harkness golfed, Casta and I shopped. She wanted to grab a pizza slice in the mall, but I insisted on lunching in a decent sit-down restaurant. This time Deke was only ten minutes late. We had just ordered when he dropped by our table.

"Excuse me," he said. "Are you by any chance Helen Spall?"

"I am, yes," I admitted.

"You probably don't remember me. I'm Deke Brennan."

I pretended to take a few moments to place him. "Oh, yes, Deke. How are you? Your son used to play with my boy Kyle. Let's see, what was his name?"

"Jamie."

"Right! They were great pals in preschool. Uh, by the way, this is my daughter Casta."

Beaming smile from Deke; barest nod of acknowledgment from Casta.

"Casta," said Deke. "That's an unusual name."

No reply from my daughter.

"She was named after her grandmother," I said. "Casta, tell Mr. Brennan what your name means."

"Torpid sloth," she muttered.

"I hardly think so," I replied. "Casta's a bit preoccupied because we've been clothes shopping. Well, it was nice running into you, Deke."

At that point, the plan called for Deke–his curiosity satisfied–to excuse himself and depart. Instead, he said, "I hate dining alone, Helen. Do you mind if I join you?"

Before I could reply, he pulled out a chair and sat down. Instantly, I could sense the gears in my daughter's head start to churn.

"Er, no, I suppose not," I stammered.

So commenced an elaborate one-act play of "distant acquaintances" pretending to catch up with each other, while my (mostly) silent daughter observed warily. Barely deigning to look at him, she resisted every effort by Deke to engage her in the conversation. And every statement he did manage to extract from her was a falsehood or impertinent fabrication. Very torturous as the minutes dragged by and my lunch went untouched. It got even uglier at the end when Deke insisted on picking up the check while I pleaded in vain with the waitress to split the bill. Didn't that idiot realize how my daughter would interpret his action?

By the time we were saying our goodbyes, I was radiating nearly as much hostility as my chilly daughter. Nevertheless, Deke felt compelled to give each of us a farewell hug. As he strolled away, Casta gave me The Look.

"Er, sorry about that fellow," I stammered. "He was always sort of a pest. That's why your father and I stopped seeing them."

"He's kind of cute for an old guy," she replied. "I can see why you slept with him. But what is he, some kind of pervert?"

"I have no idea what you're talking about, Casta."

"He was hitting on me, Mom. Big time. Even a blind person could see that."

"Don't be silly. You're imagining things. He's old enough to be your, uh, uncle. And I certainly never slept with the man. The very idea! Now, let's go check out Macy's for shoes."

April 2 – On my way back to Euclid this morning I stopped at my mother's rest home and dropped off the box of photos.

"I've got a nice job for you, Lorraine," I said. "I'd like you to go through these photos and identify everyone you recognize in pencil on the back."

"Why the hell should I do that?" she demanded.

"So we'll know who they are, of course."

"Why do you care who they are, Maddy? Have you joined some cult of ancestor worshippers in your old age?"

"Just write down their names, Lorraine. It will be a pleasant activity for you."

"That's what you think. I've spent the last 92 years trying to forget these people."

"Just do it. Your daughter will appreciate it."

"If you see my daughter, tell her that her mother sends her regards."

"I tell you what. You go through all these photos, and I'll have Helen pay you a nice long visit."

"A nice visit with that girl would be short, not long. The shorter the better!"

Later, as I was down in the basement trying to pry open a door to an old coalbin, Deke phoned.

"Our daughter is enchanting!" he exclaimed.

"Uh, she's my daughter, Deke, not yours. And I didn't appreciate your imposing yourself on us like that."

"I had to talk to her, Mok. Surely you can understand that?"

"That's not my name. And she completely misinterpreted your interest. She thinks you're a pedophile."

"What!"

"She thinks you're some pervert slobbering after underage girls."

"I trust you assured her otherwise."

"What was I supposed to say? I let the topic drop as quickly as possible. The whole thing was a big mistake, Deke."

"She's got that Brennan spark, Mok. Anyone can see that."

"Well, it was interesting seeing you, Deke. I wish you all the best. Got to go now."

"I'd like to see her again, Mok."

"I don't see how that would be possible, Deke. You don't really fit into her life. Or mine."

"I have some rights here, Mok. I'm prepared to assert them."

"Oh, really? And would you like to pay your share of the $1,300 tab I ran up buying her clothes yesterday? And while we're at it, how about chipping in for her college education? Want to send me a check for $100,000 as a down payment?"

"I would if I could, Mok. You know that."

"Sorry. I don't know that. I don't know that at all."

I finally got the coalbin door open by prying the pins out of the hinges. Dank smelly place was found to contain coal. Search through pile with rusty shovel uncovered no hidden treasure.

April 3 – My neighbor Grace and I have agreed on the terms of my senior-abuse loan. I am borrowing $3,000 at six percent interest. At my insistence, I am putting up the Beast as collateral. I'm not sure under what circumstance it could be worth $3,000. Perhaps if it were the last minivan on earth.

Got my $38 G.A.L. paperback in the mail today. That greedy jerk sure took his time shipping it. I keep expecting a fall-off in quality, but so far every one of Gloria Anne Lenore's novels has been a gem. This one's about an aspiring young dancer who gets both of her legs broken in a tragic car wreck. One might almost suppose I was similarly impaired from the way this book is keeping me pinned to the sofa.

Gabby's energetic handyperson showed up to give me an estimate. She's a large black woman in her forties named DeeAnn. She'll strip all the wallpaper, prep the walls, and paint the entire interior for $2,300. Seemed very reasonable to me.

"Shall I go with you to the paint store to pick out the colors?" I asked.

"My estimate's for Navajo White, Mrs. Spall. That's what everyone uses. A nice light neutral is what you want. I buy it in bulk, so I get it for a cheap price. Covers in one coat and hides the defects. And it looks like you got plenty of defects with this old plaster."

"Oh, right. Whatever you say."

It does seem ironic that distant, hogan-dwelling Navajos are imposing their aesthetic on the housing market of greater Cleveland.

"When can you start, DeeAnn?"

"I'll be here day after tomorrow. Bright and early."

"Is there anything I can do to help?"

"No, ma'am. Just stay out of my way."

At last, a task even I can accomplish.

April 4 – I called Joe Ducowski to report my basement was still rat-free and invite him over for lunch.

"I'd love to come, Helen. But I better not."

"How come, Joe?"

"Because you're Helen Manders. If I see you again, I'll fall in love with you for sure. And how will I explain that to my kids and grandchildren?"

"OK, Joe. I understand. So how come you never asked me out in high school?"

"You know why, Helen. I was never in your league."

"Sure you were, Joe."

"Nope, Helen. Not even close."

April 5 – It turns out there *is* a wallpaper-removing machine. DeeAnn and her cute twenty-something daughter Beverly dragged in what looks like an oversized shop vac that loosens the paper with steam. They press the steam-emitting end against the wall, and the paper unrolls like a large limp noodle. Damp and sweaty work though. Even with the windows open, the humidity in here is about 99 percent. I did my bit by making coffee and laying out a plate of cookies. DeeAnn switched off the steamer and called for a five-minute break.

"How much you going to ask for this place, Mrs. Spall?" inquired Beverly.

"I'm not sure yet. But it won't be much. I'm hoping to net enough to buy a decent car."

"Should we buy it, Mom?"

"Don't need another house, Bev. I got too many already."

It seems that DeeAnn owns eight houses that she is renting out, plus the one she lives in.

"Isn't that a lot of work and responsibility?" I asked.

"I suppose, ma'am. But I was never one to sit still for long."

That could have been a dig, since I expect Gabby had blabbed to her about my home renovation paralysis. But I decided it was just a statement of fact.

"My mother's totally organized and all business," said Beverly. "Her tenants know they can't mess with her. She's like a drill sergeant in the marines."

"I crack the whip when I need to," admitted DeeAnn. "Now back away

46

from those cookies, Bev, and let's get to work."

"Your aunt was some crazy free spirit," said Beverly, not budging.

"You think so?" I replied.

"It's too bad you have to strip away all the character to sell her house," she added. "It sort of feels like a desecration."

"I know what you mean," I admitted.

"I'll be desecrating your ass, girl," said her mother. "If you don't get that steamer cooking."

Beverly sighed, put down her coffee cup, and resumed her work.

April 6 – Amazing progress. All the wallpaper has been stripped from downstairs, and DeeAnn and her daughter are now tackling the upstairs. It really does pay to hire pros. If only I could hire someone to be Helen Spall, doting mother and loving wife.

Under the sunflowers in the kitchen lurked a green paint of stomach-churning hideousness. I don't see how anyone could have cooked any-thing appetizing in that kitchen–let alone eaten it in there. It makes the brown paint in the living and dining rooms seem positively cheerful by comparison. The Navajo White cannot be slapped on soon enough to suit me.

Found another Gloria Ann Lenore novel on Ebay. The seller claims it's quite rare because it was withdrawn from publication. Doesn't say why though. Kind of a mystery. I am now high bidder at $2.78. Three days to go. Too bad the seller didn't specify a Buy It Now price.

Got the box of photos back from my mother. Don't know why I wasted my time. She identified people as Rudolph Hess, Rita Hayworth, Calvin Coolidge, Charlie McCarthy, Elmer Fudd, etc. Wrote it in ink too, which pretty much wrecks the photos. So much for passing a legacy on to my children (not that they care).

I returned two hours later with a mystery to unravel. I showed my mother a photo of her and her sister placing flowers on a grave.

"What's the story on this, Lorraine?" I asked.

"Don't get senile on me, Maddy. That's when we visited Don's grave in Maine. All the Manders get buried up there in the frozen tundra. I hope to hell you're not planning on shipping my corpse up there."

"The headstone gives his years as 1919 to 1953."

"So?"

"So if he died in 1953, how could he father a daughter who was born in November of 1954?"

"And who might that be?"

"Your daughter Helen."

"Oh, her."

"So?"

"So no big deal. It was a goddam typo."

"A typo on a headstone?"

"Don't look at me, kiddo. It was his flaky mother who did it. You know how when you write a check after New Years half the time you write the previous year's date?"

"I suppose."

"So his mother wrote the wrong year on the form she gave to the stonecutter."

"And she didn't bother to change it?"

"Not easy to do with granite, Maddy. You can't chisel a '3' to look like a '4.' You'd have to redo the whole thing. Cost you some dough, and all those Manders were tight with a nickel."

"So all these years my father has had the wrong date on his headstone?"

"Sure. No big deal. It's not like anyone gives a flying. . ."

Mother stopped and peered at me suspiciously.

"You're such a little sneak, Helen. How come you're trying to pass yourself off as my sister? What the hell have you done with Maddy? And how on earth did you get to be so old?"

April 7 – Back home for the weekend. Casta had some news for me.

"That creepy boyfriend of yours is trying to friend me on Facebook."

"Deke Brennan is not my boyfriend, Casta. I told you that."

"I'm thinking of reporting him to the FBI."

I grabbed her by her shirt, dragged her into her bedroom, sat her down on her messy bed, then shut the door.

"What did I do this time?" she cried.

"Nothing, honey. I need to tell you something that I hope you will keep confidential. You are misinterpreting Mr. Brennan's interest in you."

"What? He's only interested in my ripe young mind?"

"There is a possibility that Mr. Brennan is, uh . . . your father."

Casta gave me The Look and chewed her gum.

"I'm sorry if that's a shock to you, Casta. I broke it off after you were conceived, and only saw him again last week. We haven't done any sort of paternity test, but you do resemble his sister when she was in high school."

Casta, master of inscrutability, continued to stare at me blankly.

"Uh, are you going to say anything, dear? Do you have any questions?"

"Are Monica and Kyle also bastards?"

"No one is a bastard here, Casta. But there's no question that they are your father's . . . that is to say, Harkness's children."

"You did it with him in some sleazy motel?"

"No, it was actually quite a nice motor lodge. We always used a condom, but we may have, uh, slipped up."

"And you were also doing it with Daddy?"

"Well, these things happen, Casta. When you're older, you'll understand. I don't claim to be perfect."

"So just because he's some slipshod, overeager sperm-blaster, that doesn't mean I want to have anything to do with him."

"Right. Well, I thought you should know the situation. If that's your position on the matter, I could make it clear to him."

"Please do, Mom. So his kid Jamie could be my half-brother?"

"Uh, I suppose so."

"And Monica might only be my half-sister?"

"That's right."

"Well, that's some good news. And now I know my mother has done at least one unexpected thing in her life."

"It really would be best, Casta, if you didn't say anything about this to anyone. Can I trust you on this?"

"Sure, Mom. Well, as much as you can trust me on anything."

April 8 – I'm still high bidder on *Ruth of Riverside Ranch*. The bidding is up to $11.34. The other bidders should just drop out now because the sky's the limit for me.

Made waffles for Harkness as a change of pace. He was pleased to hear that the wallpaper stripping is going well at last. I didn't tell him that I borrowed money and hired a crew to do the work. Husbands, I've learned, don't really need to know the nitty-gritty details.

Baked my 28th consecutive Easter ham. Just the three of us here for dinner. Well, more like 2-1/2, since Casta spent the entire meal texting on her phone.

April 9 – Spent the night again in Pepper Pike in case Harkness wished to avail himself of my charms. He didn't. Had to rush back to Euclid in the early a.m. to let in DeeAnn and her daughter. Every hour or so Bev hauls down a big garbage bag filled with steamed-off wallpaper. Four layers in the master bedroom. No wonder the walls were squishy to the touch.

Emailed Deke the news about Casta ejecting him from her life. Expressed a strong wish that he honor her decision and respect her privacy. I'm kicking myself now for contacting him in the first place. People my age should stay away from sites like Facebook that encourage wallowing in nostalgia.

Very depressed. *Ruth of Riverside Ranch* sold for $728.61. I was high bidder up until the last few seconds at $512. I never imagined one obscure book could command such a price. I hope the winner is an actual Gloria Anne Lenore fan and not some book collector just after it for its rarity and speculative value.

Of course, I realize spending over $500 for a book I could read in a few days is a bit extreme. But now I feel sick for not bidding at least $800.

April 10 – Pleasant springlike day. Oppressive clouds have all sailed off to bother Buffalo. The last of the wallpaper has gone out the door– even from the closet containing Uncle Phil's safe. Have donated all the vintage threadbare towels to DeeAnn for use as paint rags. Paste is being washed from walls, to be followed by spackling. Kind of damp sleeping here last night. Like bedding down inside a giant mushroom.

Got a rant-like email from Deke. Apparently Casta sent him a "Dear John" message rejecting his Facebook friend request. He accused me of poisoning her against him. I did no such thing, but I didn't reply to his email. I'm hoping he will get the message and go away.

I'm pretty sure at one time I loved him. Might have loved him again if things had turned out differently. At least my relations with men have been consistent: as in consistently disappointing.

April 11 – Got a curious email from Cmprof4lit, the spendthrift twit who outbid me on *Ruth of Riverside Ranch*. He said he regretted the bidding "got out of hand," and offered to mail me a photocopy of the text (for free!) when he receives the book. Smells like a scam, but I replied with my address just in case there is some benevolence left in this world.

A zillion cracks and holes in my walls are now wearing little white patches of spackle. DeeAnn and her daughter are so fast and competent I feel like a useless parasite. I try to be semi-useful by keeping them supplied with drinks and snacks. Also made a run to the hardware store for more spackle, which DeeAnn says my walls "eat like candy."

April 12 – Monica phoned this morning to get my recipe for Bachelor's Casserole, a quick and easy ground-beef dish that never fails to please. I gather Roland has been less than thrilled with the eats. And to think, only a few weeks ago he was dining out of dumpsters.

She reported that they are nearly done with their script.

"Would you like to be in our movie, Mother? There's a part for an older woman who gets crushed under the freight elevator."

"Uh, well that sounds intriguing. How crushed would I be?"

"It's all done by editing. First we see you cowering in the elevator shaft. Then we cut to the elevator coming down. Then we hear your blood-curdling scream. Also some body-crunching noises. Then there's a close shot of blood oozing out from under the elevator."

"Sounds great, dear. You can count me in. I always wanted to be a movie star."

"It's just a small part, Mother. Only one scene."

"Well, everyone has to start somewhere. Shall I practice my scream?"

"Not necessary. You can employ your standard one that you used on us."

April 13 – Big transformation. Primer paint has been rolled onto my spotted walls, burying all those vile hues under pristine white. Aunt Maddy's living room no longer feels like the Psych Ward in "Snake Pit." You no longer expect to encounter catatonic wraiths chained to the walls. But now I'm thinking I don't dare rehang those dreary drapes. What sort of value-enhancing window coverings can I scrounge up on my budget? I need something fresh, bright, and cute for about forty-nine cents. Too bad Woolworth's went out of business.

Had a debate with DeeAnn about painting the odious kitchen cabinets. She claims painting wooden cabinets is always a mistake. Paint shows all the dirt and inevitably chips. Then you have to repaint. Pretty soon you have six layers of paint and doors that no longer close.

"Then what on earth can I do?" I wailed.

"Just wash them down and spray on furniture polish. Make 'em look like new."

"But they were ugly as sin when they were brand new!"

"Well, what color would look nice with those orange counters?"

She had me there. "Couldn't we also paint the Formica, DeeAnn?"

"The short answer is no way, Mrs. Spall."

Paralyzed with indecision, I put off dealing with the issue.

Paint fumes are a bit overpowering. Grace has taken pity and invited me to spend the night in her house. For our potluck dinner, I'm making Bachelor's Casserole.

April 14 – Back in Pepper Pike, I found Harkness in a frenzy of last-minute toil over our tax return. For a guy in that business, he always procrastinates until the eleventh hour. I think it has to do with his fervent belief that All Taxes Are Theft.

"Where's Casta?" I inquired.

"Haven't seen her," he replied, bent over his computer keyboard.

"Since when?"

"Uh, let's see. Since Wednesday, I guess."

"What! You haven't seen our daughter for three days! Do you know where she is?"

"Not really. I expect she's staying with friends."

"Harkness, you can't just abandon your role as parent here!"

"Oh? Isn't that what you've been doing, Helen?"

No answer on Casta's phone. I called her friend Marie, who may have known where Casta was, but she wasn't saying.

"Was Casta in school yesterday?" I asked.

"Gosh, Mrs. Spall. I didn't really notice."

"Don't you take most of your classes together?"

"I'm sure she's fine, Mrs. Spall. If I hear from her, I'll tell her to call you right away."

Phoned two more of Casta's friends, who also claimed ignorance of her whereabouts. I grabbed my car keys and told Harkness to call me immediately if he heard from her.

My GPS guided me to Deke's address, which turned out to be a shabby little house on a dead-end lane in a rural part of Medina. His rusty Mustang was parked in the driveway.

Casta opened the door when I rang the bell.

"Hi, Mom. All the pizza's gone, but there's some salad left."

I let loose with the tirade that had been building on the drive down from Pepper Pike. Both Casta and Deke were defiant and unapologetic.

"Like what was I supposed to tell Daddy?" Casta demanded. "I'm going off to see my real father?"

"You should have called me!"

"I didn't know you cared."

Only a powerful force of will kept me from slapping her face.

"Harkness will have to be told eventually," said Deke.

"Don't you dare!" I exclaimed. "And if you want to have anything to do with my daughter, you clear it with me first. I could have you arrested for kidnapping."

"And get laughed out of court when the DNA evidence comes in," he replied.

"Get your things, Casta," I said. "We're leaving. Now!"

She gave him a warm hug on the cluttered front porch.

"See you soon, Dom," he said. "You take care."

"Thanks, Fom," she replied. "It's been fun."

I pried some of the story out of her on the drive back.

"He offered to take me to see the Flying Hatchets," she said. "They were playing in Kent."

"What's that?"

"Only the coolest band ever. They were awesome."

"Where did you sleep?"

"In the virginal guestroom, Mom. Gee, I'm not into incest, if that's what you're thinking."

"What's this Fom and Dom business?"

"Dom is daughter of mine and Fom stands for father of mine. He's my father, Mom. Hell, I look just like him."

"You do not."

"I do so. If you took a photo of you and a photo of Deke, morphed them together and subtracted all the wrinkles and decrepitude, it would look just like me."

"That doesn't prove anything."

"You're in denial, Mom. Get over it."

Casta said she feels sorry for Deke because he thinks his life has been a failure.

"Why's that?" I asked.

"Well, first his wife left him, then you dumped him, then his business failed, then he got cancer. Did you know he almost died?"

"I think he mentioned it."

"And now his son's in jail."

"What? He told me Jamie was working as a car mechanic."

"He was, but now he's in prison in Columbus. Some drug dealer got shot. The only fingerprints on the gun were Jamie's."

"Did the guy die?"

"Nope, but Jamie's in for at least eight years. Deke doesn't think he'll live long enough to see his son get released."

"That's awful."

"Yeah, so we have to cut him some slack."

"But what will we tell your father?"

"We'll tell him I was at Marie's. We'll say I left my phone on and the battery died. Daddy's very gullible, as you know."

I didn't appreciate her smug smile. Or her attitude. But that was nothing new.

April 15. Tax day. Since it falls on a Sunday, Harkness has an extra 24 hours to find ways to diddle the government. I hope the IRS appreciates that I only sign our tax returns under duress.

While Harkness cooked the books in the den, I Googled Gordon Efflemberger on my iPad. I met Gordon sophomore year when he was clerking in a copy shop in downtown Elyria. He got very snotty when I asked him to clean the drum before Xeroxing my term paper on Edna St. Vincent Millay. When I returned for my copies, he further offended me by predicting my paper would earn a B+. He said the typing was crummy and there were too many misspellings. A strange form of flirting, but I went out with him for the next two years. He was my first serious love. We even talked about marriage a few times as college kids with $4 in the bank sometimes do. Gordon was a geology major, which at the time I thought was the dullest subject on earth.

Unless there are multiple Gordon Efflembergers on this planet, he is now pastor of a Baptist church in Indian Wells, Oklahoma. Don't ask me how he made the transition from rocks to God. I recall his parents were religious, but I never saw him enter a church. Gordon has seven children and a wife who looks incredibly sweet in her photo. He now sports a bouffant hairdo and was fully swathed in Christian polyester, but he appears to be the same fellow I used to sneak into my dorm room.

Very strange to think that I might have turned out to be a minister's wife living in tornado alley. All in all, I think I prefer Pepper Pike. At least I had the foresight to fall in love with a guy who later would be an easy Google find. Must be tough for those gals trying to locate their long-lost

Ed Jones and Tim Johnsons. And even harder for fellows hoping to re-connect with former sweethearts who've taken their husbands' names.

Harkness was pleased to see that all his juggling yielded an antici-pated refund of $1,312. After screwing the government, he was sufficiently aroused to do the same to me.

April 16 – As I write this Navajo White is being industriously rollered onto my walls. Much brighter in here; I may have to start wearing my sunglasses indoors. Gabby dropped by and was pleased with the progress. She recommended cabinet refacing, granite counters, and all new appli-ances for the kitchen, but I told her I'd be lucky to be able to afford replacement washers for the dripping sink faucet.

Kyle phoned from New Orleans to report that he was having a blast on spring break, but the city was proving far more expensive than they'd anticipated.

"How much do you need?" I sighed.

"I could really use another $500, Mom."

"What a coincidence, dear. So could I."

"Well, I can't ask Dad because he doesn't even know I'm down here."

Why am I always entering into conspiracies with my children? Is that a normal feature of modern parenting?

I told him I'd wire him $300 from my dwindling house-renovation fund.

Beverly offered a possible solution for my drapes crisis. She has a B.A. in art and does drapes-painting as a sideline. She proposed to do a "Jack-son Pollocky" repaint of Aunt Maddy's old curtains in tones of cream and gold. She uses her mother's surplus latex paint and claims her customers are "always thrilled" with the results. She promised a "fresh new look" for a mere $250. I said I might consider it for $200, so we compromised on $225.

My walls are greatly improved, but now my old linoleum looks even more like evil incarnate. Do you suppose Gordon Efflemberger offers discount home-decor miracles as a sideline? Would the cad even remem-ber me?

April 17 – Finished my last Gloria Anne Lenore novel last night in Grace's cozy guestroom. I am now bereft. The light has gone out of my life.

April 18 – Paid off DeeAnn and added $50 as a bonus. I would like to have offered more, but I'm so strapped. Bev promised to return on Fri-day with my renovated drapes.

Bought some ammonia, rubber gloves, and furniture polish for dreaded kitchen-cabinet renewal. I have absolutely nothing to distract me from my work now except the fine springlike weather. Lake Erie looking very blue on my morning walk. Felt like calling Joe Ducowski, but I know I don't dare.

Is it a sign of desperation that I've removed the bowling ball from my basement floor drain?

April 19 – A miracle happened in Aunt Maddy's mailbox this morning. The postperson delivered a heavy envelope containing the promised photocopy of *Ruth of Riverside Ranch*. Attached was this note typed on Carllon-Melnegie University stationery:

> Dear Ms. Spall,
>
> Enclosed is the copy we discussed. As you can see from the title page, the novel was published in 1957, but was soon withdrawn by the publisher. I have not been able to determine why. If you have any insights, I'd love to hear them.
> Best wishes,
> Leigh Mulcahy

It appears Cmprof4lit is female and a possible Gloria Anne Lenore fan. Her stationery identified her as a Professor of English. I immediately dashed off an effusive email thanking her. I added that I would love to hear *her* insights about my favorite author, especially since Ms. Lenore was connected in some way with my aunt and uncle.

Got this email in reply:

> Helen,
>
> I'm intrigued by your aunt and uncle's involvement with G.A.L. Would love to discuss this with you. Could you send me your phone number and also note the best time to call?
>
> Btw, back in the 1950s a few boy babies got stuck with the name Leigh, myself included.
> Best,
> Leigh

I replied, then checked out Prof. Mulcahy on the Carllon-Melnegie website. His photo revealed him to be a thin fellow with one of those nose-clogging 19th Century mustaches. This text appeared under his photo:

> **Program: Cultural and Literary Studies**
>
> My research focuses on contemporary American fiction, especially those genres where science and imagination intersect. Recently I have explored how the changing technology of writing has altered the creative process. My book, *The Genius Inside the Typewriter*

(Buoyford Press, 2009), discusses how the development of mechanical writing systems affected the prolixity of three generations of prominent writers.

Looked up his book on Amazon.com. It had seven reader reviews, five favorable and two in the category of rabid nitpicking (no doubt by rival academics). Probably not my cup of tea, but I ordered it anyway. It was the least I could do for the guy for sending me Gloria Anne Lenore's very first novel.

April 20 – Half-way through *Ruth of Riverside Ranch*. Nothing objectionable so far, though the story is quite a bit darker than her other novels. It's about a girl from a western ranch family who goes out with the banker's son, is raped by him, and is now attempting to conceal her pregnancy.

No call from the Pittsburgh professor yet. Bev is here installing my repainted drapes. Definitely a different look. Very stiff from the dried paint. More splotches of gold on cream than the splatters I'd been expecting. All in all, rather artsy and in your face. Will have to get a second opinion from Gabby. Naturally, I've told Bev I'm thrilled and have paid for them. She's such a sweet kid, I don't want to disappoint her. Hope I'm not sounding like Aunt Maddy did back when the giant cabbage roses appeared.

Prof. Mulcahy phoned after lunch. He apologized for the delay, saying yesterday was his busiest day for teaching. I told him no problem, I was just loitering in my kitchen trying to avoid washing down my repellent cabinets.

"Are you succeeding?" he asked.

"Very well. I'm being nicely distracted by Ruth Berwin. She's in quite a pickle."

"I know how it turns out."

"Well, don't tell me. I have many more chapters to go, thank God."

"Why thank God?"

"Because this is the only book by her I haven't read. I don't know what I'll do when I finish it."

"Have you read *The Cosmopolitan Chorus Girl?*"

"No, I've never even heard of it."

"Hardly anyone has. As far as I can tell it's her only comic novel. It's a complete delight. Shall I make you a copy?"

"Do you really have to ask?"

We talked for nearly an hour. He appears to be as much of a Gloria Anne Lenore nut as I am. In fact, he's driving here on Monday from Pittsburgh to examine my trove of G.A.L. papers.

So far, I have two firm thumbs-down on the drapes. Invited Grace and

Peach over for dinner. Grace's exact words: "Sorry, dear. They look like something from Dracula's crypt." Peach's comment: "Look on the bright side, Helen. You won't have to redecorate for Halloween."

April 21 – Spring is sprung, the grass is riz, I seldom know where my daughter is. According to Harkness, Casta spent last night at Marie's. So I called there, and Marie's mother confirmed they were both still asleep. Call me gullible, but I accepted her word for it.

Perhaps to get back at me for abandoning them during the week, my husband and daughter leave the kitchen a complete mess. I'd pitch a fit, but I don't want to hear their rebuttals. I can only cope with so much guilt.

April 22 – I'm an emotional wreck. Poor Ruth got kicked off her family's ranch by her scandalized parents, was taken in by a kindly spinster aunt (and her suspiciously butch housemate), delivered a healthy son (after 36 hours of horrific labor), gave up the baby for adoption, then promptly died in the 1918 flu pandemic. I really wasn't ready for that. The good news is the banker's vile son also croaked. And Ruth's parents realized– too late–how they had wronged their daughter. At the cemetery they pleaded with the aunt to reveal the location of their grandson, but she turned her back on them and walked away.

Sounds a bit melodramatic in the retelling, but it was quite beautifully written. Somehow her sentences just seem to sparkle on the page– all without apparent effort. Nothing seems forced or self-consciously literary. Her words flow so smoothly and naturally, they somehow connect directly to your inner being. It's almost spooky how she pulls you into the story and takes command of your mind and heart.

I was so emotionally spent I couldn't face making dinner. So I had Harkness take us out. We went to a retro steakhouse he loves in Cleveland where the waitresses all dress up as serving wenches. More pushed-up boobs in your face than I care for, but they serve an excellent prime rib. We shared a bottle of wine, so Casta got drafted to drive us home. I don't know what's scarier–her driving, her smoking, or her loose tongue. Several times I thought for sure she was going to drop the name of a certain putative relative in Medina. Now I understand why rich people send their kids away to boarding school. It's to cover up their transgressions.

April 23 – Examined my drapes with fresh eyes. It occurred to me they look like something from a stage set. These could be the curtains for a production of "The Little Foxes" by Lillian Hellman. Tallulah Bankhead could be standing in front of them and watching her husband slowly expire because she's withholding his medicine.

Prof. Mulcahy arrived right on time at 11:30. He was taller and better-looking than I expected from his photo–although the graying soup-strainer under his nose was even bushier in person. I immediately put him on the spot by asking his opinion of my drapes.

"They appear to be carved from stone," he observed. "Are you going for a faux marble look?"

"I'm just trying to make this house presentable enough to find a buyer. Do you need a weekend retreat? It's only a block from the lake."

"It's kind of a trek from Pittsburgh."

"True, but you can breathe the air here."

"You can breathe it in Pittsburgh now as well. All the steel mills have closed."

I gave him the ten-cent tour of the premises, then asked if he was interested in lunch.

"One does expect some modest collation at midday," he conceded.

"You sound just like a professor of English."

"I can switch off that effect, Helen, if you like."

"Please don't. I know a place we can walk to where you can get a filling lunch for 85 cents. How does that sound?"

"It sounds like a step back in time."

"Actually, it's more like a step into the future."

The senior center was serving chicken wings stewed in tomato sauce. We loaded up our plates and got a table for two.

"Do you come here often?" he asked.

"Only with my elderly neighbors. This is the first time I've tried it on my own."

"They didn't halt us at the door."

"How tiresome of you to point that out," I replied with a smile.

Discussing *Ruth of Riverside Ranch*, neither of us could think of a reason why it was withdrawn by the publisher.

"Typically, books are canceled if someone is libeled or there's an allegation of plagiarism," Leigh said. "And neither seems to be the case here. Or author misconduct could be another reason. But Gloria Anne doesn't seem like the type to have been a hell-raiser."

"Could she have been exposed as a communist? It *was* the 1950s."

"Most of those contretemps were over by 1957. And she didn't seem to have had any trouble getting her other novels published."

"The publisher was Hamilton House," I said. "I never heard of them."

"I found out it was a short-lived small press started by a woman named Bernice Hamilstein. Her husband was a big-time auto parts jobber."

"I don't suppose she's still around."

"Alas, no. They had one daughter, who killed herself by jumping in front of a subway train."

"Or was pushed–by Gloria Anne Lenore!"

That got a big laugh from Leigh. I liked his laugh.

"That's a thought," he said. "She might have written her books in a women's prison somewhere."

"So how did you find out all this?"

"I put my students to work on it. That's how most work is accomplished in academia."

I asked him how he came to be interested in an author who penned novels for teenage girls.

"It *is* a bit peculiar," he admitted. "I'd never heard of Gloria Anne Lenore. And American fiction is alleged to be my field. I had a student last year who turned in a paper on her. Praised her extravagantly and compared her to Edith Wharton and Willa Cather. Well, I'm used to my students and their enthusiasms. Usually it's for Stephen King, Tom Clancy, or some other popular writer. I was dubious, so I couldn't give her more than a B."

"Oh, dear. You *are* a philistine."

"That was pretty much her reaction. So she plops this book down on my desk and dares me to read the first three chapters."

"Which novel was it?"

"*Seventeenth Summer.*"

"Ah, one of my favorites. A good choice."

"I almost didn't read it. I'm sorry, Gloria Anne, but your titles are so insipid. It's as if Shakespeare finished his play about Romeo and Juliet and decided to call it *Troubled Teens of Verona High.*"

"Come on, Leigh. Her titles aren't as bad at that."

"Well, they aren't *The Grapes of Wrath* either. Face it, Helen, *Seventeenth Summer* as a title lacks gravitas. And *Ruth of Riverside Ranch* is much too alliterative to be taken seriously."

I conceded his point. "So did you change her grade?"

"To an A. And I very seldom change a grade."

"And now you're hot on the trail of Ms. Lenore?"

"Well, it's a pretty cold trail. It's like she was some kind of a ghost. There's hardly a trace of her anywhere. The papers in your uncle's safe are the first new evidence I've encountered."

"You should talk to my neighbor. She saw a woman visiting my aunt and uncle who may have been Gloria."

"Good. A physical description would be helpful."

I pointed out he had tomato sauce on his mustache. He apologized and daubed at it with his paper napkin.

"What's the theory on that mustache?" I asked.

"This? I've had it since I was 18."

"That's the history, I asked for the theory."

"Oh, right. This is my tenure mustache."

"OK, I'll bite. What's that?"

"Well, to obtain tenure at a university you can do brilliant original work, publish in all the leading journals, and win the grudging admiration of your peers. Or, you can grow a vigorous mustache and look like some sort of intimidating, old-school intellectual. The latter was my strategy."

"You're not doing brilliant original work?"

"I swim too far out of the mainstream, Helen. I get distracted by obscure topics."

"Like Gloria Anne Lenore?"

"Yes, a prime example."

"You're a full professor, Leigh. You must have got tenure by now."

"I did indeed. And I give all the credit to my upper lip."

We walked back by way of the lakefront. Some sporadic sunshine and not too windy. We knocked on Grace's door, but she wasn't home. We talked to Peach, but she didn't have much to add. She said she had never been introduced to the Fishbys' elegant visitor and really only recalled the "dainty briefcase" she carried.

Leigh said he had to get going. I gave him the stack of Lenore papers and he gave me the photocopy of *The Cosmopolitan Chorus Girl*.

"I'll make copies of these right away, Helen, and send you back the originals."

"I'd rather you brought them back, Leigh. I wouldn't want to risk their getting lost in the mail."

"Of course, I understand. I'll check my schedule and let you know when I can return."

I waved from my front stoop as he drove off in his old green Saab.

I hoped my ploy wasn't too transparent; I wanted him to return the papers in person so I could see him again.

I have to admit I liked everything about that man–except his mustache and the wedding ring on his left hand.

April 24 – Took my morning walk along the lakefront with Grace, who asked me if the man in the Saab was my husband. I filled her in on Professor Mulcahy, but she didn't seem much interested in meeting with him. She said she had told me all she could remember about that elegant visitor of decades ago. She said she decided that the woman was most likely a fellow employee of the greeting card company. Or possibly Uncle Phil's boss.

"It's all conjecture, dear," she added. "I shouldn't stick my nose in where it doesn't belong."

"Well, we don't have much to go on. Every little bit helps."

"I'm surprised you're so interested in that forgotten writer."

"She was quite extraordinary, Grace. It's time more people knew about her."

"If you say so, Helen. But I think people are mostly interested in their computers and telephones these days."

Shocking news: Gloria Anne Lenore's chorus girl may have actually slept with a man. At least the simultaneous passing of the wee hours in one room containing a bed was implied strongly. Nothing so gauche as an actual sex scene. But talented showgirl Sophie Dinkle is certainly more cosmopolitan than Gloria Anne's other heroines.

Leigh called after lunch with an update. He said he had drawn two conclusions from G.A.L's contracts and royalties statements: "Everything's in her name, so it's likely that Gloria Anne Lenore was her actual name and not a pseudonym. I'm having some of my students see if they can find that name in any genealogical records."

"Good, Leigh. Any biographical information would be helpful."

"Right. Especially since we have zero now. Her books are out of print, but her movies are still being shown on television. And her film contracts call for payments to be made for such use. Therefore, it would seem likely that the studios are sending checks somewhere."

"Oh, right. Of course."

"I'm not sure if they'll part with that information, but I put my most enterprising grad student on it."

"Good."

"Are you washing your cabinets, Helen, or reading *The Cosmopolitan Chorus Girl?*"

"Do you really need to ask? It's a total hoot. I'm a bit scandalized, though, by the implied sex."

"Well, keep reading. It gets even racier."

Leigh said he could return on Friday, if that worked for me. I told him that sounded fine.

I shouldn't obsess about that fellow, but my years at Oberlin taught me one thing: I have a dreadful weakness for English professors. One example: my hopeless crush on a certain creative-writing prof precipitated my final breakup with Gordon Efflemberger. I guess some guys can sense when you're fantasizing about someone else while you're doing it. Fortunately, Harkness's ego screens out any such disturbing perceptions.

April 25 – Does it mean you've failed as a parent if you only hear from your children when they want something?

Casta phoned from school to say Deke wants to take her to Columbus this Saturday to visit Jamie in prison. They would stay in a motel and return on Sunday. I was very skeptical.

"Jesus, Casta, we hardly know the man."

"Well, Mom, you knew him well enough to have a kid by him. Or did you sleep with a lot of different guys?"

"You're not going to get my permission if you keep up that attitude."

"Well, I can always ask Daddy."

"And how are we supposed to explain your absence to him?"

"Don't worry, Mom. We'll just say I'm staying over at Marie's. Daddy won't mind. He loves it when I'm out of his hair."

I can understand that impulse.

"I don't know, Casta. I'm really uncomfortable with all this deceit."

"Deke is a responsible adult, Mom. He knows this cool restaurant he wants to take me to."

"No economizing, Casta. I insist you have separate motel rooms. And have him call me to discuss the details."

"OK, Mom. I'm really looking forward to meeting Jamie. And I promise not to be any trouble."

"For the rest of your life?"

"Hah! Don't you wish."

April 26 – Woke up this morning realizing that letting my daughter go by herself on an overnight trip out of town with my ex-lover was perfectly insane. I called him at 6:45 a.m. to inform him that I would be going with them. Deke said it was OK by him as long I chipped in on the expenses, we used my car, and I wasn't expecting any "hanky panky" in the motel room. I told him I would be sleeping with my daughter in a separate room, thank you very much.

Later I called Harkness at his office to tell him I was planning a weekend trip with Casta to see a major exhibition of glass at the Columbus Art Museum.

"Glass what?" he asked.

"Uh, glass sculpture, of course."

"Since when are you interested in that?"

"I've always been interested in glass, Harkness. Remember that nice glass vase I've got?"

"The one that came with your aunt's funeral flowers?"

"No, darling. The one my mother gave us for our 25th anniversary. It's blue. Made in Denmark."

"OK, if you say so. And Casta wants to go on this trip?"

"Of course. She's very artistic. We'll be back on Sunday."

"In time to make my pancakes?"

"Uh, probably not. But I'll make you a nice dinner, I promise."

"Well, OK. Try not to sprain the credit card."

"Thanks, honey. You're such a doll."

"I hope this weather holds. I might be able to get in 36 holes."

Let's hope so. Golf: it's the opiate of husbands.

April 27 – Finished *The Cosmopolitan Chorus Girl* over my morning coffee. Rather a shock that Sophie married the ventriloquist instead of the handsome bond salesman. Reading between the lines (and including her undiscussed wedding night), Sophie appears to have slept with three different men. Pretty risqué for Gloria Anne Lenore. I'm surprised this book wasn't sold under the counter in a plain brown wrapper.

Prof. Mulcahy was waiting in my driveway when I got back from my emergency appointment with Rafael, my hairdresser. I apologized for my delay; he said a neighbor had dropped by from next door to assure him that I would return shortly.

"That was Grace, Leigh. She's decided the person she saw likely wasn't Gloria Anne Lenore after all."

"I know, Helen. She introduced herself and explained her misgivings. Too bad. Still, we've made some progress."

He brought me up to date over lunch in the eastern-European restaurant (scene of my recent debacle lunch with Deke). One studio had divulged that they were sending payments to Gloria Anne Lenore in care of Buck, Circo & Everwood, a big law firm in downtown Cleveland.

"Another connection with this area," I pointed out. "What did the law firm say?"

"Nothing, Helen. It's like talking to a stone wall. They have a policy of strict confidentiality. They wouldn't even tell me if she's alive or dead."

"Bastards. I hate lawyers."

"Oh? Aren't you married to one?"

"Sort of. How do you know that?"

"Student researchers."

I felt flattered that he'd gone to the trouble.

"You've been married a long time, Leigh. I can tell."

"How so, Helen?"

"Your wedding ring. It's so thin from wear."

"This was my father's wedding ring. I wear it as a remembrance of him and to discourage concupiscent students. My own wedding ring I sold to a pawn shop six years ago for its gold content."

"Then I take it you're divorced. Any kids?"

"None. Janice didn't mind children, but she had an abhorrence of babies."

"I'm just the opposite. I adore babies. It's when they get older that I want to strangle them. I suppose you know how many kids I have."

"Could be. But tell me how this being 'sort of married' works."

"Well, I'm married, but his tenure is under review."

"Ah. Would it help if he grew a mustache?"

"Just the opposite in fact."

Leigh confessed that he was "sort of" engaged to a professor of literature at the University of Essex in Colchester, East Anglia, UK.

"And she'll move here when you marry?" I asked.

"No, Fiona has a permanent appointment there. We'll be living apart."

"I see, Leigh. Married but separated by the Atlantic Ocean. That sounds cozy."

"Well, that's academic life for you, Helen. You go to conferences and you meet people. Then you cope with the consequences."

"Does Fiona have children?"

"Not yet."

"So how old is this babe?"

"She claims to be 34, but I have reason to believe she's 36."

"And you are?"

"Old enough to be her father. I know, even I'm appalled."

"And what does Fiona think of Gloria Anne Lenore?"

"Well, she's British. She exhibits their typical prejudice against American letters. She's willing to concede that Henry James was not entirely incompetent."

"Didn't James live most of his life in England?"

"Only from about age 20 until his death. The guy was as American as apple pie."

When we got back, I discovered Leigh's book had arrived in the mail. I asked him to sign it for me.

"Are you sure, Helen? You could return it for a full refund if I don't."

"Don't be silly, Leigh. I intend to treasure it always."

As he was signing it, I asked him what Fiona thought of it.

"She hasn't really said," he confessed.

"Why not?" I demanded.

"I'm attributing it to her natural British reserve. I'm sure it's not her cup of tea. Nor do I expect you'll find it all that scintillating."

"You must be a riot at your bookstore appearances. A real advocate for your work."

"Fortunately, publishers of academic books don't expect us to do that sort of thing. They trundle our books into the marketplace, where the reading public politely ignores them."

Leigh wrote in my book:

> To Helen,
> May you come to glory in your own G.A. Lenore story.
> Best wishes, Leigh.

I offered to make some tea, but he said he wanted to beat the traffic through Youngstown. He paused on his way out the door. "Helen, I don't expect you'd like to come to Pittsburgh sometime? I could give you a tour of campus."

"I'd love to. Anything to avoid my work here. How about some day next week?"

"Great."

He said he would check his schedule and email me. No kiss (not even a hug), but he gave me a bit of a pat on the back as he was leaving.

I found Fiona Clark's page on the U of E website. Super smart and also a beauty if you go for that intense, bookish look. Her area of interest is 17th- and 18th-century poetry. You'd think a gal that attractive could find a husband her own age in her own country—instead of running after some inappropriate (although admittedly adorable) American. At least she's stuck far away on the other side of the world. Whereas, I'm only 145 miles away and virtually unattached.

April 28 – Woke up early and read some of Leigh's book in bed. Very well written and not at all dry. I was surprised to learn there were so many unsuccessful attempts at creating a typewriter before someone (C. Latham Sholes) got it right in 1867. Even then, many popular early models hid what you were typing behind the mechanism. Must have been frustrating typing blind like that. The technology got better over time, rendering obsolete the elegant penmanship once cultivated by overworked office scribes.

Fortified myself with a hearty breakfast, then drove to Piper Pike to drag Casta out of bed. She hadn't even bothered to pack. Bombed down to Medina as fast as we could, but arrived 45 minutes late. Deke said that was fairly prompt for someone traveling with a teenager.

I'm amazed how Deke can get Casta to open up about herself. On the two-hour drive to Columbus he pried more personal details out of her than I have in the past five years. Not sure how much of it was true, of course. Unlike me, Casta enjoys lurking behind a web of deceit.

Grabbed a fast pizza for lunch (I paid), then drove to the prison. I was all for staying in the car, but Deke said Jamie would be "heartbroken" if I didn't come too. My first time inside a state prison. I can't imagine being confined in such a grim place for a day, let alone for eight years.

Jamie's appearance was a shock: goatee, bulging muscles, and all those tattoos. Quite a change from the cute little four-year old who loved my peanut-butter-and-honey sandwiches. I could see he was making an effort to be pleasant, as if socializing under the watch of armed guards was an ordinary occurrence in a young man's life. Casta also tried to act normal, and they managed to have something of a getting-acquainted conversation. They discovered they listened to some of the same bands and both were making a stab at learning Spanish (news to me). Not much physical resemblance that I could see, except for their stubby fingers with shallow, childlike nails. (If Deke's fingers were any stubbier, they'd look like misplaced toes.)

Our allotted 45 minutes finally crawled to a end. As we were leaving, Jamie asked me to say hi to Kyle for him. I said I would.

"Tell him we like getting letters here," he added.

I said I would give Kyle his address, but I suppose we both knew that my son was unlikely to write.

Not much was said on the drive to the budget motel by the interstate. We got rooms a few doors apart on the second floor. Casta flopped down on one of the giant beds and switched on the TV with the remote.

"You know, Mom," she said, "if you had left Daddy for Deke, things might have turned out differently."

"That's right, Casta. You'd have grown up in poverty."

"You don't know that. Deke might have been more successful 'cause we were with him. We might have been a happy, loving family. Just the four of us. Jamie might not be in prison now."

"Contrary to what you think, Casta, the bad things that happen to people are not always my fault."

"Deke said it took him forever to get over you."

"Well, he should have kept that information to himself. It's not really any of your business."

"I won't mind if you want to sneak off to his room later."

"Sorry, dear. Not on my agenda. Are you going to dinner looking like that?"

"Better get out your book, Mom. I intend to take a bath."

She was in the bathroom 86 minutes by the clock.

April 29 – Deke's picking up the tab for our debacle Euclid lunch and mall rendezvous turned out to be an anomaly. Dinner last night and brunch this morning were both on me. I'm beginning to think the guy's wallet is chained to his pants. At my insistence we went to see the glass show at the museum. One can't lie credibly to one's husband without at least a few facts at one's command. It turned out to be the highlight of the trip. Even Casta seemed enthralled by the rainbow of iridescent colors and exquisite workmanship. We really should go to a museum more than once a decade. Makes a nice change from the tawdry effluvia of everyday life. It's good to be reminded that some people on this planet have higher aspirations than washing down their kitchen cabinets or loafing through high school.

Picked up a honey-cured ham on the way home for Harkness's promised dinner. While the potatoes were baking, I showed him some postcards I bought in the museum gift shop of the glass art on display. His comment: "I bet they're knocking off that stuff in China now for one-tenth the price."

Harkness's putter and irons weren't cooperating this weekend, rendering him not in the mood to invade my nightgown. Just as well. I'm beginning to think that sleeping with Harkness is worse than not sleeping with anyone at all.

April 30 – Got up early to make Harkness his Sunday pancakes on Monday. I asked him if he was still friends with Maurice Circo of Buck, Circo & Everwood.

"I golf with him occasionally, though I don't know why. He always cheats, and you could die of thirst before he'd ever buy you a drink."

"Do you think you could ask him about a client of theirs? It's Gloria Anne Lenore, that writer I'm interested in."

"What do you want to know?"

"Anything would be helpful. An address would be wonderful. At the very least, we want to know if she's still alive."

"Who's we?"

"Uh, me and Gabby. We both love her books."

"I'll ask if I run into him. You might call Perla to have her remind me."

Perla was Harkness's amazingly efficient secretary, who always speaks to me as if she were patiently indulging a witless three-year-old.

After a weekend away, my drapes in Euclid still came as a rude shock. I keep hoping that they'll start to blend in with the decor. Got an email from Leigh suggesting we meet at his office on Wednesday. I replied that I was looking forward to it. Read more of his book as a diversion from kitchen cleaning. Took a few notes on my iPad so I can demonstrate my interest by asking semi-intelligent questions.

Gabby showed up right before lunch for a surprise inspection. She was none too pleased.

"God, Helen, I should have warned you about Beverly and her artistic impulses. How much did she charge you for ruining the drapes?"

"$225."

"Well, what's done is done. DeeAnn said you were going to renew your kitchen cabinets."

"I am. See I've got the ammonia, rubber gloves, and polish."

"And you were planning to start when?"

"Right after lunch."

"I hope so. I've scheduled an agents' tour on Wednesday."

"What's that?"

"All the agents in the area drop by, tour the house, then note down an estimated selling price on their business cards."

"Can't do it this Wednesday, Gabby. I'm busy."

"You don't have to be here, Helen. In fact, it's better if you're not. Just give me a spare key. And I want this place neat and sparkling."

"I'll try."

"Don't try, Helen," she said, lighting a cigarette. "Just do it. We're going to have to market this as a starter home that needs updating. We'll play up the near-lakefront location."

"It's an entire city block from the lake, Gabby."

"No, Helen. It's only steps from beautiful Lake Erie."

Real estate agents live in a sugar-coated world where even the humblest shack stands tall as a "charming bungalow."

May 1 – My favorite month of the year. Although snow is not an impossibility, winter is mostly a bad memory.

Managed to bear down and do a slapdash cleaning of my repellent kitchen cabinets. I suppose they look marginally better. Also cleaned the big gas range which had starred for over 60 years in its own Festival of Grease.

I made a neatly lettered card that I placed on an end-table beside the sofa. It read: "Hand-painted draperies by noted designer Beverly Johnson."

As some marketing whiz once said: "Reality is what your hype makes it."

May 2 – Only 145 miles to Pittsburgh, a major American city, but I had never been there before. We Ohioans have everything we need right here. Probably wouldn't have found my way across the state line if not for the invention of GPS. The English department was holed up in one of the older buildings on campus. Not exactly decrepit, but you could tell no one was throwing big bucks at the humanities. Leigh had one of the messier offices along the corridor. Bookshelves to the ceiling, and somewhere under that enormous pile in the center I suspected a desk might lurk. He seemed happy to see me.

"Helen Spall, what a surprise!"

"I'm here exactly when I said I would be, Leigh."

"I know. But it's still a surprise to see you. I mean, here in my office. Does that make sense?"

"Not particularly."

"It's just that I associate you with blustery shores of vast inland seas."

"Next time I'll wear my sailor suit. How long did it take you to achieve this effect in your office?"

"You should have seen it before I straightened things up. Are you hungry?"

"Starved as usual."

We walked to a pleasant restaurant called The Chophouse Grill on a nearby commercial street. Our student-age waitress greeted Professor Mulcahy by name and eyed his guest with interest. At Leigh's suggestion we started off with pints of his favorite local ale.

"I've been reading your book," I said after we clinked glasses.

"That explains your look of desperate boredom."

I told him I was enjoying it and asked my first question. He declined to answer on the grounds that it sounded too much like an exam question.

"I wrote that book years before it was published, Helen. I can barely remember what sort of point I was making. I'm sure it was preposterous. You've altered your perfume."

"Nice of you to notice."

"What's this one called?"

"Firing Squad," I confessed. "The bottle is shaped like a bullet."

"Oh, dear. I can see I'll have to be on my guard."

I blushed to the tips of my ears. Despite the foam on his mustache, I wanted to kiss him right then.

"You should try being a little less charming, Leigh. As I recall, you're practically engaged."

"Could be, but she's so damn far away. And Fiona tends to smell like the inside of a book bag. How's your sort-of husband?"

"Frankly, it's not looking good for Harkness. Did you have much trouble deciding to leave your wife?"

"I suppose. Marriage is the process by which endearing quirks become intolerable irritants. At some point you have to call it quits before the mayhem starts."

"So do you want children, Leigh?"

"Why? Do you have a surplus?"

"Come on. You must have thought about it."

"I missed the boat on kids, Helen. I'm too darn old. And I've heard infants can be disruptive to one's dotage."

"Well, you know your girlfriend's time is running out. If she wants kids, it's really not fair to string her along."

"True, but Fiona has said she'd rather have me than all the babies in the world."

Score one for the crafty Brit.

"Oh, well, I'm sure it will work out, and she won't come to resent you later on for her childlessness."

Score one for the intrepid Yank.

"How did we get on this distressing topic?" he asked.

"Don't look at me. You started it."

"Beer always makes me want to nuzzle someone's ear," he observed, sliding closer in the booth.

"That must be a handicap when you're out drinking with the boys."

"This particular ear smells especially enticing."

He was obliged to move away when the waitress brought our food. I asked him if he was from Pennsylvania.

"Not me, Helen. I'm a California boy. Born and bred in the wild hills of Hollywood. My father was a camera technician at Paramount for over 30 years."

"Really? What movies did he work on?"

"He wasn't on the glamor side. He worked in the machine shop keeping their cameras repaired. Dorothy Lamour never dropped by in a sarong to chat."

"So how did you wind up in Pittsburgh?"

"Have you ever tried to get a job in academia? You pack your bags and go where they want you."

"Pittsburgh must have been a shock after California."

"Yeah, I'd heard stories about the Midwest, but I never quite believed it actually existed. Are you from elsewhere?"

"No, I lived in the Cleveland area all my life."

"Good for you. You enjoy all four seasons, the modest cost of living, the humidity, the snow, the mosquitoes. The gray cities with their empty factories. The innumerable Polish restaurants. The winter landscapes that look like Chernobyl after the meltdown."

"You make it sound so inviting. Would you rather live in England?"

"I'd rather live no more than four blocks from the beach in Santa Monica."

"That's not impossible. We could become producers and make a movie of *The Cosmopolitan Chorus Girl*."

"Good luck buying those rights, Helen. The only Gloria Anne Lenore my students have been able to find was born in Connecticut in 1816. And that one spelled her middle name without the 'E'."

"Then perhaps it is a pen name."

"Or she took her husband's name. Or she was born abroad. Or they Anglicized Lenorski or Lenorcweiz. The possibilities are endless."

"Are you giving up?"

"Not as long as I've got you riding shotgun."

"I'm with you, cowboy."

May 3 – Passed my first night in Pennsylvania. Not entirely satisfactorily–I spent it in Leigh's guestroom. After touring the campus, he asked me if I wanted to see his "austere post-divorce condo." It was much nicer than he made it sound. He has a large apartment on the fifth floor of a swanky 1920s brick building that got made over into condos in the 1990s. High ceilings, modern kitchen, tiled baths, and tall windows looking southeast toward the towers of downtown. We shared a passionate clinch in the elevator going up, but I got the letdown in his surprisingly neat living room.

"I have three rules I live by, Helen," he said. "I don't read books by authors under 25. I don't buy cars from guys named Mario. And I don't sleep with married women."

"How come not?"

"Because things get messy and far too complicated. Plus, it's a good way to get yourself shot."

"My husband's not the jealous type."

"Every husband is the jealous type if you rub his nose in it. I speak from experience."

"Then why did you kiss me, Leigh?"

"Because you're tremendously attractive, intensely alluring, I like you immensely, and your perfume is excessively inflaming."

"Well, that's nice to hear. I like you too. So kissing is not off-limits?"

"Kissing is permitted within reason."

So we sat on his leather sofa and necked like we were back in middle school. Very stimulating, and I didn't even mind the mustache that much. I could tell he was aroused, but there was no groping of provocative areas. Eventually, we scrounged up some dinner from his bachelor's kitchen and continued our conversation. I told him about last weekend's cultural excursion to Columbus, omitting the ex-lover and prison visit. He told me about growing up in California; I talked about life in Ohio in the 1960s and '70s. We talked about family, friends, books, our travels–all those windows into a person's life you explore when you first meet.

Then it got too late for me to drive back. So we parted for the night in the hallway outside his guestroom.

"If my husband finds out that I spent the night in your condo, you could still get shot."

"True, but I'll have the satisfaction of knowing that I died an innocent man."

"I feel like I'm in the middle of a Gloria Anne Lenore novel."

"Is that so bad?" he asked, embracing me.

"Not really," I said as our lips and bodies met.

I got out of bed when I heard his shower running. He had a 9 a.m. class, so we made do with a quick breakfast of coffee and toast.

"Will I ever see you again, Leigh?" I asked.

"Don't be an idiot, Helen. Of course, you'll see me. The sooner the better. I wish you didn't live so damn far away."

"I'm closer than Fiona."

"Yes, you get credit for that. Now all you have to do is shed that pesky husband of yours."

"Why? So I can be left desolate when you run off to marry Fiona?"

"Well, no date has been set for that disaster. And she may come to her senses."

"You could come to your senses instead, Leigh."

"It's complicated, Helen. One is, uh, conflicted."

We agreed that he would come to Euclid some day next week. We rode down in the elevator together, kissed, then parted in the parking lot.

Is it just another English professor infatuation, or have I met the love of my life at the inconvenient age of 58?

May 4 – Gabby brought over the listing papers for me to sign. The price estimates had ranged from a paltry $35,000 to a delusional $119,000 (that agent also wrote "Nice drapes!" on her card). Gabby suggested we ask $69,000 and hope to get $65,000.

"That would make us very competitive with the other listings at the bottom of the market," she pointed out. "We might get some investor interest. A smart investor could rent this place out as-is and be close to positive cash flow."

"I'd rather sell it to a nice young couple looking for their first love nest."

"Yeah, well, we'll take what we can get. How come you had your phone off all day yesterday? And don't tell me you were home, because I called there twice."

"You didn't say anything to Harkness did you?"

"No, I talked to Casta. Helen, have you been straying?"

"Not nearly as far as I'd like to."

I confessed to my middle-school indiscretions with Leigh and chaste night in Pittsburgh.

"Doesn't sleep with married women," she commented. "Well, I'll give him points for integrity–assuming he's not gay."

"I'm totally stuck on the guy, but he's engaged to some brainy gal in England a fraction of his age."

"Do you know what she looks like?"

I fired up my iPad and called up Fiona's bookmarked page. Gabby studied her photo with interest.

"Do you suppose she has thick ankles and a horsey laugh?" I asked.

"I wouldn't count on it, Helen. But she could have bad teeth. See, she's smiling, but keeping her lips closed. Those English are notorious candy munchers. And most of them don't even own a toothbrush."

I switched to Leigh's university page; Gabby checked him out.

"His photo doesn't really do him justice," I hastened to add.

"He's cute, Helen–assuming he's not hiding a hair-lip under that mustache. I like his eyes. What are they, green?"

"Kind of a soft greenish grey. They sparkle when he laughs."

"He's got a Ph.D. though. Those types can be stuffy."

"Not Leigh. He's very self-effacing and not at all full of himself. He's ideal in every respect."

"Probably not, but then no one's objective at your stage."

"I'm competing with a 36-year-old, Gabby. Tell me it's not hopeless."

"It's not hopeless, Helen. But it's definitely all-out war."

May 5 – Had a half grapefruit for breakfast. I figure if Leigh's going to delay sleeping with me, I might as well use the time to shed some flab. Fifteen pounds (!) gone would bring me down close to my college weight, when wolf whistles were a fairly frequent occurrence. Let's face it: Leigh already has slept with Fiona, making her–for better or worse–a known quantity. I, on the other hand, remain a tantalizing unknown to him. This may serve to keep his interest from flagging. I suppose it's why savvy girls in the old days were disinclined to put out.

Drove to Pepper Pike and found the house in its usual disorder. Harkness had left for the golf course. Casta was nowhere to be found. No note from her either. Sat in my messy kitchen and had a long cry. Too much to cope with these days. Also, I expect my blood sugar was low from not eating.

I thought about my finances. If the house sold for $65,000, I'd have a bit of a cushion for leaving Harkness–assuming he didn't expect me to pay child support for Casta and half of Kyle's college expenses. That could leave me broke in a matter of months. Then what?

Monica phoned to say they'd started shooting their movie. She said they needed Casta and me "on set" tomorrow morning at 7:15.

"Casta has agreed to be in your movie, dear?" I asked.

"Well, I discussed it with her, Mother. I'm counting on you to get her here on time. Tell her lunch will be provided and there are some cute actors coming."

"OK, dear. I'll do my best. Are you going to kill off your sister in some gruesome way as well?"

"I'm afraid so, Mother. Only in her case I wish it wasn't faked."

Do you suppose my daughters get along so poorly because they're only half-sisters? Being an only child, I have no experience with siblings. Growing up, I always thought a sister would be a wonderful addition to one's life. Hell, I would have settled for a cousin.

May 6 – Casta was disinclined to participate, but I pointed out that being in her sister's movie might be a first step to a real acting career, sparing her from life as a prostitute on the mean streets of Cleveland. Amazingly, we were only 15 minutes late, considering I had to drag Casta out of bed, make Harkness his pancakes, and find my way to Monica's storage facility.

"There's where your daughter's shacking with that creep," noted Casta as we drove by a rundown old house. "The neighborhood lowlifes prob-ably have already cased the joint with rape on their minds."

"Casta, must you devote your life to torturing me?"

"Gosh, Mom, I'm just telling it like it is. I expect Roland will be useless when they burst in."

To my surprise, there were nearly 20 young people gathered "on set" inside the storage lot's main gate. Roland, wearing evidence of his break-fast, was striding about in his bossy genius mode. Casta selected a donut from a box on a card table, but I–thinking of Leigh–settled for just a cup of coffee. Monica brought over actor's releases for us to sign. These legal forms assured us that even if the movie made millions, our compensation would remain zero. I asked Monica how things were going.

"Don't talk, Mother. Rest your voice. We need you at maximum volume for your scene."

I suspected she enjoyed telling me to shut up.

Phyllis (Monica's boss) has volunteered to be wardrobe czar. She introduced herself and gave Casta a frilly white blouse that she was to wear in her scene. My daughter, having no shame, changed into it right on the spot. I was relieved to see she was wearing a bra for a change.

Roland strode over, grabbed a donut with a none-too-clean paw, and looked me over.

"Good, Mrs. Spall. I see you've followed Monica's instructions to dress as matronly as possible."

I smiled and did not point out that she had neglected to tell me what to wear.

Casta got killed first. She was beheaded by a large metal NO TRESPASS-ING sign that blew off a fence. First they shot the sign flapping in the wind. The flapping was accomplished by having a tall fellow named Todd pull on a length of fishing line tied to a corner of the sign. The tripod-mounted camera looked like an ordinary SLR still camera, but Monica assured me it was capable of capturing high-quality video. A microphone inside a furry pod on a long pole fed sound via a cord into a small digital recorder that was being watched over by an Asian girl named Brie wearing headphones.

Next, Todd whirled the sign around in a circle (held by the flimsy-looking fishing line) while Casta edged as close as she dared to the arc of its swing. Very nervous-making to the mother of the potential casualty. Roland did several takes of Casta reacting in fright as the sign approached. Seemed convincing to me, and even her sister flashed her a thumbs-up sign.

The final setup involved a hole previously dug in a patch of grass outside the office. Phyllis took back Casta's white blouse and put it on a "beheaded" mannequin. Roland then ordered my daughter into the hole so she could be buried up to her neck by the two flunkies standing by with shovels and rolls of fresh sod. To my amazement, she meekly complied. After they leveled the dirt and installed the sod, Roland smeared fake blood on an edge of the sign and placed it beside Casta's disembodied head. He put the headless mannequin about a foot away and liberally doused on more blood, much of it on Casta's hair.

"OK, Casta," he said, "I want you to look terrified and mouth the words: Oh, my God! Help me!"

"Wouldn't I be more likely to scream what the fuck?"

"Probably. But too many fucks get you an R rating and we need this to be PG-13. And you can't scream because you're just a head. You have no lungs. OK, remember, you're experiencing your last view of God's green earth. So mouth the words and try to make it convincing. I want to feel you dying!"

Since they weren't burning through expensive film, Roland felt free to record 14 takes of my dismembered daughter mouthing assorted last oaths. Then the fellows dug her out of the hole, and everyone broke for lunch.

"God, Mom," said Casta as I helped clear off the dirt and fake blood, "that was tons of fun. Did I do OK?"

"You were great, Casta. You were extremely convincing as a suddenly beheaded person."

When Casta lit up a cigarette after lunch, Roland slammed down his pizza slice. "Damn! We should have had her smoking! Of course! It would be so cool if she were still puffing away with her head chopped off. Monica, let's reshoot it!"

"Forget it, Roland," she replied. "You can also get an R rating for too much smoking."

"God, I hate that fascist ratings board!" he exclaimed. "They're why cinema has lost its edge!"

It took them less that 45 minutes to crush me under the elevator, then they were off to mangle a handsome young actor in the hydraulic tailgate of the storage lot's big rental truck. At first Roland wanted to be in charge of the red button that stopped the descending elevator, but luckily for me Phyllis insisted on performing that function.

Roland kept shouting, "Louder screams! I need louder screams!" until I felt like socking him in his fat face. But in reviewing the takes on the video monitor, I had to admit that my later ones packed more punch. The guy may be something of a director after all.

May 7 – While Harkness was chewing through his Monday morning bowl of Special K cereal, I reminded him of my request for Gloria Anne Lenore information.

"Oh, didn't I tell you?" he replied. "I ran into Maury Circo at Hennessy's on Friday."

Hennessy's was a watering hole for lawyers near the Federal Building.

"No, you didn't tell me. What did he say?" I asked eagerly.

"Not much. He was three sheets to the wind, and it was barely noon. He said your author doesn't exist."

"What?"

"He said they forward those Hollywood checks to some old lady in a rest home. He said the checks are barely enough to get you a round of golf on a public course."

"What's the old lady's name?"

"That he wouldn't tell me. Said it was confidential."

"Where's the rest home?"

"He said it was the Shady Oak Grove in Parma. Why have I heard of that place?"

"It's where my mother lives."

"Oh, right. I knew it rang a bell for some reason."

I found my mother undoing a sweater in the crafts room. She was back to regarding me as her deceased sister. I asked her what she was doing.

"What does it look like I'm doing, Maddy?"

"I didn't know you'd taken up knitting."

"I haven't."

"Then why are you unraveling that sweater?"

"Because I enjoy it. And it pisses off the knitters no end."

"So that's not your sweater?"

"Of course not. I could never create something this ugly."

I demanded my mother tell me if she were Gloria Anne Lenore.

"Have you been skipping your Alzheimer's medication, Maddy dear?"

"Don't lie to me, Lorraine. I know for a fact that the author of her novels lives in this rest home. And I suspect it might be you."

"In case you hadn't noticed, Maddy, this place is lousy with old ladies. The men cycle through like they're on a conveyor belt to the grave, but the gals hang around long past the point where their conversation flags. Not that any of them had much to say in the first place."

"There are so many Gloria Anne Lenore connections to this family, Lorraine. I demand to know what's going on. I know you're hiding something from me."

"Maddy, you used to be such a pleasant person. Would you like some socks to unravel? How about a scarf? It's marvelous therapy for the nerves."

"If you're not Gloria Anne Lenore, then who is? You know everyone in this place. She would be a refined person. Very intelligent."

"I'm the only one here who fits that description. But I never wrote a book in my life. Too busy taking care of my ungrateful husbands and daughter."

Two frail, white-haired ladies entered and began to cry out in alarm. Mrs. Whistman, the day-shift supervisor, swooped in to deal with the crisis. She looked at me reproachfully as she led my mother back to her room. Later, in the hallway, I apologized and inquired if any of their residents had been writers.

"Well, we have several schoolteachers and a fairly well-known ceramicist, but I can't think of any writers. Why? Would you like to volunteer to start a writing group?"

"Uh, no. Just wondering. Have any of your residents ever mentioned Gloria Anne Lenore?"

"Just your mother, Mrs. Spall. She said her sister is obsessed with that woman. But I was under the impression that her sister was deceased."

"Right. She is."

It was a wild stab in the dark to suggest to my mother that she had been a secret novelist. I couldn't quite bring myself to believe it. Growing up, we'd owned a little Hermes Rocket portable typewriter, but on those rare occasions when I retrieved it from the high shelf in the hall closet I always found it covered in dust. Nor was there any evidence at any time that any sort of literary composition was underway in our home: no notes, no papers, no manuscripts, no mail from publishers, no unexplained phone calls. Plus, the sort of person Gloria Anne Lenore revealed herself to be through her writings did not correspond in any way with my mother. I would place them on opposite ends of the personality spectrum.

All this I pointed out to Leigh when I called him after I got to Euclid.

"How many residents does that rest home have?" he asked.

"About 200, I think. Probably 85 percent of them are women."

"Well, this narrows the search considerably. But it seems shy Ms. Lenore wants to conceal her identity to the last."

We arranged that he would come to Euclid on Friday.

"Shall we scout out the rest home?" I asked.

"Good idea, Helen. A couple of English majors like us ought to be able to sniff out the writer in a group that small."

May 8 – Finished Leigh's book. What a clever darling he is. I'm not sure I entirely agree with his thesis that the trend toward less prolix prose after 1900, with fewer dependent clauses, was a result of the mechanics of composition moving from the mega-muscles of the hand and arm (as in handwriting) to the micro-muscles of individual fingers (as in typing on a machine). I think that the pace of life simply speeded up to the point where readers no longer had the patience to work their way through all those convoluted sentences.

Gabby brought over more forms for me to fill out and papers to sign, one of them being an Owner(s) Disclosure of Known Defects. I wrote down: "Kitchen faucet drips. Landscaping overgrown in rear."

Gabby said that was fine. She said since I inherited the house I wasn't expected to know all the faults like a long-time owner. "And whatever you do," she added, "don't tell me about any, since I'd have to disclose it."

"My lips are sealed, Gabby dear. Were you happy with your divorce lawyer?"

"Carl? Oh, sure. He was a sweetheart. Very aggressive but not antagonistic. An excellent negotiator. We took that rat to the cleaners and he never knew what hit him. You want his number?"

"I'd appreciate it. I'm not sure if divorce is really practical. I'd want the kids to be provided for and I don't want to be left penniless."

"I wouldn't worry about that, Helen. You've got nearly 30 years invested in your marriage. You deserve a big share of the pile."

"But I'm the guilty party, Gabby. I'd be the one ending the marriage."

"No, Helen, you're the victim. You want out because of intolerable mental cruelty. And you have a right to be supported in the lifestyle to which you've become accustomed."

"Really?"

"I kid you not. We're not living in the 9th century, darling. You're not shackled to some serf 'til the end of time."

May 9 – A FOR SALE sign went up in my front yard this morning. Not an uncommon sight in this neighborhood. The house has to be kept spotless and unnaturally tidy at all times from now on. I'm feeling a bit torn, since if it sells, I'll lose my refuge away from Pepper Pike. And it will be harder to see Leigh.

Have starved myself for days and lost one-half pound. Every morning it gets a little harder to face the bathroom mirror. I don't see how women in their sixties can even get out of bed.

Invited my neighbor Grace to have lunch with us in Parma on Friday, but she politely declined. She said even if it was the same person who arrived by cab to visit my aunt and uncle, she'd be unlikely to recognize her after nearly 40 years.

Haven't worked up the nerve to call Gabby's divorce lawyer. Thought I'd run it by Leigh first. Still feeling very unsettled by it all.

May 10 – Phoned Monica to discuss Casta's situation. She tried to put me off as usual, but I persisted.

"I met your boss, Monica dear. She thinks the world of you. I don't think she'd begrudge you a few minutes of the company's time to talk to your mother."

"Oh, OK, but make it quick."

"Your sister really enjoyed working on your movie. It was the first time I've seen her enthusiastic about anything since she threw out her Barbie dolls."

"We don't need her hanging around the set, Mother. All she'd do is flirt with the guys and belittle me with her sarcastic comments."

"No, I think she really wants to be helpful. She's very intrigued by the whole process. And it might be a good way for you two to get a little closer."

"We despise each other, Mother. We always have."

"Well, that's a sorry state of affairs for sisters. You're the older, more mature one, Monica. I think you should see this as an opportunity to repair your relationship."

Long period of silence.

"Are you there, dear?" I asked.

"OK, Mother. You get your way, as usual. Casta can come here on Saturday. But if she causes any trouble, I'm throwing her out."

"Good. I appreciate your making the effort, dear. And how are things with you and Roland?"

"Some customers just came in, Mother. I have to go."

Have I completely failed as a parent if my daughters hate each other? Or is it a case of Harkness's genes clashing with Deke's?

In the interest of science, I phoned my son with a question.

"Kyle, if you were in a burning building with your sisters and could only save one, which would you pick?"

"Wouldn't you rather ask if I'd choose my girlfriend or you?"

"Unfortunately, I already know the answer to that question. Come on, dear, which one would you save?"

"Is this before or after I dialed 9-1-1?"

"There's no time for that, Kyle. The flames are coming right at you."

"OK, I'd save Monica."

"Can I ask why?"

"I don't know. She's always been there for me. Plus, knowing Casta, she probably set the fire."

Just as I suspected: Those Harkness genes stick together.

May 11 – More enthusiastic but chaste necking when Leigh arrived this morning. How acute is my desire to be ravished by him. I've decided he's one of those types that's very good at delaying gratification. Whereas, I wish to rip his clothes off right on the spot. I restrained myself, of course, but it was a struggle.

Leigh told me the latest news as we rode to Parma in the Beast. They have tracked down Bernice Hamilstein's grandson in Paterson, New Jersey.

"He said his grandmother never forgave Gloria Anne Lenore," said Leigh. "*Ruth of Riverside Ranch* was withdrawn at the author's request. Gloria Anne returned the advance and eventually repaid the printing costs, but Bernice felt it cost her credibility as a publisher. She blamed the failure of her firm on Ms. Lenore."

"Did she say why she wanted it withdrawn?" I asked.

"Apparently not. That's another reason his grandmother was pissed. She'd taken a chance publishing an unknown writer and then got stiffed by her. Plus, the whole affair annoyed her husband who was putting up the money. She never spoke to Ms. Lenore again."

"I'm amazed Gloria Anne had the nerve to write another novel after that debacle," I commented.

"Yeah, well I figure she needed the money. Dickens wrote all those novels because every time he had sex with his wife she presented him with another mouth to feed."

"I promise not to do that to you, Leigh."

"Thanks, Helen. I appreciate that."

"How many children did Dickens have?"

"Ten, but one died in infancy."

"Do you suppose Gloria Anne Lenore had any kids?"

"We may soon have a chance to ask her."

I introduced Leigh to my mother, but she didn't know quite what to make of him.

"My sister's a lesbian, you know," she announced on the way to the dining hall.

"No one here's a lesbian, Lorraine," I retorted.

Mother winked knowingly at Leigh and whispered, "Still in the closet, poor dear. Are you by any chance Joseph Stalin?"

"I told you, Lorraine," I interjected, "He's professor Mulcahy from Pittsburgh. He's going to give a talk after lunch in the common room."

"On your next Five Year Plan?" asked Mother.

"No, Mrs. Manders," replied Leigh, "on American fiction from 1950 to 1980."

"Actually, you look more like Thomas Dewey," said Mother. "I'd have voted for you, had I been old enough."

"You were plenty old enough, Lorraine," I pointed out. "In 1948 you were 28."

"She never could keep her big mouth shut," grumbled Mother.

As arranged, Mrs. Whistman introduced Leigh and announced his forthcoming talk. The big crowd of white-haired diners applauded politely, then returned to their gristly Swiss steak.

Mother embarrassed me by flirting with Leigh all through lunch. God knows what he must think of my family. I hope he wasn't thinking: "There in 34 years goes Helen."

Twenty-three residents showed up for Leigh's lecture. The two gents and Mother I immediately disqualified, leaving us with 20 possible candidates. Alas, none of these was elegantly dressed or wearing white gloves. Three I disqualified for falling asleep during Leigh's lively and amusing talk. Two more interrupted him with extremely dumb questions. That left us with 15 prospective Gloria Anne's.

I was in charge of distributing the post-talk questionnaire devised by Leigh's teaching assistants. I asked the audience members to write their names at the top and answer the three pages of simple questions.

"Are we going to be graded on this?" asked one old lady, looking worried.

"Not at all," I replied. "It's just a survey into the reading habits and tastes of your generation. It's part of Professor Mulcahy's on-going research."

"Are we going to get paid?" demanded one of the newly awakened snoozers.

"Very possibly," lied Leigh, "if you attend all 27 lectures in our series."

"I doubt I'll live that long," she replied sourly.

Leigh eagerly looked over the questionnaires as I drove us back to Euclid.

"It's always possible Gloria Anne Lenore missed that lunch," I pointed out. "Or had a previous engagement this afternoon. Or was too ill to come. Or finds college professors tedious."

"You *are* a worrier, Helen. Too bad you're not free and easy like your mother."

"My mother is senile. I apologize for every word out of her mouth."

"You said that already. I found her extremely charming."

"I suppose you've met Fiona's mother?"

"We're not opening that can of worms, darling. And stop distracting me."

By the time we reached Euclid, Leigh had selected his three top candidates. We sat in my excessively tidy living room and he nuzzled my ear while I looked through the stack.

"I notice you're sticking with Firing Squad," he observed.

"Well, it seems to be doing the job–sort of."

I agreed with his choices. Our candidates were Muriel Wadge, Clare Hendom, and Inez Frinezen. They appeared to be serious readers who could have been inclined to write.

"What's the next step?" I asked.

"Next, Helen, we separate the wheat from the chaff."

May 12 – Leigh slept over last night, although not with me. A bedroom wall and my surplus husband kept us resolutely apart. Nor is Leigh being at all helpful on the question of my divorce. He says it's entirely up to me to decide. I suppose men his age, burned by bad marriages, are naturally slippery when it comes to commitment. I overheard the rat conversing with someone early this morning. Couldn't make out what he was saying but the vocal tones suggested pillow talk with his bride-to-be. He's already confessed that he speaks with her over his laptop via Skype to save money. The webcams let them see each other too. I hope they don't disrobe and fondle each other remotely.

Just to show him that two could play those games, I phoned Harkness. I told him I had some house hunters coming to tour my place and asked him to take Casta to Monica's movie location. The usual grumbling, but he assented at last. Men are such trouble I'm sometimes amazed that lesbianism is not rampant across the land.

I prepared a romantic breakfast for us, but it was spoiled when Leigh let drop that Fiona wants him to come spend the summer with her at her family's place in Scotland. Apparently they own some land and a moldering manse overlooking scenic Cromarty Firth, whatever that is. The lovebirds intend to firm up their plans when they meet at a conference in Toronto in two weeks.

"So I may not see you all summer?" I asked, feeling sick.

"Well, it might only be July and August and part of September."

"Right. All summer."

"It's not yet decided, Helen."

"Right. Like a lot of things in your life."

"I'm sorry I upset you, but I thought I should, uh, keep you informed."

"Thanks. I like to be kept up to date on what you and your girlfriend are doing."

"It's a difficult situation, Helen. I suppose I should leave."

"No, don't go, Leigh. Eat your frittata. I just need a moment to digest all this."

He left about an hour later. We agreed that he would return one day next week. I kissed him goodbye as cheerfully as I could, but was feeling awful. We hadn't even experienced much of the good things and already were deep into the pain and suffering stage.

May 13 – Mothers Day. I found a cute card waiting at Pepper Pike from Kyle. He thanked me for my assistance and added that he had a great time.

"What did he mean by that?" asked Harkness.

"I really couldn't say, dear," I lied. "Perhaps it's a reference to being born."

No card from Monica or Casta. After Harkness got off the phone with his mother (who thoughtfully had moved years ago to Flagstaff), we drove to Parma and picked up my mother.

Lunch was at her favorite overpriced colonial-style inn. Years ago it had been a popular restaurant, but unnoticed by Mother the food had deteriorated as the place had gotten shabby. As was its custom on this special day, every lady was presented with a white rose and served a "complimentary" glass of sweet champagne.

The presence of Harkness was enough to tip Mother back to recognizing me as her daughter.

"It's too bad you're such a stranger, Helen," she said, motioning to the waiter for more champagne. "We had a fascinating lecture by Thomas Dewey last week."

"I'm sorry I missed it," I replied. I asked her if she was friends with Muriel Wadge, Clare Hendom, or Inez Frinezen.

"Never heard of the bums."

"They're residents of your facility, Mother."

"Well that's no claim to fame. What's your husband eating?"

Mother doesn't speak to Harkness directly because she never approved of my marrying him.

"He's having the prime rib, Mother."

"More like the unprime rib from the looks of it. He should have ordered the ham."

She was right, of course.

As she often is.

May 14 – I slept last night with darling Leigh via the brisk proxy service provided by Harkness. There's something a bit queasy-making about my husband getting so amorous on Mothers Day. Still, it's fortunate that I'm able to experience a rich fantasy life.

I called Carl Zyzinski, Gabby's divorce lawyer, when I got to Euclid. We have an appointment for Friday morning. He wants me to bring copies of our tax returns for the past three years, plus the latest bank and brokerage statements. These I'll have to sneak out of Harkness's filing cabinet while he's at work. Good thing I know where he hides the key.

I'm coping with all this by rereading Gloria Anne Lenore's oeuvre. I also Googled Muriel Wadge, Clare Hendom, and Inez Frinezen, but found nothing about them on the Web.

So far the chaff is very much adhering to the wheat.

Two agents showed up today with house seekers. It's amazing how candid perfect strangers can be in discussing the shortcomings of your home right in front of you. Both parties singled out my drapes in particular for ridicule.

One chubby gal in an unflattering sweatshirt asked me the color of the walls.

"Navajo White," I answered with a smile.

"God, that is so boring," she replied.

May 15 – Another party of skeptical house buyers (with agent) trooped through. This time a fellow asked me, "What's up in the attic?"

"What attic?" I replied, startled.

"You tell me, lady. There's an access hatch in the ceiling of your linen closet."

That was news to me. I hadn't thought to check that closet since

DeeAnn had cleared out the mountain of threadbare towels. I brought up the stepladder from the basement and retrieved a flashlight from the glove compartment of the Beast.

Fetid darkness, sun-warmed heat, cobwebs, four dusty cardboard boxes. These I passed down to the surprised house-seeker, then he took my place on the ladder and looked around.

"Nice high-pitched roof," he commented. "You got enough headroom up here to build a new master suite. Might get a view of the lake too."

"An excellent idea," I lied.

When they finally left, I dived at the boxes, then immediately phoned Leigh.

"You won't believe what I just found in my attic," I said.

"What, darling?"

"Four cartons of Gloria Anne Lenore manuscripts."

"You're kidding."

"Nope. Some are typed originals and some are carbons."

"That's fantastic."

"It gets better. At least three of them have titles I don't recognize."

"My God, Helen."

"Yep. I'm thinking these could be unpublished works."

Leigh screeched into the driveway two hours later. By then I had been through all the boxes and had uncovered another unpublished manuscript. The four new titles were *The Solitary Simpleton*, *Streetcar for Adventure*, *The Trek to Zion*, and *Her Placated Heart*.

Leigh kissed me (rather perfunctorily), then hurried into the kitchen to examine the manuscripts I had stacked in neat piles on the chrome dinette.

"Are there any with hand-written corrections?" he asked.

"A few. All in the same very precise printing. Not at all similar to our three suspects, but then their samples were written in script, not printed."

"We should try to get samples of their printing."

"Assuming these corrections weren't written by some editor."

"True. Too bad we haven't found any letters by Ms. Lenore. She must have written to someone in her life."

"I'd be thrilled with even a grocery list."

"OK, Helen. What do you want to read first?"

"*Her Placated Heart*, of course."

"A not unexpected choice. I guess it's *The Solitary Simpleton* for me."

We broke for dinner a few hours later when the Chinese food was delivered.

"How's your book?" asked Leigh.

"Excellent. It's about a girl who's volunteering in a hospital and meets a youth who was found injured by the side of a highway. So far he can't remember a thing, including his identity. How's your book?"

"Very intriguing. It seems to be a murder mystery. There's a corpse, but the only witness is a fellow everyone believes to be profoundly retarded."

"Well, don't tell me any more. I want to read it next."

"You have to give credit to Ms. Lenore for her versatility. She seems to have dabbled in many genres."

"These works should be published, Leigh."

"Well, we'll try to talk her into it–assuming we find her."

"By the way, I have an appointment with a divorce lawyer on Friday."

"Excellent, darling. What a day for welcome surprises."

May 16 – Divorce lawyer or no, we still slept separately–though our clinch in the upstairs hallway at bedtime was several degrees warmer than before. Both of us were bleary-eyed at breakfast from reading into the wee hours.

"How's your book now?" yawned Leigh.

"Kind of anxious-making. The girl suspects her new love might be wanted as an army deserter."

"Has he remembered anything yet?"

"Not that he's admitting. How's your simpleton?"

"Do you really want to know?"

"Don't tell me a thing. Is it good?"

"Excellent. Very atmospheric. I'd put it right up there with Raymond Chandler's best."

"Wow. Kudos to Gloria Anne."

Not content with poking his head up the attic hatch, Leigh decided to brave the spiders and go exploring. He had to tread carefully along the ceiling joists, lest he fall through the lath and plaster. Behind the brick chimney, hidden from view of the hatch, he found another dust-covered cardboard box. This one contained several old photo albums, flat boxes filled with papers, and a manila folder labeled "Contents of Safe."

That locksmith had been right. Written on the folder was the combination to Uncle Phil's safe. Inside was a typed sheet listing all the contents, including "Mother's diamond and sapphire ring," "Grandfather's diamond stickpin," "Aunt Moira's pearl necklace," and "143 Mexico 50-Peso gold coins."

The coins we looked up on the Web. They were going for about $1,500 apiece these days. According to Uncle Phil's vintage adding machine, 143 of them totaled a cool $214,500.

"So what happened to the treasure, Helen?" asked Leigh.

"Stolen by my daughter's funky boyfriend, Leigh. And I can't prove a damn thing."

Feeling newly impoverished again, I had Leigh take me out to lunch at the senior center. More bad news: A sign posted by the door announced the price for lunch would rise to 95 cents as of June 1. On the way back we stopped at a package shipping store, and I faxed Uncle Phil's typed list to Monica at her office. Not that I expected anything to come of that.

Spent some more time looking through the box, the contents of which all related to Uncle Phil. Perplexed by what we found, we had to interrupt our reading to drive to Parma to see Mother. We found her sprawled on the grass in the rear courtyard. She wasn't dead, she was sunbathing topless. Not at all a pleasant sight. What poor Leigh must think of my family.

Mother smiled and tugged up her brassiere when she saw Leigh.

"Ah, Governor Dewey," she said, "how nice to see you again."

"Good afternoon, Mrs. Manders. You're looking well."

"I don't usually display quite so much of myself, but the sun was so inviting. You look awful, Maddy, you should get out more."

"I'm not Maddy, I'm Helen, Mother. We need to discuss Uncle Phil."

"Haven't seen the man. As I recall, he may be dead."

"We found his family photo albums and his grammar school report cards. The photos show a family consisting of a father, mother, and two daughters. All his report cards are in the name of Philippa Tishby. Care to explain that?"

"The Tishby family learned a valuable lesson," replied Mother.

"What's that?" I asked.

"When you hire a doctor to circumcise your son make sure he's not drunk."

"Oh my," I said.

"Apparently, he botched the job so badly, they decided to chop off the rest and raise their kid as a girl. At least that's the story that got whispered to me. All the frills and lace didn't take though. When Philippa turned 18, she decided to move to another state and start buying her clothes in the men's department. I guess Phil's shortcomings didn't phase my sister. God knows what they did in bed all those years. I asked her, of course, but she told me it was none of my business."

"I'm sure it wasn't, Mother. Frankly, I'm surprised you kept their secret all these years."

"I had my reasons."

"So let's have the truth. Was Uncle Phil Gloria Anne Lenore?"

"Jesus, Helen, you sound like some kind of broken record. Your Uncle Phil was a no-talent doggerel writer. He found his niche and he rose to his level of incompetence. End of story."

"Then how did he come to have 143 gold coins in his safe?" I demanded.

"Gold used to sell for $35 an ounce, Helen dear. You could pick up those Mexican coins for pocket change. I might have a few myself tucked away in my safe-deposit box. You'll find out when I croak–assuming you don't predecease me. Really, Helen, you should try to look a little nicer for the governor here."

"I like your daughter just the way she is," said Leigh.

Mother flashed him a quizzical look. "Now I understand why you lost to Truman."

Monica phoned a few hours later. "I checked with Roland, Mother. He said that must be an old list. He said none of those valuables were in the safe when he opened it."

"Right, Monica. That's what I expected him to say."

"I believe him, Mother."

"Good, dear. It's important to trust the person you're, uh, living with."

May 17 – Leigh left after breakfast. What a treat to spend two whole days (and two gruelingly celibate nights) in his company. Not sure how I'm going to cope without him. For the next few weeks he expects to be busy with end-of-semester chores, plus he has to get ready for three days of wild, passionate sex with Fiona in Toronto over the Memorial Day weekend. Just across the lake from Cleveland. He's lucky I don't have an inclination toward stalking.

Leigh made me promise not to tell anyone about our Gloria Anne Lenore discovery. He's afraid if word gets out, it will drive her even further underground. Finished *Her Placated Heart*. It turns out the amnesia victim's twin brother was the army deserter. Our hero was revealed to be a star student at a Catholic seminary. After some tense days of anguished soul-searching, he decided to go for the volunteer nurse instead of life in the priesthood. All of which got me thinking about Aunt Maddy. I can't help but wonder if she was so big into crafts because of her husband's impairment. But how important is sex to most people? If it were a high priority for me, I probably wouldn't have stuck with Harkness all these years.

Two thoughts on Uncle Phil: Considering the hand dealt him by fate, it seems surprising that he devoted his life to composing cheerful little verses for greeting cards. And I remember once when I was a kid we went with Maddy and Phil to Geauga Lake. Since it was a hot day, everyone went into the water–except Uncle Phil. He lay on the beach in his street clothes and watched us swim. Looking back, I wonder if he was shy about appearing in a bathing suit. I remember he said he couldn't go swimming because he had to come up with "99 fresh ideas" for Valentine's Day cards. (In his business they worked far in advance of the calendar.) So that afternoon we had everyone on our section of the beach suggesting new variations on the theme of love. Uncle Phil wrote some of them down, but I never found out if any got used.

Did my clandestine copying for Carl, the lawyer, then had lunch in Rocky River with Bodana, my beautiful sister-in-law. We went to an inexpensive Russian restaurant she likes. Bodana thinks my divorcing Harkness is a Big Mistake.

"No husband is perfect, Helen," she pointed out. "Harkness gives you nice big house and minivan. He doesn't cheat on you. Every night he comes home to you. He pays for education of your children. He is boring maybe, but not so unpleasant. OK, you leave him for some other man. Big uproar and dislocation. Then what? Maybe your new man has roving eye. He finds younger babe soon. Or he makes you get a job. So now you have to work at some job you don't like that swallows up your whole life."

"But I met a man I really love."

"So that is great, Helen. Harkness gives you plenty of freedom to see your new man. You are happy and he doesn't have to know."

"It won't work, Bodana. The man I met doesn't sleep with married women."

"Why not?"

"Well, he has scruples. I respect him for that."

"If he loved you, no scruples would keep him out of your arms. I don't understand what is wrong with such American man. Where is his passion?"

"He's also engaged to an attractive woman who's 20 years younger than me."

"And for that you are thinking of divorcing your very successful lawyer husband?"

"Well, I haven't really decided."

"Good. I pray to God that you come to your senses."

"You won't mention any of this to Eliot will you?"

"Such talk we women do not share with husbands."

"Right. Do you, uh, have anyone else, Bodana?"

"Me? No. Eliot is plenty sexy. Always I check his pockets and credit card statements. He is not straying. He tells me he loves me and I know he is not deceiving. After Russian men I know, Eliot Spall is a gift from God. And very good salary he makes too."

"You're a lucky woman, Bodana."

"I make my own luck, Helen. That is what I always do. And you should too."

May 18 – I called up and cancelled my appointment with Carl, the divorce lawyer. Now I kind of hate myself.

May 19 – Took Casta to Monica's storage lot for more movie work.

Casta is now in charge of the sound recorder, since it turns out that she does a better job of keeping the audio levels where they're supposed to be than Brie. She also relieves the boom man when his arms get tired.

"People don't realize it, Mom, but sound is at least as important to the impact of a film as what you see on the screen," she remarked on the drive over.

"Really? That never occurred to me."

"It doesn't to most people. Bad sound is the kiss of death for independent productions. You don't stand a chance of getting distribution."

"I'm sure you're doing a good job. How are you getting on with your sister?"

"We tolerate each other. It's nice to know we're only half related."

"You're keeping that to yourself, right?"

"I haven't said a word."

"Good. Have you heard from Deke?"

"He sends me messages on Facebook."

"And?"

"I don't know. I'm kind of busy these days. I'm just a kid. I don't need to hang out all the time with some old guy my mother used to sleep with."

"You certainly don't, Casta. You shouldn't let him pressure you. I'm hoping he'll lose interest."

"Yeah, me too. Why should I bother with Deke when it took me so many years to get Daddy trained?"

When I dropped Casta off, Roland waved from the other side of the fence. It felt right somehow seeing him behind metal bars. It was a struggle, but I managed to return his wave with all of my fingers extended.

May 20 – Harkness was easier to take back when my days with him seemed numbered. Now that I've returned to being shackled for life, his presence grows more oppressive. I worked on my neglected flower beds and made creamed chicken livers for Sunday dinner. Harkness has never cared much for this dish. Nor, come to think of it, do I.

"Now that your house is on the market," he said at dinner. "I expect you'll be spending more time at home."

"Probably so," I sighed.

"It's been very difficult trying to get by here without you."

"I know, dear. You've been extremely patient and understanding."

"I feel your absence has adversely affected my golf game."

"Sorry, dear. We can't have that, can we?"

May 21 – In defiance of my husband's expressed wishes (as he might put it) I returned to Euclid. Gabby called to say the attendance was pretty sparse at the open house she held here yesterday.

"I think it was mostly neighbors walking through," she said.

"What makes you say that?"

"Because they expressed disappointment at our low asking price. That's not usually a good negotiation ploy if you're a serious buyer."

"They think our low price means their houses aren't worth much?"

"I expect so. That's usually their concern. So tell me about your meeting with Carl."

She didn't like my response or my explanation. Gabby said her life improved 500 percent when she shed "that boat anchor of a husband."

I started in on *Streetcar for Adventure*. (Leigh took the manuscripts for *The Solitary Simpleton* and *The Trek to Zion* back with him to Pittsburgh.) This appears to be Gloria Anne's version of a boys' novel. A 14-year-old lad in Binghamton, New York–circa 1921–converts his savings into rolls of nickels and proposes to see how far west he can ride on inter-urban streetcars. His very progressive parents say, "Oh, that sounds educational, Elwyn. Go for it, dear." So off he goes with his Boy Scout pack and transit maps. He just reached Rochester and found the guided tour of the giant Kodak factory very informative. Elwyn is something of a science nerd who likes to integrate expositions on chemical processes into his narrative. He also suggests simple experiments that the reader can perform at home using common everyday items. If Gloria Anne Lenore isn't the most versatile writer on the planet, I'd like to know who is.

I had some news for Leigh when he phoned after lunch. "All the manuscripts after the mid-1960s appear to have been typed on Uncle Phil's Underwood typewriter," I said.

"Really, darling? Are you sure?"

"Well, I'm not the FBI Crime Lab, but it's the same Elite font. And if you put a ruler under a line, you can see that the upper-case 'T' is slightly elevated and the lower-case 'M' is a bit crooked. It's the same on the manuscripts and the sample line I just typed. They match perfectly."

"Do you have any examples of your uncle's handwriting?"

"I found some of his cancelled checks in a drawer. I'm no expert, but his printing looks to be the same as the corrections on the manuscripts."

"Jesus, Helen, that's pretty convincing. But if your uncle was Gloria Anne Lenore, why is a resident of your mother's rest home getting checks from movie studios?"

"I thought about that, Leigh. Uncle Phil had a sister. She could still be alive and his heir."

"Was her name Muriel, Clare, or Inez?"

"Unfortunately not. I expect, though, you'll appreciate her name."

"What was it?"

"Fiona. Fiona Tishby."

"Well, Fiona's a fairly common name."

"Yeah, too common. Except in Mother's rest home. I checked with them. They have no resident by that name."

"Damn. I could see why the surname would be changed, but not the given name."

"Fiona may not have liked her name. It doesn't do much for me."

Since we were edging toward the topic, Leigh asked about my visit to the divorce lawyer. Like Gabby, he didn't care much for my change of heart. I gave it to him straight.

"I need some reciprocal commitment from you, Leigh, if I'm going to turn my world upside down."

"Like what, Helen?"

"Like a commitment to refrain from sleeping with Fiona in Toronto. And to inform her that you've met someone else."

"Wow, that's asking quite a bit."

"Not as much as dissolving a 27-year marriage."

"Can I think about it, Helen?"

"Please do, Leigh. You know where to find me when you make up your mind."

May 22 – To keep from dwelling on Leigh, I've been thinking about Uncle Phil. It's still a mystery what he did with all his earnings–if he was indeed Gloria Anne Lenore. And why did he continue at his greeting card job if he was earning those big Hollywood bucks? Did he choose that pen name because the initials spelled G.A.L, which the world had tried to make him but failed? And did he spend all those years inhabiting the hearts of teenage girls in his fiction because he'd spent his first 18 years masquerading as a girl?

Looked through Phil's attic box again for any clues about his sister. I think I remember meeting her once at Christmastime when I was kid. All I can recall were Aunt Fiona's severely plucked eyebrows and the tin she gave us of home-baked, rock-hard holiday cookies. You had to dunk them forever or risked breaking a tooth. If I remember correctly, she wasn't married then. And I don't recall ever hearing that she did get married. She was a photographer's assistant in faraway Fresno, which I imagined at the time to be a sun-drenched California beach town.

Her big sister, Philippa Tishby, was more than a little boyish-looking in her photos. I expect Philippa got teased a lot. Not many photos of her smiling, but then nobody in her family was big on that–at least not when a camera was pointed their way. Philippa got mostly As and Bs on her report cards. Under "Deportment" her fourth-grade teacher wrote: "Overly boisterous at times. Philippa needs to learn to be a lady." I imagine her parents shuddered when they read that ironic comment.

Had dinner next door with Grace and Peach, who said some of the neighbors resent that I'm asking so little for my house. I pointed out that it's been on the market for more than a week at that "bargain price" without attracting a single offer so far.

Both were supportive of my decision to stay married. Grace said she hoped to meet my husband and children someday, and was curious why they never came to Euclid. I said they were too busy. They probably deduced that things weren't going so well with the fellow in the green Saab, but both were too polite to mention him. I didn't bring him up either.

We discussed Uncle Phil's mysterious sister. Grace met her a few times and recalled her as being rather shy. She said she was sensitive about her disability.

"What disability?" I asked.

"Well, it may not have qualified as a disability per se. One of her arms was several inches shorter than the other."

"Really? I never noticed that."

"She wore long-sleeve blouses to disguise it. The arm also was a bit misshapen, but it functioned perfectly well."

How odd that both siblings had something physical to conceal.

Grace didn't know if Fiona was still alive. "She was younger than Phil, but I expect she would be nearly 80 now."

"Well, 80 is the new 70," I pointed out.

"I hope so, dear," said Peach. "But I doubt it."

May 23 – Finished *Streetcar for Adventure*. A fine story that held my interest throughout–and I'm not a teenage boy. I'm clueless why it and *Her Placated Heart* never got published. Young Elwyn made it all the way to Elkhart Lake, Wisconsin by traveling from one streetcar system to the next. Along the way he toured a steel plant in Erie, a sewing machine factory in Cleveland, a glass factory in Toledo, and watched Fords being assembled in Detroit. At dusk he would politely ask a farmer if he could pitch his tent in their field. They invariably assented just as politely. In the morning Elwyn would bathe in a stream or pond, then assist the farmer by gathering eggs in the henhouse or by milking cows. Then the farmer's wife would fix him a hearty breakfast that would sustain him until dinner. Off he would trot to the nearest streetcar stop for another day of westward travel on his bottomless supply of nickels. Always Elwyn was polite, resourceful, energetic, curious, congenial, and optimistic. He had no tattoos or piercings, did not listen to heavy metal on his iPod, was not sullen or hostile, and evinced no signs of being Fixated on Sex. Perhaps he represented some ideal childhood that most of us (Uncle Phil included) never had.

May 24 – Lunched with Mother in her dining hall. I took along some photos of young Fiona Tishby to see if I could spot her aged visage among the diners.

Playing it cagey with Mother, I asked her if she'd ever noticed any residents with arm deformities.

"I suppose you're obsessing now over that repellent sister of Phil. What was her name?"

"Fiona Tishby. What happened to her?"

"Don't you remember? She drowned when the *Andrea Doria* went down in 1956. Couldn't swim a stroke with that bum arm of hers. She yelled for help, but everyone found her so obnoxious they thought it best just to let her sink to the bottom."

"Then how was she baking us Christmas cookies in 1964?" I asked.

"Oh. Was that her?"

"Yes, Mother. Is she living here? Is she Muriel Wadge, Clare Hendom, or Inez Frinezen?"

"Oh, dear, Helen, you are losing it. Your poor brain must be even more ravaged than your exterior. And people tell me I've lost my marbles."

"You can't offend me, Mother. I've ceased to believe a word that comes out of your mouth."

"Well isn't that a deplorable state of affairs. And so soon after Mothers Day too."

Mrs. Whistman, the day-shift supervisor, looked at me peculiarly when I inquired if any of their residents had arms of different lengths.

"Not that I am aware of, Mrs. Spall. Of course, we do not measure their body parts when we admit them. Is this in regards to some knitting project you've undertaken?"

"Uh, no. I'm looking for an elderly relative we've lost track of. She may have changed her name. One of her arms is slightly stunted."

"Sorry, can't help you there. We've had several amputees in the past, but they have all passed on. Some of their prosthetic limbs are preserved in the chapel as a memorial to their memory."

May 25 – Leigh called before he left for Toronto. He said it was a six-hour drive, depending on the traffic through Buffalo and the backup at the border.

"Are you taking a detour through Euclid to give me a pre-Fiona squeeze?"

"I'd love to, Helen, but I better not. Guess what, darling?"

"You shaved your mustache?"

"Hardly. I started reading *The Trek to Zion*. It's Gloria Anne Lenore's masterpiece. It's an amazing, stupendous book."

"Really?"

"Hell, even the title is decent. It's about a painter and his young daughter who escape to Nevada after the 1906 San Francisco earthquake. They get outfitted with horses and supplies, and head out overland toward Zion country in Utah. Along the way they meet up with Paiute indians.

While Dad is sketching the dramatic landscape and having ecstatic visions in tribal sweat lodges, his daughter just wants to get back to her tea dances and social life in Frisco."

"Don't tell me anything more. I want to read it."

"It's Gloria Anne Lenore with all the stops pulled out. Every sentence thrusts its way into your brain on the point of an icepick. I've never read anything like it."

"That's fantastic, Leigh. Do you think we can get it published?"

"In a heartbeat, if we can untangle the rights. Or finally track down Ms. Lenore."

I told him about yesterday's frustrating conversation with Mother.

"I'm intrigued that Fiona Tishby's arm was stunted. Because the daughter in *The Trek to Zion* has the same disability."

"One arm is shorter than the other?"

"Well, Gloria Anne describes it as 'slightly deformed.' The kid is pretty self-conscious about it. That's one reason her dad wants to take her into the wilderness: to prove to her that she can handle any adversity."

We talked a few minutes more, then Leigh said he'd better get started on his drive. I asked him if he'd made any decisions about his "British entanglements."

"It's such a mess, Helen. Why does life have to be so fucking complicated?"

"I don't know, Leigh—not being involved with a person who lives on the other side of the world."

"No, he lives right in your bed."

"Good luck, Leigh. Don't have too good of a time in Toronto."

"I'll try not to, Helen. And I'll be thinking of you."

"I hope so. Shall I call you every hour on the hour?"

"Better not, darling. I'll see you next week."

That sounded like a promise, but you never know.

May 26 – Memorial Day weekend. Like clockwork, Harkness uncovered the pool, serviced the chemicals, and switched on the heater. He sets it at three notches below "Low." Not being a polar bear, I sneak into the pool house when he's not looking and adjust it.

Drove Casta to Monica's storage facility. She was feeling a bit low because the movie shoot wraps this weekend. So far, Roland has slain 37 victims in interesting and creative ways.

"Does he explain why all these people are being killed?" I asked.

"It's a metaphor, Mom. They're dying because they have so much stuff, they have to rent a storage locker to hold their excess. What he's really saying is these people are dying inside because they're ruled by their material possessions."

Spoken by my teenage daughter who once owned two dozen Barbie dolls and had suitcases jammed with tiny (but costly) outfits for every occasion.

Trying not to imagine what Leigh and Fiona have been doing all day. I'm hoping they've been locked in endless boring seminars with absolutely no time to themselves.

May 27 – Got a bad headache from Harkness's Sunday morning pancakes. No golfing for him today because he says the courses are "too jammed with riffraff" on holidays. He especially objects to the throngs of women golfers. He says you can get beaned just waiting at a tee from the balls they send careering off in all directions. So he spent the morning riding the mower over our five acres, while I lay on the sofa in the den and tried not to obsess about Leigh.

Got a surprise call in the late afternoon from him.

"I've got some bad news, Helen," he said.

I felt my stomach drop and the blood drain from my head.

"You've eloped with Fiona? You're married?"

"Of course not. This is serious. When I stopped for gas in Dunkirk, someone lifted my briefcase out of my back seat."

"So that means what? You can't give your presentation?"

"That's the least of my problems. In my briefcase was the manuscript of *The Trek to Zion*."

"Tell me you made a copy of it, Leigh."

"I was going to, but the copy machine was down."

"Oh, my God."

"I didn't discover the theft until I got to Toronto."

"You're sure you didn't leave it back at your office?"

"Of course, I'm sure."

"Did you alert the police?"

"Yeah, both the police and sheriff. I'm here now. They've got the Boy Scouts out looking for it in case the thieves tossed it somewhere."

"You're not in Toronto?"

"No, I'm in Dunkirk."

"Where the hell is that?"

"It's on the thruway about 50 miles south of Buffalo. Oh God, Helen, I've lost a major work of American literature. It's a fucking disaster."

"Is Fiona with you?"

"No, she doesn't see what all the fuss is about. She thinks I'm an idiot for leaving the conference."

Poor strategy by the Brit; she may not be as crafty as I thought.

"Could you possibly come here, Helen?"

"Certainly, Leigh, if you want me to. I could be there in a few hours."

"That'd be great. I'd really appreciate it."

I told Harkness that Gabby needed me right away in Euclid to discuss an important house issue. Five minutes later I was hurtling down my driveway in the Beast.

On the way out of town I phoned Gabby and asked her to cover for me should anyone in my family call.

Thought of Mother as I crossed the state line and drove north on the Thomas E. Dewey Thruway (known to locals as the New York turnpike). Dunkirk was a sleepy town along the eastern shore of Lake Erie. A block or two of old red-brick buildings made up its forlorn downtown. The sun was low over the lake when I found Leigh's hotel and tracked him down in the bar of the adjoining restaurant. He was gulping Scotch and looking miserable. I gave him a kiss and dragged him over to the buffet right before it closed. We filled our plates, sat in a booth, and he brought me up to date.

"I talked to the local newspaper and got interviewed by a Buffalo TV station. I said it was the typescript of a rare manuscript. I told them the title, but said I was still trying to determine the author. I'm offering a $5,000 reward for its return."

"Good, Leigh. That should stir up some interest. Why don't you eat something?"

"I'm not hungry."

I cleaned my plate and went back for dessert. Yes, it was a major disaster, but at least darling Leigh was not sleeping with you know who.

May 28 – Memorial Day. Minor breakthrough for Leigh and me. We passed the night in the same hotel room–collegially in separate king-size beds. At 2:12 a.m. he announced: "I lied about the copy machine being down, Helen. I was just too pressed for time to make a copy."

"That's OK, Leigh," I yawned. "These things happen. It's not your fault."

"I went into the gas station to pay, but the line was longer than I expected. I should have locked my car."

"Try to get some sleep, darling. I have a good feeling about this. I think someone will find it."

"Or it could already be at the bottom of Lake Erie. I keep thinking about Thomas Carlyle."

"What about him?"

"In the 1830s when he was writing his monumental history of the French revolution, he gave the manuscript to his pal John Stuart Mill to critique. Mill's maid mistook it for scrap paper and used it to start the household fires."

"Oops."

"It was Carlyle's only copy. He had to start all over again."

"Well, I'll bet his second version was much improved."

"Right. Only Gloria Anne Lenore may be deceased. Even if she's alive, I suspect she's in no condition to recreate her masterpiece."

"Try to get some sleep, darling. Things will look better in the morning."

At least the day dawned clear and beautiful. The hotel let us crank out some flyers on their copy machine. These we taped to poles around town. Hardly any businesses were open, but we managed to score some coffee at the same gas station where the theft occurred. We sat in Leigh's Saab and munched on day-old pastries.

"Have I gotten you in trouble with your husband?" Leigh inquired.

"More with my daughter Monica. I'm supposed to be hosting a wrap party for their movie cast and crew this afternoon."

"My apologies to Monica."

"Oh, they'll cope. They always do. What are you going to do now, Leigh?"

"Drive to Toronto and pick up Fiona."

"I imagine she can get a ride to the airport on her own."

"She's coming back to Pittsburgh with me."

"Oh. You hadn't mentioned that."

"Well, Toronto is rather far to come for just a conference. So she's staying over for a time."

"Right."

"I guess I should get going. Fiona doesn't like to be kept waiting."

"No, I imagine not."

When he leaned over to kiss me good-bye, some teenagers at the gas pumps rudely blasted their horn.

May 29 – My popularity has sunk to a new low with certain members of my family. That's OK, I'm not too thrilled with myself either.

Saw the photos from the party. Quite a mob scene around the pool, with Harkness in the background looking angry and lost. I'm glad I missed it. The sight of Roland in a skimpy bathing suit is not something I'd wish to endure in the flesh. The hand-blown Danish vase that was an anniversary gift from Mother got broken. And I noticed my pearl earrings have gone missing from the case on my dresser.

May 30 – Email from Leigh saying the manuscript remains lost. I made copies of *Her Placated Heart* and *Streetcar for Adventure*. Now I have copies in two separate locations. Wish we'd taken that precaution in the first place.

May 31 – Got an offer on my house: $45,000, contingent on physical inspection, bank appraisal, and my clearing up the "rat infestation in the basement."

Gabby told me I had three days to think it over and said I should call an exterminator. I phoned Joe Ducowski and explained that I wasn't trying to seduce him, but my rats were back.

"I wonder how they got in this time," he said.

"I think some real estate agent must have moved the bowling ball off the grate," I lied.

Joe showed up within the hour and did his thing in my basement with the traps and sticky paper. I was resolved to keep my hands off him this time, but we wound up again in the big walnut bed. We do fit together so nicely. And I love the dusky olive tone of his smooth, muscular body. His scent reminds me of a freshly opened can of mixed nuts.

"Well, now you've done it, Helen," he said, nuzzling a part of me that rarely gets nuzzled. "You've made me your personal slave."

"I think everyone should be permitted two families, Joe. I pick you for my second one. We can be together Mondays, Wednesdays, Fridays, and every other weekend. Do you think your wife will agree?"

"Sure, but you'll have to make do with my bloody corpse."

June 1 – We countered at $60,000, giving the buyer 48 hours to respond and ten days to remove his contingencies. It was all Gabby's strategy; I just gulped and signed on the dotted line.

Another curt email from Leigh reporting no progress on recovering the missing novel.

Too bad he only read part of *The Trek to Zion*. If Leigh had finished it, we could try placing him under deep hypnosis and chipping the text out of his brain word by word.

Last day of the school term for Casta. She appears to have passed her classes. So far, her summer plans consist of working on her tan by the pool.

June 2 – Very summery weekend. People may not realize it, but Ohio gets wildly lush and tropical this time of year. Like Hawaii without the palm trees, looming volcanoes, and pesky tourists. Our property looks its best in late spring: with the grand sweep of green lawn and my roses and hydrangeas in bloom. Driving by, a stranger might think that there is the home of one lucky family.

June 3 – Kyle arrived back from Lafayette in time for dinner. He's a bit bummed because his current girlfriend (he's had lots) went back home to Missouri for the summer. He'll be interning at an electrical engineering firm in Cleveland this summer, but that doesn't start for a week or so. I asked him as he was helping me clear off the table what he liked about electrical engineering.

"I don't know, Mom, I just dig it. Nikola Tesla is my god."

"What did he do?"

"Well, among other things he gave the world the single- and polyphase AC motor. If it wasn't for him, you'd be laboring 18 hours a day over your housework."

"Who says I don't?" I asked.

"Me for one," piped Harkness.

June 4 – No communication from Leigh and my wannabe house buyer. Gabby says it's just as well. She says he (the buyer) was a bottom-feeder looking to score a bargain at my expense. His offer was certainly puny, although at this point $45,000 sounds way better to me than zero.

June 5 – Finally got a call from Leigh–suggesting to my suspicious mind that Fiona at last departed the continent. He said he'd had 500 flyers printed, and asked if I wanted to help him distribute them around the Buffalo area.

"You don't think the thief was a local?" I asked.

"Nothing has turned up in Dunkirk, Helen. And that gas station gets a lot of business off the thruway."

"They could have been headed south instead of north."

"I know, Helen. But I have to do something."

"Right, Leigh. I understand."

We agreed to rendezvous at the hotel in Dunkirk, have lunch there, then head for Buffalo. I told Kyle I had to go to Euclid for a day or two, and asked him if he'd be OK.

"Sure, Mom. I know how to scrounge."

"If you microwave something, make a little extra for Casta."

"OK, if she's around."

"And try not to mess with any of her friends. They're only 16."

"Right, Mom. I know jailbait when I see it."

June 6 – Leigh Mulcahy is one of those people who likes to bring up Big Issues in the middle of the night. At 3:07 a.m. he announced to our pitch-dark hotel room (separate beds as before): "Fiona is pregnant."

That got me awake in a flash.

"OK," I said. "We spent all day leafleting the Rust Belt, and you tell me that now?"

"Well, it's been weighing on my mind."

"How far along is she?"

"Ten weeks."

"Really? When did you last see her?"

"Over winter break."

My groggy brain attempted the math.

"Uh, Leigh, darling, that's not adding up."

"Oh, she's not pregnant by me. That would be reckless. She says my

99

sperm is much too old. According to the latest studies, you really don't want to be impregnated by anyone older than 28."

Well that explains Casta.

"OK, so who's the father?"

"One of the young postdocs in her college. Some fellow in the physics department. Very brilliant and athletic. Plays rugby."

"He inseminated her artificially?"

"No, Fiona doesn't go in for that sort of thing. She'd figure out when she was ovulating and give him a jingle. Took them quite a few tries to get one going."

"Fiona was having sex with some young stud? Don't you mind?"

"Well, it doesn't fill me with unalloyed delight."

"So now what? She expects you to raise some other fellow's kid? How do you feel about that?"

"Again, I am not awash in warm feelings of delight."

"So what did you tell her?"

"Well, you have to understand that Fiona only undertook this effort to get pregnant because she expects us to be married. She has no interest in being a single mother."

"So you're engaged and you've set the date. When is it?"

"August 4, St. Andrew's Cathedral, Aberdeen, Scotland."

"Sounds like a major shindig. I take it her family has money."

"Scads."

"How do they feel about you?"

"Not overly awash in warm feelings. I am judged a most inappropriate choice."

"Well, at least some members of her family have sense. So what are you going to do?"

"I'm trapped, Helen. I'm ensnared. There's no gentlemanly way out."

"Well, you don't have to be a gentleman all the time, Leigh. Some backsliding is permitted. You could ditch Fiona and have reckless sex with a married woman. There's one available right now, for example."

"I'm not a cad, Helen. I have to do the right thing."

Just my luck to fall in love with an honorable guy.

"August 4, huh? You realize you'll be getting married on my mother's birthday?"

"That's odd, darling. It's also Fiona's birthday. She picked that date to make it easier for me to remember our anniversary."

"Smart move. I expect she's anticipating the imminent onset of your descent into Alzheimer's."

June 7 – I parted from Leigh with no mention of when (or if) we'd meet again. I love the man, but how much more pain do I need in my life?

I think Leigh may be drawn to Gloria Anne Lenore novels because her characters reside–as he aspires to–in a world that's better than our ugly real one.

Joe trapped three rats in my basement. I don't see the attraction–there's nothing to eat down there and who really wants to live in somebody's dank basement? After my frustrating night in Dunkirk with Leigh, it was a pleasure to enjoy Joe's relaxed company in Maddy's walnut bed. Wish I could hire the guy to give lessons to Harkness. Or a personality transplant, that might work too.

One really doesn't expect to have the best sex of one's life with an exterminator, even if he does revere you as the ultimate former high-school goddess.

June 8 – Another miserly bid on my house: $30,000 with $500 down and they want me to carry the loan. I'm surprised they didn't ask me to wash their car, shampoo their carpet, and walk their dog. Gabby told them politely to go away.

June 9 – Casta phoned while I was at the supermarket.
"You better not come home, Mom."
"What have you done now, dear?"
"It's not me, Mom. It's Daddy. Deke sent him a letter. He just got it."
Not the best news to receive in the frozen foods aisle.
"That's, uh, unfortunate. Do you know what Deke wrote?"
"Well, Daddy was grilling me about our trip to Columbus. He looks pissed, Mom. He called up and canceled his golf date."
Truly an ominous sign.
"OK, Casta, don't worry. I'll be home shortly."
"It's all my fault, Mom. I should never have unfriended Deke on Facebook."
"You're allowed to choose your own friends, dear. It's just as well this is all coming out."

June 10 – Harkness was remarkably angry yesterday and not inclined to discuss matters dispassionately. So Casta and I are taking a break in Euclid. Kyle is holding down the fort with his father in Pepper Pike. Harkness refused to let me see Deke's letter. I suspect he regards it as Evidence of Culpability and didn't want to risk my ripping it to shreds. Remind me never to marry another lawyer. Knowing Deke, he likely slanted his letter to maximize the hurt. You'd think a cancer survivor would be striving for more serenity in his remaining years.

Slept about two hours last night. I don't feel that bad about Harkness–just stressed by all the turmoil. Very unsettling to have your life in such an uproar at my age.

Casta is not too impressed with Euclid. She says "even for free" my house is a "major dump." She says I should sell it fast before global warming puts the whole neighborhood under water.

"Perhaps the lake will expand only a block and we'll be right on the shore. This house could be worth a fortune then, Casta."

"I'd rather have a nice heated pool in Pepper Pike. I hope, Mom, you're not planning to hire some budget divorce lawyer."

"No one's talking about divorce, Casta."

"Hah! That's what you think. I just got a text from Kyle. There's a locksmith there right now changing all the locks."

"I'm surprised your father would call a locksmith on Sunday. I'm sure they charge extra."

"Better hit the ATM, Mom–before Daddy cancels all your cards."

Too late as it turns out. I inserted my ATM card and the mechanical bastard impounded it. No cash was disgorged either. Pooling our resources, Casta and I scraped up $26, and headed over to the local pizza shop for dinner. We walked the six blocks to conserve the Beast's precious fuel supply.

I don't know where I'd be sleeping tonight if I didn't have this house. Since Monica currently despises me, I doubt she'd take me in. And they discourage overnight guests at Mother's place.

The nerve of that man locking me out!

June 11 – Had an emergency meeting this morning with Carl Zyzinski, Gabby's divorce lawyer. He's a short, broad guy with a super abundance of hair. Very hairy wrists and one of those heavy Nixonian beards that looks like it would abrade razor blades. Carl was sympathetic and assured me that he would "make some calls" to deal with the immediate issues. He then opened his desk drawer, removed an envelope, and handed it to me.

"Here's some walking-around money until I slap some sense into that husband of yours," he said.

The envelope contained ten crisp $100 bills. I was amazed that cash ever flowed in that direction from lawyer to client.

Carl was pleased that I brought the copies of our financial records. He said he would look them over, then phone me to discuss strategy.

"Do you want a divorce, Mrs. Spall? Or are you amenable to reconciliation?"

"Oh, I don't know. Do I have to decide that now?"

"Well, it would be helpful to know which way you are inclined."

"I suppose a divorce–if I don't wind up penniless."

"I wouldn't worry about that, Mrs. Spall. Your husband is a prominent attorney in this town with a very successful practice."

"But aren't lawyers harder to divorce?"

"Not harder," he smiled. "Just more interesting."

"But Harkness has evidence of my infidelity."

"Fortunately, the courts don't care much about that these days–as I'm sure your husband is aware. I would refrain from conversing with him or agreeing to meet with him. My secretary will give you our handout that explains the security precautions you should take. If he gives you any trouble, call me any time. And if you can't reach me, call 9-1-1."

"Oh, I don't think it will come to that. Harkness is not a violent person."

"Marital discord can bring out the worst in people, Mrs. Spall. It's best to err on the side of caution."

"Right. Is there any chance you can call me Helen instead of Mrs. Spall?"

"No problem, Helen. Around here, we consider all our clients to be family."

Family or no, Carl was still charging me (actually Harkness) $345 an hour for his time. He also had me sign a receipt for the cash.

June 12 – Awake at 2:00 a.m., so I took an inventory of my choices. The men in my life include Leigh (engaged), Joe (married), Deke (petty, vindictive, impotent), and Harkness (ranks golf higher than his wife). Seems to be a trend in my family. Mother married a man whose occupation proved fatally dangerous. Aunt Maddy chose a husband with a pronounced anatomical deficiency. My elder daughter is living with a fellow I regard as a liar and a thief. And my younger daughter has never brought home a boyfriend that I didn't find appalling.

Kind of makes you wonder if any of us is ever destined to get it right.

A courier knocked on my door at 9:52 a.m. and had me sign for an envelope. Inside was a new ATM card and a checkbook for a new bank account (in my name alone). A half-hour later Carl Zyzinski called with an update.

"Your husband has agreed to vacate your Pepper Pike house," he said. "He'll turn over the keys to my associate on Thursday, and you and your daughter can return on Friday."

"That's great, Carl. I was beginning to run out of ideas for keeping my daughter entertained."

"I've reviewed your financial statements, Helen. Considering Mr. Spall's prominence and client list, I can only conclude he is substantially underreporting his income to the IRS. Forgive me for asking this, but are you at all complicit in this deception?"

"Certainly not. My husband does all our taxes. He doesn't consult me. I just sign the forms."

"Just as I thought. I also strongly suspect your husband is concealing assets. As your attorney, Helen, I must advise you to cease filing joint income-tax returns with Mr. Spall."

"I can do that if I'm divorced, right?"

"That is correct. Of course, this gives us some leverage over your husband in our negotiations. Attorneys are officers of the court. We're expected to refrain from cheating too flagrantly on our taxes."

"Harkness hates paying taxes. He's like that hotel woman Leona Helmsley. He thinks only the little people should have to pay."

"That attitude is going to cost him in his settlement with you. I'll make sure of that."

Well, that call brightened my day.

June 13 – Since Harkness was phoning every 20 minutes, I finally broke down and answered.

"Helen, have you gone mad?" he demanded.

"Be civil, Harkness, or I'm going to hang up."

"I can't believe you involved Carl Zyzinski in our affairs. Don't you know that man's reputation? He's notorious in this town! You really should have consulted me first."

"Sorry, dear, but I'm not letting you pick my divorce lawyer."

"Divorce! Really, Helen, that is so preposterous. I don't know what's got into you. Anyway, I have some good news."

"Yes, dear?"

"I've decided to forgive you. The man who wrote that letter must be deranged. Anyone can see Casta looks just like me."

"Of course she does, dear. But I have some bad news for you."

"What?"

"I don't want to go to prison for tax evasion. So I think an amicable split is best for all. Now, I have to go, dear. If you wish to communicate further, please go through my lawyer. You have his number."

"Helen, wait . . ."

"Bye, dear. Got to go. Thank you for calling."

"Was that Daddy?" asked Casta, looking up from her book: *The Summer of Romola*.

"Uh, yes."

"So I find out you're getting divorced by overhearing a phone conversation. That's typical of this family."

"Well, I kind of just made up my mind, Casta. Are you OK with that, dear?"

"Sure, Mom. Most marriages are ridiculous anyway. Yours was pretty absurd from the get-go."

"I don't know, Casta. Your father and I got along most of the time."

"Except he wasn't really my father. Don't forget that part."

"We don't know that for a fact. Are you enjoying your book?"

"It's OK. This girl so needs to get laid. Her obsession with horses is just a substitute for you know what."

I sighed. And somewhere on this planet I suspect Gloria Anne Lenore also was sighing.

June 14 – Monica called me from work to berate me for destroying my marriage and ruining her father's life. She also was incensed that I was evicting him from his own house. I tried to present my side of the story, but she wasn't hearing any of it. Then my sister-in-law Bodana phoned, but I begged off, saying I had an appointment and had to run. I already know her point of view, and I don't need her to reinforce my insecurities. They're doing quite well enough on their own.

Got a package in the mail from my engaged friend Leigh. It was a copy of the manuscript for *The Solitary Simpleton*. He enclosed this note:

> Dear Helen,
>
> I know you're anxious to read this. Could you send me copies of *Streetcar for Adventure* and *Her Placated Heart*? Sorry, I don't have better news for you on any front. Have you had time to investigate the three ladies at your mother's rest home?
> Always,
> Leigh

Always what, Leigh? Always disappointing? Always infuriating? Always nibbling away at my soul?

Sorry back at you, Leigh: I've been a little distracted lately by the disintegration of my life. But I hope to return to ferreting out lost authors real soon.

June 15 – Casta spent nearly six hours yesterday absorbed in *The Summer of Romola*. Then at noon today I had to drag her away from her book when we went next door to Grace's house for lunch. Casta was fairly well behaved by her standards. Not a total embarrassment for a change. She spoke in complete sentences and didn't say anything too outrageous when we got around to discussing my divorce. Grace was sympathetic and supportive as usual. What a compassionate friend. I'll miss her company when my house sells. I offered to repay her loan from my new bank account, but she said she was fine waiting until the house sells.

After lunch we packed up and returned to Pepper Pike. Another locksmith was there changing the locks again. They must do a nice business from marriage bust-ups. He gave me six shiny new keys and had me sign a receipt. I offered to pay him, but he said the service was being billed to Carl Zyzinski's account.

Harkness had taken some of his clothes and most of his golf paraphernalia. I asked Kyle if he knew where his father had gone.

"He called Uncle Eliot, but Aunt Bodana nixed moving in with them. So he's in one of those extended-stay hotels out by the expressway."

"How does he seem?"

"Kind of shell-shocked, Mom. I don't think he saw any of this coming. Are you really splitting up?"

"I'm afraid so, Kyle. But don't worry. We'll still be paying for your college. And things will start to calm down soon. Everything's going to be fine."

"I hope so, Mom. It's been a wild few days around here. I thought people married as long as you guys were stuck together for life."

"No, sometimes we come unglued."

"Dad's pretty pissed that it happened right before his big charity golf tournament. It's this weekend you know. He's the chairman this year."

"Some charity, Kyle. They bus kids from the inner city so they can work as caddies. They don't even pay them the minimum wage."

"Well, some of them get pretty big tips."

"Sorry, dear, I'm not impressed."

Waiting for me was a letter from Deke, which went unopened into Harkness's shredder. I have also blocked his number from my phone. If a large meteor hurtled out of the sky and decimated Medina, Ohio, I wouldn't be that upset.

Casta brought along her book and three more Gloria Anne Lenore novels from my stash. She is under strict orders that they are not to be removed from this house, written in, defaced in any way, or loaned out to her friends. That last point I stressed with the greatest possible urgency.

"Gee, Mom, chill out," she replied. "I only want to read them, not have sex with them."

June 16 – Kyle's spending the day helping his father with the golf tournament. My son played basketball and baseball in high school, but–being a Spall–in his heart golf reigns supreme. Its appeal escapes me. I suppose it could be regarded as a form of exercise, except these days everyone rides around in those little carts. Very expensive hobby too. We could have taken the family on a luxury cruise around the world with all the money Harkness has sunk into golf. And had plenty left over to buy a replacement for the Beast.

Gloria Anne Lenore appears to have more contemporary appeal than I gave her credit for. Casta finished *The Summer of Romola* and is now reading *The Artful Miss Amelia*. It's about a girl who's painting a water-color beside a duck pond when she is befriended by an elderly widow, who invites her to be her companion on a tour of the art capitals of Europe. Casta read the description on the back of the book and commented, "I know what that old dyke's after."

"Really, Casta, there's nothing like that in the book."

"Hah! I'll be the judge of that."

June 17 – Big hubbub in the middle of the night when Casta was awakened by a prowler. I was about to call 9-1-1 when Kyle came in and said it was only Ally. She and Kyle were a handsome and popular couple their senior year in high school. Kyle moved on, but Ally so far hasn't. The past few years she's been a bit of a polite and apologetic stalker. Kyle went back to bed, but since I was awake anyway, I invited Ally in for a cup of tea. After several minutes of abject apologizing by the back door, she accepted my offer.

We sat at the kitchen table and drank tea and ate sandwich-creme cookies out of the package. I could afford to splurge. Over the past week I've lost four pounds purely from stress. Ally was still as cute and bubbly as she'd been when Kyle escorted her to the senior prom. Slim and blond with a nice figure. She would make someone a fine daughter-in-law if she could ever get over her fixation on my son.

"Kyle was looking a little tired," she observed.

"He'll be perkier in the morning."

"Oh, right. Sorry."

"So how's your job, Ally?"

She had gone to vocational college and gotten a certificate degree in dental hygiene.

"Fine, Mrs. Spall. I like it except for sticking your hands in people's mouths. That can get gross at times. But it's pretty secure. People aren't going to be getting their teeth cleaned over the Internet. Or sending them off to China. And it's nice meeting new people. It's a very social job, which is what I need."

"I imagine you must meet quite a few young men that way."

"I do have male patients. It's not like being a stylist in a women's hair salon. Do you know if Kyle is still with that girl Megan?"

"Oh, I think she's several spots back in the pack now. I think his latest is named Briana."

"Is she in this area?"

"Back in Missouri for the summer. I probably shouldn't be telling you this."

"I'm getting better, Mrs. Spall. I didn't come by all winter. I was trying to be quiet, but the sprinklers came on. That's why I let out that squeal."

"No harm done."

"Is Mr. Spall away on business?"

So I confessed to our stalker about my marital breakup. She was very sympathetic and expressed the hope that it wouldn't be emotionally damaging to Kyle.

Ally had a confession of her own: she'd been hard at work in her off-hours researching the genealogy of our family.

"Er, why's that?" I asked.

"Mostly to see if our families have any ancestors in common. Plus, you do have to worry about those recessive genes when starting your family."

"And do we?"

"I haven't found any so far. You guys are mostly English, Irish, and Dutch. We're mostly German, Danish, and Polish. I hope you don't mind me saying this, Mrs. Spall, but there's kind of a gap in your family tree."

"Oh? What's that?"

"Kyle's maternal grandfather. He's sort of a question mark. Your mother was married to Donald G. Manders, but he died in 1953 and you were born in late 1954."

"No, according to my mother he died in 1954–and she should know."

"I went to city hall and checked with the clerk's office. Donald G. Manders died July 17, 1953 of acute appendicitis."

"It must have been a different one. My father was a bridge inspector who died in an accidental fall."

"No, this was the same Donald G. Manders who was married to your mother. He was a shoe repairman by trade."

"That's impossible, Ally. When I was a kid we lived on his pension from the state."

"Well, that's not what the city records show. His death certificate was signed by the doctor at the hospital where he died. You could look it up."

"You're sure about this?"

"I'm very persistent, Mrs. Spall. And very thorough. There's no point in my tracing the Manders line if Donald G. Manders was a genetic dead end."

"No, I suppose not."

"I don't mind Kyle going out with other girls. Well, I mind, but I accept it. He has to sample other girls so he'll appreciate me."

"My son is rather frivolous, Ally. He likes to party and have fun. He may not want to settle down with anyone until he's 30."

"That's OK. I can wait."

"In the meantime, you could sample other fellows."

"Not necessary, Mrs. Spall. I know perfection when I see it."

"He's going to be bald like his father," I pointed out.

"Not a factor. The superficialities don't matter to me."

At breakfast I had a question for Kyle.

"Tell me, dear. Did you sleep with Ally?"

"Gee, Mom, that's kind of personal."

"Were you her first?"

"Yeah, I guess so."

"You know, she's completely devoted to you."

"Yeah, since kindergarten–or so she claims."

"And how do you feel about her?"

"She's OK. But a guy can't go to college and be stuck on some girl back home. That would be such a drag."

"Right, dear. I see your point."

Later, I got an annoying email from Monica. She's given me the back of her hand as only a filmmaker can. She's edited me out of her movie.

June 18 – I'd been planning to visit Mother anyway, so I went there for lunch. I found her in her room putting on a neon orange wig.

"What's the occasion, Mother?" I asked.

"Bad Wig Monday. Are you my sister?"

"No, I'm your daughter Helen."

"Well, you've got a suitable wig. The winner voted ugliest wig gets to choose all the movies next week."

"This is my own hair, Mother."

"That's OK. You're still in contention. They say it's to improve morale, but I think these lunchtime fests are just to divert attention from the food. Where's the governor?"

"He went back to Pittsburgh. Mother, I'm getting divorced."

"From that tall, bald fellow?"

"Yes, from Harkness. I've been married to him for 27 years. We had three children."

"I never approved of him, you know. You could have done better."

"Well, I'm inclined to agree with you now."

"Could have saved yourself a whole lot of bother by listening to your mother."

"You're right. I apologize."

"Looked down that long nose of his at the world. Always curling those skinny lips into a sneer. Never could stand the man."

"As I recall you never liked any of my boyfriends."

"For good reason. They always came express from Losers Inc. You'd have been better off with the Fuller Brush man."

We strolled to the dining hall. There were only slightly more bad wigs in evidence than on a typical Monday. Over lima bean casserole I broached the subject again of my alleged father.

"I found out, Mother, that Donald Manders was a shoe repairman who died of a burst appendix 16 months before I was born."

"Well, aren't you the busy little snoop."

"I think I have a right to know who my father was."

"For your information, Don was not a mere shoe repairman. He made very expensive custom orthopedic shoes. The man was a genius with feet."

109

"Well, he wasn't inspecting bridges. So no pension from the state. So what were we living on when I was a kid? You didn't have a job. Where was the money coming from?"

"Uh, bad news for you, Nosy Nellie. I'm too damn old to remember."

"And my father?"

"I suppose I could have been sleeping with someone back then. But the only name that comes to mind is Milton Berle. Was he on TV?"

"Don't play games with me, Mother. I'm sure you remember the man who made you pregnant. And why was a man dead for 16 months listed as the father on my birth certificate?"

"Or was it Bob Hope? He was from Cleveland, you know."

A lady in a pink and white polka dot wig won first prize. Mother says she never wins any of their contests because the knitters have formed a cabal against her.

She did win the contest versus me. As usual, she imparted no useful information.

June 19 – Kyle says he likes his new job. They have him calculating voltage loads, whatever that is. In my day, summer jobs paid actual cash wages so you could save money for college. These days kids slave away for free in internships and are grateful for the opportunity to be exploited.

I phoned Ally early to ask if she knew whether any of my mother's relatives were still living.

"Let me call up that page on my computer, Mrs. Spall."

"Why not call me Helen, since I won't be Mrs. Spall much longer?"

"Sure, if you wish. Here it is. Your mother's brother and sister are both deceased; they died without issue. Your mother's mother also had a brother and sister, both older, who had a total of five children."

"Right. My mother's cousins. Are any of them still alive?"

"Uh, it's possible one of them might be: A woman named Florence Okarness. That's her married name. Born in 1919. No issue."

"I think I remember my mother mentioning a cousin Flo. Could you possibly find a phone number for her?"

"I can try."

Forty minutes later Ally called me back with a phone number in Palm Springs, California. I thanked her and asked if there was any way I could repay her kindness.

"You could have me over for dinner some evening when Kyle's there."

"Of course, dear. I'll arrange it and get back to you."

"What are you arranging?" asked Casta, shuffling into the kitchen. "Some midnight rendezvous with your sex-crazed boyfriend?"

"I'm having Ally over for dinner."

"Wow, Kyle's not going to like that: being stalked right at the dinner table."

"Don't be silly, dear. Nobody's stalking anyone."

I called cousin Florence from the (relative) privacy of Harkness's den. She answered, but I practically had to shout for her to hear me. They make phones with amplified handsets; I can't understand why old people don't use them. Finally, Flo stuck in a hearing aid and was able to comprehend who I was.

"Helen, what a surprise to hear from you. I suppose you're calling to tell me your mother died."

"No, she's still going strong. She'll be 93 in August."

"A mere babe. I'm nearly 95. And how's your aunt Maddy?"

Flo was sorry to hear about Maddy's death. Eventually, we got around to the subject of my mystery father.

"You really should ask your mother about that, Helen. It's not my place to discuss that matter."

"My mother is mentally incapacitated, Florence. She has dementia."

"Sorry to hear that, honey."

"You're pretty much my last hope."

"Well, what little I know I got second-hand. I'm a bit vague on the details. You know, of course, that you were adopted."

"Uh, no, that's the first I've heard of it."

"I suppose your mother had her reasons for keeping it from you."

"Do you know who my real parents are?"

"Not actual names no. I believe it was the usual story of an unfortunate unwed girl."

"My mother was a widow without a job. How could she adopt a baby?"

"Well, as I recall, they went through informal channels. It was handled by a lawyer. Your mother had recently lost both her baby and her husband. I suppose everyone felt she needed someone."

"My mother had a child who died?"

"Yes. A little girl. She had birth abnormalities and lingered only a few months. It was very sad."

"What was her name? Do you recall?"

"I believe it was Helen."

"Do you know anything at all about my birth mother?"

"I'm sorry, honey, I don't. It was all so long ago. And I was never on very good terms with your mother. The little I know I heard from cousin Maddy."

"Did you know about Maddy's husband?"

"We all knew about that, dear. But no one ever mentioned it except cousin Tommy when he was drunk. I remember several Thanksgivings when he embarrassed Phil dreadfully. It was terrible because Maddy's husband was just the sweetest person."

"Thank you, Florence. You've been a great help."

"I hope you don't find all this too disturbing, Helen. I know your mother always tried to do her best for you."

Well, that explains why I never looked much like my mother. I was the second Helen Manders in her life–the ersatz substitute one.

Mother's always been so keen on keeping secrets. But what really is the point?

All in all, I'm rather relieved I'm not her daughter. When I was a kid and would say something nasty or hurtful to a friend, I'd think, "Oh, that's my mother coming out in me." When we were at loggerheads (as we often were), I'd think, "Why couldn't my brave father have lived and my annoying mother fallen off that bridge?"

I never once suspected I was adopted. That's the weird part.

June 20 – Carl Zyzinski checked in to say that Harkness got served with the divorce petition yesterday. Now comes the discovery phase when he's supposed to come clean about his income and assets. I expect that to be a struggle.

I called Ally and invited her to dinner on Saturday. I also told her in confidence about my being adopted. She was shocked.

"Oh dear, Mrs. Spall, I mean, Helen. Half of Kyle's genealogical background is now unaccounted for."

"Sorry, Ally. I could be Hungarian-Armenian for all I know. Does that mean you'll be giving up on my son?"

"Hardly."

"Feel free to poke around, dear. I'd love it if you could come up with something."

"Like what, Helen?"

"Like who I really am."

SUMMER

June 21 – Finally heard from Leigh. He called to thank me for sending him the manuscripts. He said he had raised the reward to $10,000 and put an ad in the Dunkirk newspaper. I told him all my news, some of which he found surprising.

"I never thought you'd do it, Helen."

"I'll be free in a few months, Leigh–should you decide not to ruin your life in August."

"It's rather out of my hands."

"No one ever got stoned in the marketplace for refusing to marry a woman pregnant with another man's child."

"But Fiona thinks of it as my child. She's convinced he's going to be very talented."

"At what? Rugby?"

"She's hoping for something more intellectual. I hope the kid doesn't start bugging me with a lot of questions about astrophysics."

"It has a sex now?"

"Yes, it's a boy. His chromosomes are all in order."

"Are you getting excited?"

"I feel like I'm rolling through the streets of Paris in a tumbril."

"Are angry mobs clamoring for your head?"

"Yes, quite vociferously."

We discussed getting together, but I explained how that would be more difficult now that I was the sole parent living at home. I told him he was welcome to stay in my Euclid house if he wished to make the drive.

"Do you want to see me, Helen?"

"Do you want to see me?"

"I want to see you, but I don't want to make you angry or upset."

"I want to see you, but I can't promise I won't yell at you. Or give you a good shaking."

Stuck at that impasse, we decided not to make any firm plans for now.

No, I didn't tell him I found out I was adopted. I'm not feeling very close to him these days.

Ally stopped by on her way home from work and dropped off some printouts of Ohio adoption law. I can petition the state Department of Health in Columbus to see my adoption records and original birth certificate. I thanked her and said I would be mailing off my request pronto. Ally said all she needs is a name (mother or father), and she can dig up the rest.

I asked her why, if I was adopted, Mr. and Mrs. Manders were listed as parents on my birth certificate. Ally said she found out that after an adoption goes through, the state issues a fake birth certificate for the child. According to her, the state would have listed Mickey Mouse as the father on my birth certificate if my mother had requested it. Thus, dead men can legally "father" children.

Well, now I know.

June 22 – Gabby called with some good news. Someone has made a full-price offer on my house. No contingencies either, except conveyance of a clear title. They are paying cash, so no appraisal or mortgage approval is required. They want escrow to close in 15 days!

"And who is this blessed buyer?" I asked.

"It's something called the Dixon L. Hamlin Trust."

"What's that?"

"I never heard of them, but I'm sure their offer is legit. They're being represented by a big law firm downtown."

"What law firm, Gabby?"

"Uh, Buck, Circo & Everwood. Ever hear of them?"

"Uh, I have, as a matter of fact."

"So do I have your approval on the deal?" asked Gabby.

"Did the offer come with any earnest money?"

"Only a certified check for 10,000 glorious dollars."

"OK, they sound serious. Let's go for it."

"Fine, honey. We're on!"

A Google search for the Dixon L. Hamlin Trust produced zero results. I was disappointed, but not surprised. It was all par for the course.

June 23 – Casta is now reading her fourth Gloria Anne Lenore novel. If she picks up another one, it will be time to report this miracle to the Vatican.

Harkness phoned Casta and said he needed to get some of his things from the house. So we arranged that he would come by while I was out doing marketing for tonight's special dinner. I hate to put Casta in the middle like that, but Carl is adamant that I'm not to see or speak to Harkness. I feel bad treating my husband like some kind of infectious plague victim, but that's the wonderful world of divorce for you.

Left a message inviting Monica and Roland to dinner, but I haven't heard back from them. I'm not sure how long Monica intends to go on hating me. Like it or not, she only has one mother and that happens to be me.

I told Kyle his attendance at tonight's dinner was compulsory because his grandmother was coming. Rather sneaky of me not to mention that Ally also was invited. Casta I threatened with a cut-off of her reading materials if she spilled the beans to him. I don't know why I'm forced to act like Catherine de' Medici to manage my family.

I had Kyle drive to Parma to pick up Mother. Ally, looking very nice in a neat blue frock, was arranging olives on a plate when they arrived. As usual Mother was a bit confused.

"Monica," she said to Ally, "I've never seen you looking so glamorous."

"This is Alicia Lund, Grandma," said Kyle. "She's, uh, an old friend from high school."

"And who is this young person with a bolt through her nose?" inquired Mother.

"It's only a small silver stud," replied Casta. "I'm your granddaughter Casta."

"When you blow your nose, do you project snot out that hole and

114

across the room?" asked Mother.

Casta laughed. "Not yet, Grandma, but I'll have to try it."

"And this elderly person in the unsightly apron," said Mother. "You must be the maid."

"I'm your daughter Helen," I replied. "You're looking well, Mother."

"The Grim Reaper will have us both soon, from the looks of you. When did you start combing your hair with a rake?"

"I think she looks beautiful," lied Ally. "What would you like to drink, Mrs. Manders?"

"Something wet and alcoholic," she replied. "Do you mind if I ask if those breasts are entirely yours? One never quite knows these days."

Ally blushed nearly as red as Kyle.

"Yes, it's all me," Ally replied.

Mother mellowed slightly after she had her glass of sweet white wine. She let Ally cut her pork chops for her, and didn't totally dominate the conversation. I felt like asking her if she'd adopted any children lately, but held my tongue. Casta and I both pretended to be oblivious to the drama going on between Kyle and Ally. Mother, however, missed my subtle signals.

"Kyle, honey," said Mother, "your friend Miss Lund is remarkably alluring. I suppose you must find it extremely satisfying being part of a generation for whom sexual restraint is virtually unknown."

"We're just friends, Grandma," replied Kyle.

"I've only slept with one person," added Ally. "I was under the impression at the time that he loved me."

"Casta, tell us about the book you've been reading," I interjected.

"Too boring, Mom," she replied. "Nobody's interested. I'd rather hear about Ally's job. So, Ally, do people gossip in your chair all day like they do at a hair salon?"

Fortunately for the flow of conversation, Ally had a lot to say about what people confess as she's probing into their gums.

Mother couldn't stay late. She said she had to get up early tomorrow to go act in a movie. The part called for her to be crushed under a runaway freight elevator.

When Kyle returned from taking Mother home, he asked if I was trying to fix him up with Ally.

"No, she's helping me on some genealogical research so I invited her for dinner. I hope you don't mind."

"It's a little awkward, Mom, since we used to go out."

"You're both free for the summer. You could take her to a movie sometime."

"She'd misinterpret my interest. She wants to marry me, you know."

"And how do you feel about that?"

115

"Me? Sorry, that's not on my agenda."

"I hear you and some of your frat brothers have a pact that you're not going to get married until you've slept with 100 girls."

"That Casta has a big mouth."

"So how many are you up to now, dear?"

"Uh, this conversation is terminated. See you in the morning, Mom."

June 24 – Someone rang our doorbell at 8:47 Sunday morning. I peeked out a window and spotted a rusty blue Mustang in the driveway. I shook Casta awake and asked her if she wished to speak to Deke. She didn't. So I had my large and muscular son tell him to go away and never come back. That man really has perfected the art of being a nuisance. Dumb, dumb, dumb move getting in touch with him again. I can hardly believe I was ever that desperate.

Phoned Leigh to tell him about the offer on my house.

"That's odd," he said, "because Dixon Hamlin was the name of the painter in *The Trek to Zion.*"

"Really, Leigh? Do you suppose Gloria Anne Lenore wants to buy my house?"

"Could be, Helen. The 'L' in Dixon L. Hamlin Trust could stand for Lenore. Have you looked it up on the Web?"

"Absolutely zero information about them. Why would she want to buy my house?"

"My guess is she's interested in the contents of the attic or your uncle's safe. Or both, most likely."

"All she has to do is call me and I'd share them happily!"

"Well, for some reason she hasn't figured that out."

"How do you suppose she found out the house was for sale?"

"Could be by talking to your mother in the rest home. She got worried that her manuscripts would be discovered or trashed–a nightmare I made true for her."

"So she could be spending $69,000 to secure a manuscript that's already been lost?"

"That is entirely possible."

"Should I cancel the sale, Leigh?"

"I don't think so, Helen. We're just speculating here. Who knows why this mysterious trust made the offer? Perhaps you could learn something by doing business with them."

"Maybe so. And I could use the money. My lawyer charges nearly $350 an hour."

"Remind me not to get divorced again."

"What you need is someone to remind you not to get married. When are you leaving for Scotland?"

"I'm resisting making up my mind on that point."

"Good, Leigh. That should be your mantra: Resist!"

Which do you suppose is the greater lost cause: Kyle for Ally or Leigh for me?

June 25 – Phoned Ryan Tatlock, the lawyer at Buck, Circo & Everwood who represents the Dixon L. Hamlin Trust. I told him I knew Gloria Anne Lenore was behind the trust and asked him why they were buying my house in Euclid.

"Is there some problem with the sale, Mrs. Spall?" he asked.

"No, I just want an explanation for your interest in my house."

"I'm afraid I'm not at liberty to discuss that."

"Why not?"

"Because I have been involved merely to facilitate the sale."

"Can you tell me if you are representing Fiona Tishby?"

"I know no such person, Mrs. Spall."

"She would be an elderly woman with a slightly stunted arm."

"Sorry. No one connected with the trust fits that description."

"If I send you a letter for Ms. Lenore, can you forward it to her?"

"I'm afraid you have been misinformed, Mrs. Spall. There's no one by either of those names associated with the trust."

"Then who are the people behind it?"

"Sorry, I'm not permitted to disclose that."

"Can you forward a letter from me to the people at the trust?"

"I can try."

"Good. I'll email you my letter right away."

In a few short paragraphs I expressed Prof. Mulcahy's and my admiration for the novels of Ms. Lenore. I said we had discovered the manuscripts in the attic and her business records in my uncle's safe. And I expressed regret that one of the manuscripts (*The Trek to Zion*) inadvertently had been lost. I concluded by urging Ms. Lenore or someone else from the trust to contact me as soon as possible to discuss these matters.

I emailed it to the lawyer.

Now, all I can do is wait and hope for the best–while I sit here reading *The Solitary Simpleton*.

June 26 – Went to Parma again to visit Mother. I suppose it's good to see her frequently, since a 92-year-old woman can't have that many years left. At least, that's what I keep telling myself. I found her in her room watching a video of herself on someone's cellphone. She was being crushed under an elevator, but I recognized the screams as my own.

"Where did you get that cellphone, Mother?" I asked.

"From that fat fellow Roland. It's his old one. He gave it to me for starring in his movie. It does everything except curl your hair and cut your toenails. And in my day we found it miraculous that you could hear Harry James on a radio the size of a packing crate."

"We've offered to get you a cellphone many times, Mother."

"I don't need a lot of pests calling up and annoying me. Speaking of which, what brings you to my humble abode?"

"I'm here to discuss my adoption."

"Aren't you a bit old for that, Helen? But hand me the papers and I'll sign away my rights to you. I hope you and your new parents will be very happy together."

"Don't play games, Mother. You know what I'm talking about. I was adopted by you as an infant, and I want to know who my real parents are."

"Adopted, huh? I guess I dreamed that part about the 22 hours in labor."

"You had a baby girl, Mother. Then she died and you adopted me."

"Says who?"

"Says your cousin Florence."

"Oh? Are you holding seances now and conjuring up the dead?"

"Your cousin Florence is alive and well, and living in California. I have her phone number if you'd like to call her."

"That interfering busybody is still alive?"

"Very much so."

"Well, this adoption business is news to me. Looks like you'll just have to dig up more of my senile and/or dead relatives to gossip with."

"I'm getting to the bottom of this, Mother. You pretend you don't remember, but I know better. So who here have you told that I'm selling Aunt Maddy's house?"

"Nobody. Zilch. Zero. Nobody here cares including me."

Probably a lie, but she said it like she meant it.

"I wish you'd stop playing that video, Mother. Doesn't all that scream-ing bother you?"

"Not particularly. Monica told me whose voice they dubbed in. I rather enjoy hearing you scream."

Well, that didn't surprise me.

June 27 – Kyle came home late last night. It was after midnight when I found him drinking a beer in the kitchen. He had been to a Cleveland Indians night game–with Ally Lund. I tried not to let my eyebrows rise, but he felt the need to explain.

"She likes baseball, remember? She played softball in high school."

"As I recall she had a very good pitching arm."

"Ninety percent of her hitters would strike out or ground out to first. The company has season tickets. Nobody wanted to see them play Se-attle, so the tickets got dumped off on the intern."

"You don't have to explain, dear."

"Yeah, well, just don't jump to any conclusions."

I took pains not to show that I approved of his seeing Ally. A mother's approval, I know, is usually the kiss of death.

I'm enjoying *The Solitary Simpleton*. I don't usually read mysteries because I find their cavalier approach to death off-putting. Someone gets murdered, and that's when the wise-cracking and fun starts. But in this book all the characters' lives change profoundly when glass merchant Roger Bunvion is discovered with a sliver of optical glass piercing his throat.

June 28 – Carl my lawyer faxed me the financial disclosure form he received from Harkness. I knew about the IRAs and 401K accounts, but the $758,000 invested with a New York hedge fund was a surprise. Then there was the jaw-dropping $1.8 million socked away in a Cayman Islands bank. Here I am driving around in a nine-year-old minivan with nearly bald tires, and my husband's sitting on millions. Not to mention having to borrow from an elderly neighbor because Harkness wouldn't advance me a dime to get my aunt's house ready for sale.

When Carl called a few minutes later, I expressed my surprise at the figures–and at Harkness's forthright accounting of his secret wealth.

"Well, we'll see how forthright he's been," said Carl. "But it's a start. He couldn't blow us off entirely because of my reputation for playing hardball. That's why I have a permit to carry a gun, have been known to wear a bulletproof vest, try not to be too predictable in my movements, and sometimes say a little prayer before I start my car."

"People threaten you?"

"It's been known to happen, Helen. I deal every day with big issues: love, sex, money, property, and children. Emotions can run a little high."

I told Carl about Deke showing up uninvited at my door last weekend, and asked if he could send a letter warning him to leave us alone.

"I haven't found letters to be very effective, Helen. I'll have one of my associates pay him a visit."

"He lives pretty far away–in Medina."

"Not a problem. Cyrus enjoys a drive out of town."

Carl said he would draw up a proposed settlement; we made an appointment for next Monday to discuss it.

June 29 – Got a reply in the mail from the Department of Health. Didn't take forever as I'd assumed. Probably a form letter run through a word processor to make it look more personal. They rejected my request because my birth mother had filed a denial of access form. My father hadn't filed such a request, but they regretted to inform me that they had no information on file about him.

I suppose I can understand her reasons. Having a child out of wed-lock was a much bigger disgrace in the 1950s than it is now. People get on with their lives, and may not wish to be reminded of some long-buried indiscretion. Anyway, there's a good chance that my birth mother is now deceased. Her children (if she had any others) might not appreciate some unknown half-sibling suddenly butting into their lives.

The fact that my birth mother hadn't named the father suggests to me he might have been married. Half my genes could have come from some cheating bastard. No wonder I strayed in my marriage.

I called Ally and told her that Kyle's maternal forebears were likely to remain a mystery. She was disappointed, but said she understood. She added that she had found a Fiona R. Tishby, born in Oconto, Wisconsin in 1936 who had a sister named Philippa.

"That's my uncle's sister, Ally. Have you found out if she's still alive?"

"Not yet, Helen. Nor anything else about her. But I'm still looking."

"Thanks, dear. Any information about her would be helpful."

Gabby checked in to report my house sale is going swimmingly. The title report came back "as clean as a baby's butt," which is often not that clean in my experience, but Gabby likes to scramble her similes. The mysterious buyers don't even want a walk-through before closing.

Gabby was disappointed that Fiona the Brit appears to have won the battle for Leigh. She says I threw in the towel too soon.

"What am I supposed to do, Gabby? Fiona is with child and the wed-ding is set for August."

"It's time for desperate measures, Helen."

"Yeah, well, if you think of any, let me know."

June 30 – Over three weeks since that cuddle in Euclid with Joe. As the saying goes, you don't miss the water until the well goes dry.

Speaking of s-e-x, I'm hoping that's not the reason my son took Ally to the country club tonight for dinner and a swim.

Casta is spending the night at Marie's, so it's just me here alone in our 4,300 square feet of suburban house. A comfortable home, but I find I'm missing the welcoming environs of Euclid.

Finished *The Solitary Simpleton*. All the clues were there, but I missed them entirely. I suppose that makes for a good mystery, but—sorry, Gloria Anne–I resent it when you make me feel stupid. Still, it's another novel that should have been published.

July 1 – Sunday morning. I found myself wondering if Harkness was having pancakes in some restaurant somewhere. I'm not exactly missing him, but there is a void where my family life used to be. For 27 years he was a presence behind the newspaper across the breakfast table. He was someone to talk to (sort of). I would talk and he would grunt occasionally. Now I have to eat my cornflakes with the perky people on morning TV.

Kyle returned from his golf match with Harkness. He said his dad was looking better, but his shots were all over the course. Nor was his putter cooperating. It seems Tiger is not the only golfer whose game went to hell when his marriage collapsed. Harkness has moved out of the hotel and into a rental condo in Mayfield Heights that his secretary Perla found for him.

Kyle had a message for me from Harkness: "He said to tell you that he has disclosed every last dime. And he's still willing to start over if you are."

"Right, well I'm afraid it's a bit late for that."

"Should I call him and tell him that, Mom?"

"No, dear. I don't want to put you in the middle of this mess. So how was your date with Ally?"

"It wasn't a date, Mom. We just went to the country club together. I was going there anyway."

"Right. Just buddies. I get the picture."

"Her dad is available. Should I fix you up?"

"What happened to his wife?"

"He came home from work one day and found all of his clothes in the pool. They got divorced."

"She probably had her reasons. I think I'll pass."

"Well, keep him in mind. I'm sure Ally would be open to a double wedding."

July 2 – Not the start of our annual vacation trip to Quebec. Harkness liked to go to Canada this time of year to escape the din of July 4th celebrations. Firecrackers make him as jumpy as a nervous dog. Just a one-day drive north and you're in an entirely different culture. We had our favorite restaurants where I could practice my feeble French. Harkness would wear his beret and look almost like a native.

Leigh just phoned with some amazing news. Delivered in today's mail was a large brown envelope containing the manuscript of *The Trek to Zion*. Gloria Anne Lenore's masterpiece hasn't been lost after all!

"Who sent it to you?" I asked. "Do they want the reward?"

"It's not the manuscript that was stolen, Helen. That one was a faint carbon copy. This one's a photocopy of the typed original. It came anonymously, with no note or return address."

"Leigh, it must have come from the author herself!"

"Or someone acting on her behalf. The postmark is smeared, but it looks like Cleveland."

"That means she got the letter I sent via the lawyer for the trust!"

"Could be, Helen. Have they canceled the sale?"

"No. Why do you ask?"

"They know we have the manuscripts and the contents of the safe. That must mean there's still something in the house they want."

"Uncle Phil's box that was hidden in the attic?"

"That's a possibility."

"Why would they pay $69,000 for my uncle's old report cards and family photos?"

"You're right, it doesn't make sense."

"Then there are the four filing cabinets filled with Uncle Phil's greeting cards. I advertised them on Craigslist, but didn't get a single call."

"A lifetime's worth of seasonal verse. I doubt that's what they're after. There must be something else in the house that we've missed."

"Want to come help me search for it?"

"I could be there tomorrow at my usual hour."

"Great. Let's do it."

Back from my meeting with Carl Zyzinski. While I was waiting to see him, an immense black man came over and told me he'd had a "cordial discussion" with Deke Brennan about avoiding me and my family.

The man handed me his business card. "If he bothers you again, Mrs. Spall, you just give me a call. Next time I won't be so nice."

I tucked his card in my purse, expressed my heartfelt thanks, and assured him I would do just that.

Carl's proposed settlement seemed dramatically lopsided–in my favor. I looked it over and said it seemed a bit harsh on Harkness.

"Well, you know your husband better than I do, Helen. If we propose something eminently equitable, is he likely to say, 'Yes, that's reasonable. I accept it.' Or will he say, 'OK, that's their first offer. Let's see how much I can shave off '."

"Harkness is a bargainer," I replied. "He never pays retail if he can help it."

"Then let's be bold, Helen. And offer him the full financial root canal–without an anesthetic."

"OK, Carl. You're the expert."

July 3 – After all that time away, my remodeled drapes shocked me afresh. This time I saw them without the gilding provided by my previous desperation. No doubt about it: they were ghastly. And the stark expanse of Navajo White–complementing none of the furnishings or floor coverings–was just as jarring. I was selling my favorite author (or her estate) a pig in a poke and apparently laughing all the way to the bank. Was I that callous? Did I completely lack a moral compass because I'm an orphan?

No kiss from Leigh when he arrived. All those weeks apart (plus Fiona) had taken their toll. He handed me my own personal copy of *The Trek to Zion*. I asked him if he'd had time to finish it.

"Yes, at 1:30 this morning. It's spectacular. I've never read anything like it. The thought that it might have been lost forever leaves me weak in the knees."

"Don't you think the fact that Gloria Anne or someone connected to her sent us the replacement manuscript proves that she wants us to get it published?"

"Well, it would have been helpful if they'd attached a note saying so. I'm tired of her fucking reticence. What has she got to hide?"

"Could she be some well-known writer using another name?"

"I know of no writer living or dead who could have written *The Trek to Zion*. It's as unique in American literature as the stories of Edgar Allen Poe. Or Nabokov's *Pale Fire*. This ain't no run-of-the-mill novel."

"So what are we looking for today?" I asked.

"Something that a very shy author would pay a big chunk of cash to get her elderly hands on."

"God, I hope she's not after that Tiffany lamp I broke."

"You broke a Tiffany lamp?" asked Leigh, shocked. "A real one?"

"Uh, I think I'll plead the Fifth Amendment on that."

We started in the basement and worked our way up. Big excitement when Leigh pried off a loose panel in the back of the broom closet. Stashed behind it was a yellowed and dusty *Cleveland Plain Dealer* dated February 21, 1962. The banner headline read: John Glenn Orbits Earth.

"My God!" exclaimed Leigh. "Gloria Anne Lenore is actually a famous astronaut!"

I gave him a sharp poke in the ribs.

"More likely it's somebody's idea of a time capsule," I replied. "Anything else in there?"

"Just a spider or two. Couple of mouse turds. Say, do we know for a fact that your uncle Phil actually died?"

"Well, I saw him laid out in his coffin. He could have been faking it, I suppose. Looked pretty deceased though, and Aunt Maddy seemed genuinely grief-stricken."

"OK," replied Leigh, "there's another idea shot down. Want to break for lunch?"

"I thought you'd never ask."

Since the pending house sale and Carl's squeeze on Harkness had improved my financial prospects, we splurged and went to a fancy Italian restaurant. I talked about my divorce and Leigh told me about his. He'd also had the full root canal, which is why he drives a car that's even older than mine. He said that one good thing about going through a searing divorce is it snuffs out any lingering feelings you may have for the departing spouse.

"Replacing love with hate is a good thing?" I asked.

"Hey, it worked for me. Blow-torching those emotional ties can do wonders for your mental outlook."

"So my taking Harkness to the cleaners is actually expediting his healing process?"

"Right, Helen. For us guys recovery doesn't start in the heart, it starts in the wallet."

Too soon we returned to resume our frustrating search. Hours later Leigh surprised me in the master bedroom.

"I saw what you just did," he said.

"What?"

"You daubed Firing Squad behind your ears."

"And a few other places too. You want to make a federal case out of it, buddy?"

We embraced and he kissed me. Busy hands began to explore my body.

"Professor Mulcahy, you are pawing a married woman."

"Married, but filed for divorce. Puts you in a whole different category."

All this was going on right beside Aunt Maddy's big walnut bed; its magnetic appeal proved irresistible.

I don't normally sleep with engaged fellows, but I figured if I was going to pine away for Leigh I might as well know what I'd be missing. Plus, I could give him a valuable preview of what it might be like to have sex with his wife in 22 years.

I'm beginning to think there's something magical about that bed. Another marvelous coupling that banished all thoughts of Joe, my sexy exterminator. Probably not quite as good for Leigh, since I made him don a condom. (I had no idea with whom Fiona's jock physicist had been sleeping–not to mention that bookish temptress herself.) For a guy with all that hair on his upper lip, Leigh had very little body hair. More muscular than I expected with just a bit of an academic's paunch to complement my flab.

"That was extraordinary," he said as we lay entwined. "How do you contrive to be so, uh, tight down there?"

More confirmation that for men the sex act wasn't about love, it was about friction.

"Easy," I replied, "I just pretend I'm a boa constrictor."

(In fact, I take the time to exercise those vital kegels every morning.)

I looked at the clock beside the bed.

"My kids will expect dinner on the table in 17 minutes."

"Couldn't you call Kyle and have him take Casta out to dinner somewhere?"

I was impressed that Leigh remembered the names of my children.

"I could if I were a bad, uncaring mother."

I rang up Kyle. He said, "Sure. No problem."

I tried not to feel guilty as we started in on Round Two.

July 4 – I invited Leigh to stay overnight in Maddy's house (without me, of course), but he opted to drive back to Pittsburgh. As he was leaving, he dropped the bomb: he's departing for Scotland on Tuesday.

"I thought you were delaying making that decision," I said.

"I was. Fiona mailed me a ticket."

"It's a good thing I love you too much to call you a wimp."

"Right. Well, that would be the appropriate pejorative."

"I don't suppose I'll see you before you leave."

"Uh, probably not. It promises to be a hectic week."

"Well, have a nice life, Leigh."

"Don't say that, darling. We'll see each other again."

"Sorry. I don't sleep with married men. It's one of those rules I live by."

We never did find anything in our search. The appeal of my house to the Dixon L. Hamlin Trust remains a mystery.

Kind of a gloomy Fourth of July around here. We're out of practice celebrating that holiday. I'm supposed to go watch the fireworks in the park with Kyle and Casta (and Ally), but I may beg off.

Beginning to think that sleeping with Leigh may have been a mistake.

July 5 – Casta reports they saw Monica and Roland in the park last night. Monica had some news. A rough cut of their movie "Store Rage" has earned them an invitation to the Barberton Film Festival. Barberton, Ohio is a small town south of Akron where they used to make matches.

Since Kyle was at work, I felt free to inquire of Casta how he seemed to be getting along with Ally.

"Well, they were holding hands. That was a shock. Guys don't usually do that with stalkers."

"I wish you wouldn't call her that, Casta. Ally is a very nice girl. I hope Kyle doesn't take advantage of her regard for him."

"Not much chance of that, Mom."

"Why do you say that?"

"I hear Ally laid down the law. The next time she'll sleep with him is on their wedding night."

"Well, good for her. That's something you might well emulate."

"Yeah, if I was living in 1903."

"Aren't you learning anything of consequence from all those Gloria Anne Lenore novels you're reading?"

"I am, Mother. Nice girls don't . . . have any fun."

July 6 – Gabby phoned with an update: The house is set to close on Monday. Relief, then instant panic.

"Jesus, Gabby, how am I going to get rid of all that furniture?"

"Relax, Helen. I got them to take the place as is–with all the crummy furniture included."

"Really? Do you suppose any of it's valuable?"

"Only if all the other furniture on earth disappeared overnight. Then you might get a hundred bucks for the lot."

"Do you think they'd mind if I took that carved walnut bed?"

"Why? What have you been doing on it?"

I confessed to Gabby about my farewell fling with Leigh.

"You mean he wasn't gay after all?" she asked.

"Quite the contrary. Now I'm feeling even worse that he's marrying that Brit."

"Did your professor give you any hint of your grade?"

"Well, he seemed to be having a good time. He was rather complimentary. We did it twice."

"Good. Now he can compare and contrast you and Fiona. She could be all brains and totally lame in bed."

"Somehow I doubt it. She's been practicing with that hot rugby jock who knocked her up."

"Never say never, girl. You want me have DeeAnn give you a bid on moving that bed?"

"Would you? I'm kind of attached to it now."

July 7 – DeeAnn and a helper transported the bed for $100 and my pricey old bed in exchange. It doesn't match my bedroom decor, but now I can retire without being reminded of all those dreary encounters between the sheets with Harkness.

"I bet Monica would have taken your old bed," said Casta, helping me rearrange my bedroom furniture. "She's sleeping on the floor, you know."

"If your sister needs a bed, Roland can buy one for her."

"You're right. It would probably gross her out to sleep on a bed that her parents were using for sex. Are you going to miss those monthly Sunday nights?"

"What? Were you spying on us?"

"Just living here and trying not to notice the predictability of your intercourse. Kyle thought it was related to the phases of the moon, but I wasn't so sure."

"I continue to be amazed, Casta, that people ever bother to have children."

"I know, Mom. It's a lot of trouble and expense. A Chihuahua or two is all anyone really needs."

July 8 – Kyle had another non-date with Ally last night. I notice his nightly phone check-ins with Briana in distant Missouri seem to be tapering off. Richie of the sparse adolescent sideburns and much-stickered skateboard doesn't seem to be pestering Casta lately. All of which means my kids' STD Risk Index is slightly less worrisome than usual. Monica is a different story, but she continues not to return my numerous phone calls.

I started reading *The Trek to Zion*. Gloria Anne Lenore certainly has a way of putting you right there on the trail amid the heat, dust, scorpions, snakes, and howling winds. Day after day the horses plod relentlessly on. I have to take frequent breaks just to keep from getting saddle sore.

Kyle and Casta helped me clear the last of my stuff out of Maddy's house. Kyle said he vaguely remembered the house from Uncle Phil's funeral. He helped himself to a birthday card from a filing cabinet for Ally's upcoming birthday. My son does exhibit those Spall tendencies at times.

Grace came over to get introduced to Kyle and say goodbye. While she was there, I wrote out a check for $3,500. She protested that it was too much, but I insisted she take it—pointing out that if it weren't for her generosity I might still be scraping wallpaper. Then Gabby arrived to give the house a last look and to collect my keys. She will turn them over to the buyer tomorrow.

Not to count my chickens prematurely, but this house ordeal soon may be over. Kind of a drag at times, but it certainly altered my life in major ways. Thank you, Aunt Maddy!

July 9 – The Euclid house is sold. The buyers didn't come to their senses at the last minute as I feared. Ryan Tatlock, the lawyer for the trust, showed up at the title company's office this morning with his certified check. Quite the handsome young man in a sharp gray suit. One of those chiseled chins that bespeak integrity. Tasteful blue silk tie that matched his eyes. Pardon me for thinking like a mother, but he'd make such a nice alternative to Monica's repellant Roland.

As usual, the paperwork was conducted without the seller's presence, but I made an appearance afterwards to shake Ryan's hand and introduce myself. I also thanked him for forwarding my letter.

"I did my best, Mrs. Spall."

"Please tell them that we received the manuscript."

"Er, right. Whatever you say. I looked up that person you were talking about. What was her name?"

"Gloria Anne Lenore."

"Right. I found out she was an obscure author of teen romances."

"Yes, among other things."

Ryan's apparent unfamiliarity with Ms. Lenore appeared sincere, but I reminded myself that lawyers were not renowned for their sincerity.

I asked him if he knew what the trust intended to do with Uncle Phil's library of books and his four cabinets of greeting cards.

"I'd hate to think it's all going to be trashed," I pointed out.

"You needn't worry about that, Mrs. Spall. I understand that nothing in the house is to be disturbed."

"Really? Then why did they buy it?"

"I'm not at liberty to say, Mrs. Spall. But we appreciate your cooperation on the sale."

"All I did was say yes when you offered my full asking price."

Ryan smiled his most radiant jury-pleasing smile. "Then it's a win for everyone, Mrs. Spall. Have a wonderful day, and it was great meeting you."

No doubt about it, he's way, way too nice for Monica.

I was afraid I wasn't going to hear from Leigh before he left, but he phoned tonight to say he was all packed. I told him I had looked up Cromarty Firth on my iPad.

"It looks like quite a scenic location, Leigh, but rather remote."

"I know, darling. I'm packing as many books as I can carry."

"How-to books for the expectant father?"

"Uh, no, not exactly. How are you enjoying *The Trek to Zion*?"

"It's marvelous. I've never read anything like it. She must have devoted thousands of hours to research."

"I know. It's extraordinary how she's captured that gritty wilderness milieu."

"So how's the wedding planning going?"

"It's all out of my hands, Helen. The guest list is over 200 and still climbing."

"And how many will be there representing the groom?"

"Oh, possibly a handful if they can score decent deals on airfares. Not many airlines are competing to fly folks to Aberdeen."

I told Leigh about selling my house and what Ryan had said about the trust not disturbing its contents.

"How very strange, Helen. They just intend to let it sit there?"

"Well, Grace, the next-door neighbor, said she'd keep me informed if anyone shows up and does anything."

"Good. In which case I suggest you visit them promptly."

"I intend to. What time is your flight tomorrow?"

"Early: 6:05 a.m."

"Well, I hope you sleep in and miss it."

"Yeah, darling, so do I."

July 10 – A gloomy morning as I knew Leigh was winging his way east and out of my life.

Bodana, my Russian soon-to-be ex-sister-in-law showed up at my door unexpectedly after breakfast. I made some tea and we sat out by the pool. It soon became apparent that she was there as an emissary of the Spall clan.

"Your husband is very much shocked, Helen," she said.

"Is he?"

"In my country for a wife to make such greedy demands, very, very unsafe for her."

"How so, Bodana?"

"Husbands would retaliate. They hire men to accost her. They do nasty things with acid. Or maybe they tamper with her brakes. Or she have bad accident in the subway."

"Right. Well, I'm glad I'm living here instead of there."

"We're both very fortunate ladies, Helen. So there is a possibility that you are flexible with Harkness?"

"Not about ending the marriage. But the settlement proposal was just a starting point. He's welcome to make suggestions if he finds anything objectionable."

"Very good, Helen. I think he may be relieved to hear that. Every night he calls my husband in a most agitated state. He thinks you have been brainwashed by your lawyer."

"Nothing of the kind, Bodana. I already was resolved to get divorced, as you know. My lawyer merely has been advising me on the particulars of the process."

"Good for you, Helen. You are cagier than I thought. I was worried that you would be too soft-hearted and wind up with nothing."

"No, Bodana, I've found that being nice about these matters doesn't really pay."

"Very true, Helen. A girl has to look out for herself and her children."

"That's just what I intend to do."

Things got a little cheerier in the afternoon when Gabby dropped off a bank check for $63,481.72. That's my net after Gabby's commission and the various escrow fees. I was tempted to run out and blow some of it on a new car, but I don't dare until Carl has nailed down the settlement details with Harkness. Part of me still worries that I may not get a dime, and this modest check will have to last me for the rest of my life.

July 11 – Casta is bummed because Marie and two of her other friends are away at cheerleading camp. My daughter is pretty enough to be a cheerleader, but she never has shown the slightest interest in any extracurricular activities at her school. She is a complete non-participant. In my day, such students lurked on the fringes and were nearly invisible. But Casta is a popular kid. I hope her non-participation is not in reaction to my busy, high-profile high school career.

To cheer us both up we went to the mall to check out the new fall styles. Very little restraint was shown. I'd ask myself, "Do I really need this?" And then I'd remind myself of Harkness's Cayman Islands bank balance.

July 12 – No call from Leigh. I haven't heard of any planes crashing in Scotland, so I'm assuming he's arrived there.

Carl Zyzinski faxed me Harkness's counteroffer to our proposed settlement. A far cry from our pie-in-the-sky fantasies, but it seemed quite generous to me. I said as much to Carl when he phoned, but he thought there was room for "serious tweaking." I told him to give it his best shot.

Since Casta's future was being decided as well, I let her see the faxes. I figured it would be a good learning experience for her, since–considering her choices in men–she may be in a similar situation some day.

"Why is there no mention of a car for me?" she demanded.

"Because you are spoiled enough, and I'm terrified every time you get behind the wheel."

"Duh, Mom! I got a C+ in driver's training!"

"Only because you flirted shamelessly with your teacher. How many feet of chain-link fence did you wipe out?"

"Fat Alice Stadnik in the back seat was totally blocking my rear-view mirror. I couldn't see a thing!"

"Then why were you driving in reverse?"

"Because Mr. Dunmore instructed me to!"

"You may get a car when you turn 18, Casta. If your behavior and attitude improve."

"And you may get another husband someday. If you lose a hundred pounds and get a face lift!"

Just the two of us stranded here on five lonely acres. It promises to be a long summer.

July 13 – Casta informed me that Monica and Roland are renting one of the theaters at the local mall for a screening of their movie Saturday morning (tomorrow). Admission is by invitation only.

"I'm going with Kyle and Ally," announced Casta. "We're picking up Grandma on the way. I understand Daddy has already accepted. He's bringing Perla, his secretary."

"Good. Then your grandmother will have someone to talk to–since Perla is practically her age."

"It's unfortunate you're not invited, Mom."

"I'll live."

Later I got a surprise phone call from Roland inviting me to see their movie.

"Are you sure my daughter wants me there?" I asked.

"I don't know why Monica's being so vindictive, Mrs. S. It's not a very attractive quality. But you must come. Your scream is the best thing in our movie."

I told him I would think about it.

July 14 – Since Casta slept in, we barely made it to the theater in time. Both Monica and Perla were cutting me dead, but Harkness managed a wary "hello." He looked thinner, older, and balder. I hoped for his sake the stress of divorce doesn't accelerate hair loss.

The theater–one of the smaller ones in the multiplex–was nearly three-quarters full. Mostly cast and crew, plus their friends and family. Also rumored to be in attendance were several local bloggers who write about film. And possibly an arts stringer for the *Plain Dealer*. Plus a film festival honcho, who had driven all the way from distant Barberton.

Roland, wearing evidence of a hasty breakfast, walked to the front to introduce his movie. "Good morning, film lovers! Are we excited!!?"

A few lackluster cheers.

"Right, guys, I know it's early, but don't worry, we'll be serving snacks after the screening. OK, please remember what you're seeing today is a work in progress. The music right now is generic, copyright-free stuff. [Loud belch.] Oops, excuse me. But we hope to have better soon. And we're still correcting the color. So if your face is green, don't panic, we'll be fixing it. We're doing this just like a Hollywood sneak preview. Did everyone get their comment card? Please fill it out at the end of the movie. And be honest, we want to know what you think. Don't worry about hurting our feelings. We are sincerely interested in finding out how much you love our movie! OK, thrill-seekers, I give you . . . Store Rage!"

Frankly, I was expecting 90 minutes of cinematic torture, but "Store Rage" proved surprisingly entertaining. Sort of a spoof on horror and/or slasher films, it set a menacing tone right from the start. Very cleverly edited to sneak in numerous shocks and surprises. The simple but coherent story held the audience's interest throughout. Many big laughs as the oblivious victims were dispatched one by one. Mother's look of mild astonishment as the elevator descended–while the nutcase on the soundtrack screamed her heart out–got a big roar from the audience.

Both filmmakers died on-screen. Monica was blinded by the laser beam of a cash register scanner, then lurched about until she impaled her eye socket on a coat rack. Shockingly realistic as blood gushed in great spurts and she writhed about with the hook penetrating her brain. Rather more than a mother could take; I had to look away.

Roland perished appropriately by biting into a donut upon which a bee had alighted. After a great deal of strenuous thrashing, he suffocated as his tongue swelled to the size of a football, then kept on expanding until an enormous red blob knocked against the camera lens and filled the entire screen.

Hearty applause as THE END flashed on the screen, and the credits began to roll.

"I know," shouted Roland, "isn't it wonderful? Remember, no snacks for anyone until you've filled out those comment cards. If any scene didn't work for you–which, frankly, I very much doubt–please let us know."

As I was filling out my card, I caught Monica's eye across the theater. I smiled warmly and flashed her a thumbs-up sign. She turned and looked away without acknowledging me. She also kept her distance in the lobby, where everyone gathered around several folding tables holding a coffee urn and trays of pastries. So I didn't push it, and chatted with Mother and several other older ladies whose kids had worked on the film in some capacity. When Roland strolled up to our group, I offered my sincere congratulations. I also commented on how professional his film looked considering its modest budget.

"Not bad for a camera that cost $929, huh?" he replied. "Of course, it kills me that all those highlights got blown out, and I could do without the jaggies on the pans, but that's video for you. But, hell, it looks surprisingly decent on the big screen."

"And wasn't the sound awesome!" exclaimed Casta.

"Also fairly decent," said Roland. "Of course, if any studio picks it up, they'll probably insist on doing a million dollars' worth of Foley and ADR work on it."

"I have only one question," announced Mother. "Why were all those poor, unfortunate people being killed?"

Roland smiled. "Just for laughs, Mrs. Manders. People enjoy seeing mayhem on the screen; it reminds them that they're still alive and kicking."

"Young man, you are a very sick person," said Mother.

"I know, Mrs. Manders. You have to be to make great art."

Harkness came up to me and was about to say something (no doubt annoying), but I stuck a cruller in his mouth and headed for the exit. He was always keen on crullers.

July 15 – Ally's 21st birthday. She had breakfast with her mother, lunch with her father, and dinner with us. Kyle grilled burgers on the barbecue, blackening them just like his dad used to do. I offered Ally her first legal drink, but she politely declined, saying she's not into alcohol. Casta volunteered to drink it instead, but I handed them both glasses of iced mint tea.

As I was cutting the tomatoes and mixing the macaroni salad, Ally told me she had found out something about Fiona Tishby, Uncle Phil's mysterious sister.

"I called the city librarian in Fresno," said Ally. "She recognized the name. She said Fiona was one of the editors of a magazine called *Western Vistas*."

"My God," I said, "there was a big stack of them in Uncle Phil's office. I threw them out when I was trying to reduce the clutter."

"I'd never heard of it," said Ally. "Apparently, it was a travel magazine with scenic photography. Sort of like *Arizona Highways*, except it covered the entire western United States. It was published out of Fresno and closed down in the 1990s."

"Did she know if Fiona was still alive?"

"She didn't, but she suggested I call the local newspaper. The *Fresno Bee* had an obituary on file on her. She died last year. They're mailing me a copy."

"Too bad. Did the librarian say what Fiona did for the magazine?"

"I guess she wrote quite a few of the articles. She traveled around the west in a VW bus with her maps and camera. Sounds like much more fun than cleaning gunked-up teeth."

"Was Fiona married?"

"Probably not, Helen. The obituary didn't mention any survivors."

After a pleasant dinner, the kids decided to take in a movie. I stayed home to clean up the kitchen and think about what Ally had discovered.

Fiona was a writer who likely was familiar with Monterey and its environs, San Francisco's Chinatown, northern Nevada, and Zion park in Utah–all settings for novels by Gloria Anne Lenore. Plus, she had a disfigured arm like Edith Hamlin in *The Trek to Zion*.

I imagined her in her VW bus at some remote campsite–filling her idle hours by writing romantic stories for young girls. A lonely woman who may not have known romance herself. This was before laptop computers, of course. She may have used a small portable typewriter, or possibly have written them out in longhand. If she moved around frequently, she might very well have sent her manuscripts to her brother for safekeeping. Perhaps he or his wife would retype them, then Uncle Phil would write in his minor corrections. It all seemed to fit.

Now I'm kicking myself for tossing those magazines. I could have analyzed her writing for similarities in style to Gloria Anne.

If Fiona died without an heir, she may have bequeathed her millions to the Dixon L. Hamlin Trust. So who are the people in charge of the fund? Why did they buy Maddy and Phil's old house? And why did they send that replacement manuscript to Leigh without a note?

Needing some help unscrambling all this, I sent Leigh a five-word email: "I found Gloria Anne Lenore."

Perhaps that will distract the guy from his bookish babe.

July 16 – No call or email from Leigh. Rather irritating, but perhaps it's appropriate that one Fiona brought him into my life and another Fiona is taking him away.

July 17 – Casta is upset because one of the local film bloggers gave a nasty review to "Store Rage." He said it was derivative, boring, amateurish, and not at all funny. Makes you wonder why he supposed all those people around him in the theater were laughing so heartily. He also found it "pretentious above its station," whatever that means. To twist the knife further, he claimed the lighting was murky and the sound was garbled.

I told Casta I thought the fellow needed to clean his glasses, check the battery in his hearing aid, and get a life while he was at it.

Carl Zyzinski faxed the latest and much improved settlement offer from Harkness. I told him it looked fine to me. He said he would send Cyrus around to get our signatures and file it with the court today.

I hope Harkness doesn't feel too ill-used. I don't want to alienate him totally, since we will always be in each other's lives because of the children. I hope he recognizes the value of my contributions to our marriage over these 27 years. And it's not like I administered a complete walletectomy. He still has a very large pile. And who knows what he has socked away undisclosed. I think the settlement is fair to both sides and to the kids.

He may not agree, but then that's why people get divorced.

July 18 – Still no call or email from Leigh. Perhaps he wants to break completely with me. That's odd, because it seemed like he had a genuine interest in Gloria Anne Lenore. Very unsettling.

What with all the rain we've been having, I had to mow the grass again today. Kyle offered to do it, but he's busy with his no-pay job and no-sex girlfriend. If I let Casta do it, I'm sure she'd mow down my roses just to watch my blood boil. I rather enjoy riding the mower back and forth across our green acres. It's a way of getting in touch with the land where you live. Perhaps my ancestors got into a similar state of mind as they followed a plow behind their horses. I suppose it's a big waste of natural resources–all those suburbanites in the Midwest keeping their lavish lawns neatly mowed. But who doesn't like the look and smell of freshly cut grass?

Ally dropped by after work with the copy of Fiona Tishby's brief obituary. She died last November 12 of complications from colon cancer. Probably a grim way to die; I hope she didn't suffer too much. It said she worked as an editor, travel writer, photographer, and (in her later years) as a teacher's aide in a predominantly Latino grade school. After she retired, she enjoyed traveling in her RV with her dog Osborne and panning for gold in the Sierras–once finding a nugget that was worth over $2,000.

That doesn't sound much like the lifestyle of someone who made millions from her books and movies. But as I recall, young Elwyn in *Streetcar for Adventure* had a little mixed-breed dog. And its name was Osborne.

July 19 – Someone on Ebay is selling a set of six *Western Vistas* magazines from the 1980s. I am the lone bidder at $3.14. Needless to say, if anyone else is interested, they might as well give up now.

Casta is reading her seventh Gloria Anne Lenore novel. It's really unprecedented that she should read for pleasure. I read books to Monica and Kyle when they were little, but Casta just wasn't interested. She'd always rather watch cartoons on TV or play cards. Only kid I've ever heard of who played solitaire at the age of four. And, no, she didn't cheat.

July 20 – Had a long phone chat this morning with Leigh via his laptop. He doesn't hate me after all. Fiona's manse in Scotland is so remote it has no Wi-Fi and no cellular phone reception. They do have electricity, when the gale off the North Sea isn't blowing too hard. Leigh reports he had to drive 23 kilometers to a pub in Invergordon to get his email. Fortunately, he likes the beer and was able to ditch his bride-to-be for a few hours.

He was excited to hear the latest news about Fiona Tishby, and agrees that she's the best candidate yet for being G.A.L.

"I'm glad it's not your uncle Phil," said Leigh. "I'd hate to think that the mind that created *The Trek to Zion* also excreted all those endless reams of greeting-card drivel."

"Sorry, I can't take that sitting down, Dr. Snob Professor. My uncle was the best at what he did. His verses for all occasions were always up there in the Tiffany class."

"My apologies, darling. I didn't mean to impugn your relatives."

"Your groveling apology is accepted. Isn't it a shame that we just missed Fiona Tishby?"

"Very inconvenient of her to die like that. But doesn't that make you and your mother her closest living relatives?"

"Could be, dear, except we're only related by marriage."

"Still, her copyrights could go to you by default."

"If she hasn't entrusted them to the Dixon L. Hamlin folks."

"Right. We're still in the dark about that. Speaking of matters dark, how's your divorce going?"

"Great. We worked out our differences and it's all in the hands of the court. The bastards make you wait an entire year for the final decree. I should have gone to Reno."

"Nobody goes to Reno any more, darling. You've seen too many old movies."

"Is your wedding still on?"

"It's at the aircraft carrier stage now: An immense enterprise steaming forward with tremendous momentum."

"And you're being dragged behind in the dinghy?"

"Pretty much."

"So were you this enthusiastic the first time you got married?"

"That was different. That time I was in love–the full package with all the options."

"What happened?"

"What usually happens. You discover the person you actually married. She had considerably more warts than I'd anticipated. I'm sure she felt the same way about me."

"And now you're doing it again."

"Well, this time it's without the blinders."

"How's your pregnant bride? Is she throwing up?"

"Incessantly. Like she's getting paid £500 a spew."

Poor Fiona is suffering.

Well, at least that was some good news.

July 21 – The Beast is no more. My years of bondage to a dented minivan have come to an end. Kyle agreed to give up his Saturday to help me find a car. We looked at some new ones, but all those years of living with Harkness had vaccinated me against brand new cars. I just couldn't pull the trigger, despite the best efforts of several psychologically manipulative salespersons. And for what they ask these days for a new car, you could have bought a fairly grand house not so long ago.

I bought a sweet little 2005 Thunderbird off a used-car lot. That was the last year for the retro-style 'Bird. Kind of pricey ($21,000) for a car that old, but it only has 36,000 miles on the odometer. Beautiful silver color with gray leather interior. Pretty much a case of love at first sight. Kyle was appalled that they only offered me $500 trade-in on the Beast, but I was surprised that they took it in trade at all.

Casta was excited when I pulled into the driveway, but I've already informed her that she'll have to pry the keys from my cold dead fingers.

Her response: "Could you drive me to the hardware store, Mom? I need to get a crowbar."

July 22 – Long look at my body in the mirror this morning. I seem to be missing a waist. I know I had one at one time, but now my torso resembles a thick sausage ornamented with several not-very-attractive appendages. All greatly victimized by gravity. At some point I crossed over the divide from "shapely" to "lumpy." Rather disheartening if I'm to re-enter the world of Dating Strange Men (i.e., men who are strangers to me). I don't want to wind up alone, and I really can't count on finding many more sexy guys who worshipped me in high school. Therefore, I need to get serious about Shaping Up.

I nailed the half-dozen *Western Vistas* magazines for my original bid of $3.14 plus six bucks postage. The seller will never know that I was prepared to go as high as $999. That was my limit, as I feel anything over $1,000 would be an absurd price for six old magazines.

July 23 – Things are in an uproar. Mother died this morning. They called me from her residence home. Due to staff cutbacks, they had made the waffle irons self-serve. At breakfast, Mother started a ruckus when she accused another diner of stealing her waffle. The disputed waffle wound up on the floor, and when Mother bent over to pick it up, she collapsed. It appears she died almost instantly of a stroke. Paramedics tried to revive her, but she was pronounced DOA at a nearby hospital. They expect to do an autopsy by tomorrow at the latest.

July 24 – The autopsy confirmed it was a cerebral hemorrhage. Not a bad way to go at age 92. A few seconds of pain at the most and you're done. The doctor said it was like flipping a wall switch. One good thing about having a control freak for a mother, she planned every detail of her funeral and burial. All pre-paid as well. The funeral home picked up her body, and the service is set for the day after tomorrow. They're even making the calls to the people on her invitation list. All we have to do is show up.

July 25 – Lots of folks have been phoning with their condolences. Harkness called to ask if he should go to the funeral. I told him it was up to him.

"Your mother always disliked me," he pointed out. "She never talked to me if she could avoid it. She always addressed me as 'Hey, you.' Or, 'Hey, you, bald guy'."

"I know, dear. Mother could be cantankerous and unkind. It was nice of you to put up with her all those years."

"I'd rather not come, if you don't mind, Helen."

"Not at all, Harkness. We are separated, after all. How are you doing?"

"Do you really want to know?"

I recognized that tone of voice.

"Uh, some other time, dear. Things are a bit hectic here now."

Monica also phoned. She said she would be attending the funeral out of respect for Grandma, but I shouldn't expect her to speak to me.

"I think we should talk this out, dear. I'm sorry if I've upset you."

"You're not sorry at all. I hear you just bought some fancy new car. You totally wrecked Daddy's life. And I'm sure your filing for divorce is what killed Grandma."

"That's hardly fair, Monica. My mother never liked your father. If anything, she approved of our getting divorced."

"You are such a heartless cow!" she exclaimed, hanging up.

And you, Monica, are so much Harkness's daughter it scares me. I'm not sure how much more pain I'm willing to accept from you.

Joe Ducowski called to say he'd read the obituary in the *Plain Dealer* and to ask how I was doing. I said I was OK, but I was missing him. I told him I sold the house in Euclid–rat problem and all. I also told him I was getting divorced.

"Good for you, Helen. Life is too short to be married to someone you don't love. I guess I lucked out in that department."

"Good for you, Joe. Thanks for calling. I appreciate it."

"You hang in there, Helen."

July 26 – Mother was laid to rest today in her chosen plot. Both Gabby and Grace, my old Euclid neighbor, sent wreaths. As Mother requested, the casket was kept closed during the service. Mother was always a bit vain; I'm sure she wouldn't care to have anyone gawking at her lifeless form. I was surprised to learn from the cemetery manager that she had also purchased an adjoining grave for me. At some point I'll have to decide if I want to spend eternity in Garfield Heights, Ohio.

A very dreary day. I'm glad it's over. It was sweet of Ally Lund to take off work and be such a comfort. Even Roland was on his best behavior. Only Monica seemed determined to add to everyone's distress with her undisguised coldness toward me.

I've heard of people being permanently estranged from their children, but I never thought it would happen to me. My mother was a constant trial for 58 years, but I always found a way to look past her faults and keep her in my life.

July 27 – We have five days to clear out Mother's room, or we have to pay another $4,137 in rent. Fortunately, she downsized radically when she moved in seven years ago. So we're not dealing with an entire house full of stuff as with Aunt Maddy's place. Casta made a beeline for her jewelry box, and I headed for her little two-drawer filing cabinet. I was hoping to find out something about my adoption, but nothing has turned up so far.

Now that we have to haul a bunch of stuff, I'm missing the Beast. Dare I ask Roland to borrow his van?

Later: I'm in shock. According to Mother's financial records, she has over a million dollars in her main account. She wrote some instructions on the folder. She said in case of her disability or death I should contact Maurice Circo of the law firm Buck, Circo & Everwood.

July 28 – No one on Mother's corridor has expressed any sorrow over her death. Nor do the administrators appear at all distressed or eager to assist with the removal of her belongings. It appears she was even less popular than I'd assumed. So I decided to try to get the move over as quickly as possible.

Not only did Roland loan us his van, he helped Kyle haul all of Mother's stuff to our garage (into the empty space where Harkness used to park his Jaguar). I figured it would be easier just to sort through it here. Kyle reports that like many fat men Roland is quite strong, but tends to run out of wind fast. I offered to pay Roland for his trouble, but he declined. Nor would he accept any payment for gas. Perhaps he feels he has enough of my money already. Let's hope so!

It's odd that these days I'm finding Roland less obnoxious than my own daughter.

July 29 – Maurice Circo delayed his golf game to see me on a Sunday morning. He even came to the house, which was another surprise. Harkness never visits clients in their homes; he feels such informalities can breed an indifference to the prompt payment of his fees.

Mr. Circo was not the dissolute drunkard I'd been expecting from Harkness's description. He was quite a pleasant older gent in coordinated golf attire (in shades of yellow and lime). He had been my mother's attorney for nearly 40 years (news to me). My mother's entire estate has been left to me. All of her accounts are jointly registered in my name, so probate will not be required. The total comes to just a hair under $2 million.

"This is all extremely shocking," I said. "Where did my mother get all of this money?"

"Well, she lived frugally, Mrs. Spall, and many of her investments did well. She took a hit in the 2007 financial panic, but had recovered most of her losses."

"But where did the original money come from that she invested?"

"Well, as you know, she had an income from movie royalties."

"No, I didn't know that. Royalties for what?"

"Uh, I believe it was for books that were adapted into films."

"Are you telling me that my mother wrote novels under the name Gloria Anne Lenore?"

"I'm not sure of the particulars. Your mother was rather secretive about the sources of her income. The checks had dwindled substantially over the years. As you can see from this quarter's statement, the last check received was for only $112."

"And if she wrote novels, who owns the copyrights on them?"

"I'm sorry. I cannot advise you on that matter."

"Does she have another lawyer?"

"Not that I'm aware of."

"Your law firm represents the Dixon L. Hamlin trust, which I believe is connected to Gloria Anne Lenore. What can you tell me about them?"

"Nothing, I'm afraid, Mrs. Spall."

"Why not?"

"Confidentiality requires it. We must maintain a firewall between our clients–at all times. I'm sure you understand why. If we didn't, we wouldn't have any clients."

"Was my mother connected to that trust?"

"No, she wasn't. That I can tell you."

"Did you handle my adoption?"

Mr. Circo blushed. "Uh, I would have been in grade school at the time."

"Oh, right. Sorry."

He looked at his watch, then brought up the subject of my pending divorce. He said that since the petition for dissolution had been filed before my mother died, a case could be made that this "windfall" was not subject to community property division.

"You mean I don't have to share it with Harkness?" I asked.

"In my opinion, no. There is no reason to disclose the full amount, or even indicate to him that it constitutes a substantial sum, should he inquire. I advise discretion on these matters, of course. No lavish spending, luxury cruises, or overseas travel until your divorce is final."

Mr. Circo gave me a thick packet of Mother's files and the key to her safe deposit box (which I'd been searching for desperately for two days). I thanked him and asked him if he'd like to be my lawyer too. He said that would please him very much.

I'm in total shock. It wasn't Muriel Wadge, Clare Hendom, or Inez Frinezen receiving those checks from movie studios. It was Mother. The evidence cannot be ignored or explained away. My cynical, ill-tempered, narcissistic, unromantic foster mother was Gloria Anne Lenore!

Now I'm glad I didn't pay $999 for Fiona Tishby's old magazines.

July 30 – Sent Leigh another terse, five-word email: "Major Gloria Anne Lenore news." I hope the rat gets back to me before the wedding.

I was waiting at Mother's bank when it opened this morning. Alas, no adoption papers in her safe-deposit box. But it did contain a gaudy diamond and sapphire ring, a diamond stickpin, a wonderfully lustrous pearl necklace, and 143 gleaming Mexico 50-Peso gold coins. They were the missing baubles from Uncle Phil's safe that I had wrongly accused Roland of stealing. No wonder my daughter hates me.

Also in the box were Mother's birth certificate, her expired passport, the license for her first marriage, some stock certificates and bonds, and a sheath of letters tied in a pink ribbon. Not old love letters, but fan mail addressed to Gloria Anne Lenore in care of Paramount and Universal, the two studios that distributed her movies.

I left everything behind except the letters, which I brought home to read.

July 31 – In *Seventeenth Summer* (by you know who) Bonnie Callahan tries to get a head start on her senior year English studies by reading *The Pickwick Papers* over her summer break. She finds it such heavy going, she falls in love with handsome balloonist Vince Fuller instead. Likewise, I had a high-school Christmas vacation ruined by being compelled to read that classic "comic" novel. Try as I might I couldn't get past the first dozen pages or so. Boring characters, torpid pace, and nothing at all to catch my interest. When he penned *Pickwick*, the prolific Mr. Dickens was producing words by the ton, but that batch just didn't appeal to me. Every day was a struggle to crack open that heavy tome; endless and non-stop were my complaints to Mother.

So far, that's the only connection I can draw between Mother as I knew her and the works of Gloria Anne Lenore. I've decided that she must have rented an office somewhere where she did her writing. Then, when I came home from school, she'd be back–pretending to be her usual idle self.

Considering the extravagance of the praise in the letters from her fans (and these gals truly gushed out their love), you would think–at least once in her life–Mother might have shared a bit of her acclaim with her only daughter. No, she was secretive to the last. Not just secretive but actively paranoid: let us not forget how she yelled at me that time I brought home one of her novels.

I admit it: I don't get it at all.

Called Monica at work and managed to blurt out an apology for misjudging Roland before she hung up on me again. And she calls *me* a heartless cow.

Also heard from Harkness, who said he had run into Maurice Circo at the country club last Sunday.

"He told me your mother left barely enough to get herself decently buried."

"Oh? Did he say that?"

"That's what he said. And Monica told me she was embarrassed by the cheapness of her grandmother's casket. She blames you, of course."

"Well, it was Mother's choice, Harkness. I had nothing to do with it. And how fancy a box does one need to go into the ground?"

"I agree, of course. Anything beyond sturdy cardboard is a waste of money. So you didn't pay for any of the funeral expenses?"

"No, I didn't Harkness. You needn't be concerned on that point."

"You bought a new car?"

"It's not new at all. It's a 2005. I'm trying to economize here. I'm not spending your money recklessly!"

"So you claim. This ridiculous and ill-considered divorce is costing me a fortune, Helen."

"Uh, really, Harkness, I'm very busy dealing with Mother's estate. If you wish to communicate with me, I suggest you contact my lawyer. Goodbye, dear."

Thanks to that conversation I no longer feel the slightest remorse for concealing my assets from Harkness. I pity his next wife, should she predecease him. There's a gal who won't be going out in style.

August 1 – Only three days until Leigh commits marital hara-kiri in Aberdeen. Still no word from him. I fear Fiona has put her foot down and forbidden any more pub excursions. Or perhaps Leigh's too busy swabbing up vomit to get away. Me, I'll take a bracing hot flash over morning sickness any day of the week.

Finished looking through the rest of Mother's papers. Nothing about my adoption and nothing further relating to her secret life as Gloria Anne Lenore. I've told the kids that they and their friends can have anything they want from the pile in the garage; what's left I'll give to Goodwill.

Thus will end Mother's physical presence on this planet, except for her headstone which is already on order. She picked out the design (plain granite slab) and specified the inscription: "A life too soon forgotten."

Needling me to the last, that was Mother.

Today was Monica's 25th birthday. I expect she's celebrating with Roland and/or her father. I sent her a card, but I confess I picked out a rather ugly one. The text inside was not at all sentimental. No gift this time. I'm not sure why people receive gifts on their birthdays, since it's their mothers who did all the work. Monica should try it some time and see how she likes it.

August 2 – According to Casta, Roland has told the Barberton Film Festival to take a hike. Their movie has been accepted by the much more prestigious Telluride Film Festival next month. Actual studio scouts and executives attend that one. The Telluride folks are known to be picky and generally don't accept films that have played elsewhere.

Casta, of course, is dying to go. I'd considering taking her, if Monica weren't being so hateful. I don't need to go all the way to the Rocky Mountains to be snubbed by my daughter.

August 3 – Received the magazines in the mail today. A total of eight articles by Fiona Tishby, though she may have written some of the unsigned ones as well. Someone must have told Fiona that a sentence should not contain more than eight words. Made for fairly choppy prose. Annoying after a while. Just one thought per sentence. And on and on. Not Gloria Anne's style at all. So there you have it.

Walked into the den this evening and surprised Kyle and Ally. Just necking, but some clothing was awry. Rather embarrassing for all, but I told them to continue on and excused myself. It wouldn't bother me a bit if they wanted to retire to Kyle's bedroom, but according to Casta, Ally has vetoed that venue.

She's such an attractive girl, I'm not sure how my son is coping. But I don't suppose a mother should speculate on such matters.

August 4 – Mother would have been 93 today. Wedding bells are ringing in faraway Aberdeen. Really, too much to cope with; I'm going to the mall with Casta.

Ally called later to apologize for the scene in the den last night. I told her things like that happen, and not to give it another thought.

"I'm not sleeping with your son," she stressed.

"Ally, dear, what goes on between you and Kyle is none of my business. You have my blessings for whatever you two decide to do."

"Well, you know how I feel about him."

"And I only hope he's worthy of your love."

I brought her up to date on the recent revelations about my mother.

"I'd appreciate it, Ally, if you didn't mention to anyone this business about my mother leaving me money from her writings."

"Not even Kyle?"

"Unfortunately not, since he's in frequent contact with his father."

"Of course, Helen. I understand. Is there anything I can do for you?"

"Would you like to look into my late mother?"

"Sure. What do you want to know about her?"

"Anything you can discover. For example, if she ever rented an office anywhere, say from the 1950s to the 1970s. And her connection to the Dixon L. Hamlin Trust."

"OK. I'll look into it."

August 5 – No word from Leigh. I'm feeling this more than I expected to. Too wretched to do more than pace and fret.

August 6 – I finally heard from Leigh. He sounded very tired and far away. I asked him how he was doing.

"I don't know. I think I've slept about two hours in the last four days."

"Was it a hectic wedding?"

"Not really."

"Are you on your honeymoon?"

"Not really."

"Uh, where exactly are you?"

"My kitchen in Pittsburgh. Got here early this morning."

"Is Fiona there with you?"

"Not really."

"Is she coming later?"

"Not really."

"Are you capable of speech beyond 'not really'?"

"Not really."

"I'm kind of confused here, Leigh. Did you get married?"

"No."

"Really? Why not?"

"Had a disagreement."

"About what?"

"*The Trek to Zion*."

"You had Fiona read it?"

"Tried to."

"She didn't like it?"

"Said it was tedious and overwrought."

"The nerve of that woman. What did you say?"

"Said if everything that was tedious and overwrought were extracted from her body of work, there wouldn't be enough left over to line the bottom of a birdcage."

"That's telling her, honey. What did she say?"

"Lots. Got pretty cutting and nasty. Said my book on the mechanics of composition was an embarrassment that she previously had been willing to overlook."

"She said that? That's terrible!"

Big sigh from Leigh. "Don't know. She made some valid points. Since the gloves were off, we got into a candid assessment of each other's scholarship."

"I suppose that can get fairly ugly when two Ph.D.s go at it."

"Massive bleeding from all orifices. Had to call off the nuptials."

"Canceled or just postponed, Leigh?"

"Canceled for this millennium."

"What's she doing about the baby?"

"Having it. Been some sparking with her obstetrician. The poor bastard is a poetry lover, don't you know."

"Was her family upset?"

"Bummed about the expense. Thrilled to see the last of me."

"This is all wonderful news, darling."

"Thought you might be pleased. [Big yawn.] You have some news?"

"Yes, my mother died."

"Oh, sorry to hear that. I liked her."

"You may have more reason to like her. She was the recipient of those movie studio payments. My mother was Gloria Anne Lenore."

Long silence on the phone.

"Are you there, Leigh?"

"I'm punchy, Helen. Did you just say what I thought you said?"

"I did. Mother was Gloria Anne Lenore. She had $2 million in the bank. I found fan letters for Gloria Anne in her safe-deposit box."

"Wow. I've slept with a great writer's daughter. I feel like Tolstoy's son-in-law."

"Well, her adopted daughter. When can I see you, Leigh?"

"Got to sleep five or six days. Will phone again when hibernation over."

"Good, darling. You rest and take it easy. I love you."

"I love you too."

That Brit wasn't so smart after all. On the eve of her wedding she decides to be Brutally Frank in her literary criticism. Now, I have to admit that I kind of agree with her re: *The Trek to Zion*. Personally, I think Gloria Anne Lenore was at her best bringing two love-starved teenagers together. This business of marching through the wilderness, sketching tall rock formations, getting sweaty in steamy lodges with nude Indians, and having ecstatic visions can get a little tiresome when stretched out over 400 pages. But would I admit such a thing to Leigh?

No. Because I've been around the block a few times. I lived with Brutally Frank for 27 years.

I know when to be candid. And when to smile and keep my mouth shut.

Scary thought: If that mysterious trust hadn't replaced the missing manuscript, Leigh would be married right now to Fiona.

August 7 – Been thinking about Leigh's aborted wedding. Now if it had been a movie, they would have had their "disagreement" right there in the cathedral as the ceremony was about to start. The lovesick obstetrician would have been an invited guest–sitting in a rear pew next to Hugh Grant and Kristin Scott-Thomas. Fiona would have walloped Leigh in the jaw, stormed down the aisle, grabbed her startled doc, and kissed him in front of the stunned congregation. But Leigh's version works fine for me too.

Leigh phoned in the early afternoon. He sounded much more alert this time. We arranged that he would come here tomorrow at his usual hour.

At dinner I broached the subject of overnight male visitors with Kyle and Casta.

"So who is this guy?" asked Kyle.

"He's a college English professor," I replied. "Very nice fellow. I think you'll like him. He lives in Pittsburgh."

"That's a lot of gas to burn just to drive here and see you," observed Casta. "What's in it for him?"

"We have a lot in common, dear. We've known each other for months. He's an expert on Gloria Anne Lenore."

"Why would a man be interested in such a total chick writer?" asked Casta.

I explained that Ms. Lenore wrote other highly regarded works besides her teen romances.

"What's he look like, Mom?" asked Casta. "He sounds like some creepy dude with thick glasses who likes to correct people's grammar."

"He's nothing like that at all. He's about my age and has a mustache."

"Like Hitler?" she asked.

"Not at all. If you object to his staying here, he can always get a room at the motel out by the expressway."

"I don't mind, Mom," said Kyle. "We were just saying we hoped you wouldn't be alone forever and get all weird like Grandma."

"Yeah, he can come," said Casta. "But if you guys get too rowdy, we may have to ground you. Does he have any kids?"

"No. He was married before, but they didn't have any children."

"Good," said Casta. "I am so not ready for a blended family. Having to pretend some strangers are your new brothers and sisters has got to suck big time."

August 8 – Went to the Cleveland Museum of Art with Leigh and Casta. A world-class museum right here in my home town, and the last time I visited there was on a field trip in high school. Room after room of van Goghs, Monets, Goyas, Turners, Matisses, Botticellis, Caravaggios, etc. A reminder of the time when this area was bustling with industry and those barons of wealth in Shaker Heights were generous with their dollars.

Casta got over her shyness and soon was teasing the adults about the nude statues and paintings. She didn't disgrace me completely and seemed to enjoy discussing Lenore novels with Leigh over lunch in the museum restaurant.

The four of us had dinner at home. Kyle and Leigh deliberated over the Pirates vs. the Indians (baseball teams). Casta somehow inveigled out of Leigh his recent near-miss at matrimony in the UK.

"You were going to marry some chick in England, but live in different countries?" she asked, amazed.

"That was the plan, Casta," he replied. "Some people manage to do it."

"I could see it," said Kyle. "That way you don't get sick of each other so fast."

"Well, Pittsburgh is pretty far from Pepper Pike," said Casta. "That might work for a while too."

"It makes for a lot of driving," observed Kyle. "What year is your Saab?"

"Uh, a 1993."

"That could get risky come winter," replied my ever-helpful son.

"Well, I'm not moving to Pittsburgh," announced Casta. "So, Mom, you can forget about that plan."

"No one is moving anywhere, Casta," I replied, coloring.

Leigh glanced my way and smiled.

Dating with children–it may be why so many of those divorced parents out there remain single.

August 9 – We offered up Leigh's jet lag last night as our excuse for retiring early. After we made love, I tried to reassure him.

"You know Kyle will be going back to school in a few weeks, and Casta's pretty independent most of the time."

"You don't have to apologize for being a parent, Helen. I like your kids. I wouldn't be a college teacher if I had a problem with young people. And your kids are nicely past the infant stage. The only diapers I need look forward to changing are my own. Or yours."

"You missed the real terror: my older daughter. Fortunately, Monica's moved out for good. I hope you're OK staying in my house."

"It's fine so far–assuming no enraged husbands come storming in."

"The doors are locked and he doesn't have a key."

"Good. It's a nice house. I didn't realize your property was larger than some countries."

"It's only five acres."

"You'll have to show me the serfs' huts tomorrow."

I wanted Leigh to stay at least another day, but he had to leave after breakfast for a department meeting. I took him into my bedroom and showed him the four feet of closet pole I had reserved for him. Also the five newly emptied bureau drawers.

"I take it you'd like me to return," he said, kissing me.

"Please do. Just think, sweetheart, summer vacation in Cleveland–it doesn't get any better than that."

August 10 – Roland phoned this morning and offered to sell me ten percent of his movie for $50,000. I take it Pacalac Productions is running low on funds. I said I would consider it if Monica would meet with me so we could iron out our differences.

"Not much chance of that, Mrs. S. She heard about your gentlemen caller and pitched a major fit."

"Oh, really? Did she call me a whore and a slut?"

"Uh, I'd rather not answer that."

"Well, draw up a contract, Roland, and I'll have my lawyer look it over. But leave out the weasel clauses. I won't invest a dime if I think you're trying to pull a fast one."

"Damn, Mrs. S, you sound like the second coming of Lew Wasserman."

I didn't know who that was, but I accepted it as a compliment.

"And make it twenty percent for $50,000," I added.

"Gee, I couldn't go any higher than fifteen."

"Deal."

August 11 – Leigh returned at his usual hour–this time with a larger suitcase. I offered to help pay for some of his gas, but he said he lacked the appropriate pencil-thin mustache to pass as a gigolo. He did accept my offer to cruise by my old house in Euclid and buy him lunch.

Someone had mowed Maddy's front lawn and cleared out the jungle in back. No other signs of occupancy though. I was hoping to check in with Grace, but her car wasn't in her garage. No answer at Peach's house either. So we went to a nearby Chinese restaurant I'd been meaning to try. Pretty mediocre as it turns out.

"What did they use to tenderize this beef–a nuclear device?" said Leigh. "It feels previously chewed."

He also pointed out that the sauces were bland and much too thick.

"Somebody in the kitchen went wild with the cornstarch," I agreed. "Cornstarch! Of course!"

"You've had a culinary revelation, darling?"

"My mother was very big on her pet peeves, Leigh. She didn't see the point of cornstarch. She wouldn't have it in the house. She thickened her fruit pies with tapioca and her gravies and stews with flour."

"Very enterprising, I'm sure."

"But you'll recall in *Seventeeth Summer* when Bonnie first met her balloonist, he asked for a sprinkle of cornstarch on his ropes to help untangle some knots. But she had used up the last of her supply making butterscotch pudding for her kid sister."

"OK, if you say so. I take it you have some sort of photographic memory."

"Not at all. I just kept re-reading that book to take my mind off your impending marriage. My mother was never much into puddings, but she would have used egg yolks and cream of tartar."

"Proving what?"

"Proving nothing, but suggesting to me that Mother didn't write *Seventeenth Summer*."

"What? You think she had a collaborator?"

"Hell no. I don't think Mother wrote any of them."

"But you were so sure she was the one."

"All the evidence is there, but there must be some other explanation."

"And cornstarch is the linchpin of your argument?"

"Hey, I knew my mother. Her affections frequently wavered, but she was very consistent in her hates."

August 12 – Sunday being Harkness's agreed-upon visitation day with Casta, we heard him blow his horn in the driveway. Of course, she (and everyone else) was still in bed. I scrambled around to get her ready, and when she finally got out the door she immediately returned to report that someone had slashed all four of Leigh's tires.

I could tell Harkness was shocked to see a man in a bathrobe exit the house in the company of his estranged wife.

"Harkness, did you do this?" I demanded.

"I don't know what you're talking about, Helen. And who is this person?"

"This is Dr. Leigh Mulcahy, a friend of mine. Leigh, this is Harkness." They nodded barely perceptible greetings.

"He's a doctor?" said Harkness. "Is someone sick?"

"Not that kind of doctor, Daddy," said Casta. "He's a college professor. That's why he drives such a crummy car."

"It's dripping oil on my driveway," Harkness pointed out.

"I believe it is *my* driveway now, Harkness. He can drip all the oil he wants. Are you keeping Casta through dinner?"

"I expect that is the plan," he replied icily.

"Have a nice time, Casta," I said, giving her a hug.

"I hate divorce," she pouted. "No one my age spends a whole day with their father!"

"Get in the car, Casta," said Harkness. "And let us leave this sorry scene behind."

Harkness roared off in his uncharacteristically less-than-pristine Jaguar. He also needed a haircut. The man had really let himself go.

"That was my husband," I said to Leigh as he contemplated his flattened tires. "I don't really think he did it."

"Any suspects in mind?" he asked.

"Possibly a fellow I used to know named Deke Brennan. Possibly Monica, though I hope not. Possibly some boy Casta's annoyed. Possibly Fiona if she changed her mind, wants you back, and followed you here."

"Uh, I think we can rule out that last suspect."

"I'm so sorry about this, dear. I'll pay for new tires, of course. What did you think of my husband?"

"That fellow? He doesn't seem like your type."

"No. He never was really."

August 13 – Leigh's car was winched onto a flatbed truck and hauled away to get new tires. Since the tires were four years old, he insisted on paying half the replacement cost. I had the rest of Mother's stuff carted off so Leigh can park safely away from vandals in the garage. We also made a report to the Pepper Pike police, but with no witnesses it is unlikely they'll find the culprit. It's the first crime of any sort we've experienced here. I hope it's the last.

We took a drive in my T-bird through the scenic Cuyahoga Valley National Park. Visitors are surprised to learn there's a national park along the meandering Cuyahoga River between Cleveland and Akron. This is before the river gets to the sprawling industrial flats in Cleveland where it once caught on fire.

Living far apart makes for a different sort of interaction than if we lived in the same city. Instead of a friend that I might meet for dinner or a show, Leigh is by default a houseguest that one feels obliged to keep entertained. I'm happy to do it, but I hope it doesn't become tiresome for him. I am so out of practice at this business of loving someone new.

Speaking of tiresome, Casta had very little good to say about her day yesterday with Harkness. The only fun she had was in making up outrageous things to tell him about Leigh. I can only hope Harkness didn't believe any of it.

August 14 – To my surprise Leigh was not interested in touring the Rock and Roll Hall of Fame. He said he already had a perfectly satisfactory one in his head. So he answered his email on his laptop, while I caught up on my housework. We spent most of the afternoon in bed. I'm working off a sex debt accumulated over several decades. As for Leigh, I'm not sure what his excuse is.

After dinner Kyle asked if he could speak to me privately. I feared he was going to complain about Leigh's continued presence, but he asked if he could borrow $3,000 to buy an engagement ring.

"This is for Ally?" I asked, surprised.

"Yeah. I don't want to give her a ring with one of those embarrassingly puny diamonds. I'll pay you back after I graduate and get a job."

"You're sure she's the girl for you? I thought you weren't interested in marriage."

"I wasn't, but things have kind of changed."

"They appear to have changed quite radically. She's not expecting is she?"

"Not very likely, Mom."

"Right. Well, of course I'll give you money for a ring. You don't have to pay me back."

"Nah, a guy should pay for his own engagement ring. We'll consider it a loan."

I pointed out that I had inherited a diamond ring and stickpin from his grandmother, and suggested that perhaps he and Ally could design a ring incorporating one or more of those heirloom stones.

"But don't girls like to be surprised with a ring?" he asked.

"Some might, dear, but I'm not so sure about Ally. It might be better to involve her in the process. After all, she's the one who will be wearing your ring."

"Yeah, you're probably right."

"And when are you thinking of getting married?"

"In June when I graduate."

"So you'll be apart for another school year?"

"Nah, Ally got a job at a dental clinic in Lafayette. She just told me last night."

"And you're going to live together there?"

"I very much doubt that."

"You don't want to?"

"I'm all for it, but she doesn't like the idea."

"Right. Well, I'm sure she has her reasons. So congratulations, dear. I think you picked a wonderful girl."

"Yeah, I'm kind of glad she didn't give up on me."

Kyle is rather young for marriage, but he's always benefitted from structure in his life. And I think Ally is just the girl to give him that.

August 15 – Maurice Circo called to say he had reviewed Roland's draft contract and regarded my buying into their movie as a very dubious and risky investment. I replied I knew that already, but wanted to know if the contract as drawn was fair to me and protected my interests.

He replied that in the unlikely event that the movie produced any income, there would be no way they could deny me fifteen percent of such proceeds. So I called Roland, and told him the deal was on. Within the hour, the contract had been signed and the check passed to his grubby hands. Leigh, I'm sure, thought I was nuts, but he didn't say anything. Roland opened the bottle of champagne he'd brought, and we all toasted the future success of Pacalac Productions. May it soon put Cleveland on the movie map.

I hope Monica appreciates my gesture of support. Fifty thousand dollars may not be enough to buy her love, but you'd think it would be sufficient to garner a thank-you phone call.

No such luck so far.

August 16 – Casta heard about her brother's engagement. At lunch (breakfast for her) she said Ally's success will be very encouraging to stalkers everywhere. I warned her there would be severe repercussions if she expressed such a thought to either of them.

"Don't worry, Mom. I won't wreck it. I know those two are your only hope for grandchildren–although I expect Roland is beavering away nightly at the job."

"Let's not go there, dear," I replied.

Casta gazed at Leigh. "Still here, I see. Did you like, move in?"

"No. Just visiting."

"The neighbors are scandalized, you know."

"They are no such thing, Casta," I replied. "The neighbors have no interest in what goes on here."

"I thought college professors preferred to sleep with their students," she continued.

"Some do," Leigh replied. "But the administration frowns on it."

"Do your students dig your mustache?"

"I expect the vast majority of them have no opinion on it."

"Could be, but my mother would be thrilled if you shaved it off."

"That's enough, Casta," I said. "Eat your cereal or leave the table."

"I've got some good news for you, professor. I'm going over to Marie's house again this afternoon. So you'll have hours of uninterrupted privacy."

"That's thoughtful of you, Casta," he replied. "We both have some reading to do."

A rude snort got her banished from the table.

Later in bed I suggested to Leigh that we have a dinner to celebrate my son's engagement.

"Shouldn't your husband be involved in such an event?" he asked.

"Well, it wouldn't be very festive with Harkness there. Divorce always complicates these family functions. Ally's parents are divorced too, so at least the tension won't all be from our side."

"They could always elope."

"I'll have to feel out Ally on the topic. I have no idea what sort of wedding she wants. It's all up to her; I know you men don't care."

"No, a simple ceremony of spitting on the hands and rubbing the palms together is all we require."

"Remind me not to marry you."

"I don't suppose you'd like to."

"What?"

"Marry me."

"Is this a proposal?"

"It's as fancy a one as you're likely to get from me."

"I suppose it helps that we're naked."

"Some nudity does facilitate the process. Any interest?"

"Where would we live?"

"Eventually, in Pittsburgh, if that suits you. I foresee two years of going back and forth, then consolidation there after Casta graduates from high school."

"You'd be willing to put up with all that driving?"

"Hey, it beats living on different continents."

"I'd love to marry you, sweetheart. But I recognize that you're on the rebound. If you're still for it in a year when my divorce becomes final, then I'll be delighted to marry you."

"You're so goddam sensible, Helen. I like that about you."

"Yeah, well, just don't cross me, buster. I have one more question: Where do you set the thermostat in winter?"

"All my family is weak in the thyroid. That's probably why we wound up in balmy southern California. I know you're supposed to set it at 68 to save energy, but I usually have it quite a bit higher. Is that a problem?"

"Not at all, darling. You passed the test."

August 16 – Leigh went home to check his mail and take out the garbage. We've decided to keep our engagement under wraps for now. There's no need to overshadow Kyle or annoy Harkness (assuming he cares). I suppose Mother's money makes me somewhat more marriageable. I'd like to think that Leigh isn't mercenary. I remind myself that he turned his back on Fiona, whose family also has money. And that was before he found out about Mother's legacy to me. It's kind of scary how well things are going with us. I'm not used to this much happiness.

August 17 – We had a pleasant celebratory dinner at that new restaurant in University Circle that got all the magazine write-ups. Just the sort of trendy place that I could never drag Harkness to. Mostly excellent, although Casta didn't care much for cracking cow bones to scrape out the marrow. There were six of us: Kyle, Ally, Casta, Leigh, Roland, and me. Monica was a no-show as I rather expected. You'd think she'd make an appearance just for her brother's sake.

I brought the ring and the stickpin. Ally decided that the diamond from the stickpin would work well in a ring. I'm no expert, but it appears to be at least two carats. She knows a talented young jeweler whose work she admires. It's a good thing we consulted her, because she's not a fan of prong-set solitary diamonds (what Kyle had in mind). She doesn't like that look and says they can snag on your clothing. How fortuitous that Kyle picked such a practical girl. She really is a beauty and they looked so happy together.

To make up for Monica's absence, Roland ate two entrees. He was calling me "partner" for a while, but I put a stop to that. As is his custom, he made a bad first impression with Leigh. But Leigh said that once you get over his "obnoxious pomposity and poor hygiene," Roland can be an interesting dinner companion–as long as you don't mind "the main topic of conversation being Roland Pacalac."

As we were leaving the restaurant, I casually asked Roland if Monica had been out late the previous Saturday night. He said she'd been home all evening, but left before dawn on Sunday to go jogging.

"Does she do that often?" I asked.

"That was a first, Mrs. S. I told her if she had any money left when the muggers got done with her to bring me back some donuts."

Does my daughter hate me so much that she'd vandalize Leigh's car?

August 18 – Bad news. I checked in with Grace, my old neighbor in Euclid, and a woman named Jody answered. She said she was Grace's niece. Grace had fallen on her cellar steps and was now in intensive care with swelling of the brain. I asked Jody if she was permitted to have visitors. She said Grace was in a coma, but the doctors were welcoming visitors to sit and talk to her.

"Does she respond to what you say?" I asked.

"Not so far, but they're getting the swelling under control. My aunt took care of herself and is in pretty good shape for her age, so that's a big plus. They're saying she has a fighting chance to recover."

We arranged that I would come to the hospital tomorrow afternoon.

Kyle returned from his golf game with Harkness. He reports his father was not very enthusiastic when he told him about his engagement.

"I think Dad's kind of burned out on marriage," said Kyle.

"Well, don't let that grump discourage you," I said. "Lots of people have very happy marriages."

"Could be," said Casta. "But they don't live in Pepper Pike. You should see Marie's parents go at it. Her mom likes to hurl stuff. The breakage is incredible."

"That's enough, Casta," I said. "We're not interested in your gossip."

"It's not gossip, Mom. It's the truth."

August 19 – Casta left reluctantly on another enforced Sunday with Harkness. I hope he puts some effort into thinking of fun activities for them to do together. It doesn't have to be a dreary day.

Leigh and I had a relaxing morning together, then he departed again for Pittsburgh. Unfortunately, he has more meetings this week as they start to gear up for the fall term. I broached the subject of retirement with him, and even planted the idea of someday relocating to California. I'm not sure this will be possible though, if my kids all remain in Ohio. Leigh didn't think much of retiring. He said the males in his family have a tradition of dropping dead within six months of their last day on the job.

I was shocked by Grace's appearance. Of course, no one looks their best in a hospital bed with tubes running in and out of them. I held her withered hand and apologized for not coming by her house to see her. I told her I had gotten swept up by my college professor and that we were now engaged. I filled her in on his near-miss with Fiona, my mother's death, and my troubles with Monica. I told her about Kyle's engagement and the resolution of my divorce. If she heard any of it, she was getting the full story on my life–as was the ICU nurse, who I could tell was listening with interest.

August 20 – I spent about two hours with Grace, then took a break in the hospital cafeteria with her niece Jody. She was a good-natured gal a few years younger than me, who–like me–had gotten a sensible haircut and ditched most of her cosmetics. I was doing a slightly better job of fighting the battle of the bulge.

Jody said that Grace was the last surviving member of that generation. Big families had been the rule, but those five sisters weren't much interested. Jody said she was the sole offspring except for Grace's.

"But Grace told me she didn't have any children," I said.

"Oh, right. That's kind of the family secret. Grace had a child out of wedlock."

"Really? Well, that's not so unusual."

"Still, Grace wouldn't want me to talk about it."

"No, I suppose not."

"It's pretty tragic. And not at all her fault. But that generation was sensitive about those things. I had to drag the story out of Mother when she was dying of cancer."

"Which sister was your mother?"

"Hope. She was the second oldest."

"I'd like to hear about it, if you don't mind."

"They grew up in a little town in Wisconsin you never heard of. Grace did very well in school, but the family didn't have much money. Grandad raised pigs and sometimes found work as a machinist. Grace worked for a year after high school and saved enough to go to business school in Chicago."

"When was this?"

"Uh, early 1950s, I guess. Back then you could be a nurse, secretary, or teacher–those were your options. Grace was training to be a secretary. So there's this classmate she gets friendly with. Some clean-cut guy whose father owned a big car dealership in Indiana—one of those luxury brands they don't make any more. Uh, Packard, I think, or maybe Hudson. He invites her out on a picnic. It's their very first date, and Mr. Rich Kid rapes her in one of his daddy's fancy cars."

"And she got pregnant?"

"Right. So my grandparents, being sticklers on morality, kicked her out of the house."

"That's awful. What did she do?"

"Her best friend from high school took her in. A gal named Philippa Tishby, who later shortened her name to Phil."

"She had the baby?"

"Yes, a daughter."

"Why didn't she keep it?"

"According to my mother, Grace wasn't sure she could love it–you know, considering the circumstances and all. She didn't feel it would be fair to the child. Philippa, I mean Phil, knew this lawyer who arranged for it to be adopted."

"And that's the last that Grace had anything to do with it?"

"Not hardly."

"How so?"

"She supported that kid. And from what I hear, the foster mother too."

"How did she do that?"

"She worked her tail off. She got a job in a factory where they made welding machines. That's where she met her husband Gergo. But he was your old-world Hungarian. He didn't want her to work after they got married."

"Did he know about the kid?"

"He may have, but they never talked about it. Personally, I don't think he did. That's why Grace had to scramble to continue making those support payments."

"What did she do?"

"She wrote a book–kind of based on her story. She had a publisher and everything. Then the child's father got wind of it. His family threatened to sue for libel. Grace was afraid they were going to try and make a legal grab for the child. So she asked to have the book withdrawn."

"And then she wrote other books?"

"Yeah, a whole bunch of them. I never knew this growing up, because Grace never told anyone in the family. Her husband knew she dabbled in writing, but he never found out how successful she'd become."

"Why didn't she tell him?"

"Oh, they had a happy marriage, but it was strictly the old-fashioned kind. When he came home from work, she always had supper on the table. They watched TV and went to bed. For vacations they went on fishing trips. They lived quite modestly."

"That was enough for her?"

"I guess so. She never complained. I think she was sorry they never had any children of their own."

I wiped my eyes with my napkin. "You know, Jody, I was the child she gave up for adoption."

"I kind of figured you were, Helen. That's why I told you the story."

Later, in the hospital parking lot I phoned Leigh with the news. Then, when I got home, I retrieved Uncle Phil's box from my closet. Now that I knew what to look for, I found Grace Hoetchans right away in a photo taken at Philippa's high school graduation. I had noticed that pretty, dark-haired girl before, but hadn't made the connection to my elderly neighbor. The same calm intelligent eyes, but otherwise unrecognizable. No resemblance at all to me that I could see.

Tucked into a small notebook in the box was a decades-old business card for Morris G. Korjath. I looked him up on the Web. His son, Morris G. Korjath, Jr., was the man I was after. I found an obituary for him from 2003. It was quite laudatory. He had taken a single car dealership and built it into a multi-state chain with annual sales of over $300 million. Also very active in civic affairs, including leadership posts with several charities. On the boards of numerous community organizations. Active patron of the arts. Three children by his first wife, and another by his second. Enjoyed hunting, skeet-shooting, golf, and never missed the Indianapolis 500.

I studied his photo for a long time. It was like looking at a male version of myself. Still handsome, but all that good living had taken its toll. The obituary went into more detail about his life, but nowhere did it mention that he was a scoundrel, rapist, and destroyer of lives.

August 21 – I had quite a bit more to say to Grace at the hospital today. I told her when I was growing up I never wanted for anything. I went to an expensive private college and never thought to question where the money was coming from. Or why I was spared the necessity of working or taking out student loans. I said I understood now why she wanted to meet my kids (her grandchildren) and my husband. Why she was saddened by my unhappy marriage and so interested in meeting that charming college professor from Pittsburgh. I said I marveled that she kept silent while I babbled on about my enthusiasm for Gloria Anne Lenore–not realizing that I was in the company of that remarkable writer and person. I said I realized now that Aunt Maddy left me her house so I could meet her special neighbor.

Perhaps I imagined it, but at one point it seemed like there was some slight response from Grace's frail hand. I said a lot more too–all the while working my way through a box of tissues as the ICU nurses tiptoed around me. I can't imagine what they must have thought.

August 22 – Invited Jody to stay in our guest room so we can get to know each other, car-pool to the hospital, and catch up on family history. I like my cousin a lot. She's married to a post office manager and has two grown sons. Starting her sixth year as an assistant principal at a junior high school in Fort Wayne, Indiana. Right now, she's trying to work out the class schedules for 957 students from 200 miles away. I told her I admired her courage for working in a middle school–considering the challenges posed by that age group. She says somebody has to mind the asylum while they get all that bad behavior out of their systems.

Casta and Kyle weren't quite sure what to make of the news that the elderly neighbor they met in Euclid was their maternal grandmother– and the writer of all those novels. I told them how I found out that I was adopted, but didn't go into detail about my conception. When Ally dropped by, I said she could cancel her research on Mother and filled her in on my discoveries. She wrote down the names and said she would start looking into my family history.

August 23 – Grace isn't doing so well. Her kidneys are failing and her pulse is weak. She had signed a do-not-resuscitate directive with her health plan. At some point, we may be asked to pull the plug. I don't really see how I could do that.

August 24 – Grace died early this morning. Both Jody and I were with her. She never regained consciousness. She was 78 years old. For the past year, she had been treated for pancreatic cancer, a fact she never mentioned to me. I suppose she didn't want to cause me to worry.

I can only pray she heard at least part of what I said to her.

August 29 – The last few days have gone by in a blur. Things are better since Leigh came back. Had a service for Grace in a church in Euclid. Very well attended by her friends, neighbors, and old-time work buddies of her late husband. She was cremated, and they've given me her ashes. I'm thinking there should be a memorial for her somewhere that her fans and readers can visit. There's no need to keep silent about her any more.

August 30 – Leigh, Jody, and I were interviewed today by a reporter for the *Plain Dealer*. We went into depth about my mother, her novels, and her remarkable secret life as Gloria Anne Lenore. Jody was very helpful in filling in details, but she–like us–had never found out how or why Grace came to choose that pen name.

I've surmised that at some point Grace must have assigned the movie royalties to Mother. The studios, having only one address, also forwarded the fan mail–which she opened, read, then stashed away. How tacky was that?

August 31 – Jody went back to Indiana today. She wanted to stay longer, but said it would be too crazy at her school if she didn't get back. We promised to stay in touch, and I hope to visit them in the fall.

September 1 – Leigh's 57th birthday. Yes, the cad had the effrontery to be born nearly two years after me. I keep telling him it's all for the best, since wives usually live longer than their husbands. He said he appreciates the "historical perspective" that an "older woman" can bring to a relationship.

"Like what?" I asked. "Like the fact that I watched a couple more years of Captain Kangaroo than you did?"

"It all adds up," he replied. "The cultural advantages of your 655-day head start are nothing to sneeze at."

So thoughtful of him to have calculated it down to the day, but I took him out to dinner anyway at that nice seafood place we like on the lake. He also claimed to like the tie, jacket, and book I gave him. I wanted to buy him a better car, but he firmly nixed that idea.

"Why not consider it a gift from Gloria Anne Lenore?" I asked, sampling a bit of his fried perch. "After all, you've helped immeasurably in getting out her story."

"I'd like to accept a car, darling. Something rakish and expensive, but I don't have the mustache for it. Or the wardrobe of Italian silk suits."

"You and your damn mustache. That thing is going away, buster, before I let you drag me to the altar."

He did let me pick up the check for his birthday meal.

September 2 – Harkness knocked on my door early this morning. He handed me my Sunday *Plain Dealer*, and asked me if I'd read it.

"Not likely, dear, since I just got out of bed, and you just retrieved it from the lawn."

"There's an article in it that mentions you, Helen. It's quite extraordinary."

I invited him in for coffee while I went to rouse Casta. He took his old spot at the dining table, and Leigh settled in opposite him to read the long feature story on Gloria Anne Lenore.

When I returned from Casta's room, they were discussing it like two civilized, mature adults.

Excellent article that quoted Leigh at length. The reporter also had interviewed several of Grace's friends and Cleveland's head librarian. The story identified me as "her daughter from a previous relationship," which is a polite way of putting it.

Monica phoned from Colorado while I was serving the coffee. In her excitement, she may have forgotten that she hates me. Or perhaps Roland has informed her that I'm dating a fellow whose father had a long career behind the scenes at Paramount. Her big news: Their movie was a surprise hit at the festival. They have received three offers so far, the highest for $1.2 million, and were still waiting to hear from Harvey (whoever that is).

I told her that was wonderful news and I was very proud of her. We chatted for a few minutes, and then I handed the phone to Harkness. Bit of an awkward moment as he explained to her that, no, we hadn't reconciled.

When Kyle got up, I sent him to the store to buy ten more copies of the paper. Casta was excited to hear of the movie's success. She suggested that since we're now all "such buddies," she and her father could just hang out by the pool today. But I gave her a hug and sent them both on their way.

Later, Monica called back to say that Harvey had passed, so they were accepting the offer for $1.2 million. We talked about the festival, then had a long conversation about my mother, including how she came to be pregnant with me. Monica wants to do that as their next project: a movie about the life of Gloria Anne Lenore.

When Kyle came in from washing his car, I expressed my surprise at his sister's change in attitude.

"Oh, I can explain that, Mom. Ally called her and gave her hell for being a dick."

"Well, that was sweet of her."

"Yeah. Ally's big on family harmony."

September 3 – Labor Day. Even though it's a holiday, I've gotten calls from the *New York Times*, the *Wall Street Journal*, and *Publishers Weekly*. They all want to do articles on Gloria Anne Lenore. A producer for a local morning news show also called. They want me to come in tomorrow to discuss my mother and her books. Me on TV? A truly terrifying prospect, but somehow I've agreed. Yikes!

A low-key holiday. We had a farewell barbecue on the patio. (Kyle and Ally are leaving for Lafayette early tomorrow morning.) Leigh had dressed for the steamy weather. To his credit, he doesn't look as silly in shorts as Hugh Grant did in my favorite movie. I noticed Leigh observing Ally in the pool. She does a great deal more for a bikini than I would–not that I'd dare wear one these days. But men are programmed to look, so there's no point taking offense. Harkness always did too, and he has the sex drive of a sloth.

I asked Leigh what he was reading, and he held up my high school yearbook.

"You didn't tell me you were the Britney Spears of your high school," he said.

"Well, you didn't ask. People have differing trajectories in their lives. I peaked at age 17. And how'd you get that book?"

"I sneaked it out of your den. It's very educational."

"Yeah, well, I'll be expecting to read yours too."

Ally reports her jeweler measured the diamond, and it came to 2.3 carats. It has one small flaw, but don't we all. She showed me a sketch of their design: a smooth expanse of gold that curves up to encircle the stone. Simple and classic. I told her I approved. I also thanked her for speaking with Monica.

"No problem, Helen. She's coming to see that the divorce wasn't all your fault. And it's best for both parties."

"You think it's best for Harkness too?" I asked.

"Of course. Now he has a fresh start. And a chance to find his true love."

She could be out there, I suppose. One of those flashy trophy blonds with more chest than brains–he might go for that.

September 4 – First day of school for Casta. I had to put Leigh in charge of getting her there, since they wanted me at the TV station no later than 6:45. Barely had time to say goodbye to Kyle and Ally. I hope she fits in with his college friends and life. They're driving both cars to Indiana convoy style. Both vehicles were packed to the roofs with Ally's worldly goods.

Incredibly nervous getting made up in the TV studio. But unwound a bit once we got started. Don't think I totally disgraced myself. Leigh told me I was great, but he's expected to say such things. It helped that the interviewer had read a few of G.A.L.'s novels in high school and was still a fan. Her male co-host was something of a pest. All he wanted to talk about was her book on streetcars.

Leigh went back to Pittsburgh after lunch. Each separation gets harder. Two more years of this! How will I ever cope?

September 5 – Many more inquiries and phone interviews. I may be on National Public Radio next week. I'm hoping radio is less terrifying than TV. If *60 Minutes* calls, I'm telling them to drop dead. I don't think I can take the strain on my nerves.

This afternoon I met with Maurice Circo and his junior colleague Ryan Tatlock. Ryan was wearing blue pinstripes today and looked like the tastiest hors d'oeuvre on the plate. The first thing I told Maurice was my daughter had sold her "little" movie for $1.2 million–meaning I had more than tripled my investment in less than a month. So much for his cautionary legal advice.

Maurice smiled and congratulated me on my talented family. He also expressed his condolences over the death of Grace Hoetchans, my birth mother.

I thanked him and asked if they were ready to breech the "firewall" now.

"I'm sorry, Mrs. Spall, if I left you with the impression that Mrs. Manders, your adoptive mother, was the author Gloria Anne Lenore."

"I found out who really wrote those novels, Mr. Circo. It was my birth mother Grace Hoetchans."

"Good. Then we're on the same page. As you may have surmised, she was also the entity behind the Dixon L. Hamlin Trust."

"You mean my mother bought the house I was selling?"

"Yes, and she has left it to you in her will, plus the adjoining real property which was her own residence. You are the beneficiary of her entire estate, except for a bequeath of $500,000 to Mrs. Herbert S. Treggs."

That was my cousin Jody.

Like Mother, Grace had lived frugally and made some wise investments. My share came to over $3 million, plus the Euclid houses, plus full control over her copyrights.

More than a little mind-boggling.

How kind of Grace to buy my aunt's house from me. And then she went to all the trouble of hiring a crew to clean up the yard–while suffering from cancer. She must have known her days were numbered since I hear very few recover from that kind of cancer.

I can't help but think that at least some part of her wanted her secret to come out. Perhaps that's why she hadn't retrieved her manuscripts from Maddy's attic or her papers from Uncle Phil's safe when they were still alive. And why she sent that replacement manuscript to Leigh.

She'd earned all that money, but not much recognition. And that must have hurt.

Maurice had also structured Grace's estate so that probate wasn't required. He handed me both sets of keys for the Euclid houses.

Those ugly drapes and stark Navajo White walls are back in my life.

September 6 – Having so many houses to choose from, I've been shuffling them around in my mind. If I thought Harkness could look after Casta, I'd give him back his house–with her in it. I could live in Pittsburgh during the week, then she could stay with us in Euclid on weekends. I don't want to spend two entire years having a commuting relationship with Leigh. And who knows who he might meet next at some conference? But can Harkness be trusted to watch over my trouble-prone daughter? He wasn't minding the store very well last spring when I was staying in Euclid.

How about Harkness, Casta, Monica, and Roland all reunited under the Pepper Pike roof? Casta would get lots of supervision, but the mix of personalities might prove volatile–as in the cops being called out to deal with the bodies.

I phoned Leigh and told him my net worth was now pushing $5 million. He replied that such a bankroll could be nudging him by default into the gigolo category.

"Shall we get you fitted for those silk suits, honey?" I asked.

"Why not, dearest? And while you're at it, sign me up for tango lessons. Swines like me will do anything for a rich woman. Just don't ask me to change my name to Porfirio Rubirosa. That one's already been taken."

In truth, I only get to keep part of my pile. Maurice warned me that I may be facing a sizeable bill for estate taxes.

How ironic that what I need now is an unscrupulous tax attorney.

September 7 – Met Monica for lunch at the European cafe in Euclid. She had some news: her father is now living with Bodana's cousin, a woman named Ludmila.

"So that's what Casta was alluding to," I said.

"She told you?" asked Monica.

"No, she offered to sell me a hot piece of information about Harkness for $25. I told her I wasn't in the market for gossip. Have you met her?"

"Not yet, but his secretary was implying strongly that she was a gold-digging tramp."

"Oh, I wouldn't pay any attention to Perla. She just wants him for herself."

"But she's 95 years old!"

"Not quite, dear. But she could be retired and collecting Social Security if she wasn't so stuck on your father."

"Does Daddy have any gold left to dig? I was under the impression you cleaned him out."

"Hardly, dear. He has quite enough to keep Ludmila in the furs of her choice."

Monica's second piece of news was that she and Roland are moving to Los Angeles. As soon as the check arrives from the distribution deal, she's quitting her job and heading west.

"Are you sure you have to go, dear?" I asked. "The movie you made here is doing well."

"Strictly an amateur effort, Mother. But it got us a foot in the door. It vaulted us past all the other wannabes with no credits. Now we have a chance to be real filmmakers. You have to go to L.A. for that. So, tell me about this college professor of yours."

I filled her in on Leigh, making it clear that this was no summer fling. Felt a bit odd justifying my love life to my daughter–especially in light of her chosen partner. Didn't say that, of course, since I learned my lesson about Monica: That girl can be touchy.

After lunch we went to look through Grace's house. Peach came over and I introduced her to my daughter. Monica now regrets that she never got to meet her grandmother. I didn't point out that she'd have had the chance had she helped me with the wallpaper scraping. One has to do quite a bit of self-censoring around Monica, whereas I can say the harshest things to Casta, and she just laughs at me.

In the top drawer of Grace's desk I found this note addressed to me:

> Dear Helen,
>
> If you are reading this, then you know about your background. I'm so sorry for abandoning you. I soon

realized that I had made a dreadful mistake, but by then it was too late to alter our circumstances. I did what I could over the years to make amends for my impulsive and ill-considered act. I hope you will find it in your heart to forgive me.

I treasured getting to know and meeting your lovely children. Please forgive my deceitfulness. Since your mother chose not to tell you that you were adopted, I felt I could not reveal myself to you.

Forgive me also for misleading you about the visitor. The elegant lady who used to arrive by taxi was my long-time literary agent Anna Vierny. I would meet with her in your aunt's house to conceal her visits from my husband. I felt it best to keep my family and work lives separate.

It warmed my heart to hear that you appreciated my books. That was the best gift of all you could have given me.

All my love,
Grace

I handed the note to Monica and shut myself in the bathroom for a time. How strange that Grace should feel the need to apologize to me after all she did for me. And I never treated her as anything more than a casual acquaintance.

In an upstairs bedroom, the door to which always was closed on my previous visits, we found two large fire-resistant file cabinets containing manuscripts and research notes. Exciting find: another unpublished manuscript. This one is titled *Views across the Bay* and appears to be a memoir of Grace's childhood on the farm in Wisconsin. There were two copies, so Monica and I didn't have to fight over it.

September 8 – Had to make a copy of *Views across the Bay* so Leigh and I could read it simultaneously. Wish I could have read it when Grace was alive. I love finding out about her (my) family, but I have so many questions. The bay in the title refers to Green Bay, a long arm of Lake Michigan that extends into Wisconsin. Their farm was north of Oconto, a couple of miles inland from the shore. Grace was just a tot during the grim 1930s. Things had improved by the war years when she was in grade school. Everyone had to pitch in, and not just on farm chores. Local machine shops with defense contracts jobbed out work to her dad, who made parts on a little nine-inch South Bend lathe in his barn workshop. Grace showed an interest, so he trained her and her sister Hope. Each put in a two-hour shift after school on the lathe. Their sister Charity inspected parts for accuracy with micrometers and measuring jigs. Grace was the one who suggested they could speed up production by using a rotary tool post to turn it into a makeshift turret lathe. Hard to believe my mother was turning out parts for munitions at the age of 10.

Her parents were church-goers, and her father was pretty strict about what radio shows they could listen to. They don't sound like fanatics though. From her description of them, I'm surprised they were so un-feeling in their rejection of her in her time of need.

September 9 – Leigh and I both finished *Views across the Bay*. He thinks it could be the next *Little Women*. By high school Grace's friend Philippa had become like the sixth daughter in the family. The Tishbys lived in town; Philippa's father had a jewelry store and also repaired watches. Hope (Jody's mom) was the boy-crazy sister. Grace and Philippa were the dreamy ones. They liked to ride bikes to a shady cove on the bay and read novels and poetry. It was a way to escape the harassment they both suffered from classmates and locals over their friendship.

The text ends the summer after they graduated from high school. Grace was working two jobs: at the public library and also on-call as a switchboard operator at the local telephone exchange. (To call someone in their pre-dial town, you picked up the receiver, and a girl at the other end said, "Number please.") She and Philippa had talked of going to business college together, but Philippa decided she'd had enough of small-town Wisconsin. She bought a bus ticket to Cleveland, where an uncle had promised her a job at his printing company. When Grace went to see her off at the bus station, Philippa had cut her hair and dressed for her journey as a boy. They promised each other that they would remain friends forever.

It was a promise they kept, but I can't help but wonder if Uncle Phil yearned for more. Do you suppose he drew from his hopeless love for Grace to pen all those Valentine verses?

September 10 – Leigh left for Pittsburgh this morning. The weekends go by much too fast around here. All in all, I'm glad someone sabotaged his car. At least I know he's traveling all those miles on new tires.

I've decided to leave Grace's house exactly as it is until I've had time to think about things. Two more literary agents phoned today. That makes about a dozen inquiries since the stories came out in New York. I've asked them all to send me information about themselves. Then Leigh and I will decide which one we wish to work with.

Casta had some news about her Sunday with Harkness *et al.* Her father is now sporting a toupee. He dyed his remaining hair brown and got a rug to match. I asked her how he looked.

"He looks like a totally different person, Mom. I mean, it's amazing. Too bad his personality stayed the same. It's helpful that he's tall. You don't really get a good look at his new hair until he sits down."

"How convincing is it?"

"It's not awful. You can sort of tell it's fake, but it doesn't look silly. Ludmila likes it, so I guess it's staying."

"And how do you like her?"

"She's OK. It's way easier being with both of them than just Daddy. That was lame in the extreme."

"Is she pretty?"

"I thought you'd ask that. So I took a bunch of photos with my phone."

She was very pretty indeed. Those Russians sure know how to do bone structure and creamy complexions. Nice curves too. It took me a second or two to realize that the strange man standing beside her in the mirrored aviator sunglasses was my ex-husband-to-be.

I asked Casta what Ludmila did for a living. She said she would sell me that "intriguing" information for her usual price.

I passed.

September 11 – Phoned Bodana to make some discreet inquires about her cousin. She was immediately on the defensive.

"You kicked him out, Helen. He was so miserable. I thought why must my husband's brother suffer so much?"

"Really, Bodana dear, I don't mind at all. I'm happy that he's found someone!"

"Really and truly?"

"Yes, really. I just was curious about her, that's all. She's your cousin?"

"Sort of. She's a cousin of a cousin."

"And what does she do?"

"She has very good job. She does escorting."

"Really? Does Harkness know that?"

"Of course. He see her many times in the past in the courthouse."

"Oh, my."

"Ludmila is very pretty girl. Very popular with men, but I tell her Harkness is special."

"So she's stopped being an escort?"

"No. Why she quit such a good job?"

"And Harkness doesn't mind?"

"I expect if they get married, he make her stop."

I was finding this all extremely hard to swallow. Had my daughter spent yesterday in the company of a call girl?

"So Harkness knows that she's still working?"

"Of course. He sees her get ready every day. It can be dangerous, but she has a gun."

"Your cousin carries a gun!"

"Always. And a big black stick. It's part of her uniform."

"Her uniform? What sort of escort is she?"

"She escorts prisoners from the jail to the courthouse. She's a deputy sheriff. She has a degree in criminology from Youngstown State."

"Oh. That's a relief. Has she ever been married?"

"No. I tell her to wait for someone special. She's picky like me."

"How old is she?"

"Not so old. In one month she will be 38. Would you like to meet her?"

"Uh, I don't really want to interfere, Bodana. I was just curious. Do you know if she likes children or teenagers?"

"She does volunteer work sometimes with juvenile offenders. For that she should carry a gun, but no, she doesn't take it."

An interesting conversation. Harkness is now living with a pretty, 37-year-old, Russian-born cop. I'm finding it a struggle to bend my mind around that concept.

September 12 – I did 42 minutes on National Public Radio today. It was much less terrifying than TV. You go into this little booth at your local station and face a microphone while wearing headphones. The interviewer was in Philadelphia, but you pretend like you're in the same room. The headphones make it sound like she's God speaking to you from the center of your brain. Disconcerting at first, but I got used to it. I said my mother Gloria Anne Lenore was a sadly overlooked writer, and her recently discovered unpublished novel, *The Trek to Zion*, was one of the great novels of the 20th century. I added that her unpublished memoir, which I had just discovered and read with delight, was destined to be hailed as a classic. All rather brash of me, but Leigh says if you don't make bold claims, no one will pay any attention.

I held nothing back this time. I talked about the rape, her parents' reaction, her friendship with my uncle Phil, my adoption, her marriage to a factory worker, and her secret life as a writer to support me and my adoptive mother. I never thought I was particularly articulate, but this time the words just flowed out of me. During a break in the recording the producer had to remind me to speak slower. I guess I was feeling inspired!

September 13 – Big reaction to my radio appearance. Too many phone calls and emails to cope with. People are calling from Hollywood inquiring about the rights to Grace's story.

I'm in over my head. I need some professional guidance.

September 15 – Leigh and I decided to go with a New York agent named Susan Floster. She's about my age and was a fan of Gloria Anne Lenore as a teenager. I know she's enthusiastic because she flew to Cleveland on her own initiative and knocked on my door yesterday. (She arrived here in a cab.) She's staying the weekend in my guest room. She had been one of my top choices, but going the extra distance clinched it for me. We also had an immediate rapport. She has many important clients, and her agency has a west coast branch in Beverly Hills. She seems to know everyone out there too.

How plugged in is Susan? She had seen "Store Rage" in Telluride. She recognized Casta as the unfortunate girl who had been beheaded by the flying sign.

We only see Susan at mealtime; the rest of the time she's holed up in the guest room reading.

September 17 – Just took Susan to the airport. She was most enthusiastic about Grace's memoir, *The Trek to Zion*, and *The Solitary Simpleton*. She thinks she can get multiple offers from publishers for them. She thinks if those books do well, there will be interest in republishing the romances–leading off the series with *Her Placated Heart*. *Streetcar for Adventure* she says will be a harder sell, since not many young adult readers are interested in streetcars these days. Too bad, it's such a fun book.

Susan's confident there will be movie interest in the memoir and *The Solitary Simpleton*. She's not so sure about *The Trek to Zion*. She loves *Her Placated Heart*, but suspects the story may be too old-fashioned for Hollywood. Still, she says some producer may surprise us with an offer.

I told her Monica was interested in doing something with Grace's story. Susan was discouraging on that point. She says there's too much interest now from major studios to leave the project in the hands of beginning filmmakers–however resourceful they proved themselves to be with "Store Rage."

Damn. I hope Monica doesn't go back to hating me when I tell her that.

September 18 – I heard from Ally this morning. They found her a nice apartment, and she's started work at her new job.

"I have something else to confess, Helen," she said. "I hope you won't be upset or get angry."

"What is it, dear?" I asked, alarmed.

"Kyle and I went to the courthouse yesterday. We were married by a judge."

"Really?"

"Uh-huh. I was happy waiting until June, but he was getting kind of antsy. I felt it might help him to be focused on his studies this year. It would be good if he could get his grades up by the time he graduates. I hope you don't mind."

"Not at all, dear. You have my hearty approval. I'm just a bit surprised. My congratulations to you both. Are you going on a honeymoon?"

"No time for that now, Helen. Classes have started."

"Do you have enough money? Would you like me to supplement the allowance he gets from his dad?"

"No, we're doing fine. My job pays pretty well and our rent isn't bad. I found out that some of Kyle's ancestors on your mother's side were Serbian. He's very proud of that."

"Er, why's that?"

"His hero Nikola Tesla was from Serbia."

"Oh, right. Well, welcome to the family, dear. I hope you will both be very happy together."

"I hope so too, Helen. We're giving it our best shot."

After we said goodbye, I immediately phoned my son. He was at his frat house shooting baskets with some buddies. I said I had just heard the news.

"Oh. Ally told you, huh?"

"She did. I told her I was very happy for you both."

"Good. That's a relief."

"I hope you're taking this seriously, Kyle."

"Sure, Mom. Marriage is a big step."

"Do you ever read the obituary page?"

"Heck, Mom, I don't even read the paper. Nobody my age does—except maybe the sports page."

"Well, you should read the obituaries sometime. Lots of people you read about were married for 60 or 70 years."

"Yeah, so?"

"So good marriages can last forever, dear. But you have to work at it."

"I know, Mom. We're doing that."

"Good. Because I've got something to tell you."

"What?"

"Ally is a very sweet girl. You are so lucky to have her. So don't mess it up. If you break her heart, I'll break your face. Got it?"

"Got it, Mom. Geez, I thought you were calling to congratulate me."

"I just did. And I'll be sending you a check. Don't blow it all on beer."

"OK, Mom, I love you too."

When I got off the phone, I wrote them a check for $5,000. I know mothers are supposed to have adversarial relationships with their daughters-in-law, but I for one am thrilled. I'm grateful that my son is in such capable hands.

So I'm part Serbian. There's a place I know almost nothing about. Didn't they have a war there recently?

FALL

September 22 – Leigh and I hosted a farewell dinner today for Monica and Roland. They're leaving tomorrow for California in Roland's van. We limited the invitations to family: Casta, Harkness, Ludmila, Harkness's brother Eliot, and Bodana. To my surprise, they all decided to come.

Ludmila was a bit aloof at first, as I suspect Harkness had portrayed me as The Evil Wife. But she warmed up when I gave her a tour of the house and garden. I asked her how she had gotten Casta to give up cigarettes.

"I told her it was dirty, stupid, and would ruin her looks," she replied.

"I said the same thing to her," I pointed out. "She laughed at me."

"Sometimes kids are more likely to listen to strangers than their parents. I told her I smoked for a year, but quit when my boyfriend at the time refused to kiss me because my breath was so gross."

I found Ludmila very easy to talk to and not at all full of herself like Bodana can be. It helps that I'm not in the least jealous that she's sleeping with Harkness. I hope he's putting more effort into the act than he did with me.

I'm gradually getting used to the new Harkness. I found the contrast between his youthful hair and 59-year-old face somewhat incongruous. At least his faux hair went nicely with his hip new wardrobe. The guy had seldom looked so trendy, even when we were first married. Of the two brothers Eliot always had been the sharper dresser, but now Harkness was giving him competition–and more than matching him in the arm-candy department. I noticed Roland could barely keep his eyes off my husband's date. If Roland gets to be a big shot in Hollywood, Monica will have to work harder on her appearance to retain his interest. (Or not would be fine with me too.)

Monica hasn't said anything more about working on Grace's story, so I've dropped the subject as well. Roland is hot to do a comedy about a highly contagious brain virus that turns its victims into raging sex maniacs. They're already one-third done with the script.

Later, as Monica was helping me clear the table she slipped me a check for $162,000. It was my share of their distribution deal, minus agents' commissions. She took me aside in the kitchen and said she had a confession to make. She and Roland had heisted the valuables from Uncle Phil's safe. She said it was the only way they could finance their movie. They sold the entire lot of jewelry and gold coins to Mother for $30,000.

"We figured all the loot would come back to you eventually," she explained. "So we thought of it more as borrowing than stealing. I hope you don't mind."

"I'm not sure how I feel about that, dear. It seems to me you were taking advantage of an elderly person afflicted with dementia."

"Hardly that, Mother. We sold them to her for one-eighth their actual value. Grandma never could resist a bargain."

"Now that we're getting things off our chest, dear, did you sabotage Leigh's car?" I asked.

"I didn't know it was his car, Mother. I thought you were keeping company with Casta's lowlife father. Would you like me to pay for the damages?"

"Not necessary, dear. But let's not allow things to get so bad between us in the future. At least return my phone calls, OK?"

"OK, Mother. It was making me pretty miserable too."

It's unnerving that Monica proved such a good liar. At the time I really believed that Roland was the thief and my innocent daughter was being duped by his denials. It never occurred to me they were Bonnie and Clyde hawking stolen property to my aged mother.

September 24 – Phoned Harkness at his office this morning. I asked him if he would like to have his house back.

"Is this some kind of joke, Helen?" he demanded.

"Not at all, dear. I'm prepared to move out and hand it back to you. I have just one condition."

"What's that?"

"You have to live there with Casta and Ludmila. You can take care of Casta during the week, and she'll stay with me in Euclid on weekends. But you'll have to watch over her and be a real father. And Ludmila has to stay there too. If she leaves, the house reverts back to me."

"That sounds like multiple conditions."

"No, it's just one condition with multiple parts. What do you say?"

"Why are you so interested in my staying together with Ludmila?"

"Because I like her and I think she's good for you. And Casta likes her too. I think Ludmila could be a good influence on our daughter."

"Are you serious about this, Helen?"

"Harkness, we were married for 27 years. Did you find me to be a frivolous person?"

"That shyster lawyer of yours won't like it."

"You let me worry about him, dear. Is it a deal?"

171

"Let me get this straight, Helen. You don't want any compensation for the house?"

"No, Harkness. It's yours as long as you meet my condition."

"I'll have to talk it over with Ludmila. Can I get back to you?"

"Sure, but do me one favor."

"What?"

"Don't pay any attention to what your secretary may say about it. I suspect she's listening in."

We both heard a gasp, followed by a click on the line.

This residence always felt more like Harkness's house than mine. I don't need five acres, a pool, and 4,300 square feet of stately home to keep clean. I will miss my garden, I suppose. But I think he should have the property. He likes Pepper Pike, most of his golfing buddies live here, and it's close to his country club. By making his ownership of the house contingent on Ludmila living here, I'm hoping it will encourage him to treat her better than he treated me.

I think this divorce may have taught him a few things about women and marriage. I hope so at any rate.

September 25 – The house-transfer deal is on. Harkness, Ludmilia, Leigh, and I are all for it. Casta is willing to go along for a substantial increase in her allowance. Perla, however, has tendered her letter of resignation.

September 26 – Met with DeeAnn and Beverly at my old house in Euclid. They are going to repaint it from top to bottom–this time in the colors of my choice. I'm also putting in carpet to go over the vomit-inspired linoleum–mostly a neutral grayish berber. I'll make do with the kitchen as it is for now, since we'll be using it mostly as a weekend house. New furniture is a must; I may borrow some pieces from Grace's house.

The new drapes will go in after DeeAnn and Beverly leave. I decided I can't live with the old ones. Too jarring to the nerves.

September 28 – More good news from Susan in New York. She's closed two more deals. Gloria Anne Lenore is having a big second act in publishing and movies.

September 30 – A quiet Sunday with Leigh in Pepper Pike. He's been helping me sort through stuff and pack. It's endless. I knew I was a packrat, but I didn't realize I was a full-fledged hoarder.

We've been listening to a CD he gave me. In 1896 a man named John Wesley Waters raped a 12-year-old girl. From that act of violation came the great jazz singer and actress Ethel Waters. I especially like her sprightly version of "Taking a Chance on Love." She's become one of my spiritual grandmothers.

Yielding to constant supplication, Leigh at last brought along his old high-school yearbook. He was in several clubs, but wasn't the manic overachiever like me. I was surprised to see his photos revealed that he has a small wine-red stain under his nose. I suppose that birthmark made him self-conscious growing up. I expect he was teased about it. So he retreated to the world of books and became a college professor. Such a small thing, yet it can make a big difference in someone's life.

I'd like to think I'd have been interested in him in high school, but perhaps not. Knowing me, I might have asked myself how he'd look escorting me to the winter dance. He was a good-looking kid, but he might not have made the grade for Suzy Shallow. She was into those flashy guys back then.

Now I was feeling bad for harassing him about his mustache. I ventured an apology, but he told me to think nothing of it. So I gave him a kiss and told him I loved him—mustache and all. He said he would value mine as well, should I develop one in my dotage. What a charmer I've got on my hands.

After lunch I took a break to jot down a few thoughts on my iPad. Leigh asked me what I was writing

"Kyle gave me an app last Christmas for keeping a diary," I replied. "I've been giving it a whirl."

"Really? That's great. The journals of Gloria Anne Lenore's only daughter. That sounds spectacular. Can I read it?"

"Certainly. When I'm dead."

"Oh? You have something to hide?"

"Of course, dear. That's how you know I love you."

Brenda the Great

Chapter 1

I BLAME my parents for making me fat.

In the first place they named me Brenda, which as everyone knows is a fat girl's name.

Brenda Blatt.

String a concrete block on a motorcycle chain, hang it around your neck, and that's the psychic weight of my name.

Then my parents had the audacity to bring both sets of crazed fat genes to their marriage bed. They are both big people. My mother, for example, likes to embarrass me by careering around Walmart on those battery-powered carts they provide for the lame and infirm. But she's not handicapped, she's just obese. Not one stitch of clothing in her closet is of a non-stretchy fabric. As long as I've known her she's never left the house without committing a major fashion felony. Then there's my father, who has not been able to cut his own toenails since the age of eight. Lately, his feet have been receding even further from view and are probably now a distant memory.

So I have a double dose of flab in my DNA. I could limit myself to 50 calories a day and five years later I'd still be fat. I was chubby as a baby, chunky as a toddler, tubby as a kid, and now porky as a teen.

Even if they invented a machine that could blast off your fat, I'd still be big. Petite I'm not. For example, the last time I measured my chest I had a 37" bust. Sounds promising, but about 35 inches of that is my capacious, big-boned rib cage. With my shirt off I look more like Arnold Schwarzenegger than Sophia Loren.

The irony is I think I could do beautiful so well. I wouldn't be condescending and stuck-up like the pretty girls in my high school. I'd be gracious and charming to all—even to the plain Janes.

I guess I always knew it wasn't to be. When I was four I got a Perky Princess cosmetics case for Christmas. Full of little rouge samples, face glitter, mascara, blusher, lipsticks, and perfumes. I unwrapped the package and remember feeling very embarrassed. Like suddenly I was some kind of imposter. I knew even then, this wasn't for me. So I put it aside and tossed my new football around with Buford, my lunky big brother.

Yeah, he got a fat boy's name too.

A mental game I used to play: If not beautiful, why not pretty? If not pretty, why not shapely? If not shapely, why not petite? If not petite, why not slim? If not slim, why not blonde? If not blonde, why not . . . and so on.

In every category of attractiveness, I always struck out.

So if fat and plain was my destiny, why not a numbing dose of stupidity? I could have been one of those jolly fat girls beloved by all.

Or, why hadn't I been born a boy? After all, I had a 50 percent chance of that. Ugly fat guys often get dates with attractive chicks. They seem to have no trouble finding someone to marry them. They're happy and contented drinking beer, watching sports, shooting forest creatures, and driving their big-ass pickup trucks. No one thinks less of them for sporting a massive gut.

Well, I suppose some people do. But it's got to be way easier being a fat guy than a fat girl.

For example, I know for a fact that my brother has had sex with at least four girls. Whereas, I'm still waiting for that first (insane? retarded? desperate?) guy to ask me out.

* * *

My sneaky parents are upset. They snooped around on my Facebook page and discovered I only had four friends. And one of them is Harold, my autistic cousin. The other three are amateur Korean tap-dancers whose videos I've watched on Youtube. None of them is particularly adept, so they're very appreciative when you send them complimentary messages.

My parents think I should put more effort into "being social." I've had a few "friends" in the past, but they always wind up stabbing you in the back. Pretty soon they're making snide comments about your appearance. Or looking reproachfully at you every time you stick a potato chip or cheese curl into your mouth. So far, I've had much more rewarding relationships with snack foods than with people.

I find the kids in my high school divide neatly into two categories: moronic or hostile. So I pretty much don't associate with any of them. I did try out for the golf team last year, just to get my father off my back, but all the guys on the team proved so hateful I walked off the course during our first match. And I was leading by three strokes at the time.

My brother is better at "being social." He made friends by playing football and hockey. I could be a jock if I put my mind to it, but golf and football are the only sports that appeal to me. Basketball, like infancy, involves way too much dribbling. Soccer only makes sense if you've had both arms torn off in an industrial mishap. Volleyball and tennis are for the quick and agile, not the large and lumbering. Wrestling might be fun, but our school restricts that activity to boys. Nor are girls welcome to try out for our perennially losing football team.

So I'm stuck being the fat outcast of the junior class.

* * *

My grandmother rolled into town today. Rather ominous. We usually see her at Thanksgiving and Christmas, but her arrival in August is unprecedented. As usual she was driven up from her mansion in Montecito (el supremo ritzy beach town down near Santa Barbara) in her immaculate black 1964 Chrysler Imperial (its eye-searing shine is like something out of a Stephen King novel). She stays in our guestroom (my brother's old bedroom), but her chauffeur Manny has to bunk with his cousin in San Lorenzo. God forbid Grandma should spring for a motel room for the guy.

My father's mother is our one anomalous relative, being both scrawny and wealthy. How rich she is we're not sure, but I can point out that my mother always goes out of her way to be nice to Grandma, even though she's despised her forever. My late grandpa made his pile importing canned hams from eastern Europe. They were so cheap the bargain-minded housewives of the Cold War overlooked their Communist origins. Growing up, I ate a lot of fatty Polish and Rumanian ham, which may be another reason I'm so heavy. A truck used to deliver cases of them (all expired date), which kept us from starving when Dad failed to get tenure at Hayward State. Now he teaches California history and driver's ed at a high school in Oakland. We've remained here in the flats of Hayward so that every morning when my dad bends over painfully to pick his newspaper off the stoop he can flash the finger up to that campus on the hill that snubbed him.

Grandma greeted me with her usual question: "How's the diet going, Brenda?"

"Great, Grandma. I gained 14 pounds so far this summer."

"What! Are you taking those diet pills I sent you?"

"Sure, Grandma. They haven't suppressed my appetite, but I've been feeling terrifically homicidal."

"I hope you're kidding, Brenda!"

"I used to crave Ben & Jerry's Heath Bar Crunch ice cream. Now I'm jonesing for a Glock 20 Gen4 semi-automatic pistol."

Mom chuckled nervously. "She's just pulling your leg, Enid."

"I hope so," said Grandma, looking at me askance.

"Of course," I added, "a nice simple strangulation can be just as fulfilling."

* * *

I should have kept my big mouth shut. My parents want to stick me in some school for maladjusted girls in Stockton. That's that grungy town in the Central Valley that recently filed for bankruptcy. The school fees are pricey, which is why Grandma was called in. She has been prevailed upon to open her purse to save me from a life of lonely ostracism and (possible) mayhem. My only alternative is a fat girls school in distant Nebraska that guarantees "significant" weight loss every semester. So I have a choice of moldering with misfits in boring Stockton or starving on the prairies with a bunch of chubby Cornhuskers.

Or I could strangle my entire family and run off to Mexico with Manny. I wish that guy wasn't nearly as old as my granny. I'm so ready to shack up with some hot Mexican desperado. Lots of those hombres, I've heard, like 'em large and limber.

I have put my size 12 foot down and informed all concerned that I will NOT be leaving home to be incarcerated against my will at some crummy boarding school. I added that as far as I was concerned, the subject was closed. I said if Grandma really wanted to help me, she could buy me a plane ticket to New York and lease me a studio apartment in Greenwich Village.

"Those places are full of roaches and bed bugs!" wailed my mother, horrified.

"We'll have no high school dropouts in this family," said my dad. "Besides, you're barely 16."

"You'd be raped within a week," added Grandma. "That city is crawling with degenerates."

"I can take care of myself," I replied. "It would take a fairly determined rapist to tackle this hunk of muscle. Besides, I'd be packing heat."

"That's it," announced my mother. "I'm taking you off those diet pills!"

Well, the joke's on her, because the only thing I'd been doing with those pills was sneaking them into her morning orange juice.

Not that they appeared to be doing much good.

* * *

Dateline: Stockton, California. Yeah, I'm here. I arrived this afternoon with two suitcases, a footlocker, my golf clubs, $300 worth of chintzy dorm furnishings from IKEA, a very bad attitude, and my anxious mother. My father wanted to come too, but school starts today in Oakland, and he had to be there to help confiscate the weaponry.

Apparently, there are to be three of us incarcerated in one smallish room. I've met my two roommates, neither of whom will look you in the eye. They seem startled by my size, a not uncommon reaction, I've noticed.

Before she left, my mother took my roommates aside for a private confab. I hope she didn't ask them to spy on me. Or enlist their help in discouraging junk-food bingeing. That's right, Mom, embarrass the hell out of me on my very first day in this prison.

"Your mother had to turn sideways to go through the door," observed Gianna, pushing back her thick glasses. She was slim and blonde, but otherwise appearance-impaired.

"Yeah," I sighed, "notice that, did you?"

Since I was the last to arrive, I got the narrowest bed by the door to the corridor. I gave it a trial sit. It creaked loudly and sagged alarmingly.

"Is your name really Blatt?" asked Lauren, the other girl. She was petite, tanned, possibly part Asian, and verging on the pretty.

"Fraid so. Anyone want to switch beds?"

No one volunteered.

"What's that smell?" I asked.

"It's the city's sewage treatment plant," replied Lauren. "It's a few blocks away."

"We'd still appreciate it if you'd go out in the hallway to fart," said Gianna.

"Noted," I replied, feeling around in my pockets. "I take it you girls aren't new here," I said, unwrapping a Heath bar.

"We both started last year," said Gianna.

"So how do you like it?" I asked, munching away.

They looked at each other.

"It's OK," said Lauren "I hope they don't succeed."

"Succeed at what?" I asked.

"There's a secret conspiracy," she whispered. "Some girls are plotting to murder Mrs. Lumpwapht."

Mrs. Lumpwapht was the owner, headmistress, and chief disciplinarian of the school.

* * *

Ferncliffe Academy consists of a half-dozen concrete block buildings on a couple of pinched acres in a bleak, sun-baked neighborhood. Warehouses to the west; blocks of aging tract houses to the east; and some sort of swampy wetlands to the south. The campus had begun as one of those small Christian colleges that spring up, struggle along for a few decades, then go belly up. Deluxe it was not. The dreary buildings appeared to have been constructed with volunteer Christian labor and scavenged materials. The tile in the bathrooms looks like it was installed by a crew of blind four-year-olds. The grounds were completely devoid of nature except for one stunted tree outside the classroom building.

Mrs. Lumpwapht and her former husband bought the place cheap at the auction sale. All this I found out from a short girl in the restroom where I had retreated to change into the required school uniform: white blouse and ugly plaid skirt. It was not a look that brought out the best in my figure.

I'm not sure how I'm going to cope with this lack of privacy. People my size generally do not enjoy parading around in the nude. I squeezed into one of the toilet stalls and quickly changed clothes. The one bathroom on the corridor has six toilets, four semi-grungy showers, three dripping sinks, and a urinal. I guess that's for girls who want to practice letting fly while standing.

When I returned to my room, Gianna and Lauren were checking out the contents of my footlocker.

"You brought too much stuff," complained Gianna, unembarrassed to be caught snooping. "You only get two drawers in the dresser and two feet of the closet pole."

"These are the biggest panties I've ever seen," announced Lauren, holding up one of my non-designer cotton undies.

"You guys need to back off," I replied, grabbing my intimate apparel. "I won regionals and placed second in the state in my weight class on my high-school wrestling team. I'm not to be messed with."

"I'm not afraid of you," said Lauren. "My boyfriend Pico is one scary dude. He's a gangbanger in Modesto. You touch me and you die."

"I was just trying to be helpful," whined Gianna. "Just because you're big doesn't mean you get to hog all the space. And what's with these fucking golf clubs?"

Damn, I knew I should have picked that Nebraska diet school instead.

"You should be glad I left my golf cart at home," I pointed out.

I broke one of my precious Heath bars in half and gave it to my roommates as a peace offering. Then I unpacked as best I could and shoved the rest of my stuff under my bed.

"I'm famished," I said. "When's dinner?"

Gianna looked at her watch. "In two and a half hours."

"And I wouldn't get your hopes up," added Lauren. "The food's not that great."

"And Mrs. Lumpwapht says ladies should never ask for seconds," said Gianna. "It's just not done if you wish to be thought refined."

"That's OK," I lied. "I'm a pretty light eater."

"Uh-huh," said Lauren. "I can see that."

Impossible though it may be to believe, I was already homesick for Hayward.

* * *

Dinner in the austere cafeteria was one burger patty minus the bun, a scoop of runny cottage cheese, and two peach halves out of an institutional can. Dessert was a quarter cup of chocolate pudding in a small chipped bowl. My roommates ditched me to sit with their friends, so I took a seat at the end of one of the three long tables. The girls sitting nearby made a point of pretending I was invisible. Mrs. Lumpwapht and a dozen or so teachers dined on a raised platform that probably doubled as a stage for school assemblies.

As instructed in Ferncliffe's rules-laden "Guide for Students" handbook, I remained politely seated, waiting to be dismissed.

Mrs. Lumpwapht swallowed a small, refined spoonful of her pudding, then rose to give a welcoming speech. She was one of those over-manicured, tightly wound types with short, sensible hair and an intimidating manner. I put her age at mid-fifties. She announced the "great news" that enrollment had reached an all-time high of 266.

"As you may know," she continued, "forty-seven percent of our girls are day students from the greater Stockton-Lodi area. But now a majority is enjoying the full Ferncliffe experience of living and learning here in our warm and supportive community. Isn't that marvelous news!"

We all applauded politely.

Next Mrs. Lumpwapht introduced the three new additions to the teaching staff, none of whom looked like they would ever be getting tenure anywhere. Then she had all the new students stand up and introduce ourselves. I counted 17 of us. Very nervous-making when it came time for me to speak. I blurted out my fat girl's name, blushed despite my best efforts to appear calm, and sat down askew on my chair, which the girl beside me had slid silently to the side. (Naturally, she was one of those pretty blonde types.) A wave of tittering across the room as I floundered and flailed to keep from falling on the floor.

"Not very gracious, Miss Blatt," commented Mrs. Lumpwapht. "We must work on your posture this term."

That decided it. If any assassinations were being planned, I would not be the one blowing the whistle on the plotters.

Mrs. Lumpwapht closed by challenging all the returning students to greet "each and every new girl" with "warm words of welcome" by the end of the week. To encourage such activity, she noted that the faculty had been alerted to monitor for such exchanges.

Wow, compulsory friendship. That was a new one on me.

After dinner I walked around the campus (U.C. Berkeley it was not), then checked out the commons room in our dorm. Some old couches, a scuffed table, a few well-thumbed fashion magazines, but no TV. No WiFi anywhere on campus either. Mrs. Lumpwapht, according to the "Guide for Students," felt that computers were "more of a distraction than an aid to education." So what did she expect us to do for entertainment? Read books? Chat up our fellow students? Flirt with the Mexican janitor?

A couple of girls loitering in the commons room missed an opportunity to say a few words of warm welcome to a new student. In fact, they exuded the same sort of hostile vibe I knew so well from my old school-mates in Hayward. So I went up to my room, ate the rest of my candy stash, and stared at the walls until my roommates returned and it was time for lights out (at 9:30 p.m., if you can believe that).

Yes, world, I totally, totally hate my life.

Chapter 2

BOTH OF my roommates despise me. My tiny bed was so uncom-fortable, I tossed and turned all night. Every movement caused a loud creak, which brought moans of protest from the non-slumberers. At one point Lauren tossed a shoe at me. Finally, around 4 a.m. I dragged the mattress off the frame and slept on the floor. At 6:45 a.m. I was jolted awake by a bell ringing loud enough to be heralding the Zombie Apoca-lypse. I'm told I can look forward to that seven days a week.

Waiting bleary-eyed in the line for the showers, I was tapped on the shoulder by the girl behind me, who demanded to know my birthday.

"April 3," I yawned. "What's it to you?"

"Haven't you read your handbook?" she asked. "January through June showers in the evening; July through December showers in the morn-ing."

"And when do I take a shit?" I said. "On the third Monday following a full moon?"

"Just get out of this line before I report you!"

Breakfast was just as niggardly as last night's dinner: one scoop of scrambled eggs, two pieces of white toast (unbuttered), and half a grape-fruit. I doubt even diet schools in Nebraska would have been that chintzy. So–much to the consternation of the cafeteria crew–I went back for sec-onds.

"Didn't I serve you already?" asked the elderly cafeteria lady in the unbecoming hairnet.

I thrust out my plate. "Please, ma'am, I'd like some more."

"But didn't I serve you already?" she repeated.

"Uh-huh, and now I'm back for seconds," I smiled.

With great reluctance, she tipped meager spoonful of scrambled egg onto my plate.

"Any chance for another piece of toast?" I pleaded.

She tossed me half a slice.

I downed this bounty, then telephoned my mother. I told her it wasn't working out and I wanted to come home–immediately, if not sooner.

"But, Brenda honey, we already paid for your first semester. They have a no-refunds policy. It was thousands of dollars!"

"I'm desperately unhappy here, Mom. I need to leave."

"Just give it a little more time, hon. You've only been there a day."

"I'll be Little Miss Social back in Hayward, Mom. I'll take a Dale Carnegie course. I'll join Toastmasters. I'll have 500 close friends by Christmas, I promise. Just get me out of here!"

"No can do, Brenda. Just remember, it's for your own good. I'm sure you'll love it there once you get to know some of your classmates. Just be friendly and outgoing. Well, got to go, honey. Thanks for calling! Bye!"

Very grim: faint from lack of nourishment, potentially constipated, and stabbed in the back by my own mother. I then called my father at work and made the same pitch to him. But he didn't want me back either. I am now entertaining the notion that my parents are happy (thrilled?) to be rid of me.

As I was shuffling out of the cafeteria one of Mrs. Lumpwapht's lackeys accosted me.

"Are you Brenda Blatt?" she asked.

"I might be."

"Here's your class schedule. Don't be late."

Apparently, one did not have any choice in classes. According to the card she handed me, this semester I will be taking Expressions, Behaviors, Undercurrents, Practicalities, Vistas, and Explorations. Is it just me, or does that sound like Education Lite?

* * *

The first rule in the "Guide for Students" and the only one underlined and in bold type read: "Students may not leave the campus without a written permission slip signed by a staff member."

Fine. I would be happy to obey–assuming they were providing sufficient rations to sustain life. Impelled by my strong will to survive, I skipped my first class and strode off in search of a market. I found a little corner store about 10 blocks away in a semi-scary neighborhood. There, I loaded up with supplies, then reluctantly headed back–chewing as I walked.

Mrs. Lumpwapht herself greeted me inside the front door to the classroom building.

"Shall we have a chat in my office, Miss Blatt?"

"OK," I said, swallowing. "Care for some cheese curls?"

"I think not," she replied coldly.

Her office, although forbidding, was much more expensively furnished than the rest of the school. I took the chair facing her fancy desk and continued to crunch away on my snacks while getting my ass chewed for going A.W.O.L.

I told her flat out I couldn't be alert and attentive in the classroom on their skimpy meals.

"Our meals are planned by a trained dietician, Miss Blatt. They are nourishing and well-balanced. Surely you yourself must acknowledge that your caloric intake is excessive. And your choice in supplementary foods is appalling."

"I was hungry. And please take note, Mrs. Lumpwapht, that these cheese curls are baked, not fried."

"That's Lom-waft, Miss Blatt. The first 'p' in my name is silent."

"Then why is it there?"

"That is not the issue here. You will eat only the meals provided by the school. You will not leave campus without permission. You will appreciate this opportunity to eat sensibly, lose weight, and improve your health."

Compulsory appreciation: that was a new one on me too.

Not agreeing to any of that, I changed the subject. I told her I needed a new bed and explained the reasons why.

"Our beds do not creak, Miss Blatt—when girls who take care of their bodies sleep on them. You will have to make do with what you have."

"But it's killing my back and keeping my roommates awake."

"Then this is an opportunity for you to think creatively. And to exchange views with your roommates and negotiate a solution that's satisfactory to all."

I sat there and thought creatively, but all I could come up with was strangling her on the spot.

Mrs. L was all for confiscating my snacks, but I think the fierceness of my glare deterred her. She suggested I consume them "sparingly" until my metabolism adjusted to my new "more healthful" diet. I expect that's not likely to happen before the year 2097.

* * *

I ditched my snacks under my bed and headed off to Behaviors class—taught by a Mrs. Goldbline, who looks to be your Jewish earth mother type. I'd say she's spent way too much time in bead stores. If you like chunky jewelry that rattles and clinks, she's your man.

This class seems to assume that we're socially maladroit because we lack an instinctive understanding of the rules and customs of human behavior. Like we're all missing those Subtle Signals that normal people perceive. So it's Mrs. Goldbline's job to teach us how to interact with our fellow species. Kind of like charm school for retarded primates. Let's hope there's a lesson coming up on being nice to fat girls.

I was hoping Undercurrents was a course on scuba diving, but it turned out to be a dullish hodgepodge of civics, history, and current events. Teacher is a nervous dude named Mr. Love, who looks like he was dragged out of a truck on the interstate, handed a piece of chalk, and told to wing it.

Next was Practicalities: basic math for dummies, plus various life lessons such as how to set an elegant table, dress to impress, or host a cocktail party for 75. Could be marginally tolerable, but it's a big dive off the College Prep track. Guess I can forget about applying to N.Y.U. next year. The teacher, an ancient gal named Mrs. Swengard, dresses like some society dame circa 1962, complete with flowered hat and white gloves. Very classy elocution too, despite her loose dentures.

After a stupendously meager lunch, I dragged myself to Vistas, which is your cultural appreciation smorgasbord: literature, poetry, drama, etc. The teacher is a young chick (dressed all in black) named Miss Porteau, who could rank in the 99th percentile in Stockton for hipness. I must find out how she washed up on these bleak shores. I could smell her nicotine breath from four rows back. Believe it or not, our first assignment is to read the trendy novel *Bastard's Child*. I may have a leg up here since I've already seen the movie.

I read the first two chapters (actual sex scenes!) in study hall, then trooped off to Explorations. This is Science for Chicks, taught by a stout and mannish Miss Bronkiel. Today's demonstration was to prove Steam Is Hotter Than Water. Miss Bronkiel set up some lab apparatus over a gas burner and was hoping to ignite a piece of paper in the invisible jet of pure steam. Instead, she got a damp sheet of paper and a nasty burn.

Still to come is Expressions, which I skipped today. Can they be devoting an entire semester to making faces?

* * *

Everyone got a bit more sleep last night, since I dragged my mattress onto the floor right at lights out. Then at breakfast a girl actually spoke to me. She plopped her tray and herself down beside me and said, "Do you hate this hell hole as much as I do?"

I glanced over and replied, "Honey, compared to me, you're lovin' every minute of the day here."

"No way, girl," she replied. "Compared to me, you are in complete and total bliss. You could kiss the walls you're so happy to be here."

"Hardly the case, dude. Compared to me, you're greeting the dawn with a song and smile just from the knowledge that you can turn any corner and find yourself face to face with good ol' Mrs. Lumpwapht."

"I doubt that," she replied. "My name's Ruby Splodge."

I told her my fat girl's name.

"Ruby Splodge," I said. "That sounds like what they clean off the side-walk after a drive-by shooting."

"Well, your name sounds like a menu item in a German hofbrau. Something greasy with extra sauerkraut."

"So how come they stuck you in here?"

"It was my jealous mother's idea. She got worried big-time I was going to seduce my new stepfather."

I looked her over. Ruby was another of life's losers in the looks lottery: short and scrawny, flat as a pool table, with dingy hair and a face that was zooming way past plain to zealously ugly. Just a shade shy of hideous. It didn't actually hurt your eyes to look at her, but it was a severe strain.

"You were putting moves on the dude?" I asked.

"Hardly. He's a total creep. Just being in the same room with him could put you off guys for life."

"Is he hot for your bod?"

"Could be. He's always making these suggestive remarks. My mother marries a sicko degenerate so I get banished to Stockton. What's your story?"

"Bad attitude."

"And your parents think this place is going to improve it?"

"Yeah, they're kind of delusional. I just phoned my mother and told her that if they didn't yank me out of here fast, I'd be forced to take up smoking."

(Some girls smoke to stay slim, but I've been deterred by nicotine math: smokin' + coughin' = coffin.)

"What did your mother say?" asked Ruby.

"She hit me where it hurt. She said if she thought I was buying cigarettes, she'd have to radically curtail my allowance."

"So are you going to start smoking?"

"No way. I need all my money for snacks to keep from starving."

"I hate this swill worse than you do."

"No way, Ruby. Compared to me, your taste buds are experiencing ecstasy three times a day."

* * *

It turned out Ruby was in my first period Expressions class, where I received an awful shock. Two of them in fact. Every day, five days a week, they expect us to write an essay in this class. Then on Saturday morning we have to meet here for two fucking hours to "discuss and review" our week's output. School on Saturday! Is there no end to the horror? The essays we have to write out with a pen, and they take off points for mis-spellings and crummy penmanship. No fewer than 300 words must be excreted daily. I may die from terminal writer's cramp.

The designated slave driver for this class is a skinny Asian fellow named Mr. Ng. I expect that growing up his family was too poor to afford vowels. English appears to be a second language that he is still wrestling into submission.

Today's essay theme was "The U.S. President I Admire Most." Naturally, I devoted my 300 words to Richard M. Nixon. Too bad I missed out on his presidency and know virtually nothing about him. Most of what I wrote I made up. But isn't that what all successful writers do?

I did remember that ol' Nixon opened up relations with China, which I noted was "probably a huge mistake."

I hope Mr. Ng doesn't take offense at that.

The rest of the day was a bleak repeat of yesterday. I ate lunch and dinner with Ruby, who appears to want to become my de facto friend.

Don't ask me why.

Chapter 3

NOW IT appears my roommates loathe me with an all-consuming passion. You'd think that confining three strangers in intimate proximity in one shrunken room would lead to some sort of accommodation. Friendships might blossom and in time a sisterly affection might develop.

Hah!

Lauren (the pretty one) looks right through me as if I didn't exist. I try conversing with her, but meet with stony silence. I could drop dead from a stroke and she would go right on filing her glitzy artificial nails.

Gianna's attitude is even spookier. She never says anything either, but keeps her beady eyes fixed on my every move. No lie: she sits at her desk and stares at me non-stop. I tell her to back off with the prying eyes, but 10 seconds later she's back glued retinally to my person.

I suspect my hygiene may be giving offence. Hayward has its warm days this time of year, but Stockton really fries. Needless to say, nothing on campus is air-conditioned except Mrs. Lumpwapht's glam office. I am a large person who tends to perspire when the temperature climbs above

65. The crummy and rationed shower facilities here do not encourage gratuitous bathing. So, at times I may not be as fresh-smelling as I (or my roommates) might wish.

For that they treat me like a sub-human? For that they want to load me onto the next cattle car to Dachau?

* * *

First Saturday morning of essay reading with the ever-vivacious Mr. Ng (pronounced like you've wired your jaw shut, then stabbed yourself in the eye–which sounds like more fun than listening to the banal opinions, insipid logic, and dreary sentiments of my classmates). I fear this enforced exposure to such mangy prose can only impair one's natural facility with language.

Since the victims had to march to the front of the room in alphabetical order, I was the second reader of the morning. Got through my stuff fast as possible, then stood there squirming and sweating as "constructive comments" were offered. As usual, the hostility was ill-concealed. For example, Gianna complained that I "used too many adjectives and adverbs." I'd like to give her a sharp poke swiftly and forcefully. No matter how vicious the pile-on, Mr. Ng sat like a cypher behind his battered desk and barely uttered a word. The guy may have perfected the art of sleeping with his eyes open.

I can see now that my three essays on Dick Nixon, the inappropriateness of waking teens before 2:30 p.m., and why every form of personal expression except blogging has become irrelevant in the computer age were all much too tame. What this class needs are fiery opinions freely expressed.

After lunch Ruby and I scored day passes from hip Miss Porteau. She was leery since the last girl she let venture off campus failed to return. Three weeks later the runaway was arrested by Fresno cops while performing a sex act on a 68-year-old man in a Kmart parking lot. (I certainly hope she was doing it for money.)

We assured Miss Porteau that our destination was the city library and we would return promptly. I found out that Miss P was dragged to Stockton by her BF, a Stanford Ph.D. grad in music, who could find a job only at the University of the Pacific. Despite its location in the hairy armpit of the Central Valley, this college is alleged to be decent–graduating such stars as Dave Brubeck and Chris Isaak. Since she lacks a teaching credential, Miss P was forced to scrounge up a low-paying job at a third-rate private school. This is her second year at this institution, and she looks about as pleased to be here as the rest of us.

Needless to say, visiting the library was not on our agenda. Ruby was all for trooping off to downtown Stockton, but as we were being slow-roasted by a sirocco blowing up from Bakersfield, I nixed that. Instead we made a quick excursion to the snack aisle of a supermarket that Ruby knew of that was only two blocks away. What a delightful find! We loaded up with all my favorites and adjourned to the semi-rustic wetlands behind the school. If you fight your way through the bushes, you come to this meandering slough (rhymes with "who knew"?) that branches off from some river, probably the San Joaquin. Rather bug-laden, but we sat down on the litter-strewn bank and broke open the Diet Pepsi and cheese curls.

Since it was kind of private, Ruby decided to take off her blouse. Not that she has much to hide. I've seen larger breasts on sun-bathing lizards. She said I could take off mine too, but no way do I parade my bare flab in public.

Interestingly, although Ruby has never had an actual BF, she appears to regard herself as something of a dude magnet. Therefore, she finds attending an all-girl school to be especially confining.

"Nothing but chicks as far as the eye can see," she complained. "It's too bad there are no boys' academies nearby."

An all-male school for the blind would be just the thing, I thought. Then we could both dive into that dating pool.

I said, "Yeah, boys. They don't have much to do with me."

"You just haven't met the right guy, Brenda. Some boys go for big girls."

"Right. But do they ever visit here from Bulgaria?"

"Did you see that fat gal in the market? She had a pretty cute guy pushing her cart."

Now I see why Ruby is optimistic about her future love life. She has abysmally low standards.

"You mean the guy with the bad skin, Neanderthal brow, beer gut, and curly back hair?" I asked. "The one who looked like a drug addict?"

"You're too critical, Brenda. Guys don't appreciate chicks who run them down."

A sudden rustling in the bushes had Ruby grabbing for her blouse. She clutched it to her chest as the bushes parted and a very dwarfish black fellow emerged from the greenery.

On second glance he appeared to be an actual dwarf. A very surprised little person lugging a brown paper bag. We stared open-mouthed at the interloper.

"Care for a cheese curl?" I said at last, remembering my manners.

"No thanks. Those things are extruded from a machine like shit from your anus."

"Say what!" I exclaimed.

"Excuse me, sir," said Ruby. "Would you mind turning around? I need to cover up."

He politely did as requested, depriving him of the sight of breasts that were considerably smaller than his own.

"OK," said Ruby, buttoning up.

"You girls must be from that school," he said, checking us out.

"What makes you say that?" I asked.

"Well, not many other people are dressed in plaid wool skirts this time of year."

"I'm Ruby and she's Brenda," said my companion. "Would you like a diet soda?"

"I've got beers here," he replied. "Care to switch to the hard stuff?"

We both accepted cans of his discount, off-brand beer. He opened one for himself and sat down beside us.

"Name's Darnell Brickman, but most folks call me Brick."

Brick had broad, flat features and surely the darkest skin I had ever seen. His teeth were very irregular as if God had selected them at random from dental discards. Brick appeared to be in his early twenties. He was dressed sportingly in satiny red bloomer-style pants, red and white striped shirt, and a vintage (as in grubby) porkpie hat.

"What are you, some kind of midget?" asked Ruby.

He laughed. "The M-word is kind of like the N-word: not used in polite company these days. I got a condition called dwarfism."

Sudden revelation: I didn't score a zero in the looks department after all. I did OK in one category: I am not a dwarf.

We chatted while we guzzled our tepid beers, then Brick led us along the bank to where he hid his little floating home under an overhanging tree. It was an old sailboat, maybe 16 feet long, missing its mast, with a tiny cuddy cabin in the prow. We stepped aboard and Brick opened the door to his cabin.

"Here's where I live," he said proudly.

I couldn't have squeezed in there on a bet, and it seemed claustrophobic even for a dwarf. Inside were some salvaged pieces of foam, an old flannel sleeping bag, and a couple of small suitcases.

"Smells a bit musty," I observed.

"Well, all the wood's pretty much rotted from bein' at the bottom of this slough for Lord knows how many years."

He pronounced slough like the slow-moving animal.

"Aren't you afraid of sinking?" asked Ruby.

"Not me, Ruby dear. This here hull is fiberglass. I looked it up in a book. They expect any kinda hunk of fiberglass to last a couple of thousand years. Which means if Jesus and his crew had built my boat, it would be ready for retirement right about now."

"Does your boat have a name?" I asked.

"I call it The Andre."

"Aren't boats supposed to have girl names?" asked Ruby.

"I don't think that's required by law," he replied. "I named him after Andre the Giant. He's my hero."

Since there was a pleasantly cool breeze off the water, neither of us was in any hurry to leave. We settled down in the grungy cockpit (just big enough for three), Brick popped open more beers, and I tackled another bag of cheese curls. Heath bars also were distributed freely to help ease the alcohol into the bloodstream.

"How you girls like your school?" Brick asked.

"We hate it!" we replied in unison.

"I can dig that," he replied. "I also failed to thrive in the classroom."

"Do you have a job?" asked Ruby.

"Well, I have had a job or two," he admitted, taking a philosophical swig. "Didn't much take to them. They usually involve some bossy white dude telling you what to do. Or yelling at you for not doing it. Hard to get a job when you're my size. Not even dishwashing. You walk into a restaurant and the boss man thinks: Oh, no! Lawsuits from the N.A.A.C.P.! Or: Oh, no! I'm gonna have to spend $10,000 to lower my sinks and counters to accommodate this here handicapped midget! Sometimes I fill out an application anyway, but they don't hire me on account of my record."

"You have a police record?" asked Ruby, intrigued.

"Sure do. It's hard having any sort of interesting young life without being locked up a few times. Me and my buddies back in Turlock liked to take nice cars on test drives. We weren't as particular as we might have been about who they belonged to."

"So what do you do for money?" I asked.

"Mostly I do part-time panhandling. I have my own corner downtown. Only do it for an hour or two if the weather's nice. Sometimes I sing a little and play my tambourine if I'm feeling good. Rest of the time, I just sit there with my hat on the sidewalk and nice folks drop money in it. I'm prone to depression, which is an affliction that besets me."

"Your family lives in Turlock?" asked Ruby.

"Just an aunt. I used to live with her–since I was seven. But she asked me to leave."

"Because you got into trouble?" I asked.

"No. Because I'm gay. She's a person of righteous faith and views my sinful inclination as an abomination."

"I hate most of my relatives too," I assured him.

"I try to channel only love into my life," he replied. "But it can be a trial at times."

"Do you have a boyfriend?" asked Ruby.

"Not at the moment, Ruby. I'm not the sort of chap that draws the gaze of attractive young men."

Welcome to the club, I thought.

It was my first time drinking two entire beers. Got a bit woozy in the head, which I believe is the desired effect. Probably could be seduced in such a state, should anyone ever attempt it.

As Brick's little boat was not restroom equipped, we eventually had to excuse ourselves. He showed us a rear gate behind the school's service building that appears to be locked but can be opened easily by sliding it up on its hinged supports. He said he occasionally sees Ferncliffe students hanging out by the slough, but always avoided them lest they call the cops or sabotage his watery home. We assured him that we would keep mum about his presence.

Best news of all: Brick said he would be happy to buy snack items for me anytime I wanted. All I had to do was give him my list and the money.

Starvation may yet be averted!

Chapter 4

SUNDAY AT last!

An entire day without irksome classes. This school offers a 9 a.m. worship service in the legacy chapel, but attendance is not compulsory, and I hear only a handful of spiritual types (and/or suck-ups to Lumpwapht) show up.

Sharing a leisurely but meager breakfast with Ruby, we discussed the events of the preceding day.

"I'm worried about Brick sleeping on that dank boat," she remarked.

"I know. He must breathe his weight in mold spores every night. That couldn't be good for the guy."

"Winters here can be cold and rainy, Brenda. How will he ever cope?"

"Well, maybe he checks into homeless shelters on bad days."

"I think we should try to find him a job, an apartment, and a boyfriend."

"Good luck, Ruby. We're schoolgirls living in a glorified prison camp. How are we supposed to help him?"

"Well, we could try!"

"OK, some kind of job might be possible. But he may not want us messing around in his love life. Sure, I suppose there's someone on this planet who might be thrilled to meet Brick, but how are we supposed to sift through eight billion prospects to find him?"

"It shouldn't be so hard. Brick is pretty cute."

"Ruby, have you had your eyes checked lately? He's as homely as a toad and shorter than your average kindergartner."

"That's just your baggage as a white girl, Brenda. You should look past your prejudices to the person within."

"I'm not saying anything against Brick, Ruby. I'm just saying by the conventional standards of attractiveness, shared by many people of all races and creeds, Darnell Brickman falls a bit short."

"If he weren't gay, Brenda, I would go out with him in a minute. Would you?"

Me date a dwarf? I think not.

"Uh, he's a little old for me, Ruby. Damn, I really would like to give my sweat glands a rest today. I wonder if we're in for another scorcher?"

This whole business about boys may be moot in my case anyway. I have no intention of passing my retrograde DNA onto some pathetic next generation. As far as I'm concerned, I'm a walking genetic dead end. If some guy some day wants to hook up with me (which I doubt will happen), he'll be shooting into latex until the end of time (or my menopause–whichever comes first).

* * *

To promote domestic tranquility I decided to do my laundry in the school's coin-op machines. Ancient steam irons also were provided, but I skipped that step. I remember reading somewhere that wrinkled clothing can be slimming to one's silhouette. While I was waiting for the dryer to finish, Gianna came in with a big load and gave me the evil eye. I'm beginning to think my roommate may be somewhat off in the head.

When I got back to the room, Lauren deigned to speak to me: "You should be nicer to Gianna. I think she likes you."

"No, I believe she hates my guts."

"You're wrong there, Brenda. She's really stuck on you."

Profound incredulity greeted that statement. Recognizing a vicious mind-fuck when I heard one, I changed the subject.

"So how come you never speak to me, Lauren?"

"My boyfriend dumped me. I'm a mess."

"You broke up with your Modesto gangbanger?"

"Hey, that's my business. And quit hogging so much of the damn closet!"

Fortunately, my brother was coming to take me out to lunch, so I was able to escape that snake pit. A teacher's permission is not required for such excursions. You can leave with any adult relative as long as they show their I.D. at the front office and sign you out. Personally, I'll never regard Buford as an adult, but he passed muster with the Matron on duty.

Since my brother failed to win any football scholarships (not even to the J.C.), he decided to take a year off before starting college. He's working at a Bay Area brewery and developing quite a physique from lugging around 100-pound bags of barley malt. He could be the only Blatt in history with more muscles than flab. He says he likes the work and the pay isn't too bad, but he can no longer stomach beer as a beverage.

"Why's that?" I asked over Slamburgers at Stockton's one and only Twizzler Griddler (Buford's favorite burger chain).

"It's that damn fermentation smell, Brenda. It gets in your brain and don't let go. So I had to switch to vodka coolers."

"Isn't that a chick's drink?"

"Yeah, I guess. I'm thinking of wearing a skirt when I go out."

"What would Holly say?"

"She'd probably dig it."

Buford's latest GF had once regarded herself as a lesbian, but now had swung to the opposite extreme and was dating my brother.

"How come Holly didn't come with you today?" I asked.

"Stockton's supposed to have a good paint ball arena. I thought I'd give it a try this afternoon. Holly hates paint ball."

Somehow I knew my brother hadn't driven all the way out here just to see me.

"And how are our parents doing?" I asked. "Are they missing me dreadfully?"

"Not much sign of that, Brenda. Mom says she walks by our empty bedrooms and feels this immense sense of relief."

"She said that?"

"Yeah. She said she also likes the confidence that comes from knowing that when she opens the refrigerator the leftovers will still be there."

"What a bitch. She doesn't realize that I was the only thing keeping her from getting even fatter."

"I don't know, Brenda. She claims she's lost eight pounds since you left. She says she no longer feels competitive about eating all the groceries before they disappear."

* * *

My brother paid for my lunch and also slipped me two crisp $20 bills. He offered to take me paint-balling with him, but I declined. I learned the hard way that my size and sex make me a prime target for incoming splatters. The appeal of that "sport" eludes me. I suspect it must tap into male homoerotic ejaculation fantasies.

I had Buford drop me off in downtown Stockton. This area was once probably fairly bustling–in about 1925. Then businesses left, stores closed down, and half the buildings were torn down and replaced by nothing much. I walked around (sticking to the shady sides of the streets) and checked out a couple of junk stores. In a plaza-like space I came upon Brick sitting near an artificial waterfall that flowed into a shipping channel. His overturned hat had collected some coins and a couple of bills.

"Hi, Brenda," he said, looking up and smiling.

"Hi, Brick. How's business?"

"Kinda slow today. Too hot for tourists."

"You get tourists in Stockton?" I asked, plopping down beside him.

"Sometimes. On weekends we get day-trippers from the Bay Area."

"They must be frighteningly desperate for something to do."

"Stockton has its attractions."

"Oh? Where are they hiding them?"

"There are some nice bike rides along the waterfront if you're into that."

I wasn't, so I brought up the subject of employment.

"Ruby and I were thinking that perhaps you could get a job with Goodwill. You know–in one of their thrift stores."

Brick laughed. "Hey, I was working there last year. I was too short to man the cash register, so they stuck me in the back room to sort through the incoming stuff."

"Didn't you like it?" I asked.

"Kinda hard on my back. And it got pretty depressing sorting through people's castoffs all day. The stinky shoes were the worst. Not many cute guys in my department either."

"Did you quit?"

"No, I got my butt canned. Too many unexcused absences. The job made me depressed, so I'd have to drink, so then I'd miss work."

"That's too bad."

"It's OK, Brenda. I prefer being self-employed."

"Oh, right."

"This day isn't typical. Some days I make over $10 an hour sitting here."

"Don't you have any, you know, goals?'

"Goals, huh? Well, mostly I just want to get through the day without too much pain and suffering. How about you?"

"Me? I don't know, I have fantasies about going to New York someday."

"You should do that, Brenda. I think you'd fit right in with that sophisticated Manhattan crowd."

We looked up as a strolling Yuppie couple approached. "Can I take your picture?" asked the man, holding up his iPhone.

"Please do," replied Brick. "And I sure would appreciate a one-dollar donation."

The GF dropped four quarters into the hat, Brick put his arm around me, we both smiled, and the fellow snapped our photo.

"God bless you," called Brick as they sauntered away. He picked two quarters out of his hat. "Here's your share, Brenda."

"Oh, you keep it, Brick."

"No, girl. You earned it. You worked just as hard as I did for that sale."

* * *

Since Buford's $40 was burning a hole in my pocket, I took Brick out to dinner at a nearby Mexican restaurant that he recommended as "cheap and good." We both ordered the deluxe carnitas plate, which was excellent.

After his second beer, Brick got rather subdued. He confessed that bountiful Mexican meals always made him feel sad.

"Why's that?" I asked.

"Mexican food is so festive, it reminds me I have so little to celebrate."

"I know what you mean," I sighed.

"Love eludes me. That is my sorrow."

"You've never been in love, Brick?"

"Just the 24-hour variety. I think that counts more as lust."

"Have you ever thought of going out with another dwarf?"

"Not easy to do, Brenda. We little fellows tend to be excessively macho to compensate for our size. Not many seem willing to swing my way. Have you ever been in love?"

"Who me? Not likely."

"Well, you're still a kid. Your day will come."

"You actually think some guy's going to fall in love with me?"

"Sure, Brenda dear. Men like strong, magnetic gals."

"Ruby says she can see me as a biker chick riding with some outlaw motorcycle gang."

"Does that have any appeal?"

"Not really. I got overexposed to unrefined guys at my high school. I think they're creeps."

I ordered another beer for Brick, which was probably a mistake. He got even more morose and told me about the time he and his buddies crashed a stolen car.

"We rolled it. Like three or four times. Just missed a big oak tree which would have been the end of us for sure. This was in the middle of the night on a county road. Pretty deserted out there. Marty was driving and had that Audi going over a hundred. I kind of had a crush on him at the time. He was hurt the worst. They had to cut him out of the car. I rode with him in the ambulance. He was kind of panicking. He was all busted up and thinking he'd wrecked his body. You know, like his life was over. Like maybe he'd be stuck in a wheelchair and would have to have some attendant wipe his ass for him. So you know what I was thinking the whole ride to Modesto?"

"What, Brick?"

"That he'd walk out of that hospital all fixed up and fine, but I'd still be a dwarf for the rest of my life."

"And was he OK?"

"Yeah, pretty much. He got some girl pregnant and they moved to Visalia. He works painting houses like his dad."

"So you weren't hurt in the wreck?"

"Just bumps and bruises. None of us had buckled up, of course. Not the macho thing to do. I was bouncing around in that car like popcorn in a popper."

Chapter 5

I PHONED my mother this morning. I told her I hoped she and the leftovers would be very happy together.

"I hope you realize, Brenda, I said that to your brother in jest. Of course, we all miss you terribly."

"I can be packed and waiting by the curb in ten minutes."

"I have to go, darling. Do make an effort to fit in there. I know you'll succeed wonderfully if you just stick to it."

I feel nothing but a warm and abiding hatred for that woman.

At breakfast I told Ruby that Goodwill Industries was out as an employer for Brick. I also informed her that he preferred his present "self-employment" to any regular job.

"Darn, Brenda, if he doesn't want a job, then it will be tough to manage the nice apartment. We'll just have to fix him up with a boyfriend with money."

"And how do we do that?"

"I got it all figured out. We'll write him a nice personals ad and then screen the replies!"

Right. I can imagine that ad: "Homeless panhandler with drinking problem seeks handsome and generous sugar daddy of any race for committed relationship. Oh, did I mention I'm a dwarf?"

We had to drop the subject when Elaine sat down with her tray. Ruby lucked out and only got one roommate who hates her guts. The non-hater is Elaine, a junior like us who has sprouted to an impressive six feet four inches (and is still growing). She weighs about 100 pounds, so not many curves are encountered as you ascend the heights. She's kind of pretty in a tallish way, but has never had a date because boys are intimidated by her towering stature.

"Did you hear about the new girl who arrived last night?" inquired Elaine. "She's absolutely gorgeous."

"By Ferncliffe or Stockton standards?" asked Ruby.

"Neither," replied her roommate. "In New York, Paris, or Hollywood this girl would be a total knockout. She's amazing. I hear she's nice too."

"Impossible," I replied. "That combination is not humanly possible."

"Well, see for yourself," said Elaine. "Here she comes."

We tried not to stare as the person in question entered and walked over to the food line. OK, she was stupendously beautiful with a figure to die for. Big deal. Some people actually do win the looks lottery. Admittedly, very few score an ace in every category like this chick. Still, if you stripped her, you'd probably find a flaw or two—maybe a small mole somewhere or an unsightly toenail.

The girl got her meager breakfast, scanned the room with her stunning blue eyes, then walked over and sat down–right next to me. Naturally, I decided to ignore her. Right then a lovely translucent hand with flawlessly manicured nails invaded my personal space.

"Hello," said the creature. "My name is Marie Malencotti."

I shook the offered hand. Right: she gets a name that sounds like music; I get the fat girl's name from hell.

"Brenda Blatt," I replied. "That's Ruby and that's Elaine."

Greetings of varying warmth were exchanged. Just for the record I should note that she smelled as enticing as she looked. Like a field of wildflowers at dawn on a Tuscan hillside.

Marie sipped her orange juice and looked down at her tray. "Gosh," she said. "I hope I can eat all this food."

That did it. I officially hated her.

* * *

Lucky me: Marie appears to have the same class schedule as I do. She walked with me to every class and chatted me up like we were old pals. Turns out she's from Ventura, down on the coast north of L.A. Her parents shipped her up here because they object to her boyfriend–even though Rodney is the quarterback of the football team, made all-state in

197

hockey, and got early acceptance to Harvard.

"You're not pregnant are you?" I asked at one point.

Marie blushed in a manner that even I had to admit was exceedingly charming.

"Heavens no, Brenda. Rodney and I have taken the pledge. We're saving ourselves for marriage."

"Marriage to each other?"

"I hope so. Of course, one never knows if young love will endure. Rodney is nearly two years older than me. He's strikingly handsome and receives a great deal of attention from many girls."

Somehow I wouldn't have expected any less.

Speaking of inappropriate attention, I was publicly humiliated in Practicalities class when Mrs. Swengard upbraided me for looking like a "rumpled bed." I informed her that I had foresworn ironing as a frivolous waste of energy that was contributing to global warming. She replied that she would rather "fry on a barren planet" than go about in public looking like a slob. She, needless to say, is neat as a pin and probably irons her old lady panties and all of her other repulsive undergarments.

Mrs. Swengard then commended the new girl for looking so "eminently presentable" in her school uniform. As if Marie wouldn't look just as stylish and fetching dressed in a scavenged garbage bag.

* * *

Strange doings right before dinner. Lauren silently packed up her stuff and moved out. Five minutes later Marie arrived with her tasteful belongings. By then, I had claimed Lauren's abandoned space, so Marie got stuck with the narrow bed by the door. She didn't seem to mind.

"What a nice room!" she exclaimed. "Won't this be fun. Hello there, I'm Marie Malencotti."

Gianna blinked twice behind her thick glasses and shook Marie's hand.

"That's Gianna," I said. "She doesn't say much, but her eyes can burn holes in your flesh."

"Where, where's Lauren?" asked Gianna.

"Lauren has changed rooms. I believe she's in the other dormitory now. I know we'll all be such good friends. And where are you from, Gianna?"

"Uhmm, Paso Robles."

"Oh, that's not too far from me. I'm just down the coast a bit in Ventura. Well, I don't want to keep you from your studies."

"She wasn't studying," I volunteered. "She was staring full-time at me."

"No I wasn't," lied Gianna. "Want some help unpacking, Marie?"

"Oh, I think I can manage."

Marie kicked off her shoes and began putting away her things.

Now feet I had always regarded as these utilitarian, smelly appendages at the end of your legs that were best kept confined to shoes whenever possible.

Marie, I was shocked to observe, had dainty little feet that were nothing less than darling. We're talking feet that called out to be kissed, nuzzled, and caressed. All of a sudden I could see from where foot fetishists were coming. Who knew? Toes can be enchanting! Ankles can cause one nearly to swoon! Heels theoretically could be tongued and possibly sucked.

I sat down heavily on Lauren's bed and turned away to face the wall.

Is this how lesbianism began? Seduced by the feet? Were they the thin edge of the wedge? Did you start there and work your way up?

* * *

That evening Ruby and I sneaked out the back gate to visit Brick. He wasn't at his little boat, so we sat by the slough and watched the sun go down.

"Boy, that Marie has sure taken a shine to you," Ruby observed.

"Tell me about it. It's really unprecedented. Those types usually find me beneath contempt."

"I hear Lauren demanded to move, so the Lumpster asked for volunteers. Marie's hand shot up like a bullet."

"Were there any other volunteers?"

"What do you think?"

"No, huh? Well, at least Marie's nice to me; Lauren hated my guts. And I got a better bed out of the deal."

"Maybe she'll let you borrow some of her clothes."

"Ruby, you should know that I rarely appreciate sarcastic allusions to my weight."

"Sorry, Brenda. No offense intended."

"So, Ruby, I was wondering. What do you think about feet?"

"You mean feet versus meters? I think the metric system should take a flying leap."

"No, I mean human feet."

"Well, I'm glad I got two of them. Some people don't. Brick has fairly big feet I noticed for a little guy."

"Do you find feet attractive?"

"Not usually. You should see my mother's feet. What a disaster zone! Every time she wears sandals the whole neighborhood gags."

"I hear some people find feet to be, uh, erotic."

"Yeah, and a lot of those pervs get jobs in shoe stores. The reason that jerk of a clerk is taking so long to return with your size 9s in Moroccan brown is he's back in the stockroom masturbating like mad."

"Really?"

"It's a known fact."

"That's totally gross."

"Yeah, and a lot of those pervs specialize. Like some of them only get off on little kids' feet."

"Really?"

"Uh-huh. 'Course, those are the ones that should be dragged out and shot. So what's the deal about feet, Brenda?"

"Oh, nothing. I'm just trying to understand the many diverse aspects of human sexuality."

"Well, my advice is to stop thinking about feet and start concentrating on cock. That's what I hope to be handling soon."

I'll say one thing for ol' Ruby. She's certainly an optimist.

Chapter 6

IT'S A pleasure waking up in the morning when the first thing you see is Marie Malencotti. It's not just that she's pretty. The whole Malencotti package exudes cosmic harmony. All the diverse elements fit together perfectly, achieving some absolute ideal of beauty. It's such a pleasure to rest your eyes on any part of her. She really is an aesthetic feast for all the senses. Slumbering, she's a joy to observe, but when she opens those baby blues the entire room lights up with the force of her sunny personality. Preposterous as it may sound, my new roommate is touched with magic.

With such a dazzler in our midst you'd think Gianna would have switched to staring at Marie. Nope, I'm still the focus of her visual fixations. Gianna stares at me, I stare at Marie, and Marie smiles benignly at us both.

There are some drawbacks in having Ms. Malencotti amongst us. For one, I now feel radically inhibited in bingeing on snacks. Cheese curls really can't be stuffed into one's face with Marie looking on. (Fortunately, Heath bars still can be munched discreetly at night under the bedcovers.) Plus, I've had to retreat to the laundry room for some emergency ironing. And showering is now a daily necessity. Not to mention brushing after every meal. If only chilly fall would arrive soon, so I could cease sweating like a pig from every pore.

Marie makes a point of sitting with me at every meal. She and I met Ruby and Elaine at breakfast to go over their draft of Brick's personals ad. (We had to blab about Brick to those two to get their input, plus who could keep a secret from Marie?)

"Uh, you don't mention that he's short," I pointed out.

"We did by inference," explained Elaine. "Everyone knows that if you don't say he's tall or give an exact height, that means he's short."

"You have some expertise in this area, Elaine?" I asked.

"Elaine's big sister has been doing the personals thing for years," Ruby pointed out. "That's why I had her help me with the ad."

"And has your sister met anyone?" asked Marie.

"Just a bunch of creeps and losers," admitted Elaine. "There was this one guy who went off his meds right in the middle of dinner. He had to be subdued by the waiters."

I continued with my critique: "Nor do you mention anywhere that Brick is black."

"That's not really material," said Ruby, defensively. "We're living in a post-racial society now."

"But we do say that he enjoys the bustle of urban life," noted Elaine.

I had a few more nits to pick. "I'm not sure stating that he cherishes his 'live-aboard lifestyle' really conveys that he's homeless and residing on a salvaged hulk."

"Everyone knows there's some exaggeration in these ads," replied Elaine. "People read between the lines. We don't want him to sound like a total loser."

"I think it's fine," said Marie. "I'd be inclined to respond if I were a gay man."

"There you have it," said Ruby. "We'll put it up on Craigslist today."

"You have access to a computer?" I asked.

"Uh, we thought we'd use Marie's iPhone," said Ruby.

"No problem," smiled Marie. "I'm happy to help any way I can."

* * *

One of Mrs. Lumpwapht's toadies barged into Miss Bronkiel's Explorations class this afternoon looking for me. I got frog-marched over to Mrs. L's pleasantly cool office, where she chewed my ass big time.

"Mr. Ng is very upset!" exclaimed the Lumpster, red-faced. "He says you've threatened to kill him!"

"When? Where? How?" I demanded.

"Right here in the Expressions essay you wrote this morning," she replied, tossing the item in question down on her desk in front of me. "Your handwriting is execrable, but the evidence is clear. I'll not have members of my teaching staff threatened!"

"I didn't threaten anyone," I replied calmly. "I merely pointed out that when the revolution comes some teachers will be facing the firing squad. You'll note I didn't specify anyone in particular."

"That is totally unacceptable, Miss Blatt!"

"On the contrary, it is a historical fact. Nearly every revolution results in a purge of the intellectuals. Look at Stalin's Soviet Union and the Red Brigades in China. Mao's Great Leap Forward turned into a swift trip to the cemetery for millions. In Cambodia the Khmer Rouge killed everyone wearing eyeglasses. They figured they were the elites."

Mrs. Lumpwapht pushed up on her glasses. "There's not going to be a revolution here and no one's going to be purged."

"That's what the aristocrats thought in France in 1788. Actually, I don't think many of the teachers here have much to worry about. Not if the cadres are targeting the intellectuals."

"Your attitude is entirely unacceptable, Blatt. You will write a letter of apology to Mr. Ng and you will refrain from such outrages in the future. In addition, I am giving you a week of punishment duty in the cafeteria. You will report to Mrs. Castillo in the dishroom after dinner tonight."

"I thought Expressions class was intended to encourage the free expression of our opinions."

"Then you are misinformed, Blatt. It is to give you practice writing to prepare you for college–should any such institution have the misfortune of admitting you. Now get out of my office!"

I rose from her ritzy armchair and flounced out. One good thing about being heavy, you can really flounce when you try.

* * *

Everyone at dinner agreed that it was rotten of Mr. Ng to have gone straight to Lumpwapht without talking to me first.

"You were very brave to express your opinions so fearlessly," said Marie.

"Oh, I wasn't so brave," I admitted. "I was just trying to be outrageous in order to get expelled."

Marie looked shocked. "You want to leave us?!"

"Uh, well . . ." I stammered.

"Anyway, it's not going to work," said Ruby. "The Lumpster isn't going to give up your tuition for writing like a wacko. If she did that, we'd all be threatening to kill people in our essays."

"That's right," said Elaine. "Now if you actually murdered Mr. Ng, that would be a different story. You'd probably at least get suspended for that."

"I hope you don't leave our school," said Marie. "That would be too much to bear."

My fork froze in mid-flight. Could anyone actually have said something that nice to me?

I was thinking of sweet Marie when I located Mrs. Castillo in the dishroom. This was a hot, steamy, smelly, and noisy pit where a Mexican fellow was feeding plates into a rumbling dishwasher.

"You want me remove and stack the dishes as they come out of the machine?" I asked, hopefully.

"Naw, that's Luiz's job," she replied. "You wash those."

Mrs. Castillo pointed to triple stainless steel sinks piled high with blackened cooking pots and crusty metal trays from the steam tables.

"Uh, is there a machine to wash them?" I asked, desperately looking around.

"No machine," she replied. "Only you. And no slapdash 'cause Mrs. L she come in to inspect. Very picky lady!"

Thank God I'm assigned to shower in the evening. Two hours later–dripping with sweat and nearly dead from heat prostration–I stepped fully clothed into the shower with just the cold water blasting down on me.

The good news is I must have sweated off five pounds. Six more days in that Dishroom from Hell and I may be down to Marie's size.

* * *

Chafing has commenced. I'm starting to chafe badly from the heat in places you really don't want to chafe. Kind Marie noticed my plight and lent me some of her scented bath powder. I now smell just as nice as she does. Now, if I looked just as nice, my life would be complete. I wouldn't ask for another damn thing!

Mr. Ng didn't say much when I handed him my letter of apology this morning. In fact, he mumbled something totally unintelligible and looked away in embarrassment. I've decided he's too much of a weasel to murder. After the revolution he will be assigned to permanent pots and pans duty in the dishroom.

Today's essay topic was "Why it Is Important To Respect your Teachers." That seemed a bit self-serving, so instead I wrote my 300 words on cheese curls. I believe I made a very strong case that they as close as we are ever likely to come to the Ideal Food.

Cheese curls really are remarkable. They deliver this delectable cheesy and salty crunch to your mouth, then melt away to nothingness. It's a miracle! They must be 99% pure air and therefore virtually calorie-free. You can tote giant grocery bags full of them home from the store and your arms never get tired because they're so light. On a cost-per-pound basis they're much cheaper than boring, over-priced foodstuffs like broccoli and lima beans. Even infants or toothless old people can enjoy them. Best of all, cheese curls are a delicious warm-up to the wonderfully smooth chocolate snap of a Heath bar. Truly, a snack pairing made in heaven!

Anyway, I went on like that for my full 300 words, remembering to conclude: "And that's why I honor and respect any teacher who takes the time to enjoy a quick, energizing snack of wholesome cheese curls."

I expect that will get me back in Ng's good graces. God knows I don't want to upset my pal Marie by getting expelled from her life.

* * *

By lunch today a total of two responses had come in on Marie's iPhone to Brick's ad. Neither looked promising, although one fellow had attached a semi-blurry close-up view of his erection. We passed around the phone and studied the photo over our chicken salad (made with turkey because it's cheaper).

"I'd say he's adequately equipped," commented Ruby. "He's got everything I'd need."

"It must be weird being a boy," said Elaine. "I'd be embarrassed having such a thing sprouting from my body."

"Breasts can be a burden too," I said, adjusting a chafing bra strap.

"That's true," agreed Ruby and Elaine, both dramatically under-burdened.

"It's pretty tacky sending a photo of your anatomy to strangers," said Marie, the only member of our group whose anatomy people would stand in line to view. "I say he goes in the reject pile."

"Agreed," I said. "May he be forever consigned to lonely self-abuse."

"You know I've been reading the student handbook," Marie went on.

"Always a sure cure for cheerfulness," I noted.

She smiled. "It says we can invite a guest to dinner on the third Friday of the month."

"As long as we fork over an extra eight bucks," interjected Ruby.

"I believe this Friday is the third one of the month," continued Marie. "We could invite Brick and show him all the replies we've received."

"That's not a bad idea," said Ruby.

"We could chip in $2 each," added Elaine. "That makes it pretty cheap."

"It would be worth it just to see the look on the Lumpster's face," said Ruby.

"Well, you'll have to invite him, Ruby," I said. "I have torture duty again in the dishroom."

"I feel bad that you got punished," said Marie. "Would you like me to help you?"

Marie Malencotti slaving away in the dishroom? The world could never tolerate such an abomination.

"That's OK, Marie," I replied. "I appreciate the offer, but the Lumpster would find out and we'd both get in trouble."

"At least make them give you rubber gloves," she replied. "You don't want to wreck your nice hands."

I know that sounded like sarcasm, but it was just Marie being her lovely sincere self.

Chapter 7

OK, I'M not saying this place is Greenwich Village on the slough, but it's kind of nice getting away from Hayward, my hateful classmates, and my domineering mother and her diverse neuroses. I could do without the dishroom slaving, but Luiz finished early last night and gave me a hand with the pans. He's kind of cute (albeit muy short), and I'm known for having a weakness for Mexican guys. I'd be surprised if he's much older than 20. We were kind of flirting over the suds, but I expect I'm not his type. At least he sweats just as freely as I do. So we have one thing in common.

Such is the power of my pen: When I came into Expressions class this morning, I noticed a half-eaten bag of cheese curls on the shelf behind Mr. Ng's desk. Being a foreign-born person, it is likely that he had never before experienced that treat. What a world of flavor I've opened up to him! I trust he'll remember that when grading time rolls around (not that I care).

As a break from yesterday's downer topic, today's theme was "My Ideal Mate." Remembering that I would be reading my output in front of the class, I wrote that my ideal man was likely incarcerated at present in a state or federal penitentiary. I said that he rode a large, nine-cylinder H-D motorcycle, shaved his head, and preferred to go shirtless except for his aromatic leather vest heavily draped with chains. I said he had one glass eye (his original having been gouged out in a gang fight), a replacement brass nose (ditto), and a full set of diamond and gold grillwork on his teeth. He never left home without strapping on his Glock 20 Gen4 semi-automatic pistol and his concealed ankle dagger. He could never fly in an airplane because he had too many piercings and studs to go through the metal detectors at security checkpoints. On the center of his manly chest was tattooed a full-color life-size portrait of me, surmounted by the words "Brenda [heart] Forever!" I went on in this vein for another 275 words, concluding that although he preferred to remain wild and free, my ideal mate occasionally worked as the western regional sales manager for Heath candy bars. And, yes, he could bring home as many free samples as desired.

After Vistas class (where we were still mired in *Bastard's Child*), Miss Porteau took me aside to tell me I was now the talk of the teachers' lounge. Apparently Mr. Ng had blabbed to all and sundry about my incendiary essay.

"It was just a joke," I assured her.

"I wasn't worried," she replied, looking as usual like she was jonesing for a cigarette. "I like your spirit, girl. I sometimes wonder if all of my students have been lobotomized or just me."

"Yeah, I know the feeling. Well, I better go. Marie's waiting."

"Right. That Marie is an interesting case. We should discuss her sometime."

"Fine. I'd love to."

What do you suppose Miss Porteau meant by that? It does strike me as odd that although Marie has been exiled against her will from her Ivy-bound stud, she doesn't appear to hear from the dude. Could golden boy Rodney be so stuck up he's blown her off?

I guess all of Ferncliffe must have heard about my essay and subsequent Lumpster confrontation. Four girls I don't even know gave me thumbs-up signs in the halls today. Of course, I may be scoring some status points by walking to class with the one and only supreme knockout in the school.

* * *

By dinner we had heard from three more potential Love Mates for Brick. One was a chick who must have struck out so many times she was now mining across the aisle. Elaine was all for leaving her in, but we blackballed her on a three-to-one vote. The other two prospects sounded OK, although one guy lives in San Francisco, which is pretty far to go to get laid. You also wonder why his net is stretching out this far, since the last time I heard there was no shortage of gay guys in S.F.

"I bet he's short," speculated Ruby. "He doesn't state his height and he's a cake decorator. That's a field dominated by short guys."

"Since when?" I asked.

"Since always, Brenda. It's a known fact. Short guys are fixated on the birthday parties they never got invited to."

"Why didn't they get invited?" asked Marie.

"Because the taller kids were more popular."

"Well, I'm tall," noted Elaine. "And I didn't get invited to many parties."

"We're dealing with the extremes here," replied Ruby. "The kids at the height extremes always get excluded. So short guys want to decorate cakes."

"Not Tom Cruise," Elaine pointed out. "He became an actor."

"But how do we know what Tom does in his spare time?" replied her roommate.

206

"And what do the excluded girls want?" Marie asked.

"Good question," I said. "So, Elaine, what do you want to be when you grow up?"

She gave it some thought. "I don't know. Maybe join the Army. See the world."

"Ah-hah, just as I thought," said Ruby.

"And that proves what?" I asked.

"Think about it," said Ruby. "What do kids do at birthday parties? They play shoot-em-up video games!"

More sweaty flirting with Luiz after dinner in the dishroom. I like that he's not afraid to get right next to me at the sinks. The guy looks pretty sexy too in his long black gloves, rubber apron, and soiled wife-beater t-shirt. He works this crummy job, then toils half the night in Lodi making donuts.

"How come you work so hard?" I asked him.

"I got plans, Brenda. I want to get a taco truck and then open a bak-ery."

"What kind of bakery?"

"The usual. You know: galletas, empanadas, pan de huevos, semitas, polvorones."

"Any cakes?"

"Of course."

"I don't suppose you decorate cakes?"

"How did you know? I'm taking a class in that right now at the J.C."

Too bad. More proof of Ruby's short-guy theory, plus it means I can never marry Luiz. No way could I wed a guy who owns a bakery. I'd wind up weighing 900 pounds and have to be carted around on a forklift. Still, if he decided to make a grab for me across the dishwater I probably wouldn't scream that loud.

* * *

Not that I was looking, but I got to see Marie naked when she slipped off her robe after returning from the shower this morning. I was so wrong in my original assessment of her. She is without flaws from head to (you'll pardon the expression) feet. She's female perfection come to life. Skin like soft pink cheese, curves shaped by God when he was on some divine aesthetic high. Totally devoid of imperfections down to the sub-atomic level.

If I had her body I wouldn't be languishing in some prison school in Stockton. I'd be modeling lingerie for $2,000 an hour. I'd be dating movie stars and jetting to Paris with handsome playboys. I'd be peddling my own line of pricey lounge wear on the Home Shopping Network.

Marie's as nice as they come, but I suspect it's bad for my self-image to be rooming with someone that gorgeous. It's like being shrunk down to doll size and having to shack up with Barbie. One can't help but compare and beat oneself up for falling so short. If I weren't an inch or two taller than her (big deal) and perhaps a tiny bit smarter (who cares?), I'd be paralyzed with despair.

If I become a raging lesbian/foot fetishist, we all know who'll be responsible. In the meantime, I'm hoping to see her naked again soon. It's a very stimulating way to start your day. Even Gianna momentarily unlocked from me to glance her way.

Ruby informed me at breakfast that Brick has accepted our invitation to dinner tonight. He says he's going to get a haircut, shower at the Salvation Army, and wear his best clothes. We're keeping him in the dark about our personals campaign so he won't chicken out.

Today's Expressions theme was "How I Would Solve the Problem of Global Warming." Since ours is the generation that will be frying in the heat, blowing away in the storms, and drowning in the rising seas, I gave it my best shot. I wrote that it was useless to expect people to change or dial back their consumption mania. And corporations made their profits selling stuff, not reminding us to conserve. Therefore, scientists should get to work right now tinkering with our DNA. Future generations of humans should be at least 90 percent smaller. That way one cow could feed a whole town for a month. One house could be converted into a hundred apartments. People could still drive their now toy-sized cars and watch their tiny, big-screen TVs. Of course, some other species would have to be downsized too so we don't get menaced by rats or carried off by hawks. And while those brainy Ph.D.s were tinkering, they could take a big load off Mother Earth by switching off the genes that make people fat.

* * *

Brick, who lacks a watch, was 20 minutes late for dinner. I was beyond ravenous when he finally showed. All 150+ necks in the room swiveled as one when he made his entrance dressed in a fluorescent lime-green suit (with lapels sized like elephant ears), tangerine silk shirt, and jumbo red and orange polka-dot bow tie. His gleaming golden shoes clicked like tap shoes when he walked.

"Well, don't you look nice," said Ruby, as we approached the depleted food offerings.

"I hope this look isn't too flamboyant," he whispered. "It's my old outfit from when I used to be a magician's assistant."

"Where'd you work?" asked Elaine, "Las Vegas?"

"No. Melvin wasn't much of a magician. We mostly worked rest homes and birthday parties."

Ruby's eyebrows shot up. "Was he a tall magician?" she asked.

"Quite the contrary, Ruby. He was not much taller than me."

"How interesting," she replied, flashing us an I-told-you-so smile.

"That will be eight dollars in cash," announced the head server, scrutinizing Brick with distaste.

Marie handed over our wad of ones.

"That looks interesting," said Brick, eyeing the steam table. "What is it?"

"Fish pods," I replied. "It's like they started out to make fish sticks, but the machine ran amok."

"These are cod croquettes," corrected the server, dumping a single pod on Brick's plate.

"It looks delicious," he lied.

Everyone continued to stare as we carried our trays over to our usual spot at the end of one of the long tables. Like the gentleman he is Brick set down his tray and held out the seats for each of us in turn.

"I don't know where to start first," said Brick, unfolding his paper napkin and contemplating his lonely fish pod and sloppy mounds of mashed squash and canned corn.

"I try to eat with my eyes closed," I said. "It goes down easier that way."

"You girls are so nice to invite me," he said. "I never expected to see the inside of this school."

"Neither did we," commented Ruby. "But we're trying to make the best of it."

"Ruby's making the best of it better than me," I observed.

"Hardly," she replied. "Compared to me, Brenda is pinching herself with disbelief that she's lucky enough to be here."

"You're both in total Ferncliffe bliss compared to me," said Elaine.

"Oh, I don't know," said Marie. "It's not so bad. I've made some wonderful friends here."

Believe it or not, she was looking straight at me when she said that.

So what could I do but return her warm smile?

Brick looked a bit embarrassed when we announced that we had found six hot guys for him to date via a Craigslist personals ad. Marie handed him her phone so he could read the text of his ad.

"Well, that sounds a bit like me–sort of," he said. "I notice you didn't mention that I was on the short side."

"That was implied," said Elaine. "You have to be subtle in these ads."

"I guess," said Brick, reading through the six winning responses. "Yes, these fellows sound most interesting. Wow, one's a cake decorator. I've always been interested in that."

"Really?" said Ruby. "How interesting."

"Which one do you want to meet first?" asked Elaine.

Brick gave it some thought. "Does your phone have a camera?" he asked.

"Sure," replied Marie.

"Then why don't we take my picture and send it to the fellows?" said Brick. "I'll try meeting all the ones who are still interested."

We agree that sounded like a sensible plan. I suggested we take a photo of Brick sitting at the table, but he preferred a shot of him standing between Ruby and me. Thankfully, we managed to exclude from the shot our resident giantess Elaine. Next to her Brick might have looked even more poignantly diminutive.

As we were returning to our seats, we were intercepted by the Lumpster.

"Good evening, girls," she said. "I see you have invited a guest."

"Mrs. Lumpwapht, this is our friend Darnell Brickman," I said.

"That's Lom-waft, Miss Blatt. How do you do, Mr. Brickman?"

"Uh, fine. It's nice to meet you."

"And what is your connection to our girls?" she asked.

"He's an old friend of our family," I replied. "Darnell used to study under my father at Hayward State."

"How nice," said the Lumpster. "And what is your academic area, Mr. Brickman?"

"Urban economics," he replied. "I do field investigations into the plight of the homeless."

"Fascinating," she replied, smiling her fake smile. "How rewarding that must be for you. And are you going on from here to a costume party?"

"No, I always dress like this," he replied.

"Do you?" she said, her eyebrows rising. "And why, may I ask, is that?"

"I like a festive look, Mrs. Lumpwapht. I say if you can't be big, make a big impression."

Smart. And all these years I've been trying to do just the opposite. I'm a big person trying to make a small impression. Dumb.

"Oh, Mrs. Lumpwapht," I said, pronouncing her name correctly. "Since we're entertaining Mr. Brickman, may I be excused from the dishroom this evening."

"Certainly not, Blatt."

I didn't expect so, but it was worth a shot.

Chapter 8

MORE MARIE Malencotti nudity this morning. I'm hoping I will become inured to that sight and it will soon become very boring (as it is said to be for married people). Perhaps I'll make a study of it to see how long this process of conditioning requires. Odd that she has the same parts as I do, but mine disgust me.

Marie and I chat a lot, but I haven't found out much about her. Her father is a noted chef and her mother's a decorator. No siblings. Beyond that, she's pretty much a blank. Whereas, she's heard the full story of every humiliation I've suffered since age three. How boring that must be for her. I should learn to clam up.

My new Let 'Er Rip essay style got a warm reception in Expressions class today. I wasn't handed back my "firing squad" essay to read, as I expect Mrs. Lumpwapht is keeping it as evidence in case any of the teachers (or her) turn up with a knife in their back. But my classmates laughed throughout at the description of my ideal mate. And my solution to global warming sparked over 30 minutes of comment and debate. I hope Mr. Ng appreciates how I'm trying to make his class less boring.

Speaking of which, Marie's essays were well-written, but a bit on the dry side. No one offered much criticism, though, because she's so beautiful. Her ideal love mate sounded suspiciously like that indifferent dude Rodney. Had she specified a fat female, I might have signed up right then for Lesbianism 101.

* * *

It's the weekend so, of course, I get assaulted by cotue (Curse Of The Unfertilized Egg). Some girls breeze through their periods, but for me it's like a multi-day enrollment in a Mississippi chain gang: cramps, nausea, headache, fatigue, aches, etc. As a large person I may suffer more because I have more body volume to feel sick in. I hemorrhage like a Baghdad bombing victim, but God forbid you should want to flush anything. Our amateur Christian plumbing is not up to snuff, and *nothing* from the personal products aisle is permitted in the Lumpster's feeble toilets. Last year I'm told they had a sewage blockage that nearly plugged up the entire neighborhood.

At dinner I could barely gag down tonight's gray fatty/gristly meat substance.

"You're looking kind of listless, Brenda," observed Elaine.

"She's having her period, poor thing," said Marie, patting my hand.

"All this suffering is stupid," I groaned. "I'm never going to have any babies, so what's the point? I say give me a pill to flush the whole business out for good."

"You don't know that for sure," said Ruby. "You'll get married and then I bet you'll want to start a family."

"That's right," said Marie.

"You are both so wrong," I replied.

"I don't see why this fertility business has to start so young," said Elaine. "How many girls our age want to get pregnant?"

"Pretty close to zero," I said. "Ninety-nine percent of us are terrified of the idea."

"That's true," said Ruby. "There should be a gene that gets activated when a diamond ring is slipped on your finger."

"If guys bled like this every month," I said, "Ten thousand scientists would be working right now on a solution. Hell, I bet there'd be an Apple app that switches off menses with a simple swipe of the screen."

"Dream on," said Elaine.

"Speaking of guys," said Ruby, "have we heard back from any of Brick's prospects?"

"Not yet," said Marie.

"I hope they all don't flake out on him," said Elaine.

"I'm sure they won't," replied Ruby. "He looked so cute in that photo."

* * *

Four days later. I'm back from the planet Sickasadog. I thought the last two nights in the dishroom were going to finish me off for good. Thank God I'm finally done with that, though I'll miss Luiz, who successfully resisted the urge to lay a rubber glove on me. It probably didn't help my cause when I threw up on the floor Sunday night. Few guys find projectile heaves of stinky vomit to be much of a turn-on.

The big news is Miss Porteau is gone. The Lumpster announced on Monday that she had resigned to "spend more time with her family." What a transparent lie. The story I heard was some parents had complained about our being assigned "obscene books," plus she had been caught one too many times sneaking smokes on campus. So Mrs. Lumpwapht herself is teaching Vistas until a new teacher can be found. (A.S.A.P., we're all praying.) So our only hip teacher got canned, and I never had a chance to talk to her about Marie. Our copies of *Bastard's Child* were confiscated, and we are now mired in *The Mill on the Floss*. Or is it, *The Floss on the Mill?* I forget.

Two guys are still hot to go out with Brick, even after seeing his photo. They are the S.F. cake decorator and a house-builder in Lodi named Iilivi Ittiwangi. I'm not sure what nationality that is. Maybe Martian. Ruby feels it's a good omen that his last name contains the word "wang." I fear that girl is obsessed with you know what.

At dinner tonight Marie suggested that we get to work improving our place in the school social hierarchy.

"Why bother? I replied. "I'm fine being a social outcast."

"In any gathering of humans greater than one," said Marie, "there's always a pecking order. We should make sure we're at the top in this school."

"And how do we do that?" asked Elaine.

"I've been giving it some thought," said Marie. "I propose we start a sorority. An elite sorority with membership by invitation only."

"You need to re-read your student handbook, honey," I said. "All sororities and such organizations are explicitly banned."

"We'll make it top secret," said Marie, lowering her voice. "Everyone will know about it, of course, but nothing will be written down. There won't be a shred of evidence anywhere that it exists."

"So how would we work it?" whispered Elaine.

"We could start with six members," said Marie. "Then, once a month, two more girls would be invited to join."

"Well, I'm sure you'd never get around to inviting me," I sighed.

"On the contrary," said Marie. "You'll be our president."

"What!" I gasped.

"Marie, I think you should be president," said Ruby. "You're naturally the most popular and you'd give us instant prestige."

"No," replied Marie. "Brenda is the most forceful personality in the school. I could sense that from my first day here. She can be president and I'll be chair of the activities committee. Ruby can be vice president and Elaine can head up the membership committee. The first two girls we recruit will just be members."

"We'll need a name," said Ruby. "Should we go with Greek letters?"

"Aw, nobody knows Greek any more," Elaine pointed out.

"My brother knows some," I said. "He's been wearing an 'I Phelta Thi' sweatshirt for years."

"That's cute," said Marie. "I was thinking of The Arcadians. Arcadia is a region of Greece."

"Yeah," said Elaine. "I like that: The Arcadians. It sounds mysterious, yet kinda exclusive and classy."

"You don't think The Ferncliffians might be better?" suggested Ruby.

"Get real," I said. "Nobody would want to join a secret society with a name that lame."

"Then we're all agreed?" asked Marie.

"Agreed!" we whispered.

Wow, president of The Arcadians and I'm only 16. Have I taken a sudden turn toward social acceptance and veneration by my peers?

* * *

To get the gossip mill going about our secret sorority, Ruby and Elaine informed their hateful roommate Alicia that she could forget about being invited to join The Arcadians. The next morning I broke the same news to Gianna, who blinked and said, "The only thing you should be president of is the Stinkarians. Or the Fat Slobbians."

Resisting an urge to throttle her, I replied, "If you're thinking of applying for a transfer out of this room, that's fine with Marie and me."

"Marie is a fake and a phony."

"She's been nothing but nice to you, Gianna–as have I. What's your problem, girl?"

"I don't have any problems, Brenda. You're the one with the problems."

"So quit watching my every move!"

"I don't know why you imagine I'd want to look at you," she said, staring at me with her usual intensity. "Because I don't."

No doubt about, the girl is seriously deranged.

Just then Marie returned from the shower, and I watched her put on her makeup. She doesn't use much: just some mascara and a kiss of lipstick in a faint but flattering hue. I asked her how come she skipped the eyeliner, blusher, eye shadow, etc.

"Oh, I think all that looks so fake," she replied. "Especially on girls our age. Blatant eye shadow is the kiss of death if you ask me. I expect I'll be piling it on, though, when I get old and desperate like my mother. It must be depressing looking in the mirror when you're 46."

"Or sometimes even when you're 16," I pointed out.

Marie's smile telegraphed sympathy and encouragement. "We should go to Macy's and find you some decent lipstick."

"Lipstick on me looks like the rear view of a baboon."

"Nonsense, Brenda. It's all a matter of picking the right shade. Don't you think so, Gianna?"

"I think Brenda's right," said Gianna. "She'd look like a baboon's butt. For sure!"

I thought of Tiger Wood's angry wife and my golf clubs in the closet. If Gianna's body washed up in the slough, do you suppose they'd have any way of tracing the imprints of a nine iron on her skull back to me?

* * *

Brick has a date tomorrow night. I got the hot news when I was picking up a large snacks order from him. Our sorority caper has elevated my anxiety level, and when I get anxious I get hungry. Gianna may be right; the only organization I may be worthy of heading is the Baboon chapter of the Fat Slobbians. I'm really not sure I'm capable of being at the center of social attention. Out here on the fringe may be lonely, but at least it's semi-comfortable.

Back to Brick. Figuring a BF in Lodi beats one in distant S.F., he is going out first with the oddly named house-builder. One of Brick's regular customers gave him a pre-paid cell phone so he could arrange the hook-up. He and Iilivi are meeting in downtown Stockton, and going out for drinks and dinner at the Mexican restaurant.

"How does he sound?" I asked.

"Uh, nice, I guess."

"Does he have an accent? His name sounds African."

"No, I'm pretty sure he's a white guy. I can do that, but I usually prefer a dab or two of color."

"I know what you mean. White guys can be so, uh, white."

"I'm kind of nervous, Brenda."

"Just remember, Brick, you have absolutely nothing to lose—especially if you make him pick up the tab. It's always a crap-shoot, and if you don't hit it off, it's no reflection on you."

"I suppose so. If this works out, Brenda, maybe Iilivi will have a friend for you. We could double-date sometime."

"Sure. Maybe."

And maybe I'll catch a virus that will cause me to lose 100 pounds. Or a truck will run me over and while the plastic surgeons are rebuilding my face, they'll slip up and render me beautiful.

Meanwhile, I am rekindling my love affair with cheese curls.

* * *

Another lousy topic in Expressions today: "Twenty-five Most Important Reasons I'm Grateful for My Parents." I'm really letting down the team this week, what with me being OTR/OTL (on the rag/out to lunch) and topics straight out of the *Girl Scout Handbook*. By reason number five I had crossed over into negative territory: "I'm grateful that my parents aren't boozers and seldom blow the mortgage money on meth. Reason Six: I appreciate that to my knowledge my parents have never committed a brutal homicide." And so on.

Things were more interesting in Behaviors class where Mrs. Goldbline had us doing more role-playing. Today we were discussing with our "best friend" the fact that she was now dating our ex-boyfriend. Kind of a stretch for me since I have neither. Mrs. G was trying to demonstrate how we can deal with such issues without resorting to guns or knives. Considering the difficulty I'll have in ever scraping up a BF, I expect any slut he's two-timing me with will be in for a very bad time. Mayhem of a shockingly grizzly sort will be required.

My profile is definitely on the rise here. Lots of girls I don't even know are saying hi to me in the halls. And two girls came up to us at lunch today and whispered that they'd like to be considered for membership. They seemed nice, but they got nixed by Elaine for being "low status" sophomores. To keep The Arcadians exclusive we have to restrict membership to juniors and seniors. The plan is we'll each nominate two girls and then thrash out amongst ourselves who gets the coveted invitations.

So far, I'm finding it much easier to think of girls I don't want than any that I do. All I require is that they be nice, fairly unattractive, and defer to me in every way. Should they also revere me as their personal god and master, so much the better.

Chapter 9

AFTER LUNCH on Saturday Marie and I sneaked out the back way. A cab picked us up in the supermarket parking lot and took us to Stockton's largest mall. Marie paid with the credit card her parents gave her in partial compensation for being separated from her friends, banished from Rodney, and exiled to Stockton.

Marie bought some pantyhose for herself and three bras and a tube of lipstick for me. She said that my bra looked like something that had been liberated from a North Korean peasant. So now my tits are getting acquainted with the concept of lace. The lipstick was a tougher purchase since we were confronted with a bewildering blizzard of brands and shades.

"How come there are so many colors?" I asked.

"Because beauty is a very high calling," replied Marie. "Great artists are employed without regard to expense. That's why you will find the most subtle colors on earth right here in the lipstick department. Reds and pinks that no eye could imagine just a few short years ago. Even this far from Paris a woman has hope that she can find the perfect complement to her skin, bone structure, and coloring."

Easier said than done in my case.

After a desperate search, assisted by several overly made-up (if you ask me) salesgirls, we settled on a peachy coral. Only $85.00 plus tax. Marie handed over her credit card without flinching.

"You sure you want to spend this much?" I asked. "My mother buys her lipstick at the dollar store."

Marie stifled a shudder. "That's OK, Brenda. I think our choice is perfect for you."

I sneaked another quick glance in a mirror–never in short supply in the makeup department. A little unnaturally festive if you ask me, but I suppose I could get used to it. Way, way better than the sultry reds we had tried, which made me look like slutty trailer trash of the very dimmest sort.

Speaking of which, while we had a late afternoon snack in the mall food court several obnoxious louts tried to hit on Marie. Why is it that the cute guys smile shyly and walk on by, while the repellent lowlifes pull up a chair and grunt out the tritest pick-up lines? What makes these twerps imagine that someone like Marie would deign to have anything to do with them? And why, when she politely rebuffs them, do they look at me and sneer, "Oh, I get it. A couple of carpet munchers."? As if only confirmed lesbians would be able to resist their charms. In short, why are guys so incredibly stupid? Are their tiny, deformed brains so pickled in testosterone that they are incapable of grasping their own repulsiveness?

Sometimes it amazes me that the human race didn't die out eons ago. What sustained it?

Probably all those invading hordes raping the natives. Many, many of their descendants wound up living in Stockton.

* * *

My phone rang absurdly early Sunday morning.

"Hi, Brenda," said a familiar voice. "How's the diet going?"

"Grandma, it's barely six. Did someone die?"

"Not that I heard. When you get to be my age, Brenda, you'll regret all those hours you wasted in idle sleep."

"If you say so. But right now I'd like to enjoy them. What do you want?"

"I hear you're getting along great up there now."

"What makes you say that?"

"Well, you stopped calling your parents and begging to leave."

"I'm resigned, Grandma. I'm like those intellectuals in China hoeing the rice paddies during the Cultural Revolution. I've given in to my fate."

"Don't knock Communism, Brenda. It kept us all in ham sandwiches. I hear you're doing well in your classes and making lots of new friends."

"You're remarkably ill-informed, Grandma. Whom have you been talking to?"

"I get my reports. After all, I'm the party paying the bills."

"A tremendous waste of my inheritance. I hope you don't blow all your bucks imprisoning me in Stockton."

"I have never appreciated your attitude, Brenda. If you expect to inherit anything from me, you'll have to shape up. And slim down. What is your present exact weight? And don't lie."

"I'm tipping the scales at an even 532 pounds these days, Grandma. Far from a world's record, but substantially stout even for me. Barnum and Bailey are desperate for me to join their circus, but only if I also grow a beard."

"Liar. I hear you lost seven pounds since you got there and are down to 216 pounds."

"Are you spying on me, Grandma?"

"I just called to say keep up the good work, Brenda dear. I think there's a distinct possibility that some day soon I might be proud of my only granddaughter."

"I wouldn't count on it, Grandma. I just started injecting meth. It's wonderfully stimulating to the libido."

"I don't know where you got your weird sense of humor, Brenda. It must be from your mother's side."

"I was switched at birth in the hospital, Granny. My real parents are wanted by the feds in 15 states. They ditched me there and stole your precious little grandchild to sell on the black market."

"Well, Brenda dear, that's as likely an explanation as any. Talk to you soon. And stay away from those snacks!"

* * *

Ruby scouted the premises after breakfast and reported there was no sign of Brick by his little boat. Possibly good news, but we'll have to wait and see.

I'm still digging my new bra. Much more comfortable, plus it elevates both your tits and your mood–not to mention your perceived taste. I feel now that I was wandering unnecessarily in the wilderness bra-wise for many years. Naturally, I blame my mother.

Marie clipped off some of my brown shag and stuck me in her hot rollers for a while. I now have glam hair to go with my peachy coral lips and renovated bust line. It's all gilding the fat lily if you ask me, but I've been getting some compliments. Fortunately, the blazing temps have backed off slightly, so I no longer look like Miss Steamy Sweatbox all the time. My new industrial deodorant (formulated originally for steel workers stoking blast furnaces) also seems to be working.

After dinner Ruby and I sneaked out the back way. We found Brick on the bank by his little boat. He was grilling a sausage with a propane torch.

"Hi, guys," he said. "Wow, Brenda, what have you done to yourself?"

"She got a make-over by Marie," volunteered Ruby. "I want her to do me next."

Another impossible mountain for Marie to climb, I thought. I said, "You like this look?"

"It's very becoming," replied Brick. "Care for a hobo snack?"

Ruby demurred, but I accepted. Carcinogenic to be sure, but very tasty. While I munched, I told Brick to quit stalling and spill.

"He seems pretty nice," Brick admitted.

"You spent the night at his place?" Ruby asked.

"Yeah, I did."

"So what's he like?" I demanded. "We want details."

"Uh, he's quite a bit older than me. Mid-thirties I guess. On the tall side. Right around six feet. Very, very pale like that white asparagus they grow in the dark. Says he can't tan, just burns."

"Did he say why he has such an unusual name?" asked Ruby.

"He said he'd explain that after we got to know each other better."

"Where does he live?" I asked.

"Out in the delta. Has a nice piece of waterfront property. Used to be a prune orchard. Looks to be your normal guy, but he has a very unusual home."

"How so?" I asked.

"He lives in a dog house."

"Come again?"

"He lives in this cute house that's in the shape of a dog. It's sort of like the Sphinx in Egypt. The body is kind of rounded like a loaf of bread, then there's this dog head sticking up in the front. It's got two little crunched-in front paws, and the outlines of the back paws are molded into the sides. You enter through this wee door under the head. There's a bigger door in the back under the tail. It's, uh, very unique."

"Is it big like the Sphinx?" asked Ruby.

"Not hardly," replied Brick. "I'd say it's about eight feet wide and maybe 20 feet long–not counting the overhang of the dog head."

"It's the size of a trailer!" I exclaimed.

"Yeah, pretty much. You walk into this petite living room. In the back is a galley kitchen on one side and a weensy closet and bathroom on the other side. The bedroom is up a ladder in the head."

"So you spent the night inside a dog's head!" I exclaimed.

"A pug's head to be specific," replied Brick. "You can also have it painted to look like a Boston terrier or a puggle."

"What's a puggle?" asked Ruby.

"That's a cross between a pug and a beagle," he said. "His house is the prototype. Iilivi is all set to start making them out of fiberglass. Cost him a fortune to get the molds made. He's already got a few on order. He'll build them in an old barn on his land and deliver them by flatbed truck."

"There are people who want to live in a dog-shaped house?" I asked, incredulous.

"I guess so, Brenda. Different strokes for different folks."

"Sounds kind of pinched and dank," said Ruby.

"I don't know, Ruby. It felt pretty big compared to my boat."

"So would your average squirrel's nest," I said. "Does it have any windows?"

"A few, but most of the light comes in through crank-up skylights. He's got two round stained-glass windows in the dog's eyes. The morning light streams in and bathes you in a rich golden glow. Kind of makes for a romantic feeling, if you know what I mean."

"That is beyond weird," I commented. "Speaking of which, isn't it a little strange to sleep with someone you just met?"

"You'd think it would be, Brenda, but you kind of separate it into two piles. There's the sex on one side and the guy on the other. After you get to know him better the piles kind of get shuffled together more."

"I doubt it works that way for chicks," I replied.

"It may not," Brick admitted. "Not being a chick, I couldn't say."

"Are you going to see him again?" asked Ruby.

"I guess so. He seemed all for it. He said it was OK with him, though, if I wanted to meet up with Lonny from Frisco."

Lonny was the allegedly height-impaired cake decorator.

"I like Iilivi but I got two areas of concern," Brick continued. "One: not only is he white, he's about as white as a person can get without being chemically bleached."

"Not a problem," I replied. "Your babies will come out a nice coffee au lait. So what's your other needless worry?"

"What if he only wants to go out with me because I'm small? What if he thinks I'm the only size boyfriend that would fit in his tiny house?"

* * *

I'm totally amazed. While waiting in line to take a shower before bedtime, the two girls in front of me said I could go ahead of them. Very gracious of them, especially considering that I got the last of the hot water. (Chintzy Mrs. Lumpwapht has a timer that switches off the boiler at sundown.) I can't believe how nice I'm being treated since rumors of my presidency have been circulating. Dumb me: I should have been planting such rumors back in my high school in Hayward.

Another horrible topic in Expressions class today: "What I Would Say in a Speech to the United Nations." Seriously, is this something that 16-year-old girls think about? I mean, wake up and smell the tea Mr. Ng. Would you believe the guy is actually married? Is this what he wants to discuss when Mrs. Ng is begging him for a lay?

Better news in Vistas class today: At long last we got a replacement teacher for the departed Miss Porteau. Not only do we no longer have to face the Lumpster's daily flogging of George Eliot, but our new teacher is a complete dreamboat. Fresh from the ivy-covered halls of Sacramento State, Mr. Owen Fulm looks like a younger and blonder Brad Pitt. He has soft blue eyes, cute dimples when he smiles, and a cleft in his chin that you just want to curl up and die in. The consensus is he's not gay, because when Marie entered the room his jaw dropped about a foot. Or he could have been fixating on my peachy coral lips, since I was walking right beside her.

Poor Mr. Fulm wished to finish up our discussion of *The Chill on the Dental Floss*, but everyone was too abashed and smitten to be capable of speech. Of course, he spent most of the hour trying not to stare at Marie. The electricity flying between those two was enough to terminate several death-row inmates. It was especially dramatic when he finally called on her because everyone could sense it was mutual Love at First Sight. Totally doomed, of course, because Marie is Untouchably Inviolate, being both a student and jailbait to boot.

Our new teacher was the main topic of conversation at dinner.

"I think it's appropriate," observed Ruby, "that hot Mr. Fulm has a four-letter name that starts with F-U."

Marie blushed and looked away.

"I would do him," affirmed Elaine. "Just name the place and I'll be there."

"What's the Lumpster's motive in this?" asked Ruby. "Is she trying to torment us all? What do you think, Marie?"

"I expect Mr. Fulm was the best-qualified candidate. I thought his analysis of Miss Eliot's theme of forgiveness as culminating in the fatal flood was quite astute."

"Uh-huh," I said. "Plus, you'd do him in a heartbeat."

"That's not really relevant since he's a teacher at our school," insisted Marie.

"You won't be able to marry him until you're 18," I pointed out. "From the look on his face in class today, I'm sure he'll wait for you."

"I don't know what you're talking about, Brenda. He was looking at you more than me."

"Only because the sight of you was scorching his eyeballs," I said.

"They're going to have the cutest babies," added Elaine.

"God, yes," I agreed. "Totally adorable and smart too. I can see them at the breakfast table slurping down their porridge and discussing the Victorian novelists."

"You guys are impossible," said Marie, blushing anew.

My dark secret: I'd do Mr. Fulm *and* his bride to be.

Chapter 10

TODAY IN Undercurrents class Mr. Love was discussing the Viking invasion of England in the 9th century (as if we care). He said that when they captured the Christian Anglo-Saxon kings, they would sacrifice them to their pagan war god using the "blood-eagle" method. This involved ripping the victim's lungs out of his rib-cage and draping them across his shoulders like an eagle's folded wings. Of course, the dude was alive and conscious while this was going on. Which goes to show that being king back then was more than just jousting, bossing around your vassals, and diddling the ladies in waiting. Mr. Love advocates reviving this technique to execute our own death-row inmates–instead of "letting them off easy" with a lethal injection. The guy is quite the Nazi. You're lucky to get out of his class without losing your breakfast.

As today was the deadline, The Arcadians met in absolute secrecy (after dinner by the slough) to discuss the nominated candidates. Since Ruby and Elaine had colluded on their picks, we had six to choose from instead of eight. I nominated Ashley and Peyton, the two girls who had sacrificed their hot showers for me. I didn't really know them, but they seemed less overtly obnoxious than many of our fellow Ferncliffians.

Ruby and Elaine nominated Olivia and Naomi, two mousey types who weren't setting any speed records in looks, personality, or smarts. They didn't do much for me, and I could sense Marie had the same reaction. Her choices were much bolder: Taylor and Salma. Taylor being a popular senior, and Salma being the loudest voice at the Latinas' table. The latter was tight with my former roommate Lauren, which I didn't regard as a point in her favor. And Taylor was buddies with Chloe, the girl who had embarrassed me by pulling my chair away that first night when I arrived.

The rule, suggested by Marie and agreed to by all, was that any member could blackball any other member's nominated candidate. Therefore, the discussion got pretty heated.

"You know what your problem is, Brenda?" Ruby asked at one point.

"No, but I think I'm about to find out."

"You're totally hung up on judging people by their appearance. You never consider the inner person. That's why you dislike yourself. Since you're so obsessed with physical appearance, in your mind you don't measure up."

"All I said was I've never seen Olivia smile because her teeth are so crooked. I just think it's a shame her parents never sprang for an orthodontist."

"What's that got to do with accepting her into our sorority?" Ruby demanded. "This is a girl we're considering, not a horse."

"Well, she is kind of horsey," I pointed out. "You put a bit in her mouth and a saddle on her back, and she'd be ready for a romp around the track."

Very ugly look from Ruby.

"So what's wrong with Naomi?" asked Elaine.

"Have you heard her essays in Expressions class?" I asked. "The girl is borderline mentally deficient, and I'm being charitable here. The idea is to elevate ourselves in the school hierarchy, not become a refuge for losers. Right, Marie?"

Marie cleared her throat. "Uh, we should make an effort to pick girls who will enhance our standing in some way. What are the points in favor of your nominees, Brenda?"

"Well, Ashley and Peyton are very . . . uh, very nice."

"You know Ashley has a problem with shoplifting," said Ruby. "That's why she got sent here. All the malls in Northern California have her photo posted in their security offices."

"Really?" I said, "I wasn't aware of that."

"And the rumor is Peyton's knocked up," said Elaine. "Her days in this school may be numbered."

That's one way to escape Ferncliffe. If things get too bad, I could always rape Luiz in the dishroom and hope for the best.

In the end, all the nominees got blackballed, illustrating democracy in action. The disappointed Arcadians adjourned and agreed to try again in a few days.

* * *

Not that the competition was tough, but Vistas has emerged as everyone's favorite class. OK, our new book, *Pride and Prejudice*, is marginally more interesting than the *Frill on the Moss*. It's about this British chick, plagued with a ditzy mom and some lumpen sisters, who's on the outs with a stuck-up rich dude. No sex scenes and none likely as it was written about 200 years ago.

Of course, hardly anyone pays attention to the book because the dynamic between Owen (Mr. Fulm) and Marie is much more compelling. For 50 minutes a day they have to sit in the same room and pretend they don't want to rip each other's clothes off while we get to observe their every look, sigh, and grimace. It's way better than TV because this real-life drama is unfolding right in front of our eyes.

You'd think it would get boring because the action (such as it is) is very, very subtle, but we're all completely mesmerized. The latest development: twice today Mr. Fulm called on girls who had raised their hands with these telltale words: "Yes, Marie." He immediately corrected himself, but the damage was done. Naturally, Marie blushed both times.

It's fascinating to watch, but we're kind of jealous that the sexiest teacher and prettiest student are so stuck on each other. What are my chances that some day a guy that cute will desire me that much? Just about nil.

Naturally, Marie's been pretty moody and distracted. I forgot to daub on my lipstick this morning, and she didn't say a word about it. Even when she wasn't in love, I hardly had a clue what was going on with her. Now she's a complete mystery. And, no, she doesn't want to talk about it with her favorite roomie.

Weird event of the day: Chloe Ptucha came up to me at lunch and apologized for the "chair incident." She said it was a "dumb attempt at hazing a new girl" and added that she hoped "we could still be friends." I said sure and told her that it was no big deal to me. I hope she was sincere, but I've learned to be skeptical. Chloe was the prettiest girl in the school until Marie showed up. She leads a big crew and ranks with the big cheeses.

Things were chilly between Ruby and me for a few days, but we appear to have made up. It's always unpleasant when a friend opens up and tells you what they really think of you. Had I been as candid to her, I doubt Miss Splodge and I would still be speaking.

We're sort of linked by our friendship with Brick, who has a date tonight with the cake decorator. Since Brick is car-less, Lonny is making the long trek from S.F. A topic of speculation: If the date runs late will Brick be inviting Lonny back to his place? One positive sign: Brick reports that Iilivi is calling him daily.

Brick may soon have two BFs (thanks to us), while I remain unkissed, unloved, and un-everything-else.

That sucks.

* * *

Today's Expressions topic: "The Animal I Would Most Like To Be If I Hadn't Been Born a Human." I said giraffe because everyone looks up to them, you get a great view from up there, and predators mostly don't mess with them. Kind of hard padding it out to 300 words. Got a bit repetitious there at the end. Actually, I'd rather have been born a chipmunk. They're cute, frisky, appear to be having a great time, and you never see a fat chipmunk. They grow up fast, have lots of sex, and are spared the boredom of school and jobs. Old age is not a problem because when they start to slow down some hawk or owl swoops in and makes a quick meal of them.

Speaking of animal mating habits, Ruby has a date. She was so impressed with Brick's success with our Craigslist ad, she secretly had Marie post an ad for her (yes, complete with photo). Some Stocktonian lad named Cole replied, and they are going out for ice cream tomorrow (Saturday). Cole is 16, likes kayaking, and is active in the Accordion Club. He looks pretty normal in his photo, assuming it wasn't sent by some 48-year-old sex predator/rapist/murderer. You do wonder why a boy our age is trolling the personal ads when his high school is crawling with available chicks. I'd be nervous as hell, but Ruby is looking forward to their meeting. Marie has promised to style her hair and help with her makeup. I guess it's too late to call in an emergency plastic surgeon. (Sorry, that was excessively catty even for me.)

Meanwhile, we met up with Brick by his little boat and got the full story on his assignation with Lonny.

Not surprisingly (to Ruby), the cake decorator is short, topping out at a mere five feet, five inches. Even though his celebrated cakes (some of which cost thousands of dollars) have been written up in *San Francisco* magazine, Lonny would rather be a photographer. For the past few years he's been working on a photo book called *Nudes at 100+*.

"You mean he talked over a hundred gullible exhibitionists into taking off their clothes?" I asked.

"No, Brenda," replied Brick. "All of his subjects have to be at least 100 years old."

"Gross!" I exclaimed. "Who wants to look at a bunch of rotting, decrepit old people in the buff?"

"Lonny says they're very beautiful in their own way," replied Brick. "He says it's the one area of the nude that has never been fully explored."

"Right. For a very good reason," I said. "I don't know, Brick, the guy might be some kind of sicko."

"Oh, Brenda, don't be so middle class," scolded Ruby. "Lonny sounds like a very artistic person. Did you like him, Brick?"

"Uh, yeah, I guess so."

"So where did you and the shutterbug pass the night?" I asked.

"Well, I slept here. Lonny stayed with his parents across town. He was born and raised in Stockton, you know."

"He's a white dude?" I asked.

"Yes, and that's got me a little worried."

"Why?" asked Ruby.

"He says his parents are very prejudiced. They hate gays and black people, plus he doubts if they'd be that open to a dwarf."

"They sound charming," I remarked. "Don't they know their son is gay?"

"Well, Lonny's been dropping hints since he was 14, but they haven't been picking up on his clues."

"I'd marry him anyway," I said. "Just to have the satisfaction of watching them drop dead from shock."

* * *

This business of Ruby having a date with an actual boy has me feeling, well, annoyed. I'm not sure why. I don't think I'm jealous. It just feels like an injustice somehow. In a well-run world Ruby would be spending her Saturday hanging out with us in this boring school, not licking ice-cream cones with some accordion-playing kayaker.

I also deeply resented all the effort thoughtful Marie expended trying to gild the Splodge lily. From all the prep work being done you'd think Ruby was about to wed the Prince of Wales, not hook up with some local teen nobody. And so much effort to achieve so little. In my opinion Ruby's attractiveness inched up from a 1 (on a scale of 1 to 10) to a 1.2. Still, I joined Marie and Elaine in blowing kisses to our beaming pal as she sneaked out the back gate. Before she departed I had the foresight to have Marie snap her photo. This should be helpful to the police in case Ruby becomes the victim of heinous foul play.

When I returned to my room for a therapeutic Heath bar, I was shocked to discover that someone had cleaned out all my snacks. And emptied my purse of its cash (over $63, including my lucky Susan B. Anthony dollar coin). I alerted Mrs. Beezle, the Matron, who went off to find Mrs. Lumpwapht. Three minutes later the Lumpster herself was rummaging through my stuff to make sure I hadn't somehow "misplaced" the heisted goods. When nothing was found, she turned fiercely to the Matron and told her to "activate Code 9."

Mrs. Beezle strode out to the hall and pushed the button on the fire alarm. Ear-shattering clanging throughout the campus immediately emptied all the buildings. The staff had everyone gather in the parking lot, then the Lumpster yelled for us to go to the dining hall and remain there until instructed otherwise.

"What's going on?" one girl asked.

"I hope it's not a fucking Code 9," another girl muttered.

In the dining hall, the Matron called the roll. Three girls didn't answer. Two had been signed out for the day and one was A.W.O.L.

"Do you know where Ruby is?" the Matron asked Elaine.

"Uh, I'm sure she's around somewhere," she replied. "I think she had a headache from getting her period."

"Have you seen her?" Mrs. Beezle asked me.

"Uh, she may have gone down the block to get some Midol. I'm sure she'll be back soon."

"She should have come to me if she wasn't feeling well," said the

Matron. "Mrs. Lumpwapht will be furious if she's left the grounds."

"Why are we being kept here?" I asked.

"It's a Code 9," she replied. "No one may leave until all the rooms have been searched."

More grumbling around us. I heard one girl whisper, "Some bitch must have snitched." Another voice said, "Yeah, I just hope we find out who."

* * *

Three bags of cheese curls were found stuffed in a cupboard in the common room of the other dorm. A wastebasket behind the droopy sofa disgorged wrappers from four Heath bars. The residents of that dorm were made to line up in the dining hall, and Mrs. Lumpwapht went down the line smelling each girl's breath. A distinct chocolaty aroma was detected emanating from Kaitlyn, one of Lauren's new roommates. A search of her purse turned up $72, including a Susan B. Anthony dollar coin. Kaitlyn indignantly claimed the cash was hers, but the Lumpster dragged her off to the office to phone her parents. The rest of us were dismissed.

It appears I committed a faux pas. One does not report thefts to the school authorities. That's "snitching." You're supposed to make inquiries privately and let the big cheeses "punish" the girl responsible.

Justice was swift. Luiz will be getting lots of assistance in the dishroom. Not only will Kaitlyn be slaving there for the next three weeks, but so will four other girls found with marijuana and other contraband in their rooms. All of them, plus their friends now hate my guts.

Even though Ruby escaped punishment (kind Mrs. Beezle let her off with a warning instead of reporting her to the Lumpster), she's mad at me for not waiting until she had returned before blowing the whistle on my loss. Of course, she wasn't the one facing penniless snack-deprivation in this gustatory desert. Can anyone fault me for panicking?

"I blame myself," said Marie at dinner. "I've been absorbed in my own concerns and haven't been looking out for my friends."

"What sort of concerns?" I asked, hoping she'd open up about Mr. Fulm.

Marie didn't take the bait. "Had I been there for you, Brenda, we could have handled this matter without all the fuss."

"It's not your fault, Marie," said Ruby, flashing me a dirty look. "Now I guess The Arcadians are toast."

"Well, we'll have to put off the new members for a bit," conceded Marie. "I doubt anyone would wish to join us now."

Yes, the President screwed up big time. Now I know how George W. Bush felt when all of his wars went bad and the economy tanked.

Fortunately, we had Ruby's date to discuss, a welcome distraction from beating up on Brenda. Ruby said that Cole was "even cuter than his photo" and was coping pretty well with A.S.

"A.S.," I said. "Would that be Accordion Sensitivity? Is he allergic to his squeeze box?"

"How about Advanced Studliness?" leered Elaine.

"Or Artificially Scented," suggested Chloe, who lately had been sitting near us and eavesdropping on our Arcadian conversations. "Does he go too heavy on the aftershave?"

"He has a *mild* case of Asperger Syndrome," replied Ruby, offended. "That's why he's more comfortable meeting girls through personal ads."

Elaine was dubious. "So can you like have a conversation with him?"

"Of course," said Ruby. "He's very intelligent. He told me a great deal about the accordion. Did you know it was invented in China in 3000 B.C.?"

"Wow, that makes the polka over 5,000 years old," I noted.

"Cole is *very* talented," said Ruby. "I don't notice *you* playing any musical instruments, Brenda. Next summer he intends to paddle his kayak all the way to Fisherman's Wharf in San Francisco."

"While playing the accordion?" I asked. "Is he trying to set a record?"

"Laugh if you want to," sniffed Ruby. "But at least *I've* got a boyfriend."

* * *

The next morning I was yanked out of Behaviors class and summoned to Mrs. Lumpwapht's office. There she handed me an envelope containing $64 in cash (including my precious dollar coin).

"And my cheese curls?" I inquired.

"You'll be happy to know they have been ground up and are being incorporated into today's taco salad. And what's this I hear about your being the president of some secret sorority?"

Besides being a thief, Kaitlyn evidently was also a stool pigeon.

"We had discussed such an enterprise, Mrs. Lumpwapht, but Marie consulted her student handbook and noticed it was against one of your many rules."

"I will have no cliques at Ferncliffe, Blatt. I will have no one feeling excluded. I want all of my girls to feel equally welcome and involved. If I hear of your being engaged in any such clandestine organization, you will be severely punished. Is that clear?"

"Yes, Mrs. Lumpwapht."

"Nor am I pleased with your essays for Mr. Ng. They exhibit a tiresome superciliousness. It is time for you to grow up, Blatt."

"I'm trying," I lied.

"Yes, Blatt, you are *very* trying. Now, get back to class."

I left wondering if the Lumpster was naive or willfully blind. Hardly a bastion of egalitarianism, her school was rife with cliques.

This evening, while I was taking my daily shower, unknown enemies sneaked into the bathroom and flushed all the toilets at once. I was scalded, but I didn't let out a peep. Showing your pain only encourages them.

Chapter 11

HOW EXACTLY does eating ice cream and discussing accordion history (once!) with a person qualify him as your boyfriend? I mean, isn't he more properly termed an "acquaintance?"

Nevertheless, Ruby and I had three reasons for sneaking out the back gate after dinner tonight: 1. To meet her "boyfriend," who was proposing to convey himself here via kayak. 2. To obtain an emergency restocking of snacks from Brick. 3. To catch up on Brick's diverse love life.

We found Brick seated in the cockpit of his boat and eating a Heath bar.

"I'm not charging you for this one, Brenda," he said, swallowing hastily.

"I should hope not," I said, grabbing one from a grocery bag and quickly denuding it. "Can you believe over 24 hours have passed since I last experienced this essential chocolaty crunch?"

"Can I have one too?" begged Ruby.

"If you must," I sighed.

We took seats beside our host and munched our candy.

"Brick, have you by any chance seen a very cute guy in a kayak?" asked Ruby. "I'm expecting my boyfriend any minute."

No sightings by Brick, but he got the full story on Ruby's romantic liaison.

I felt a dose of reality was required. "She's only had one date with him," I pointed out.

"Love can blossom quickly," noted Brick. "If the stars are in accord."

"I think Cole and I are *very* compatible," declared Ruby, flashing me a smug look.

"Uh-huh," I said. "Well, I hope he shows before it gets dark. Or he may be reaching San Francisco sooner than he expected."

"Cole knows every nook and cranny of this delta. He said it has over a thousand miles of waterways. Imagine that."

"Speaking of nooks and crannies," I said, "Brick, how are you getting on with your dog-house dweller?"

Brick smiled. "Very well, Ruby. I spent all day yesterday with him. He grilled a salmon for our dinner. He told me something amazing."

"What!?" we piped.

"Well, it's kind of a secret."

"You've got to spill, Brick," I said. "We're your mentors. We can have no secrets."

"OK. I could use your perspective on this anyway. Iilivi has a voice in his head that talks to him."

"Oh, dear," I said. "That doesn't sound good."

"Well, I'm not so sure, Brenda," he replied. "It seems to be a pretty helpful voice. He first heard it a few years ago when he nearly cut off his thumb with a circular saw. So instead of dialing 9-1-1, Iilivi wraps the whole bloody mess in a towel and drives himself to the hospital."

"How macho," commented Ruby.

"So he's sitting there in the emergency room while the admitting clerk is going through his bloody wallet to see if she can find his medical card when he hears this voice say clear as day: 'Using a dull blade is poor economy after all'."

"What's that mean?" asked Ruby.

"According to Iilivi, the blade was old and dull, which is why it jumped out of the board he was sawing. Ever since then, this voice has been giving him advice. He says it's really helped him. After the housing crash he wasn't getting any work. All the contractors in the valley were going broke. It was the voice that came up with the idea of building little fiber-glass houses shaped like dogs."

"The jury may still be out on that suggestion," I pointed out.

"No, Brenda, Iilivi showed me his order book. He's got 14 firm orders so far and he gets inquiries every day. And the voice told him his name was too ordinary. That's why he changed it to Iilivi Ittiwangi."

"What was it before?" asked Ruby.

"Ed Smith."

"That's pretty dull," I conceded. "So what else has this voice told him?"

"That's the weird part," said Brick. "Last month the voice told him that soon he was going to meet his life partner."

"Did it give any details?" I asked.

"It said that from across the water would come his obverse."

"Well, that's pretty vague," I said.

"It's not vague at all," insisted Ruby. "Brick lives on the water. He's

230

short and black, and Iilivi is tall and white. They're like the opposite sides of a coin. It's destiny!"

"Uh, OK, if you say so," I said, unconvinced. "So you're not going to see Lonny again?"

"I've got a date with him on Friday."

"Did you mention that to Iilivi?" I asked.

"Yeah, I did. He said he was going to wait and see if he got any reaction from the voice."

"So what do you make of all this, Brick?" I asked.

"I guess it's kind of exciting. I always dreamed of meeting a guy with a strong spiritual side."

"Yeah, assuming he doesn't go nutso on you," I replied.

Eventually, the conversation returned to Iilivi's dangling thumb. "So did they sew it back on?" I asked.

"Well, they tried to, but it happened in August when all the good surgeons were away on vacation."

"You mean he's missing a thumb?!" exclaimed Ruby. "How does he work at carpentry?"

"Well, he couldn't, which is why they transplanted his big toe."

"Your boyfriend has a toe on his hand?" I asked.

"Uh-huh. But it looks more like a smallish thumb than a toe. It works fine."

"And how's his foot?" I asked.

"Well, he has a slight limp, but he felt it was worth it."

"That voice he hears could be the spirit of his missing thumb," speculated Ruby.

"You're right, Ruby," said Brick. "There could be much wisdom in our thumbs. After all, they are what distinguish us from other, less intelligent animals."

"And babies suck them," I pointed out.

"Meaning what?" asked Ruby.

"Meaning over-suckage of plastic binkies could be a cause of all the stupidity in this world."

I said that facetiously, but I think my companions bought it.

We stayed out as late as we dared, but no BFs in kayaks were seen. I felt this rather deflated Ruby's love balloon, but she's putting on a brave face.

＊ ＊ ＊

Today's topic in Expressions class was "Why Stealing Never Pays." Oh, really? What about all those shady bankers who wrecked the economy and are now enjoying opulent lifestyles in their oceanfront Hampton estates? Or cruising the Mediterranean in their yachts? Or sipping wine in their boutique vineyards in my home state?

Not wanting to get the Lumpster on my back again, I didn't mention any of that. I said stealing never pays because the guilt torments you until you die.

Although in the case of Kaitlyn it appears that she intends to torment me until I go insane. After another showering incident, I've had to enlist Marie to stand guard while I bathe. Fiendish Kaitlyn sidled up to me in the dining hall at lunch and whispered that I was "second on the list after the Lumpster." I told her to back off lest I "snap her bones like tooth-picks." Not wanting a shiv in my gut, I'm now watching my back 24/7.

Ruby reports she has heard from her BF. Cole got so engrossed in his accordion, he lost track of the time. He allegedly texted her that he couldn't make it, but her phone is so primitive, it doesn't receive texts. So his kayaking expedition has been rescheduled for tonight.

At dinner Chloe sat down in Marie's chair and said, "I bet I know something that you girls don't."

"What it feels like to take on an entire football team," I suggested.

Chloe laughed. "You are so funny, Brenda. I can't believe all those girls hate your guts."

"I'm coping," I said. "So do you know where Marie is?"

"I might," she smiled slyly. "It's a bit of a scandal."

"So spill," I replied.

Chloe looked around and lowered her voice. "Marie got signed out by Mr. Fulm."

Unlike Ruby and Elaine, I tried not to look shocked.

"No big deal," I lied. "They probably went to the library or a book-store."

"Or back to his apartment," suggested Chloe.

"Mr. Fulm knows better than to fool around with an underage stu-dent," I insisted.

"You think?" said Chloe. "Well, it wouldn't be the first time in the history of the world."

"They do totally love each other," Ruby pointed out.

"We don't know that," I said. "She's never mentioned anything about it to me."

"There's no use lying for your friend, Brenda," said Chloe. "Everyone knows what's going on with those two."

"You're just jealous he's not after your well-trodden bod," I retorted.

Chloe smiled. "I'm not giving up, Brenda."

"Giving up what?" I asked.

"Oh, haven't you heard? I'm trying to get your pal Gianna to switch rooms with me."

* * *

Naturally I was skeptical, but right on time a blue kayak paddled into view around a bend in the slough. Ruby let out a cry of joy and waved enthusiastically. Yes, the occupant of the kayak appeared to be a young male. He waved back.

Moments later he clambered out of his molded plastic craft, gave Ruby an awkward hug, and reached out to shake my hand.

"Hi, I'm Cole."

Improbably, Ruby was right. Her BF was way cuter than his photo. Engaging smile and intense pale brown eyes. Tan cargo shorts and an "Accordionists Do It With Both Hands" t-shirt showed off his slim build and deep tan.

"Hiya, I'm Brenda."

Shy Cole did eye contact like he had learned it from a book.

"Nice to meet you," he said. "Do you live around here?"

"I live at the same school as Ruby. Hence the matching uniforms."

"Not matching," he replied. "The sizes are different."

"Right, but that's usually a given in this context."

Cole gave it some thought. "I could debate that point, but it's relatively trivial."

"How was your journey?" asked Ruby.

"Not strenuous. I did it in 42 minutes. I had allowed 45. We can talk for 12 minutes if I'm to return before dark. The moon is in its final quarter and will be rising at 1:08 a.m. No cloud cover is expected."

"Shall we sit down on the bank?" suggested Ruby. "I have purchased two candy bars from Brenda. May I offer you one?"

This date was beginning to sound like a role-playing session in Mrs. Goldbline's Behaviors class.

"OK," replied Cole, accepting a Heath bar.

We sat down in the dirt and looked out across the still water.

"Is it difficult learning to paddle a kayak?" I inquired.

"Well, you may get a dunking or two along the way. Venturing into the ocean is more of a challenge. Then you have to learn how to right yourself if you get knocked over by a wave."

"I think I'll stick to cruise ships," I replied.

"Is your family in that business?" he asked.

"Brenda was making a joke, Cole," said Ruby. "She's known for her offbeat humor."

"I'm just a jolly fat girl," I lied.

"You're not as big as Ruby led me to believe."

Another insight into Ruby's opinion of me. Oh well, I'm used to it.

"You must have misunderstood me," said Ruby hastily. "How do you like your candy bar, Cole?"

"Very good. I also like Heath Bar Crunch ice cream."

"Right on," I said. "If they allowed us to have freezers in our rooms,

I'd be totally stocked with that flavor. Padlocked, of course."

"Dream on, Brenda," said Ruby. "Cole, honey, what have you been practicing?"

"I've been playing along to my dad's Paul Desmond albums."

"I'd like to hear you play sometime," she purred.

"We could arrange that. I could play duets with Dylan."

"Dylan is the other member of their high school Accordion Club," explained Ruby.

"I see. Kind of an exclusive group."

"I did what you asked, Ruby," said Cole. "I talked to Dylan about Brenda. He wants to meet her."

All news to me.

"Great!" exclaimed Ruby. "I'm sure Brenda is dying to meet him too."

"Ruby, dear, that qualifies as one of your more outlandish assertions. Who is this Dylan person?"

"He's Cole's best friend. I'm sure you'll like him, Brenda."

"I'll talk to Dylan," said Cole. "We'll figure out a time we can all get together."

"I don't know," I said. "I have a pretty busy schedule."

"She has the same schedule I do," said Ruby. "She has plenty of free time. And Cole, honey, let's try to make it some time when your parents aren't at home."

Uh-oh, the spider was beginning to weave her web.

* * *

When I returned to my room, I asked Gianna if she was planning on moving out.

"Who wants to know?" she replied.

"I believe the question was posed by me."

"What's it to you?"

"Well, Gianna, I've become accustomed to having your eyeballs pinned relentlessly to me. I'm not sure how I'd cope if they were suddenly withdrawn."

"Why should I do that bitch Chloe any favors? And why does she want to move in here?"

"Beats me. Then you're not swapping rooms with her?"

"That's my business. How much will you pay me to stay put?"

I gave it some thought. Could Chloe be any worse as a roommate than Gianna? Possibly. At least Gianna's obnoxiousness was a known quantity, whereas who knew what deviousness Chloe was up to?

"I could give you five dollars," I ventured.

"A day?"

"I was thinking more like five per semester."

"Get real, Brenda. You pay me $250 cash and I'll forget about moving."

More evidence that the girl was insane. I told her to forget it.

It was nearly 8:30 by the time Marie returned–too late for me to take a shower if hot water was desired. I hadn't washed my hair in four days and was beginning to resemble one of those gals who live under a bridge. Marie, however, looked even better than usual. It was apparent that wherever she had been, she had been having a good time.

"We missed you at dinner," I remarked casually.

"I had to get out of here," she admitted. "I took a long walk along the levee and had a sandwich at Subway."

"Did you sneak out?"

"No, I got a pass from one of the teachers."

"Anyone I know?"

"Mr. Fulm heard me complaining about the rule confining us to campus. He said he'd sign a pass for me anytime I wanted."

"That was nice of him."

"He'll sign one for you too. Just ask him."

"So, you didn't go off with him then?"

"Good grief, no. Is that what you suspected?"

"Me? Certainly not. I think some people were wondering."

"Sorry to disappoint them. I'm a very dull subject for gossip. Did you meet Ruby's boyfriend?"

"I did. He showed this time."

"What's he like?"

"What can I say? The girl lucked out. He seems very nice. Cute too, and only a little weird around the edges. He has a friend who wants to meet me."

"Great!"

"I'm not doing it though."

"Oh, Brenda, why not?"

"Because I don't think I can bear the look of disappointment in his eyes when he sees me."

"You don't know he'll be disappointed. You have a lot to offer. And not every guy is looking for a Playmate of the Month."

"Oh? Since when?"

"Brenda, do you ever read the Sunday newspaper?"

"Never."

"Well, perhaps you should start. Check out the wedding announcement photos. There are lots of girls just as big as you who get married every week."

"They may be big, but I bet they're pretty."

"No prettier than you. People fall in love with the person, Brenda, not the packaging."

"That's easy for you to say, Marie. You can have any guy you want."

"Not true, Brenda. I wanted Rodney, and I don't have him. OK, it may not work out with Cole's friend, but at least you'll have gotten your feet wet. Going out with guys is like anything else–you get better with practice."

"You could get some practice by going out with Mr. Fulm. He likes you."

"Don't be ridiculous, Brenda. The idea is absurd."

Chapter 12

MY MOTHER surprised me by calling me this morning. I was beginning to think my parents had changed their names and moved to Bolivia. She said everyone was "thrilled" that I was doing so well in my new school. I told her that if they were spying on me, their webcam was defective. I said I had been robbed and was now universally despised for being a snitch. I concluded by telling her that when she was aged and infirm I would be putting her in a home run by the Little Sisters of the Mafia.

"Just try to remember, dear," she said, "that we always have your best interests at heart."

"Well, I won't have yours at heart, Mom. When you get Alzheimers, I'll be dropping you off on a street corner in Tijuana with no I.D. and no dinero."

"That really is a nasty thing to say, Brenda."

"Thanks. I do my best."

"Your brother would never say anything that hurtful."

"Well, try sticking him in a prison school and see how fast he changes his tune."

"Got to run, dear. If your first report card is satisfactory, I may increase your allowance."

"Thanks, Mom. I love you too."

That last bit was expressed with the deepest insincerity I could muster. True, I don't hate it here quite so much now, but I feel my mother should be given a hard time just on general principles.

When Marie and I got back from our last class, we discovered that Gianna had packed up all her stuff and vacated the premises.

"Quick, Marie," I said. "Take Gianna's bed."

"Why? I don't mind my bed."

"Take her bed right now! Or I will never speak to you again!"

"Oh, all right, Brenda. I don't see what difference it makes."

While I was helping Marie make up her new bed, Chloe entered followed by three toadies (Aubrey, Zoey, and Jasmine) bearing her stuff.

"Here I am," announced Chloe. "The deed is done! Aren't you pleased?"

"I hope you like it here, Chloe," smiled Marie.

"I hope no one sticks mothballs up your nose while you're sleeping," I said, unsmiling.

"I'm not worried about that," chuckled Chloe, inspecting her new bed. "Zoey, how tall are you?"

Zoey was the shortest girl in the school. Despite that impairment, she had an impressive rack as my brother would say.

"Four feet, nine and one-half inches," she replied.

"Good," replied Chloe. "You'll have lots of growing room in this darling little bed. Haul it downstairs and bring me back your bed."

"OK, if you say so," sighed Zoey. "But make Jasmine help me."

"Jasmine, do your duty," instructed Chloe.

The two girls went to work dismantling Marie's old bed while Aubrey began unpacking. "Someone's golf clubs are hogging all the closet," she reported.

"Why are there golf clubs in our closet?" Chloe inquired sweetly.

"Golf is my life," I lied. "When I'm 18, I intend to turn pro. Touch my clubs and you die."

"Push Brenda's clothes up against her clubs," ordered Chloe, still smiling. "I'm sure she won't mind a few more wrinkles. Marie, I love your hair. Is that your natural color?"

"Yes, that's how it grows."

"You're so lucky. My hair untouched is the color of a dead rat."

"People often rave about my hair," I lied, patting my straggly ends. I decided I had a right to get competitive about my looks. After all, it was incontrovertibly true that the two prettiest girls in the school *had gone out of their way* to transfer into my room.

There's the tiniest possibility that I may be somewhat charismatic.

* * *

Ugly truth about dreaded events: All too soon the day arrives when you must face them. And so after dinner on Saturday, Ruby and I sneaked out the back way and headed off toward the supermarket parking lot where we were to be picked up by Cole and Dylan. Ruby had gilded the lily to an improbable degree and smelled like the smokestack of a perfume factory. I, on the other hand, had opted for a casual look in jeans and 49ers sweatshirt. No perfume, only some perfunctory hair styling, and the merest smear of peachy coral to indicate that, yes, I was equipped with lips.

I was praying we'd be stood up, but soon a dusty SUV squealed into the lot and slammed to a halt in front of us. A sticker on the back bumper read: TERMITES FEAR ME, REALTORS LOVE ME. Ruby and I piled into the back seat and off we zoomed. Dylan was driving; Cole was riding shotgun. He did the introductions (after some prompting from Ruby). Dylan said hi and appeared to be inspecting me in the rearview mirror. I prayed he'd go back to watching the road as I felt age 16 was too young to die.

Our driver was as outsized as his vehicle. Tall and wide, Dylan was one of those pear-shaped boys: all gut and butt. You'd think my fat genes would go for that, but perversely they seemed to prefer 'em slim and slight like Cole. Nor did Dylan's ragged flannel shirt, sparse goatee, and unruly scarecrow hair push any of my love buttons. All of which was a relief as it took the pressure off. Frankly, my dear, I didn't give a damn what young Dylan thought of me.

"So you go to that bad-girls school," said Dylan as a conversation starter.

"Uh-huh," I replied "It's very exclusive. You have to have committed at least three major felonies to be admitted."

"That is so untrue," said Ruby. "Don't believe anything she says."

"I'd heard rumors of that school for years," said Dylan. "But you guys are the first evidence that it exists."

"Yes, but do you exist? That is the question," I pointed out.

"Brenda is very deep," said Ruby. "You should hear her essays for Expression class."

"I'd love to read some of them," said Dylan.

"That's not happening," I replied. "Hey, isn't that a red light just ahead?"

As luck would have it, fate had not scheduled me to die at that intersection. Eventually, we arrived in a neighborhood of identical tract houses. Somehow, Dylan located Cole's house and soon we were getting settled in his teecee-teecee living room (a word invented by my mother which stands for tasteless & cheesy and tacky & cheap). Except for a scruffy micro dog named Myron, we had the place to ourselves. Cole's parents and older brother were out enjoying Stockton nightlife.

All the accoutrements of seduction were in evidence: three extra-large pizzas, a chilled six-pack of Coors Lite, a half-bottle of rum (borrowed from the baking supplies?), and two dazzling accordions. Cole's was iridescent aqua-blue and mother of pearl. Dylan's was shiny apple-red and chrome. Both crafted in Italy where the art of gilding the squeeze box had reached its gaudy zenith.

I was all for diving into the pizzas, but we had to be polite and listen to some music first. The boys did not saw away in unison. They played jazzy tunes in a syncopated style with each instrument responding to the riffs of the other. It was surprisingly easy on the ears. I did some actual toe-tapping, while Ruby put on a show of enjoyment like they were the second coming of Duke Louis Armstrong Miles Ellington.

"Amazing!" she exclaimed, when they had concluded. "You guys are fabulous! Just breathtaking!"

"You sure are," I agreed. "And I fear the pizzas are getting cold."

At least Dylan and I had one thing in common: we both preferred the pepperoni to the vegetarian with pineapple. But he liked the rum-fortified beer much more than I did. I downed a few repulsive swallows to be polite.

When the last pizza slice was split between Dylan and me, subtle Ruby said, "Cole, honey, why don't you show me your room?"

He took a final fortifying swig of his beer and said, "Sure. OK."

Off they went, leaving me and the dog alone with the goateed gorilla. He gazed up at the ceiling and emitted the loudest belch I had ever heard.

"Sorry," he said. "If you don't let out the bubbles, you can explode."

"Yes, I hear it's a common cause of fatalities."

Dylan chuckled. "You're the total package, Brenda. Looks, wit, attitude, and style."

"Thanks. That's what all the guys tell me."

He took hold of my chin. I feared he was going to pull me to his lips, but he proceeded to wipe off a spot of pizza sauce. He put the saucy digit by my mouth and I reluctantly licked it.

"That Ruby is a live one," he commented, wiping his hand on his pants.

"Yes, a bit too lively for her own good. I hope your friend has a condom."

"He does—as, come to think of it—do I."

"I think we should just talk, Dylan—since we just met and are complete and total strangers. How long have you been playing the accordion?"

"Since I was three. All the males in my family do—for untold generations. My grandfather played professionally. Ever hear of Willy K the Polka King?"

"Sorry. Can't say that I have."

"That's OK, Brenda. Nobody under the age of 90 has either. I could kill for a brownie right now."

"I've got a couple of Heath bars in my purse."

"Then what are we waiting for?"

Dylan and I munched our candy and politely ignored the rhythmic sounds emanating from elsewhere in the house.

"Eighty beats per minute," he remarked at last.

"What?"

"That's a good tempo for a sexy song. It's a common rhythm during sex. Your hips want to move at 80 beats per minute."

"Sorry, I wouldn't know about that."

"Me neither. But that appears to be the case from the auditory evidence available."

"Right. Well, they better finish up pretty fast. We have to be back in time for lights out."

So Dylan kissed me. It wasn't too awful. I liked the pizza and chocolate overtones. His goatee wasn't the tidiest, but I didn't feel traumatized for life. The clumsy paw to the breast I could have done without. I thought the cad was trying to grab me lower, but it turned out to be little Myron humping my leg.

Naturally, I was curious how things had gone with Ruby, but all I could get out of her later was that it had been "terribly thrilling and profoundly beautiful."

Yeah, like I'm going to believe a word of that.

Dylan had kissed me, but I went to sleep thinking of Cole. I liked everything about that boy except his regrettable intimacy with Ruby Splodge.

* * *

It turns out we weren't the only ones sneaking back right before lights out. Marie also had been away at an undisclosed location.

"Just out for a walk," she said at breakfast.

"Boy, a girl could die of loneliness in your room," complained Chloe.

"Not very likely," I replied, "considering your retinue of toadies."

"I do have many charming friends," she conceded.

I could tell Ruby was anxious to spill.

"I find it very frustrating," she announced. "After you've made it with a guy, it's really hard to go back to sleeping with two female roommates."

"Thanks a lot," said Elaine.

I was right: Ruby was not the sort of girl to keep her deflowering under her hat. It was discussed at length in lively whispers, but I didn't take part. I mean it's not like getting some teenage boy to sleep with you is that daunting of a task. I myself declined such an opportunity last evening. According to my brother, guys his age will jump just about anything female with a pulse. And some aren't so particular about either of those conditions.

At 11:00 a.m. sharp (more or less) the four Arcadians plus Chloe assembled by the curb in front of the school. We had been signed out for the day by the compliant Mr. Fulm, who looks even cuter in his casual weekend garb. Too bad he had to stay behind to prep for next week's classes. No one had invited Chloe to the barbecue at Iilivi's, but she begged to be included with such servility that we had to give in.

The two fellows picked us up in Iilivi's pink and gray 1958 DeSoto station wagon. Kind of a tight squeeze, so we made Chloe sit in the way back. As the bulkiest passenger I got the front window seat (squeezing Brick into the middle next to Iilivi). This gave me a good position from which to inspect the driver's right hand. No way that toe looked like a thumb. Ugly scar all around its base, but it seemed to work OK. Despite his crypt-like pallor, Iilivi was a decent-looking guy: mild blue eyes, receding blond hair, and a chin that wasn't quite keeping up with his prominent nose.

After everyone got introduced, Ruby said, "Cool car, Iilivi. Did you restore it?"

"No, my grandfather bought it new and kept good care of it. He drove it for over 50 years. Never felt the need to trade it in for something newer. A car doesn't need to be restored if it's parked out of the weather, gets regular maintenance, and isn't driven where they salt the roads."

"You don't mind all the pink and gray?" I asked.

The car was as zealously two-toned inside as outside.

"No, it's in keeping with the period," he replied. "What do you think, Brick?"

"I think this car is so very, very you."

The ancient wagon was probably a death trap on wheels, but Iilivi seemed like a competent driver. We headed north on the interstate toward Lodi.

"Oh, Brenda," said Ruby, "Cole called me. He said that Dylan really likes you."

"Gee, thanks for the update."

"Don't you like him? she asked.

"He's OK. If I ever decide to hook up with an accordionist, I'll put him on my list."

This conversational gambit gave Ruby another chance to hash over last night's exploits. The girl does like to brag on her burgeoning sex life. Elaine tried to steer the talk back to me.

"So this Dylan dude didn't impress you?" she asked.

"He seemed nice. You're welcome to audition him yourself on Ruby's next double date. I'd say he's just a few inches shorter than you."

"That sounds promising," said Elaine. "What do you think, Ruby?"

"Sure, give it your best shot, Elaine. I didn't realize Brenda was so particular."

"Some of us don't hop into bed with the first guy that snaps his fingers," I pointed out.

"What's that supposed to mean?!" she demanded.

"Be nice, girls," said Brick. "Don't make us stop this car and come back there."

Iilivi's place was pretty far out in the sticks. His land was at least ten feet lower than the water that flowed along the other side of the levee. Scattered among the old plum trees were a big wooden barn with water tower, a farmhouse that looked abandoned, several outbuildings, and the dog dwelling. Brick's description hadn't prepared us for its over-the-top pugness. It really was like a giant pug at rest on a raised platform beside the slough. For example, Brick hadn't mentioned the accurately molded dog fur, the cute red collar with silver-painted studs, and the realistic whiskers extending out from the dark-shaded snout. I could see why dog lovers were lining up to order duplicates.

The neatly furnished interior wasn't spacious, but it seemed adequate for one non-materialistic neat freak and a dwarf–assuming they liked to-getherness and never argued. We Arcadians and Chloe oohed and ahhed as Iilivi gave us the grand tour.

"I'd love to honeymoon here," said Ruby, presumptuously. "It's just so sweet and cozy!"

"And it's nice that you're so close to the water," added Elaine.

"Yes, the visibility helps," said Iilivi. "I've gotten several orders from people cruising by in houseboats."

"You can see some videos taken by boaters on Youtube," noted Brick proudly. "Iilivi did all the design from start to finish."

"And do you have a dog?" asked Chloe.

"No, I've never had a pet of any sort," Iilivi admitted.

"And why's that?" she asked.

"My mother discouraged it. She thought pets were dirty, and that I would be traumatized if they ran away or died. So pets always seemed like too much responsibility for me to handle."

"You could get one now," Elaine suggested.

"I don't know about that. My space is pretty tight."

"You could start with something small," said Chloe. "Like a turtle or a goldfish."

"I think Iilivi's got all he can handle with me just now," said Brick, giving his boyfriend's hand a squeeze.

All this chitchat was fine, but I for one was ready for lunch. Iilivi fired up the grill while Brick served tall glasses of iced lemonade. The proposed menu looked promising: chilled salmon salad, corn on the cob, melon balls in a vinaigrette, and grilled sausage sandwiches with home-made sauerkraut. A large chocolate cake occupying most of the minia-ture kitchen counter looked especially enticing.

We settled into folding chairs on the sunny deck and sipped our drinks. I could get used to such a pleasant environment–not that I'll likely ever get the chance. Why is it that gay guys always have the most enviable lifestyles?

Carried away by the bohemian atmosphere, Ruby undid the buttons of her blouse. No bra, of course, since such an appliance for her would be superfluous.

"Getting a little sun there, girl?" inquired Chloe.

"I thought I might. Any objections?"

"None worth mentioning."

I was beginning to appreciate Chloe's sense of humor. I turned to Marie and smiled.

"You OK?" I asked.

"Fine, Brenda. It's very nice here."

It was, but as usual she seemed like she was a million miles away.

I was just biting into a spicy Italian link tucked into a crispy French roll under a layer of tangy sauerkraut slathered with mustard, when a black and white sheriff's car rolled to a stop beside Iilivi's parked DeSoto. A uniformed deputy exited the car and strode up the steps to the deck. He removed his aviator sunglasses and took in the scene of suddenly silenced picnickers. I for one was thankful that Ruby had buttoned up before sitting down to eat.

"Yes, officer, can I help you? asked Iilivi, placing his sandwich on his plate and wiping his hands on a napkin.

"Is this your property?" asked the deputy, checking out the impressive dog's head that loomed above him.

"Yes, sir. I'm the owner. What is this about?"

"We got a report of suspicious activity going on here. Are these your children?"

A mind-bogglingly dumb question. Only Chloe made no effort to suppress a snort and smirk.

"No, they're just friends," Iilivi replied.

"How old are you, Miss," the cop asked Chloe.

"Sixteen. How old are you?'

"Do your parents know you're here?"

"Sure. Do yours?"

Marie felt the need to demonstrate some maturity. "We're students at Ferncliffe Academy," she volunteered. "We're properly signed out for this activity today. There's nothing amiss here."

"Ferncliffe, huh?" said the deputy. "As I recall they nabbed one of their runaways down in Fresno." He turned to Iilivi. "Do you have any filming or video equipment on the premises?"

"No. Why? Has some been stolen?"

"Mind if I check in your, uh, house?"

"No. Be my guest."

We exchanged glances as the deputy entered Iilivi's tiny home (without a warrant!).

"Eat, girls," said Iilivi. "It must be some mistake. There's nothing to worry about."

"I wouldn't be so sure," whispered Brick.

Eventually the cop returned and asked to see Iilivi and Brick's I.D.s. They handed over their driver's licenses, which he took back to his squad car. We could see him talking on his radio.

"What do you suppose this is about?" asked Ruby.

"Anybody here have really sharp eyes?" asked Iilivi.

"I have 10/20 vision," said Marie, who made a habit of excelling in every personal attribute.

"You see that house way in the distance across the slough?" said Iilivi, pointing toward the water. "Can you see anything there?"

Marie shielded her eyes with her hand and peered toward the house. "There's a window open on the second floor. Someone's up there looking out with really big binoculars."

Wow, she did have great eyes. I could barely make out the house.

"That would be Mrs. Goodhume," said Iilivi. "An elderly person with way too much time on her hands. And decidedly not gay-friendly. Shall we wave to my busybody neighbor?"

We all waved.

"She's not waving back," Marie reported.

"It's not a problem," said Iilivi. "We haven't done anything wrong."

"You hope," said Brick. "I can think of three offences I'm committing: an ex-felon in possession of a sandwich, eating while black, and violating societal norms for height. Not to mention mixing with white folks. Just you wait. That tire biter's not done hassling us."

The deputy returned a few minutes later. "My dispatcher called your school. Apparently, you're not authorized to be here. They want you back immediately."

"Surely they can finish their lunch," protested Iilivi.

"Nope. Let's go, ladies. Move it."

As we groaned and got up from the table, the deputy handed back the driver's licenses.

"These girls are all underage," he said. "I suggest in the future, you invite someone else to your barbecues."

"I'll invite whomever I choose," said Iilivi.

"Yes, well, their school authorities may not be done with you. I suggest you not leave town."

"We're not going anywhere," said Brick defiantly.

Ruby and I gave him a quick hug and waved good-bye to Iilivi as we trooped down the steps. Four of us squeezed into the back of the squad car, while Chloe claimed the front seat next to the radio, computer console, and guns.

"Don't touch anything," warned the cop, "or I'll have to cuff you."

"Wow, this is just like on TV," purred Chloe. "I'm impressed."

OK, the deputy was being a hard ass, but he was fairly young and cute. Chloe's flirtation skills certainly left Ruby and the rest of us in the dust. All during the drive back, she had that cop blushing, chuckling, or squirming in embarrassment. It was a pleasure to watch a master at work, even if I was missing out on some fabulous chocolate cake because Ruby had to show off her concave chest.

Both the Lumpster and Mr. Fulm were waiting out front when we arrived. He looked like he had had his ass well chewed. He and Marie exchanged their usual poignant glances as we got sent to our rooms.

The irony is we spend 50 minutes a day in Mrs. Goldbline's Behaviors class learning how to be social and make friends. Then, when we try to do just that, we get stomped on.

Chapter 13

OUR PUNISHMENT for attending a pleasant gathering with friends was one week's confinement to campus. Not too onerous considering we're locked up here anyway. At least we avoided the dreaded dishroom. Of course, it's still pretty crowded in there with Kaitlyn and the marijuana abusers scouring away. Ruby and I regretted that we didn't get a chance to be alone with Brick to inquire about his second date with Lonny. We're completely in the dark about one-half of his love life–always a source of frustration for friends.

Marie is the most bummed about getting busted. She's worried the incident has jeopardized Mr. Fulm's position here–since all new teachers are on probation their first semester. I assured her it will all blow over and be forgotten. Mr. Fulm's a good teacher–even when enmeshed in a tragic love affair–and I'm sure the Lumpster values his services.

As I was leaving my last class of the day (Miss Bronkiel's labored Explorations of Why Science Is Dull), the Matron informed me that I had a visitor in the lobby of the administration building (the only place where non-family visits are permitted). It was Dylan looking worried. He skipped the usual preliminaries.

"Cole says that Ruby says that you don't want to go out with me again!"

Inspired by Chloe's example, I decided this was a good opportunity to work on my flirting skills.

"Well, that's a vicious falsehood."

"Then you do want to go out with me?"

"That depends."

"On what?"

"On what you had in mind. I should point out that another session in Cole's living room is not my idea of a dream date."

"Meaning what?"

Are guys really that obtuse?

"Meaning I have my standards."

"You'd rather go to a motel?"

"I'd rather go to a nice restaurant. I'd rather go to a play. Or a concert. A round of golf might be fun. Perhaps you should consult a dictionary and look up the definition of 'date'."

"So you do like me?"

"I don't actively dislike you, Dylan. I haven't had a chance to get to know you yet. The purchase of a comb might be a good place to start. And you could shave off that repulsive facial hair."

"But, Brenda, I like my goatee. It makes me look older."

"That's fine. I'm sure there are plenty of ladies at the senior center who would enjoy hanging with you in Cole's living room. You should warn them that Myron might tear their support hose when he humps their leg."

"You're kind of a ball buster, Brenda."

"I really have no idea of what you mean by that. Come back with a concrete proposal for an interesting date, and I may entertain the notion of seeing you again. So nice of you to drop by."

"How about another kiss to tide me over?"

I held out my hand. "Only on the back of the hand, please."

Dylan smiled and gave me a semi-gallant peck on the designated spot.

* * *

More spectacular nudity in our room this morning. Not only is Chloe a champion flirt, she has the goods to back it up. I find it a bit unsettling that I'd much rather view Marie or Chloe in the buff than Dylan. As much as I enjoy looking at them, I don't really feel much of an urge to progress to the fondling stage. Now Cole, on the other hand, I could see ravishing every way possible. Too bad Ruby is clamped so firmly onto her boyfriend. You couldn't pry her off that guy with a steel I-beam.

After breakfast I phoned my mother. "Mom, I need you to call Mrs. Lumpwapht."

"Oh dear, what did you do now, Brenda?"

"Nothing too criminal. There's this boy who wants to take me out. I need you to inform her that I have your permission."

"A boy? You're seeing some boy?"

"Don't worry, Mother. It's not Love with a capital L. Or Sex with a capital S. It's strictly for P.E."

"Good God, what's that?"

"Practical experience. I need some practice dating."

"Heavens, Brenda, you're exhibiting such maturity now. I think that school is doing you a world of good."

"Just call her, Mother. Otherwise, I'll be locked down here like it was San Quentin for chicks. Please phone her today."

"I'll call her right now, darling. You've made my day!"

"Sorry to hear that. It was certainly not my intention."

"And always make him use a condom."

"Mom, I'm not having sex."

"Well, if you do, be responsible and use protection."

"Remind me again, how soon after you were married did you have Buford?"

"So learn from your mother's mistakes."

The answer to that question is five and one-half months.

She sighed and went on, "Your brother lost his job."

"Why? What did he do?"

"The brewery installed a new automated loading system so they don't need as many workers. He got replaced by some tubing and a micro-chip."

"That's too bad. What's he going to do?"

"Move back home if nothing comes up."

People have announced mass killings with more cheerfulness than my mother said that. I told her to buck up and reminded her that parenting is a life sentence. (Another reason I'm skipping the whole ordeal.)

Ruby had some news at lunch. Cole and Dylan have written a song for two accordions and singer, which they intend to post on Youtube. Ruby has been recruited to do the vocals.

"So you're a singer?" I asked with my usual skepticism.

"Of course. I mean everyone can sing, right? It's like talking, only smoother."

"Then you haven't actually done any singing?"

"Not a lot, Brenda. But I'm very musical."

"What's the title of the song?" asked Elaine.

"I Made a Kayak Built for Two, But You'd Rather Paddle Alone."

"Sounds like a sure hit," said Chloe.

"I'm sure it will go viral," replied Ruby. "After we get a million or so views we'll be famous. Then we can get a record deal and do concerts in giant stadiums."

"That'd be fun," said Elaine. "You could ride around in one of those custom-made buses."

"Mostly we'd fly from city to city in a private jet," Ruby explained. "Bus tours can be so grueling."

Clearly, another dose of reality was overdue. "Millions of people post songs on Youtube," I pointed out. "Most only rack up a few hundred views."

"I know that," Ruby replied. "But they don't have Cole's talent. Or his looks. And what's this I hear about your going out again with Dylan?"

"Yeah," said Elaine. "What's up with that?"

"What can I say? The guy showed up here to plead his case in person. I guess I don't want to break his little heart."

As I was leaving Explorations class, the Lumpster cornered me in the hallway. "A word with you, Blatt. Your mother informs me you're dating some local boy."

"Uh-huh."

"How did you meet him?"

How was that any of her business?

"I was flashing distress signals with a mirror out my window and he signaled back."

"I don't like your attitude, Blatt. Not one bit. Nor do I appreciate my girls associating with the local riffraff."

"You don't even know him," I pointed out.

"I will have no more pregnancies in this school. Is that clear?"

"I'm not having sex with him, if you must know."

"Just because a boy pays attention to you, it doesn't mean you have to sleep with him."

"I am well aware of that. Can I go now?"

"Just remember, Blatt, a pregnancy now can wreck your life."

"Thanks for the tip, Mrs. L. I certainly wouldn't want my life to be any worse than it already is."

* * *

Amazing development. We were all in my room counting down the minutes until dinner when Chloe let out a whoop. She dragged Marie over to the window.

"Tell me what you see out there, girl!" said Chloe.

"Oh my. It looks like a prostitute."

We all crowded around the window. Down the block a chunky gal was modeling hot pants and thigh-high boots, the universal symbol of sexual availability for $$$.

"She's kind of off the beaten track," said Ruby.

"I don't know," said Chloe, "lots of trucks drive by going to those warehouses. Truckers get really horny from their seats vibrating all day."

"Really?" asked Elaine.

"It's a known fact," confirmed Chloe. "See, that delivery truck is slowing down."

The truck slowed, honked its horn, then sped up.

"Wow, she gave him the finger," said Ruby, impressed.

Now, I can sort of see being a high-priced call girl with an exclusive client list. If Richard Gere wanted to buy me designer clothes and take me to expensive places, I'd consider doing him for generous payments in cash. But standing on a street corner and having to get intimate with ANYBODY who came along, that seems like a tough way to make a living. Not to mention that retailing it that way, you probably can't charge much. So you have to go for high volume. Plus, there's the boredom factor of standing around all day. Plus, 99 percent of the people who go by probably look at you with contempt. Plus, you're kind of risking harassment, arrest, injury, disease, and death.

"What does she look like, Marie?" asked Chloe. "Is she pretty?"

"I can't really tell. She's wearing quite enormous sunglasses. I hope that's a tattoo on her arm and not a bruise."

Everyone shrieked in surprise.

Mrs. Lumpwapht had crossed the street and was striding toward her.

"Oh, my God!" screamed Ruby. "What's she doing?"

"That confirms it," said Chloe. "The Lumpster's a lesbo."

In-your-face yelling quickly commenced.

"My God," said Elaine. "They're screaming at each other."

Loud cheering and stomping erupted throughout the dorm. Ms. Hotpants had reared back and punched our headmistress right in the nose. She staggered back from the blow as her assailant turned and fled.

"Holy shit!" exclaimed Chloe. "Did you see that? Cold-cocked by a ho right in broad daylight!"

"Awesome!" gasped Elaine. "Totally awesome!"

The cheering went on. In truth it was one of the great moments in the history of Ferncliffe Academy.

On the way to dinner The Arcadians held an emergency meeting in the bathroom and voted to make that free-swinging working girl our first honorary member. To simplify logistics, we also voted to induct Chloe. Ruby considered blackballing her, but I said it would reflect poorly on her–as the only Arcadian with a hot boyfriend–to be so uncharitable. Elaine, chair of our membership committee, has requested that Chloe be kept in the dark until a suitable initiation ceremony can be devised.

* * *

Empty chair at the high table during dinner. Rumor has it Mrs. L was off getting her nose reconfigured. Splint? Plaster cast? Amputation? I expect a beak that flattened will require major work.

After dinner Ruby and I tracked down Brick by his little boat. He was eating sardines straight from the can. We both declined his offer to share. He swallowed a smelly fish and apologized again for our picnic getting aborted.

"Not a problem," I replied. "The lunch was great. So how was the cake?"

"Wonderful. Iilivi made it from scratch. I brought some back with me, but I finished it off yesterday."

"And how was your date with Lonny?" Ruby asked.

"Great. He wants me to move to San Francisco and work in his bakery. And Iilivi wants me to move in with him and work on his dog houses. He's thinking I could paint the outsides."

"So what are you going to do?" I asked.

"I don't know. That's the problem. I do like them both, but the jobs sound like drudgery. If I make money, I'll start buying things and then I'll never be free again. I'll be owned by my stuff, like most people."

"But you were complaining that you didn't have a boyfriend," Ruby pointed out.

"Yeah, I know. I'm kind of mixed up."

"And summer's over," I added. "They're predicting rain for tomorrow."

"Are they? Damn. Yeah, winter's a drag here. I was thinking of heading south."

"You could try *one* of the jobs," Ruby suggested. "Just for the winter."

"I could do that, Ruby, but I'm kind of too depressed to decide."

"Your life is about to improve, Brick," she said, "but you're trying to sabotage it."

"Am I? How do you know that?"

"Because I've watched my mother do it for 16 years. I recognize all the signs."

* * *

In between scouring her pots and pans, Kaitlyn's been busy. She's started a rival secret sorority called the Delphians. Both of my former roommates are rumored to be founding members. It sounds like a promising group if you wish to hang with thieves, losers, and wackos.

Marie suggests we select another new member and hold our sacred and traditional ritual of induction soon. Otherwise, it may look like The Arcadians are copying our lowlife copycats. But can we agree on anyone? Chloe only squeaked by because I'm adept at manipulating Ruby. Unfortunately, we can't go for the third prettiest girl in the school, because that would be Kaitlyn. (Attractive, yes, but only in a generically bland way.) After her, there's a steep falloff in looks. One enters the realm of zits, flab, bad hair, poor posture, weird noses, warts, really big boobs, monster butts, missing teeth, glasses from hell, b.o., mental issues, etc. What's scary is that after descending through all those categories you still haven't reached my level. Good thing I'm President, because otherwise I wouldn't stand a chance of getting in.

The Lumpster showed up for breakfast. She'd tried camouflaging things with makeup, but you can tell she has two black eyes and a severely bruised nose. I was disappointed to see that her honker, though enlarged, was relatively straight. They must have shackled a chain to it and yanked it back out with a tow truck.

Marie found out from Mr. Fulm that our headmistress had called the cops on previous prostitute sightings, but Stockton's cash-strapped police department is so decimated by layoffs they tend not to respond to such trivialities. This time the Lumpster decided to make a citizen's arrest on her own. Too bad she forgot her gun and handcuffs.

So Marie is having private confabs with Mr. Fulm. We asked for details, but she declined. We know she's not talking to him after class, because they make a big show of ignoring each other. Of course, they are fooling no one.

Yes, it's pouring rain today. If you think Stockton is dreary when it's hot, you should check it out in the rain. I hope Brick is finding shelter somewhere. He wants to be loved, but he also wants to be a free spirit. That can be a tough combo to manage.

Chapter 14

GRADES GOT mailed today. I have no idea how I did. I'm in good with Mrs. Goldbline (Behaviors) and Mr. Fulm (Vistas). Mr. Ng (Expressions) may still be harboring a grudge for my alleged death threats. After those three, things get dicier. Mrs. Swengard (Practicalities) regards me as a hopeless slob, though I tend to do well on her sneaky pop quizzes. Miss Bronkiel (Explorations) is so incompetent a teacher that everyone's floundering in her class. Mr. Love (Undercurrents) teaches history and civics from the point of view of a right-wing, Bible-banging, conspiracy-minded, gun-loving, racist, sexist, gay-bashing redneck–so we're seldom on the same wavelength and frequently clash. Still, I'm usually awake in his class, which is more than you can say for some of my classmates.

I finally heard from Dylan. He phoned with a concrete proposal for a date tomorrow night.

"How about we grab a quick bite at Applebees and see 'The Mikado,' which my high school's drama club is putting on?"

"What's that?" I asked.

"It's a musical set in Japan by a couple of English dudes."

"Is one of them Andrew Lloyd Webber?"

"Uh, could be. I'm not sure."

"OK. I'm still under lock-down, so I'll have to sneak out. Pick me up at six in the parking lot where we met before. I expect you to look present-able and your car to be washed."

"It's my dad's car, Brenda. If I washed it, I think he would drop dead."

"Well, I'm willing to take that chance. And don't be late. Standing around in that parking lot, I don't want to be taken for a high-priced call girl."

"Right, Brenda. I'm looking forward to it."

"Well, don't get your hopes up. I have to be back here right after the play's over."

"So I should cancel the motel reservations?"

"You got it."

The Arcadians held another marathon nominating session last night downstairs in the ping-pong room. It's very private there as ping-pong is not a game that any Ferncliffian has been known to play. We went through a long list of prospects, but the only girl no one felt obliged to blackball was Chloe's short toady Zoey. So she got the nod. Her profile in the school is not high, but she's sort of pretty and has distinguished herself by being extremely short. Elaine and Ruby volunteered to notify the can-didates of their selection. They set their alarm for 2:00 a.m. and did the deed at that hour. Zoey screamed in surprise when awakened, but seemed gratified by the news. Her roommates Aubrey and Jasmine were less pleased. I was there, of course, when Chloe got the news. She said it was a dream come true, but wondered if it couldn't have waited until morn-ing.

I disagreed. Good news is especially dramatic when it comes like a bolt in the middle of the night. It's what sets The Arcadians apart from those lesser groups.

* * *

I heard some snickering in the halls as Marie and I walked to

Practicalities class. Then as I was taking my seat Mrs. Swengard adjusted her dentures and asked me what I was trying to prove–provoking titters from Kaitlyn and her lackeys.

"About what?" I asked.

"Your appearance, Miss Blatt. Your appearance."

I looked down. My blouse and skirt were as neat and orderly as anyone dared hope. Certainly no worse than usual.

"Is something wrong?" I asked.

More snickering from my enemies.

"Is that letter a comment on your grade?"

"Mrs. Swengard, I have no idea what you're talking about."

Great burst of laughter. Marie looked behind me and removed something from my back. More laughter as I saw what it was: a large "D" cut out of red construction paper. So that's what that jostling in the hall had been about. The Delphians had struck. At least it wasn't a knife in the gut.

"I'm sorry, Mrs. Swengard. I didn't know it was there."

"And what is the significance of that letter?" she asked.

"I have no idea," I lied. "It must be some childish person's idea of a D-level prank."

"Such disruptions are not permitted, Miss Blatt. Don't let it happen again."

"Yes, Mrs. Swengard. Shall I have my back surgically removed?"

"I suggest you go discuss *that* with Mrs. Lumpwapht."

So I had to go to the Lumpster's office and hand her the sealed note from Mrs. Swengard. I studied her heavily made up face as she read it. Her honker was still nicely swollen. What a punch that must have been.

Very dark frown. "Mrs. Swengard writes that you have been disruptive and impertinent. What do you have to say for yourself, Blatt?"

I explained the circumstances of my victimhood.

"So you were not protesting the grade you received from Mrs. Swengard?"

The bitch gave me a D!

"No, Mrs. Lumpwapht. I haven't seen any of my grades yet. Did I get any other Ds?"

"Two, I believe. Your parents will not be pleased. But I expect they are accustomed to being disappointed by you."

"I never received grades that low in the public schools. I hope they don't feel the need to withdraw me from your school. They know I haven't been treated fairly here."

That caught the Lumpster up short. A threat to her wallet could not be ignored.

"If as you say, Blatt, you were the victim of a prank, then some allowances could be made for your behavior. You will return to class and apologize to Mrs. Swengard. And you will try to be more respectful in the future."

"Yes, Mrs. Lumpwapht. Your face is looking better."

"I have given a full description of the assailant to the police. I hope justice will prevail, but I am not optimistic. If you should see any sort of suspicious females loitering about, please notify me at once."

"I certainly shall," I lied.

* * *

Another day of cold rain. Our room this morning was as chilly as old Mrs. Swengard's thighs. Makes it kind of tough to crawl out of bed. Chloe says we better get used to it because the Lumpster never turns on the heat until after Christmas vacation. We're all bundled up in sweaters, which is not a slimming look for me. Marie, on the other hand, fills out a sweater like some lonely sailor's dream. Life is so unfair, but I may have mentioned that before.

Speaking of which, my mother called me during breakfast to complain about my crummy grades. I got two As (from my competent teachers), a B- (Mr. Ng), a D+ (that bastard Mr. Love couldn't have swung me a C-?), and two Ds (Swengard and Bronkiel).

"What can I say, Mother? Most of the teachers here suck. They are the dregs of the dregs."

"Are you really applying yourself, dear?"

"I'm doing my best, Mom. I do well on tests. Those low marks reflect their personal animus toward me."

"Shall I complain to your headmistress?"

"Don't bother. She hates me too."

"You're not neglecting your studies for your social life, are you, Brenda?"

"I thought you sent me here to get a social life."

"We did, darling. But one shouldn't overdo things. And how are you getting on with young Dylan?"

"I don't recall mentioning his name to you, Mother."

"Oh, I'm sure you must have. Have you seen him again?"

"We have a date tonight. So you still have time to plant a webcam in his car."

"Really, Brenda, I have no interest in spying on you. But do remember to act responsibly."

"He won't be able to unclamp my knees with a hydraulic jack."

"Really, dear, the things you say!"

* * *

It was still raining when Dylan picked me up—which gave him a convenient excuse for driving an unwashed car. To his credit, Dylan had visited a barber, shaved off his goatee, and ditched the ragged shirt. Too bad he was still a big pear-shaped lump.

"You look nice, Brenda," he said, leaning over for a kiss. "You smell good too. Is that perfume?"

"No, it's my vaginal deodorant spray. Yes, of course, it's a perfume. I borrowed a spritz from my roommate. It's called Perish Before Sunrise."

"Wow, that sounds, uh, heavy."

"Heavy is not a word I appreciate your using around me."

"Oh, sorry. No offense."

Applebees was as warm and festive as a chain restaurant in rainy Stockton could be. I ordered the Bourbon Street Chicken & Shrimp; my date went for the Sizzling Double Barrel Whisky Sirloins.

"How did your recording session go?" I asked, sipping my diet soda.

"Horrible. Your basic living nightmare."

"Ruby isn't working out as your singer?"

"Well, there may be a planet somewhere in the universe where music is tuned to her scale, but it's not this one. I heard notes out of her mouth today that I never knew existed."

"So what are you going to do?"

"We were thinking of auditioning you."

"Yeah, right."

"You have a nice voice, Brenda. I know you could do it."

I sighed. "Do you have a one-sheet of your song?"

"Sure. Right here."

I looked over his dog-eared photocopy.

"Well, your tune is not bad, but your lyrics kind of suck."

"So you read music?"

"I should, I studied cello for years—until I found out it's not polite to sit around with your legs spread. You know there are more words that rhyme with kayak besides crack."

"Feel free to clean it up, Brenda. We're not married to those words."

"Well, I'll see what I can do. Who wrote the tune? It's pretty catchy."

"Cole did most of it. He's kind of a genius, but I'm better looking. And much better in bed."

"So you allege. Oh, just in time, here comes our food."

It turns out "The Mikado" was not by Andrew Lloyd Webber. It was a very silly show about a guy who gets condemned to death for flirting and all the complications that ensue. Very well done for a high-school production. The singing was competent, the players in the pit were mostly in tune, and the costumes and sets were nearly dazzling. On the drive back to school I suggested to Dylan that there were any number of girls in that show who might be good for his song.

"Not going to happen, Brenda."

"Why not?"

"Girls in my high school tend not to wish to be associated with members of the Accordion Club."

"Are you that uncool?"

"Not in my opinion."

"How about theirs?"

"Well, not many of them seem excited by the prospect of screwing me. Kind of strange because the accordion visually is the most beautiful instrument out there. Plus, it's like an entire orchestra dangling down your front. If you think about it, the whole thing is pretty darn phallic."

"Guess you were born in the wrong century."

"Probably. I bet accordionists a hundred years ago had to beat the chicks off with a stick."

We experimented with another kiss and some strenuous grappling in the supermarket parking lot. I do like kissing boys, I've decided. I'm just not sure I'm kissing the right one.

When I sneaked up to my room (well past lights out), I found a small-ish lump asleep in my bed. I gave it a probing poke.

"Leave me alone," it wheezed.

"Zoey, what are you doing in my bed?" I whispered.

"Brenda? Oh, hi. Chloe said you weren't coming back tonight."

"Wrong. So clear out."

"Do I have to? It's so warm here and such a cold, dark trip to my room."

"Are you emulating Monica Lewinski? Do you wish to sleep with your President?"

"What?"

"Never mind. Just push over. And don't thrash about."

On a chilly night it *is* rather pleasant sleeping two to a bed. Zoey gave off plenty of welcome warmth while taking up hardly any space. Plus, she smelled better than the average boy and didn't snore.

Chapter 15

EYEBROWS WERE raised in my room this Sunday morning when we were discovered sleeping two to a bed. I see nothing controversial in employing a fellow student as a substitute hot-water bottle. Though the narrowness of the bed did necessitate some actual contact, we were fully clothed at all times. The fact that my arm lay across Zoey's impressive rack I attributed to the dynamics of sleep. Should I turn out to be a lesbian after all, I now know there are some aspects of that lifestyle I can look forward to. (Probably the best thing for me would be to sleep with a boy, then compare and contrast the experiences.)

Ruby continues to exhibit major cluelessness when it comes to her BF. All during breakfast she was boasting of how well she did at yesterday's recording session. The girl has refined cognitive dissonance to a high art. I felt I better not mention that they were recruiting me to take her place.

Marie and I slipped away to the ping-pong room to unlameify the lyrics. After a struggle, we both agreed that the entire kayaking metaphor would have to go. Our revised song, titled "Riffraff," laments a jilted lover's tendency to fall for those unsavory and irresponsible types. Perhaps mindful of her neglect by Rodney the Indifferent, Marie was really getting into it. The lyrics are way clever, they fit the tune perfectly, and there are no false rhymes. Andrew Lloyd Webber eat your heart out.

Mr. Love, who seems unnaturally fixated on medieval England, was talking last week about a particularly incompetent king known to history as Aethelred the Unready (979-1016 A.D.). So I've been applying that classification system to my friends. There's Ruby the Overconfident, Elaine the Tall, Marie the Awesome, Chloe the Flirt, Zoey the Racked, Brick the Troubled, Cole the Kayaker, and Dylan the Grappler. Plus, Gianna the Gazer, Kaitlyn the Creep, Owen the Tormented, Lumpwapht the Tyrant, Luiz the Sudsy, Iilivi the Toed, Buford the Unemployed, Mom the Non-Maternal, Dad the Disappointed, etc. I'd like to be thought of as Brenda the Bold or Brenda the Great, but more likely destiny will label me Brenda the Fat.

* * *

Brick has disappeared! No one has heard from him since Tuesday. Nor is he answering his phone.

Sounding most distressed, Iilivi phoned Ruby to ask if we could check Brick's boat. We found it swamped with half a foot of murky water. The cuddy cabin was empty except for some soggy foam. No note or indication of where he had gone.

After lunch, Iilivi signed us out by showing his I.D. and claiming to be Ruby's cousin. Waiting for us in Iilivi's vintage station wagon was Lonny the Cake Decorator. Very handsome short dude who must visit the gym daily. Or perhaps he tones his pecs squeezing those tubes of frosting. One odd detail: from the neck up he looks like a cute eight-year-old boy. It's like his body matured, but his face remained stuck in the third grade. Somehow this renders him instantly lovable. Comparing notes later, both Ruby and I immediately wanted to clutch him to our breasts (assuming she had any) and give him a big comforting squeeze.

Since Lonny was a native, he knew where to look. In a gray and chilly drizzle, we toured all the homeless hangouts throughout the Stockton area. Hard to believe one moderate-sized city could pack in all that grimness. None of the people we talked to who knew Brick had seen or heard from him since last week.

The optimists (Lonny and I) thought that perhaps Brick had headed south in search of fairer weather. The pessimists (Iilivi and Ruby) were convinced that he was in trouble somewhere or some disaster had befallen him. We thrashed this out over dinner in a Vietnamese restaurant down the block from a homeless shelter.

"Why would Brick leave town without letting anyone know?" asked Ruby.

"I'm sure he would at least phone me to say good-bye," insisted Iilivi.

"Well, Darnell's not the most responsible person I've met," Lonny pointed out.

"That's right," I agreed. "Brick wants to be a free spirit. And free spirits may not pay attention to the social niceties."

"Well, if I don't hear from him by tomorrow," said Iilivi. "I'm filing a missing person's report with the Stockton police."

"That's probably a good idea," said Lonny. "I'll go with you if you like."

"I'd appreciate it. They might take it more seriously if there were two of us."

Eventually, I got around to asking Iilivi if he was still looking for workers for his dog-house business.

"I am, Brenda, but I'm kind of particular. I need someone reliable and good with his hands who hasn't picked up a lot of bad habits."

Not exactly my brother, but I gave it a shot anyway.

"Do you know if he took any shop classes in high school?" asked Iilivi.

"Both wood shop and auto shop," I replied. I didn't mention that

Buford had crafted the ugliest buffet-hutch in the history of world furniture. It was still disfiguring my parents' dining room, though my mother has designated it Wedding Gift Number One for when Buford gets married.

"Have him call me," said Iilivi. "I'd be happy to talk to him. I'm pretty far from Hayward, but I might be able to come up with some housing for him."

"That'd be great," I replied. "He wouldn't need anything fancy."

"And I'm always on the lookout for promising apprentice bakers," added Lonny.

"Probably not the best fit for my brother," I replied. "With his sweet tooth, he might put a serious dent in your profits."

After Iilivi dropped us off, Ruby said it was rude of me to talk about a job for my brother at a time like this.

"Why?" I demanded. "Iilivi still has a business to run. You heard him say he was getting behind on his orders."

"Don't you understand, Brenda? Iilivi's inner voice has told him that Brick's in trouble–possibly even in danger. That's why he's so concerned."

"How do you know that? He said no such thing."

"Well, it's not something you talk about with strangers. But if you weren't so insensitive, you would have picked up on it."

I could have debated clueless insensitivity with Ruby, but I stifled the impulse.

Before we went in, we stopped at the supermarket to stock up on essential provisions. Keeping supplied with vital snacks will be more difficult now that Brick has wandered off to parts unknown (or been abducted by aliens). I don't suppose he gave much thought to my needs when deciding to flake out.

We heard from Dylan. He's thrilled with our revised lyrics. He said Cole is impressed, but feels the original vision of his song has been compromised. I said to tell Cole that's what artistic collaboration is all about, and to get over it. I said he should be grateful we aren't charging them big bucks for our professional services.

I also alerted my mother to Iilivi's job possibility. Had I phoned my brother, he might not have bothered to follow up on it. By informing my mother, I *know* the call will be made. She liked the idea of Buford working out here so he could "keep an eye on you"–thus shirking her parental responsibilities even more. I'm beginning to think that having children was not high on my mother's list of priorities. I may be despoiling this planet as a byproduct of sloppy birth control.

* * *

Monday morning. More gloomy rain plus fog. It's like London in 1945: lousy weather, rationed food, and no TV. At breakfast we informed our prospective Arcadians of the first of five feats they must accomplish to earn membership in our elite sorority.

"I thought we were already members," said Zoey, confused. "What was that waking us up in the middle of the night about?"

"That merely was to inform you of your selection as a *candidate* for membership," Elaine explained.

"OK, so who do we have to blow to get in?" asked Chloe.

"Your first task," I whispered, "which must be accomplished today, is to give–in public–a hearty hug to our esteemed headmistress."

"No way," said Zoey. "I'm joining the Delphians."

"No, you're not," said Chloe. "OK, Zoey, you better do it now. Then I'll do it at dinner."

"Why do I have to go first?" she complained.

"Because you're plausible as a person needing a hug. The Lumpster would know something was fishy if I tried it first."

"Damn! Well, OK, here goes nothing."

Vastly ill-at-ease, Zoey shuffled over to the high table, tapped Mrs. L on the shoulder, and whispered something in her ear. The Lumpster smiled in surprise, rose from her chair, and gave the victim a warm and enthusiastic hug. A flabbergasted silence descended on the room. The hug went on and on. Eventually, Zoey squirmed free and returned to her seat.

"Well, that was pretty horrible," whispered Zoey. "And now I've disgraced myself in front of the whole school."

"What did you tell her?" asked Ruby.

"I said I had a bad night and needed a hug. How was I supposed to know she was going to hang on like a drowning rat?"

Can it be that the Lumpster was also in need of a hug?

"This is even scarier than I thought," commented Chloe. "How about I blow the janitor instead?"

"No way, girl," I replied. "A true Arcadian never backs down from adversity."

* * *

We finished *Pride and Prejudice* in Vistas class today. Everything turned out fine. Mr. Darcy gave up being a snob and Elizabeth got over thinking he was a stuck-up twit. Since the ending was so romantic, everyone paid extra attention to Owen and Marie. Both looked a bit misty-eyed while stealing some all-too-obvious significant glances. Their distress is to be expected, since they know that if they yield to their passions, they won't be living happily ever after in luxurious Pemberley on £10,000 a year. More likely Mr. Fulm will be going to jail and Marie will be trundled off to Juvenile Hall.

After our last class Ruby swiped a big can from the kitchen dumpster so we could take turns bailing out Brick's little boat. She is determined not to let it sink—even if we both perish from pneumonia. Still no sign of its occupant anywhere. Iilivi and Lonny have filed their report with the cops, who didn't seem all that alarmed that a homeless dwarf with a criminal past has gone missing. Iilivi's trying to contact a relative, but so far he's turned up no Brickmans in the Turlock area.

Somehow the word had got around. Many eyes were trained on Chloe this evening when she got up from her meatballs in cream sauce (not real cream) and headed toward the high table. To her credit, she didn't dawdle, but went right up to the Lumpster. Chloe said something while pointing toward her left eye, which she was keeping shut.

"What's she doing?" whispered Zoey.

We watched as Mrs. L stood up and began examining Chloe's distressed eye.

"She's faking it," commented Ruby.

"Yeah, what a sneak," said Zoey.

As Mrs. L directed Chloe toward a beam from an overhead light, her patient casually grasped her around her waist. The arms inched farther along as the examination continued until the embrace was nearly complete. Chloe blinked a few times, smiled, appeared to offer thanks, and briefly clasped her benefactress again. Turning her back on the Lumpster, she smiled smugly and sauntered back to her seat.

"That doesn't count," hissed Zoey.

"What do you mean?" demanded Chloe. "That was a hug!"

"It was not," insisted Zoey. "You were faking it."

"Of course I was faking it. Otherwise, everyone might take me for an emotionally needy suck-up."

"Did that count as a hug?" demanded Zoey.

Everyone turned toward their President. "It counted as a hug," I ruled. "Chloe had her arms around her. Well done, girl."

"Thanks, Brenda. Damn, I could use a hot shower right now. I feel totally contaminated by her cooties."

* * *

We awoke to a sunny morning. Then both my roommates flashed some welcome nudity while dressing. Then Juanita (my favorite server) was manning the steam table, so I got an extra-generous helping of french toast and sausages. The only flaw in my morning so far was the cheapo artificial syrup which coats your mouth like Valvoline in a V-8. I poured it on anyway.

I nibbled a bonus sausage (donated by Marie) and faced our two pledges. "Are you girls ready for today's challenge?"

"I guess," sighed Chloe.

"I suppose," sighed Zoey.

"Yesterday's task," I reminded them, "entailed some embarrassment to yourselves."

"Not to me," sniffed Chloe.

"That's 'cause you cheated," said Zoey.

"Did not."

"Did so too."

"Anyway," I continued, lowering my voice, "your challenge today is to embarrass a Delphian."

"Piece of cake," said Chloe. "Be in the hallway outside the cafeteria right before lunch. Is it OK if Zoey and I work together on this?"

"Sure," I replied. "We Arcadians are renowned for our teamwork."

My luck held in Expressions class. Taking a break from a tedious string of tiresome topics, Mr. Ng assigned us to write 300 words on "What I Hope To Be Doing 10 Years from Now." I said I expected to be the celebrated host of a top-rated TV show called "Getting Even with Your Ex." Viewers would write in with creative suggestions for exacting revenge from former spouses/lovers who had jilted, dumped, or cheated on them. The winners would get to realize their fantasies in front of a nationwide audience as the unfolding incident was taped via concealed cameras. I acknowledged that occasionally our targeted victims might sue us or be driven to suicide. Therefore my production company would be fully insured so my fabulous salary would not be imperiled. Looking on the bright side, I said these unforeseen tragedies could be great publicity for the show. I concluded by mentioning that I had already written an appropriate theme song for our show titled "Riffraff," which soon may be a Number One hit on Youtube.

Not even a slog through Undercurrents and Practicalities could spoil my morning. Mr. Love asserted today that every computer and cellphone built in "Red China" could be switched on remotely by their military to spy on Americans. In which case I expect they like to watch Marie get dressed as much as I do. Mrs. Swengard's lesson was on how to dine in an expensive restaurant. We learned that you butter your bread in little bits (not the entire slice at once), you never freshen your lipstick at the table, and you always let "your escort" pick up the tab. Too bad she never got around to mentioning by which date it was permissible to blow him under the table.

Lunchtime found The Arcadians blending nonchalantly amidst the throngs waiting for the cafeteria doors to be unlocked. Noon was the scheduled time and not a calorie could be had before then.

"Eewww! Gross!" squealed a familiar voice.

Everyone looked toward Chloe.

"Oh, my God!" screamed Zoey, pointing. "That is *so-o-o* disgusting!"

We all looked down. Clearly, there was something stuck to the side and bottom of Kaitlyn's shoe.

"God, Kaitlyn!" sneered Chloe. "You are such a slob!"

"Fuck!" she exclaimed, turning the color of a ripe tomato. "That sure as hell isn't mine!"

We all crowded in for a closer look. Adhering to Kaitlyn's shoe was what appeared to be a tampon (a used one), accompanied by a length of soiled toilet paper.

"Get it off! Get it off!" shouted Kaitlyn, shaking her foot. The bathroom debris held fast; no volunteer stepped forward to remove it. Kaitlyn reached down and gave the dangling string a tentative tug.

"Gross! She touched it!" someone commented.

"Fuck!" hissed Kaitlyn, taking a firmer grip. Tentacles of pink gum stretched away from her shoe as she tugged at the mass. She shook her hand violently–flinging the liberated debris across the hall and striking a fellow Delphian: my old roommate Gianna. She lurched back, but the mass became entangled in her hair. She let out the first truly blood-curdling scream I had ever heard. This brought the Lumpster running.

"What the hell is going on?" Mrs. L demanded.

"Kaitlyn was a bit careless with her hygiene," explained Chloe. "Now her tampon is stuck in poor Gianna's hair."

"I think it's all that gum she chews," added Zoey, helpfully.

"Gianna, go straight to the janitor's office," our headmistress commanded.

But panicked Gianna was in no condition to comprehend human speech. She was quivering oddly and her eyeballs had gone north in their sockets.

"Kaitlyn, help Gianna," ordered Mrs. L. "And I want you both in my office right after lunch."

Needless to say, our two acolytes passed that challenge with flying colors. Later, during lunch, Chloe explained how she had brought her plan to fruition. "Well, I knew Kaitlyn has a twitchy bladder. She always takes a tinkle before lunch. And naturally, she stops by the mirror on her way out. So I had positioned Zoey with the goods in the stall closest to the mirror."

"She made me reach in the garbage to pick out that tampon," Zoey confessed.

"True," conceded Chloe, "but I did my share. I chewed most of the gum. So when Kaitlyn was by the mirror, I kind of crowded her over to get her closer to Zoey."

"Then I did the deed," grinned Zoey.

"She never suspected a thing," said Chloe. "The toilet paper was unplanned."

"She picked that up on the way out," Zoey explained.

Another fortunate occurrence. And what an ideal trajectory that flying tampon took. This could go down as the luckiest morning of my life.

Chapter 16

GIANNA CALMED down after the janitor used some lighter fluid to clear the gum and other matter from her hair. She spent the afternoon reclining on the sofa in the student lounge with her feet elevated and a damp washcloth over her eyes. She's kind of high strung and lacks coping skills—not a good combination for life at Ferncliffe Academy. Clearly the Delphians are so desperate for members they'll take anyone.

Still no sign of or word from Brick. Now Ruby has to worry about that, plus a noticeable lack of calls from her BF. Cole hasn't been paddling out this way either. Could it be that one sexual encounter with Ruby is enough for any guy?

Speaking of mysteries, Marie disappeared again after dinner. I was hoping to follow her, but she has a knack for melting away unseen. I'd give up cheese curls for a week to know where she goes and who she's with. She always returns with a noticeably improved mood, which I find suspicious as hell.

More rain and thunder last night, then a breakfast only a zombie could stomach: chipped beef on toast, or as we call it Gloppy on a Floppy. Not very fortifying for a day of scholastic assaults in soggy Stockton. Thank God we still had our sorority pledges to help boost morale.

"Are you ready for your next assignment?" I asked brightly.

"I guess," sighed Chloe.

"I suppose," sighed Zoey.

"OK, yesterday, frankly, was a triumph. Today, however, may be more of a challenge."

"Why does that not surprise me?" said Chloe.

"Today's required feat," I continued, "is to be seen on campus handcuffed to a cop."

"What kind of cop?" asked Chloe.

I was wise to her tricks. "No, Chloe, it can't be that deputy sheriff you were flirting with last week. It has to be someone new. A real cop in a real uniform."

"With badges and guns?" asked Zoey.

"The very same," I replied.

Zoey glanced questioningly at her leader.

"Piece of cake," said Chloe.

* * *

Dylan phoned me during lunch. Our recording session is set for Sunday afternoon. He informed me that Cole has been fiddling with our lyrics.

"He can fiddle away, but I intend to sing it just the way Marie and I wrote it. Otherwise, you can get yourself another songbird."

"I dig it when you use jazz slang, Brenda. Can I ask you a personal question?"

"I suppose."

"Are you open to intercourse more than one way?"

"Meaning what?"

"Meaning besides the vagina."

"Sure. For example, I'm totally open to your sticking it in the tailpipe of your dad's SUV. Preferably while it's running. Any more questions?"

"You kill me, Brenda. You absolutely kill me."

"Funny, I often have exactly that impulse."

In Vistas class we were starting in on a new book (*The Grapes of Wrath* by John Steinbeck), when a commotion outside drew everyone to the window. Down below Chloe and Zoey were handcuffed to a cop, while a guy laden with multiple cameras was taking their photo and a woman with a steno pad appeared to be interviewing them. The cop and prisoners were smiling, and he was holding up a small plate of cookies.

"Well, they did it," whispered Marie.

"Yeah, so it seems."

We got the story during dinner.

"OK," said Chloe, "So I put on my sexiest voice and gave the cops a jingle."

"She called the main number," Zoey translated.

"I say to the fellow that answered: hey, I hear you guys are in financial distress. He says yeah, you got a few million you could spare? I say unfortunately not, but I'm a civic-minded student and we've baked some cookies to thank you all for doing such a great job."

"We sneaked out and bought the cookies at the market," Zoey explained.

"Yeah, and then she ate most of them before the cop even showed up.

So a reporter heard about our call, and she tags along."

"On account of it's a human-interest story," said Zoey.

"Right," affirmed Chloe. "And probably not much else was happening in boring Stockton. So they bring a photographer too. The police department sends over one of their rookie cops, who's sort of young and cute."

"I'd do him," proclaimed Zoey. "In a heartbeat. His name's Tom. He was really nice."

"Right, only Tom pretends to be annoyed that our cookies are so skimpy. I say why don't you put the cuffs on us and we'll take a pledge to bake you cookies every week. So, naturally, he plays along."

"I love being cuffed to a cop," Zoey confessed. "It's such a turn-on."

"I could tell," said Chloe. "I figured right then was when you were committing to a life of crime."

"Could be," admitted Zoey.

"So does this mean you have to provide cookies for the cops every week?" asked Elaine.

"I sincerely hope not," replied Chloe.

"What did the Lumpster say when she showed up?" asked Ruby.

"Well, at first she was pissed," said Chloe. "Then she figured out it was a chance to get some great publicity for her crummy school. Then we got sent back to class so she could bend Tom's ear about getting clocked by that ho."

"I bet if I were 18, Tom would ask me out," said Zoey. "I could tell he liked me."

"The guy had a wedding ring, you dope," said Chloe.

"Did he really? Well, that sucks."

"He was also about two feet taller than you."

"That's OK, Chloe. I'm not into short guys."

* * *

Rumor has it that Kaitlyn has figured out who was behind her humiliation. The Delphians have been put on high alert and are now on the warpath. I hope the kitchen staff is keeping a close watch over the butcher knives and cleavers. In a fair fight (fists only), I'm pretty confident I could take any girl in this school. I used to rough it up with Buford and his pals, and never failed to stomp their puny asses. Several more girls have approached me about joining The Arcadians, but I had to explain that membership is by invitation only. You can't be an elite organization if you take anyone who wanders by.

Mr. Fulm showed up at breakfast with 50 copies of the Stockton paper. Chloe and Zoey made the front page of the local news section. Very flattering photo of Chloe, but Zoey looked like a midget with breasts.

"Why do I look so short?" she complained.

"Well, you are short," Elaine pointed out.

"It was the photographer's fault," said Chloe, "He should have angled his shot up instead of down–although this way kind of disguises my enormous nose."

I should have such a petite, delicately shaped, and enchanting nose.

"You have a lovely nose," said Marie, who herself possesses one of the Supreme Noses of our epoch.

"Thanks, Marie," replied Chloe, "but it's a gross turnip compared to yours."

"Oh, I hardly think so," she laughed.

They went on gushing extravagant nose compliments until I was about to lose my cornflakes.

"Enough! Enough!" I said. "It is time to move on to the topic at hand. Are you girls ready for your next challenge?"

"I suppose," sighed Chloe.

"I guess," sighed Zoey.

"Good," I said. "I really appreciate your enthusiasm. We Arcadians have noticed that it's a real drag having classes six days a week. Your task is to get school cancelled for tomorrow."

Zoey's face sank. "But, but that's impossible."

Everyone looked toward Chloe.

"Piece of cake," she smiled.

* * *

Someone tossed a water balloon into a toilet stall this morning, drenching poor Ruby, who was already miserable from BF trouble and her monthlies. The new rule is Arcadians only go to the restroom in pairs.

I hope Ruby wasn't attacked because of her unsightly earrings. Today's eyesores featured rounds of white plastic defaced by a grid of orange and green squares. Like something your granny wore in 1977. Since we're all dressed alike in ugly uniforms, many girls express their individuality via ear ornamentation. But most of the trinkets dangling from their lobes look like something disbursed by explorers to appease hostile natives in the remote interiors of steamy jungles.

There are exceptions to the bad taste parade. Marie occasionally wears simple pearl earrings that glow with a soft lunar sheen. And Chloe daily adorns her lovely ears from her vast repertoire of flattering baubles. Today's selection: small squares that flame with a fiery red-orange light. Made from some sort of high-refractive glass and more dazzling than any gem. She's offered to let me try them on, but, of course, I never bothered to get my ears pierced. I figured the marginal augmentation of my allure wasn't worth the pain of the needle. So my bumptious ears just hang out there naked as a baby's butt.

So far I'm not digging *The Grapes of Wrath*. It's a shock that we're reading John Steinbeck, since he wasn't an English person living in the

19th Century. He was from Salinas, though, which is pretty much the Stockton of the Monterey Valley. During his lifetime he was despised by most of the locals, but now they have a museum there devoted to him. Mr. Fulm wants to organize a field trip to Salinas, but I'd be amazed if he gets the Lumpster to agree. Steinbeck won the Nobel Prize, but some critics these days sniff that he was strictly second rate. I'd say he's quite a bit duller than Jane, who kind of grabs your attention right away. I guess if you're going to write about the Depression, your prose can't be all that sparkling.

At dinner the Lumpster tapped her water glass with a spoon and stood up to make an announcement. "Attention, girls. As you may have heard, the day students have been instructed not to come in tomorrow. We are going to have to evacuate the buildings. Everyone must be in the parking lot promptly at 8:30 a.m. with an overnight bag. You will be bused to a local hotel, where you will spend the night."

Thunderous applause and crazed cheering.

The Lumpster motioned for silence. "I expect everyone to conduct themselves in a manner befitting the lofty standards of Ferncliffe Academy."

A girl named Felicity raised her hand. "Where will we be eating?" she asked.

"The hotel will be serving a buffet lunch and dinner. I expect you all to act like ladies at the buffet."

For some reason the Lumpster looked directly at me when she said that.

Kaitlyn raised her hand. "Are we going to have our classes?"

"Unfortunately no," replied our headmistress. "But I expect all of you to study on your own."

Yeah, right.

More applause and wild cheering. Clearly, it was another momentous day in the history of Ferncliffe Academy. When the cheering stopped, we all turned toward Chloe.

"How, how on earth?" I sputtered.

"Actually, it was nothing," she smiled. "I'll tell you all about it tomorrow–when we're reclining by the hotel's indoor pool."

That decided it. When I get to be a famous TV personality, I'm hiring Chloe to head up my production staff. That girl is nothing if not resourceful.

Ruby broke down and called her BF this evening. Cole said he hadn't been neglecting her, but had been working "day and night" on his song. No, he hasn't posted it to Youtube yet, on account of "unforeseen production delays." He and Dylan are too chicken to tell her that she's been replaced by another canary. I'm not telling her either, as I really don't need my eyes scratched out. Nor do I have a clue exactly how the news is going to be conveyed. We could sneak her a massive dose of sedatives and then have Marie do the job. Bad news is always more palatable when it comes from someone who is soothingly beautiful.

Brick's little boat is still deserted. And no one's heard a word from him. Iilivi hasn't heard from the cops either, which means that no dwarves have been arrested or washed up in the slough. I'm sticking to my theory that he blew town. There must be more glamorous places to make a living as a pro panhandler. Palm Springs? Newport Beach? Hollywood?

* * *

Ferncliffe Academy owns a rusty old school bus, but we got transported to the hotel out by the interstate in a fleet of those posh buses that normally haul old folks to Indian casinos. Marie and Chloe packed their swim attire, but no way do I parade around my flab in anything resembling abbreviated spandex. We were assigned room 929, which—not surprisingly—was on the ninth floor. The immense window offered a sweeping view across the tawdry expanse of greater Stockton. Discernible on the far eastern horizon were the faint outlines of some Sierra peaks. Our room has a glam bathroom, a big-screen TV, a mini bar (locked for our protection), and dual queen beds. The two beauties opted to share one bed, while the fat girl got assigned the other one.

Marie inspected a small notice posted on the entry door. "According to this, our room rents for $285 a night," she reported.

"Right," said Chloe, "except nobody pays that. They always post an inflated figure so you think you're getting a deal. Who would pay that kind of money to spend a night in Stockton?"

"Still, I bet this room is expensive," said Marie.

"I sincerely hope so," said Chloe. "I have never been a cheap date."

"I made Dylan pay for my meal at Applebees the other night," I bragged.

"Good for you, girl," said Chloe. "But next time make him take you to someplace nicer."

"Won't he expect me to put out in return?"

"You bet your life," she replied. "But don't do it in his car. That's tacky. Right, Marie?"

"Uh-huh."

"Marie's not an expert like you are, Chloe. She's still a virgin."

Chloe glanced casually over at our stunning roommate. "Right, Brenda. And if you believe that, I got a hotel here I'll sell you cheap."

Zoey zoomed in without knocking. "There's a fun center next door! We're all going down to play miniature golf!"

Now, I've always held that miniature golf is for people with miniature minds, but I tagged along with the group. The first thing I did was hit the

269

bank of gleaming vending machines. The second thing I did was kick everyone's asses at golf. It was pretty much a slaughter from the first hole.

Next, came lunch back at the hotel. Admittedly, I'm the sort of person who thrives in a buffet situation–even with the Lumpster flashing me those disapproving looks as I trot back for my fourth refill. And really, who has the willpower to resist the adjoining dessert bar? A make-your-own hot-fudge sundae with warm cherry cobbler on the side–all topped by an ocean of whipped cream. And three brownies and some peanut-butter cookies. All for no extra charge! What's not to like?

It's a good thing I didn't go into the posh pool, as I probably would have cramped up and drowned within 30 seconds. Marie and Chloe got tastefully wet, then we all reclined with our books among the fake palm trees beside the pool. Ruby, Elaine, and Zoey also were displaying their iterations of the female body in semi-revealing swimwear.

"OK, Chloe," I whispered. "Spill it. How did you do it?"

"You really want to know?" she smiled, "I left it all up to Vinny Guitierrez."

"And who exactly is that?" I asked.

"It's this amazing voice she can do," explained Zoey. "She sounds just like some Mexican dude."

"Let's hear your Vinny," said Elaine.

"Buenos tardes, señorita," said Chloe–heavily accented and deep of voice. "Would you like to go up to my room and show me your tortilla?"

"Amazing," whistled Ruby. "How do you do that?"

"I channel my inner Latino," replied Chloe. "So I call up the Lumpster and say I'm from the sewage treatment plant. I say we're installing some new valves to fix the problems that caused the blockage last year. Only there's a possibility of severe sewer gas backflow–so could you please evacuate your school on Friday between the hours of 9 a.m. and midnight."

"What did the Lumpster say?" I asked.

"She was pissed. Mucho yelling and screaming. She demanded to know why she wasn't given more notice. I say unfortunately our safety officer has just alerted us to this issue. She said what happens if I don't evacuate? I say there is a possibility of injury, dismemberment, or death if toilets get blown off their mountings. That got her attention. Then I say don't worry, we'll pay for all the costs of evacuating your school. Take your students someplace nice for the day and send us all the bills."

"Very clever," I said. "And what happens when the sewage district refuses to pay?"

"Well, that's not really my problem," replied Chloe. "I figure at the very worst the Lumpster will keel over from a massive stroke."

"I could live with that," I replied.

"Yeah, I don't have a problem with that," said Zoey. "So do we get to be Arcadians?"

"Well, we were going to issue you a fifth challenge," I said. "But I don't really see how you girls could top this. So, unless anyone objects, I say you're in. Right, Arcadians?"

Marie, Ruby, and Elaine all nodded their assent. The Elite Four were now the Magnificent Six.

Chapter 17

LOUD BANGING on the door roused us at 2:13 in the morning. It was Matron Beezle, who told us to "get dressed immediately" and to "hustle downstairs as fast as possible."

"What's up?" yawned Chloe.

"We're all the victims of a cruel hoax," she replied. "Hurry! The bus leaves in five minutes!"

Well, that was a lie. The bus (Ferncliffe's ratty old one) left a half-hour later and only with the first 40 girls. The rest of us got to lounge around the crowded lobby until our names were called for its subsequent trips. It was nearly 4:00 a.m. before Marie and I got to board. I don't see why they couldn't have let us sleep in until morning. It's not like they were going to rent the rooms to anyone else at that hour of the night. Not only was our sleep unnecessarily truncated, but no snacks of any sort were provided. And I had been so looking forward to the breakfast buffet. The hotel's officious night manager looked even more steamed than Mrs. Lumpwapht, who was beaming daggers at her usual suspects (myself included). You'd think she'd know to investigate those crank calls before running up huge hotel bills.

When we got to school, we discovered that the kitchen was closed. No breakfast was to be served! And the Lumpster posted flunkies at all the dorm exits, so no one could sneak out to relieve the famine. We Arcadians had to make do with my meager cache of cheese curls and Heath bars.

"I wonder what happened," said Zoey, crunching away.

"Probably the hotel got worried," speculated Ruby, "and tracked down someone at the sewage district."

"I talked to Mrs. Beezle after you guys left," said Chloe. "According to her, the bill for our day on the town came to over $18,000."

"That's not bad," I said, claiming the last of the Heath bars.

"It really isn't," agreed Ruby. "If you had that many guests at your wedding, the tab would be way higher."

"That's right," said Elaine. "Plus, we got both lunch and dinner. But there was no band and no dancing."

"And no flowers or table decorations," added Ruby, "And no monogrammed napkins or matches, no party favors for the guests, no wedding dress or rehearsal dinner. No bridesmaids' gifts and no photographers or videographers. And no minister, of course."

Unlike me, Ruby must have been paying attention when Mrs. Swengard discussed "planning your perfect wedding" in Practicalities class. Should I ever get married, I doubt much planning will be involved. It likely will be a spur of the moment thing, and I expect the groom will be very, very drunk. The minister may be an Elvis impersonator in a tacky wedding chapel. I'll be holding one plastic rose, and the ring will be a $29 pawn-shop special.

"Well, we better get going," said Marie.

"Where to?" I asked, startled.

"It's Saturday morning," she replied. "We're due at Expressions class."

What a nightmare. Our all-too-brief respite from school was over.

* * *

Mrs. Lumpwapht was still pissed at lunch. She delivered a loud diatribe against the "evildoers who would imperil the financial health of our school." She announced that the "party or parties" responsible for "this execrable prank" would be expelled and their parents hit with a bill for $21,487.16. She demanded that the guilty persons step forward immediately to "accept the consequences for your irresponsible act."

We gazed about with innocent interest while the Lumpster waited for someone to confess.

"If you do the right thing today," she went on, "I may be persuaded to forego criminal proceedings against you."

Zoey swallowed hard while Chloe continued to radiate righteous innocence.

Ominous silence in the room.

"I see," Mrs. L said at last. "No one intends to do the right thing."

Hardly a surprise since the promised retribution was so dire.

"In that case," she continued, "all students will be confined to campus until such time as the guilty party is found. No exceptions will be permitted!"

Muttered grumbling was instantly silenced when the Lumpster raised her hand. "I'm not finished here," she went on. "I am also offering a $500 reward for information leading to the discovery of the culprits."

A sophomore Delphian raised her repellant hand. "Is that $500 in cash or just credit on our tuition bill?"

"It is five crisp new $100 bills from my hand to yours," Mrs. L replied. "Any more questions?"

I felt like asking if her inflated payback total included the $500 snitch bribe, but decided I better not.

"Well, that sucks," said Ruby, after we were dismissed. "I'm scheduled for a hot date tonight with Cole."

"Are you gonna sneak out? asked Elaine.

"You better not," warned Zoey. "I hear the Lumpster is planning hourly cell checks just like at San Quentin."

"Not to worry," said Chloe. "This may all be taken care of soon."

"You're not planning to confess?" I whispered, shocked.

"Don't be silly, Brenda dear," she replied. "There are other ways to cook this goose. Just leave everything to me."

Marie's my greatest pal, but when the shit comes down, I want Chloe at my side holding the umbrella.

* * *

My brother phoned while I was back in my room and regretting the impulse to share which had so devastated my snacks hoard. He reported that he had been to Lodi, had discussed his vocational aspirations with Iilivi Ittiwangi, and had been hired on as an apprentice fiberglasser.

"I hear those chemicals are pretty toxic," I commented.

"That's why you're dressed in a moon suit and wear a full-face respirator."

"Sounds hot and uncomfortable."

"Yeah, I know, but fiberglassing is an essential skill if you want to customize cars."

"And do you want to do that?"

"Only since I was like three years old. Ed 'Big Daddy' Roth is my god!"

So my brother has dreams. Who knew?

"And where will you live?" I asked.

"Well, Iilivi offered me a room in his broken-down farmhouse, but Dad said I could haul up the trailer and camp in that."

Believe it or not, my family used to vacation in a camper trailer. But it had been parked for years in a storage lot in San Leandro because my mother could no longer squeeze through the entry door. We were all still trying to forget that embarrassing incident in the mountains near Lone Pine when the volunteer fire department had to be called to extricate her after a large breakfast of hotcakes and pan-fried trout.

"That sounds like a good plan," I said. "So what do you think of Iilivi?"

"He seems OK. He tried to come across as easy-going, but I can tell he's a perfectionist. They can be a drag to work for, but you do learn how to do things right. He likes that I'm your brother."

"Right, so try not to mess up too bad."

"I did OK at the brewery. I'm not a complete screw-up."

"Glad to hear it."

"I guess you know he's got a transplanted toe. Makes it kind of weird when he shakes your hand. I also suspect he could be gay."

"What makes you say that?"

"There was a swishy guy with him named Lonny. I got the feeling he had stayed over for breakfast."

Hmm, that was interesting news.

"Lonny is a famous San Francisco cake decorator," I noted.

"Geez, you can get famous for that?"

"Of course. So be nice to him—he might bring you a cake."

"I had a piece of German chocolate cake that Iilivi baked. It was freaking outrageously awesome. I'm hoping the refreshments make up for being stuck so far out in the boonies."

"Will Holly be visiting you?"

"Right away, I hope. I need to show those dudes I'm batting for the opposite team."

* * *

Ruby was none too happy when I informed her about Iilivi and Lonny.

"Well, that's as suspicious as hell," she commented.

"Uh, why exactly?" I asked.

"Brick up and disappears, and now his former boyfriends are keeping company."

"So?"

"So that's as suspicious as hell."

"Uh, why exactly?" I repeated.

"Because *nobody* has heard from Brick! And apparently they don't care! And why is that?"

"We don't know that they don't care," I pointed out.

"It's suspicious," she insisted. "Suspicious as hell."

"I don't get it, Ruby. You think they did him in? Why? So they could steal his sleeping bag or his tambourine? So they could take over his valuable panhandling corner?"

"It's all our fault, Brenda. We introduced him to those guys. We don't know anything about them. They could have been in cahoots from the beginning. How come they were so eager to go out with a dwarf? Answer me that!"

"As I recall you said you would have loved to go out with him if he weren't gay. You said he was cute."

"And so he is, Brenda. That may be why he was targeted to be the victim of some barbarous act. I'm talking hate crime here or murder for thrills. And now your brother's out there living alone with those monsters."

"Ruby, dear, you're going a bit off the deep end. Why would Iilivi and Lonny have reported him missing to the police if they were in any way responsible for Brick's disappearance?"

"To divert suspicion, that's why. God, Brenda, I think we should call the cops."

"No one's calling the cops, Ruby. Let's get a grip here. You have absolutely no evidence to back up these paranoid fantasies."

"You think I'm paranoid? I'm not the one hearing voices like Mr. Iilivi Ittiwangi. Who knows what that evil voice has been goading him to do?"

"But weren't you the girl saying how wise and perceptive that voice was?"

"We've all been naive, Brenda. You, me, and Brick. We've been shockingly naive. And now we've landed in a nest of vipers."

"Ruby, I think you should go lie down. Take an aspirin and have a rest. You'll feel better when you've had time to reflect on this calmly."

"I tell you it's suspicious, Brenda. It's suspicious as hell!"

* * *

I'm still worried about Ruby, who didn't show for dinner. We assumed she'd gone off with Cole, since the school lockdown had been canceled.

Very startling development: A snitch fingered a girl named Estebana, who confessed to the Lumpster that she made the crank call from Vinny. She's now holed up at Mrs. L's house. They're waiting for her rich parents to messenger over a plane ticket back to Monterrey, Mexico. The messenger also will be delivering a bank check for the full $21,487.16. Plus an additional $2,000 to keep the matter private (no cops).

"It was a case of one hand washing the other," explained Chloe. "Her parents sent her here to hobnob with Americans, practice her English, avoid being kidnapped, and be caged away from boys. But poor Estebana was desperately unhappy."

"Welcome to the club," said Elaine.

"Her father made a fortune in horrible-tasting candy," Chloe continued, "so the Lumpster's fee is like a fleabite to his wallet."

"But won't she be in big trouble with her parents?" I asked.

"She certainly hopes so," Chloe replied. "She's hoping to be banished to a school in Barcelona, which is where she really wants to go."

"Yeah, I'd probably take that over Stockton," I admitted.

"And the $500?" asked Marie.

"It's now residing happily in my purse," said Chloe. "If you make me Treasurer, I'll donate the entire amount to The Arcadians."

"Done by executive order," I said. "You really are too much, Chloe."

"I try," she smiled.

"How come everyone gets to be an officer except me?" complained Zoey.

"We can't all be chiefs," I explained. "Someone has to be a lowly Indian. But don't despair, honey, your day will come."

* * *

At breakfast Sunday morning Ruby was cutting me dead. Nor was she willing to discuss with the others her "hot date" last night with Cole.

The Lumpster must have been feeling flush after her windfall. Breakfast was pancakes and bacon–with the unprecedented choice of plain or chocolate chip pancakes. I had a generous sampling of both. The upgraded "maple" syrup was still artificial, but not as cloyingly fake as before. The hot tea (my usual morning beverage) tasted like more than one bag had been dipped into the giant urn. All in all, it was a very satisfying start to my day–despite Ruby's moodiness and the dark looks from the assembled Delphians.

Their leader paused by our table on her way out. "You're not going to get away with it, you know," hissed Kaitlyn.

"Get away with what, dear?" I asked.

"Our day at the hotel. I know you guys were behind it."

"That's odd," I replied. "I seem to recall you girls having quite a jolly time at the buffet and pool. But don't thank us, thank Estebana."

"I know for a fact she's just your stooge."

"Well, here's a thought. Why don't you Delphians arrange for a school holiday? And then we'll see who's the most respected and popular."

Kaitlyn scowled and flounced away. Too bad she lacks sufficient heft to flounce with conviction.

I invited Marie to accompany me to the recording session, but she said she had other plans. She smiled and declined to be more specific. Beautiful people can get away with being mysterious because the rest of us feel inhibited about intruding into their beautiful lives. It's sort of a tautology: the Tautology of Aesthetic Exclusion. There's a parallel force at work for us folks at the opposite end of the looks spectrum. People don't intrude into our lives because they couldn't care less. We're subject to the Tautology of Aesthetic Indifference. Perhaps I'll expound on this thesis further in tomorrow's 300 words for Mr. Ng.

My arms were laden with grocery bags when Dylan zoomed up in his dad's semi-dusty SUV.

"Been shopping, honey?" he inquired, leaning over for a kiss.

"No, I'm auditioning to be Stockton's youngest bag lady. And don't imagine any of these snack items are for you. They're my supplies for next week."

"Don't they feed you at that school?"

"As little as they can legally get away with. Do you have some news for me?"

"My erectile system is functioning superbly."

"I mean about Ruby. She appears to have decided she hates me."

"Yeah, Cole grew some balls and told her we were switching canaries."

"How did she take it?"

"Not too well. And the idiot told her *before* they'd done it, so pussy was off the menu."

"No wonder she was so pissed. You know Ruby claims to find sex immensely satisfying."

"That's odd because she hasn't even done it with me yet."

"Well, I think she's lying. No girl enjoys sex her first time out."

"I know a simple way to prove you're wrong, Brenda."

"Just concentrate on your driving, Tiger. I don't need to die in a giant orange cloud of crushed cheese curls."

"I can think of some kinky things we could do with cheese curls."

"You could think of kinky things to do with your grandfather's dentures. And probably with your grandfather too."

"My grandfather's dead."

"I doubt that would slow you down much. You prefer sex partners who don't fight back."

Dylan laughed. "You slay me, Brenda. You drive me absolutely wild."

"Don't talk to me, Dylan. I need to rest my voice."

"Why? The best singers smoke, drink, and have sex like mad. Hard living imparts character to your voice. You think Tom Waits rests his voice?"

I pointed to my sealed lips, then flashed him the finger. The big lump laughed with delight.

Chapter 18

DYLAN'S HIGH school was built in the 1980s (when the state still had money), and was not as decrepit as I'd been expecting. Graffiti was under control and the halls didn't smell that bad. The boys had set up for our recording in a little room off the band room. It featured actual acoustic tile on the walls and ceiling, a battery of microphones on stands, and a headphones-bedecked nerd named Wyatt hunched over a large mixing board.

"Yo, Brenda," said Cole, looking anxious and desperately cute. "Here are my revised lyrics."

He held out a sheet of paper, which I declined to grasp.

"No thanks, Cole honey," I smiled, removing a lyrics sheet from my purse. "I've brought my own."

"But don't you even want to read it?" he pleaded.

"Not particularly. You write nice tunes, Cole, but you're no Paul Simon or Biggie Smalls. You need to leave the lyric-writing to them that can. Shall we do a run-through once or twice?"

I expected to be a bit nervous, but I was surprisingly calm. We rehearsed for about 15 minutes, then recorded three takes. The last one sounded pretty darn fine, if you ask me. No accordion flubs this time and I avoided bumping my fat nose into the microphone.

"Wow," said Wyatt, when the playback ended. "That sounded almost semi-professional."

"What do you mean?" said Dylan. "It was great! Brenda, I knew you could do it. Damn, girl, you're the next Mama Cass!"

"Remind me to lay off the sandwiches," I replied.

"It was very good," agreed Cole. "So how about we try it now with my improved lyrics?"

I looked at my watch. "Oops, my complimentary time is up. From now on I charge union scale, which is $166 an hour–with a four-hour minimum."

"Is that really union scale?" inquired Wyatt.

"It could be," said Dylan. "Cole, I think our songbird is done here. You want to try it with Wyatt singing your lyrics?"

Cole's crest had fallen. "Not really. OK, I guess we're finished."

Working in a semi-professional manner, Wyatt connected some cables, pushed some buttons, and loaded an MP3 of our song into my phone.

To celebrate this musical milestone the three of us adjourned to a nearby pizza joint. Wyatt was invited, but he declined, saying he wanted to "play around" some more with the levels. I hope he doesn't make me sound like another one of those annoyingly over-processed pop singers clogging the charts.

"What happens next?" I asked, biting into cheesy pepperoni.

"You mean after we ditch Cole and head back to my place?" asked Dylan.

"No, I mean with your funktitious song?"

"Oh. Well, we play it for the actor types in the Drama Club. If it gets their dicks hard, they'll cook up some kind of accompanying video."

"I know they'll like it," said Cole. "Though I guess they won't need to borrow my kayak now."

Clearly, the guy had a one-track mind.

"How long will the video production take?" I asked.

"I'm giving them until Friday," replied Dylan. "You can't give 'em much time; otherwise they'll screw around until we've all graduated."

"And then you'll upload it to Youtube?" I asked.

"Yep," said Dylan. "Mark next Saturday on your calendar. That's the day we all become famous. Right, Cole?"

"It could happen. Hard to say really. Public tastes are so fickle. Ninety-nine percent of the music that's popular today makes me want to hurl."

"Only ninety-nine percent?" commented Dylan. "I didn't realize your tastes were so broad. What do you like to listen to, Brenda?"

I gave it some thought. "Pizzas sliding out of the oven. Chocolate cakes being sliced. Whipped cream spritzing out of the can."

"I can dig that," said Dylan. "Or how about the soft click of a bra being unsnapped?"

"I prefer the delicate crunch of a sharp knee to the groin," I replied.

"Ouch," said Dylan. "Hey, Cole. Wake up, buddy! It's all happening here."

"Sorry," he replied. "I was thinking about Ruby. She wasn't very nice to me yesterday. It's not my fault she can't sing. If you see her, Brenda, can you tell her that I broke up with her?"

"I'll do no such thing, Cole. Ruby's my friend. If you want to break up with someone, you'll have to tell her yourself."

"But I don't want to hurt her feelings. How about I just stop calling?"

"That won't work either," I said. "You'd just be prolonging her misery. Be a man, dude. Dump her properly."

"This trying to go out with girls may have been a mistake. Things get awfully complicated."

I felt like shouting, "So try me instead!" But instead I just shrugged.

"At least you got your carrot waxed," said Dylan, grabbing the last pizza slice. "You crossed that bridge."

"Yeah. I guess."

Contrary to the reports I'd received, he didn't sound like a fellow who'd experienced thrilling, spectacular sex.

* * *

As the guys were dividing up the bill, Dylan's phone rang. It was his dad requesting his car back A.S.A.P. When houses are sold, he inspects them for termites. These days he was a very busy guy because Stockton leads the nation in foreclosures. Thousands of homeowners stopped paying their mortgages when they all woke up one morning and said, "Damn, what was I thinking! Why am I living in boring Stockton?"

"Fuck!" exclaimed my date. "What should I do?"

"Well, you better go," said Cole. "I can drop Brenda off at her school."

"But the night is still young!" he protested.

"It's just as well, Dylan. I've got homework to do," I lied.

Frustrated and despondent, Dylan helped me transfer my groceries to Cole's brown Geo Metro, a car that looks like it was built behind the Iron Curtain by disgruntled communists, but apparently wasn't.

"Our time will come, baby," said Dylan, planting a pepperoni-flavored kiss on my indifferent lips.

"I hope . . . not," I grunted.

"Don't lay a hand on her!" he warned Cole.

Cole started his engine, which sounded like a blender grinding old cheese.

"Is this your car?" I inquired, being polite.

"Yeah, I inherited it when my grandmother died. They offered it to my brother, but he passed. It doesn't look like much, but it has low miles and is good on gas."

We waved as Dylan peeled out of the parking lot, then we putt-putted in the opposite direction.

"I really like your song, Cole," I commented, digging my lipstick out of my purse and slathering on a fresh layer of peachy coral.

"Thanks."

"Have you written any more tunes?"

"Yeah, lots. They come to me at night and when I'm kayaking."

"We could get together and collaborate. You could play them for me, and I could cook up some ideas for lyrics."

"I don't know, Brenda. Your idea of collaborating is to say my way or the highway."

"I didn't touch your tune, you notice. Song-writing often works best when there's a strict division of labor."

"Well, I guess we can try it."

"Good. Do you have my phone number?"

"I could get it from Dylan."

"Here, I'll give it to you." I tore a corner off a grocery bag, wrote my number on it, and tucked it into Cole's shirt pocket. I liked the feel of his warm boyish bod under the thin cotton. In fact, I liked everything about him.

"Are you going to see Ruby, Brenda?"

"I suppose. She's kind of mad at me since I took her place. Shall I tell her to expect your call tonight?"

"Yeah, I guess so."

"It can all be over in a minute or two, Cole. You don't have to offer any lengthy explanations. Just tell her you decided you're not compatible and you enjoyed meeting her. It's no big deal."

"OK, that sounds easy enough."

"But don't mention that you discussed it with me. I don't want her to think I put you up to it."

"Right, Brenda. I understand."

"Good. I really like your song. Did I mention that?"

"Yeah. You did. And I like your singing. You really put some heart into it."

"Thanks. I get a nice rumble going with this large chest of mine."

Cole glanced over and inspected my chest. "Yes, I suppose that's true."

Riding next to Cole in his ridiculous car, I felt I was beginning to grasp the connection between love and sex. Yes, it might be rather pleasant for Cole to put his arms around me, remove my delicate underthings, and do something untoward with his privates.

* * *

When I got back to my room, I played the MP3 of our song for Marie and Chloe. Both were impressed.

"It sounds great," said Chloe.

"I had no idea you were so talented," said Marie. "What a voice you have!"

"Well, you helped a lot with the lyrics," I pointed out.

We were listening to it again when someone knocked on the door. It was Elaine. "Can I hang in here for a while?" she asked.

"Sure," I replied, switching off my phone. "What's up?"

"Ruby just got a call from Cole. The creep dumped her. Now she's a mess."

"Maybe I should go see if she's OK," I said.

"I wouldn't," replied Elaine. "Ruby's lashing out at all her friends. And you're at the top of her list."

"I'll go talk to her," said Marie. "You girls stay here."

Marie checked her hair in a mirror (it was perfect) and quickly departed.

"I hope she knows what she's in for," sighed Elaine.

"Not to worry," I said. "Marie resides in the stratosphere. Ruby and I are both slogging in the mud, so she feels more competitive with me."

"We're all down in the mud compared to Marie," said Chloe.

"Hardly," I replied. "You're super attractive."

"Yeah, well, I don't haunt your soul like Marie. Notice how she's left the room, but you can still feel her presence?"

"That's right," confirmed Elaine. "She's amazing."

So it seems I'm not the only one under the spell of Miss Marie Malencotti.

"I'm surprised Ruby's taking it so hard," said Elaine. "She only went out with the dude a couple of times."

"Ruby invested a lot in the concept of having a boyfriend," I replied. "It's a blow to her ego to have him end it."

"I never take guys seriously," said Chloe. "You just can't at our age. If you want love, get a puppy."

"Pets are forbidden at Ferncliffe," I reminded her.

"Then get a protégée," said Chloe. "I get lots of loyal devotion and affection from Zoey and my other girls."

"OK, Chloe, then that's your next project," I said. "Find me a protégée."

"Wake up, Brenda. You've already got one. She just left the room."

Wow, lovely Marie as my protégée. Could it be true?

* * *

I forced myself to smile at Ruby this morning at breakfast, but got back only a scowl and a very cold shoulder. My phone rang as I was cradling my throbbing head and trying to swallow some tea.

"Yeah?" I wheezed.

"Brenda!" boomed Dylan. "The Drama Clubsters flipped over our song!"

"That's nice."

"I also played it for my dad. He said you sound like a combination Sophie Tucker meets Ethel Merman."

Those gals didn't ring any bells with me, but I suspected they'd been dead for at least 50 years. I'd have preferred Adele meets Aretha Franklin.

"That's nice. I suppose."

"Brenda honey, you're not sounding very enthusiastic."

"I've come down with an affliction that you will never suffer."

"Like what? Split ends? Nipple rash?"

"It's a monthly thing."

"Oh, that. I like chicks, but I'm sure glad I was born a guy."

"Yeah, you lucked out on that deal."

"I got a very fine dick that never gives me a speck of trouble."

"Congratulations. I'm very happy for the two of you. Now, I think I'll go throw up."

Odd but true: Marie and Chloe also got their periods today. They came equipped with the Grade A Maximum Allure female package, but for some reason I'm way sicker than they are. I ask you: is that fair?

Not sure what happened the rest of the day. I guess I ate some lunch and dinner. And possibly a Heath bar or two. Then I went to bed. Right before I lost consciousness I noticed it was still light outside.

* * *

I came down to breakfast this morning and discovered that the cafeteria staff was now dressed as zombies, witches, and ghouls. I figured that Ferncliffe Academy had descended into its final apocalyptic spasm, but then I remembered that today is Halloween. Not many girls had gotten it together to dress in costumes, though Kaitlyn appeared as the tramp she is—complete with blacked-out tooth and five o'clock shadow. The joke was on her because Mrs. L paused to upbraid her for not wearing proper school attire. I had dressed as a Rumpled Menstrual Victim, so I drew only the usual Lumpster frown.

My listless breakfast was interrupted by a phone call from my brother sounding distressed.

"F-f-fuck, Brenda! W-w-what's going on!?"

"Buford? What's up, dude? Why are you stuttering?"

"I-I-I'm freezing my balls off. M-m-my teeth are ch-ch-chattering. I just got rousted from my trailer by an ar-r-rmy of cops. They won't let me g-g-get dressed."

"What's going on there?"

"You t-t-tell me. They g-g-got a bunch of d-d-dogs sniffing all over. Is Iilivi some kind of cr-cr-criminal?"

"He's no such thing. You hang in there, 'bro. I think I know what the trouble is."

I rang off and glared at Ruby.

She glared back. "What, Brenda?"

"You called the cops on Iilivi!"

"So what if I did? Somebody had to do something. They have to find the body before the crime scene is disturbed even more."

"The only thing disturbed is your mind! You're causing innocent people needless grief. And why? Because you can't carry a tune, and your boyfriend broke up with you."

"That's none of your business! At least I care about Brick!"

"Hah! That's a laugh. All you care about is hurting people. You are really a sad case."

"Oh, yeah? Well, I'm sorry I ever introduced myself to you. You're a back-stabbing traitor!"

"OK, girls," interjected Marie. "Let's cool off here. Ruby, how about we meet later to talk? You can tell me what's going on with your friend Brick."

"Oh, drop dead, Marie," she replied. "You're just as big a phony as Brenda!"

Ruby got up from the table and flounced off.

"Wow," I sighed. "There's a girl with a chip on her shoulder."

"She's very unhappy," said Marie. "I'll try to talk to her after she's cooled off. And, Brenda dear, let's not provoke her any further."

"She started it, Marie. The girl's deranged."

"She's certainly got a temper," commented Chloe. "I hope she doesn't have access to any weapons."

"Chloe, can you do me a favor?" I asked.

"You want me to find you some body armor?"

"No, I need you to locate a missing dwarf named Darnell Brickman."

"Piece of cake," she smiled.

* * *

Today's task in Expressions class: write a scary 300-word ghost story. No profanity, sex, or violence permitted. It's always a bit awkward when Mr. Ng tries to be trendy and topical. I was feeling as inspired as a dead lizard, but I gave it my best shot. My story was about a girl who got sent to a pricey private school where they had lousy food and incompetent teachers. She died from an infected paper cut and returned as an angry ghost, who exacted a terrible revenge on all her tormentors. She gave them all severe nipple rash, which they scratched ceaselessly causing everyone immense embarrassment. Probably not up there with Edgar Allen Poe, but he never had to write spine-tingling fiction while bleeding from a major orifice.

As Marie and I were leaving Vistas class, Chloe paused for a chat.

"Brenda, you know the town of Compton?"

"Yeah, it's down south somewhere near L.A."

"I found a Brickman Dry Cleaners there. I phoned them and asked to speak to Darnell. They said he would be coming in at 4:30 for the evening ironing shift."

"Fantastic work, Chloe. Could you convey that information to Ruby? And could you tell her that I suggest she give her pal Brick a call?"

"Sure thing, Brenda."

I am so revising my opinion of Chloe. That girl is a marvel. Meanwhile, neither my brother nor Iilivi were answering their phones. I hope they haven't gone down in a blazing gun battle with the cops.

We met up with Ruby at dinner. She was looking most satisfyingly humbled.

"Hi, Brenda," she said. "I guess I overreacted, huh?"

"So it appears. You talked to Brick?"

"Yeah. I did. He was sounding OK. He's working at his cousin's dry cleaners. He says he doesn't mind ironing."

For me, ironing professionally would rank very, very low as a career pick: Just below selling my body on the street corner. And right above housemaid for Mrs. Lumpwapht.

"Did he say why he left without telling anyone?" I asked.

"Yeah, he did."

"OK, we're listening. So spill."

"Well, Brick said that when he was with Lonny, all he did was talk about how great Iilivi was. And when he was with Iilivi, all he did was talk about Lonny. And then it occurred to him that those two were kind of perfect for each other. They're both sweet guys and terrific bakers. And Lonny fits Iilivi's prophesy, being both short and coming from across the water–assuming he boated over from San Francisco."

"So why didn't Brick introduce them?" I asked.

"Don't ask me. He decided if he left, they might get together to look for him and then hit it off–which from the sound of it I guess they did. So everything turned out OK in the end. Though I've decided that Brick is pretty much a major flake."

"Still, there's the matter of the cops descending on Iilivi," I pointed out.

"It was the sheriff's department," she noted. "Yeah, I feel kind of bad about that."

"They must have had a search warrant," said Marie.

"That's right," agreed Chloe. "The cops have to go to a judge to get those. And present some sort of probable cause."

"Right, and they'd likely need more evidence than some hysterical schoolgirl's unfounded suspicions," I added.

The assembled Arcadians all gazed questioningly at Ruby.

"OK," she conceded. "I might have exaggerated things a bit."

"What exactly did you say?" I demanded.

"I said I overheard Iilivi making death threats against Brick."

"Ruby, that was very reckless of you," said Marie, shocked.

"Well, they wouldn't listen to me otherwise. I was really worried."

"So did you call off the cops?"

"Yeah. I phoned right away and gave them Brick's number. They sounded kind of pissed. They had called in the FBI on a possible kidnapping."

"You got everyone in a big uproar," I pointed out.

"Well, what can I say? I'm sorry. Next time a friend of mine disappears, I'll just ignore it and hope for the best. Say, Brenda, can I listen to your song?"

I plugged in my earbuds and handed her my phone. She listened with a mildly quizzical look on her face.

"Yeah, that's fairly decent," she commented, handing me back my phone. "But I really prefer Cole's original lyrics. The kayaking reference was such a great metaphor. So all in all I like my version better. It just sounds more professional."

"That's fine," I said. "Different strokes for different folks."

And in Ruby's case, she needs about 30 swift ones delivered to her skull with a stout stick.

After dinner the Lumpster hosted a Halloween "party" in the court-yard. Cheap candy from Costco and some watery punch. A few sad pump-kins we were supposed to carve. The Arcadians took in the dismal scene and promptly departed. When you're living Halloween every day, there's not much cause for additional celebration.

Chapter 19

MY BROTHER phoned right before lights out. His speech was slurred as if he'd been the target of vicious police brutality.

"Yo, Brenda. Did I call you or did you call me?"

"Buford! What's happening there?"

"Got some good news, girl. I'm no longer boycotting beer."

"Are you drunk?"

"Either I'm drunk or someone's outside spinning this trailer around. Wheee!"

"Why haven't you been answering your phone?"

"Been out partying. When the cops left, Iilivi took me and Jaime down the river in his boat."

"Who's Jaime?"

"Mexican dude who does the dog plumbing and dog wiring. Iilivi bought us steaks at this bar place along the river. Then we stayed for the big Halloween bash."

"What did the cops do?"

"Poked around all over the place. Asked a bunch of dumb questions while a big batch of resin got hard in the bucket. Made the boss super peeved. They did find his cat though."

"What?"

"Iilivi had this old cat that went missing a while back. The police dogs sniffed out its corpse. No bodies though."

"We found out that the person they were looking for is OK. He's working at a dry cleaners down south."

"Yeah, Iilivi was relieved to hear that. So was that Lonny dude who showed up after we got back. If he's not the boyfriend, they're like super-close buddies. What's that sound?"

"I don't hear anything."

"Oh, it's me pissing on the floor."

"Damn, Buford, are you peeing your pants?"

"Hell, I'm buck naked! I hope I haven't been having sex. There's no one out here except guys."

"Jesus, how many beers did you have?"

"Well, the boss was paying so I didn't bother to count. What is it you wanted?"

"Buford, you called me."

"If you say so. God, it gets fucking dark here."

"Good night, bro'. I hope you feel better in the morning."

No reply; I suspect he had passed out.

* * *

November has reared its ugly head. Bad news for a summer person like me. What I have to look forward to: light deprivation, cold rain, depression, binge eating, dramatic weight gains, lousy Christmas gifts. I do have one thing slim in my life: the chance of our song ever getting noticed. Plus, the very slim possibility that Cole someday might call. I hope my present mood is a hormone thing, and not a realistic appraisal of my life.

Dylan phoned to say the Drama Club was busy story-boarding the video for our song. Every shot is carefully planned in advance–just like they do in Hollywood.

"Are they borrowing someone's camcorder?" I asked.

"Hardly. We have a state-of-the-art video setup."

"Lucky you. We don't even have computers at our school."

"I thought your school was fancy and expensive?"

"No, just expensive."

"What do they do with all the money you pay?"

"Who knows? Our headmistress may be blowing it up her nose. The teachers sure aren't paid much. And the eats suck."

"Speaking of which, Brenda, we've had about 12 dates now. You know what that means, girl?"

"Time to break up?"

"Time to get it on, baby! When would you like to hook up?"

"How about five years from next Tuesday?"

"I'm thinking Saturday night. I'll pick you up at six. Wear something sexy."

"OK. How about a low-cut dress done in chain-mail and barbed wire?"

"Fine. As long as it unzips down the back. I'm a guy who really likes to unzip."

The fellow is nothing if not dogged. He has all the seductive charm of a runaway bulldozer. I may come down with a nasty virus by the weekend. Or should I just grit my teeth and get it over with?

I posed this question to Marie on a joint restroom visit.

"Just tell him you like him as a friend and aren't ready for any major commitments. He'll understand."

"But he's sort of crazy about me, Marie. That's kind of unusual. What if he's the last guy I'll ever meet who finds me attractive?"

"Really, Brenda. We've had this conversation before. You'll meet lots of fellows who will like you and want to be with you."

"Are we talking about me here or you?"

"Have some confidence, Brenda dear. You have a lot to offer. And don't let Dylan bully you."

Sometimes my best friend sounds just like someone's mother.

* * *

My off-and-on friend Ruby is being nice to me again, although she hasn't actually apologized yet for her profound and prolonged obnoxiousness. After class today she sneaked out the back way, untied Brick's little boat, and sent it adrift down the slough. He's now even more homeless than he may realize. Then at dinner she confided that following her dramatic cafeteria blowup she was contacted by the Delphians, who tried to recruit her to be a spy. Yes, those fiends were seeking a double agent inside The Arcadians. It may be time to challenge them to a rumble featuring jeers, rude gestures, and withering putdowns. I'd resort to violence, but Mrs. Goldbline insists that never solves anything.

Lightning has struck. Cole called me. We're getting together after dinner tomorrow to go over some songs. He asked me if I wanted to have Marie join us.

"How do you know Marie?" I asked, aghast.

"Well, I don't, but you wrote on the sheet you gave me: lyrics by Brenda Blatt and Marie Malencotti."

"Oh, Marie just helped with the spelling and punctuation. We'll do fine without her."

Give me credit for some smarts. When you're trying to engage the interest of a boy, the last thing you'd want to do is drag along a beauty like Marie.

What I learned in school today: The Roman army withdrew from Britain in 410 A.D., leaving the defenseless natives open to invasion by hordes of Angles and Saxons. It turns out the Romans occupied Britain for nearly as long as Europeans have been in North America, making it a wonder that we're not all speaking Italian and riding Vespas. Grampa Joad died on the journey to California and was buried along Route 66, near the site of a modern-day Motel 6. Very sad development, leaving most of us (and one girl in particular) wishing to be comforted in the arms of our teacher. If your escort fails to open the car door for you, you should wait patiently in your seat until he does so (thus missing out on both dinner and the movie). Force equals mass times acceleration, which is why it's unwise to step in front of a speeding train. People indulge in gossip in order to make themselves feel superior and have a sense of power. It is an attempt to enhance one's status within the group. Overlooked by Mrs. Goldbline: Were it not for gossip, we would all perish from the sheer boredom of existence.

After dinner Chloe and I did our laundry. She joined me in munching a Heath bar while our clothes went round and round. I asked her how she wound up at Ferncliffe.

"I was always a problem child," she replied. "If my parents told me to do something, chances are I'd do exactly the opposite."

"Why's that?" I asked.

"Just my nature, I suppose. I'm extremely exasperating to my parents."

"What do they do?"

"You mean for a living?"

"Uh-huh."

"My mother drinks as a lifestyle. My father used to sell vacation time-shares. Now he claims to be an investment consultant."

"You have doubts about that?"

"Well, I know his clients give him money. Whether he invests any of it I couldn't really say. My father is very charming. If your clothes were on fire, he could sell you a gallon of gas and make you feel like he's doing you a favor."

"You can be charming too, Chloe."

"Thanks, though I'm sure my mother wouldn't agree."

"Was it her idea to send you here?"

"I expect so. Boarding schools are for parents who are clueless and can't cope."

"Yeah, my parents were thrilled to dump me off at this joint."

"At least we have the satisfaction of knowing they're paying big bucks for the privilege of getting rid of us."

"Not me, Chloe. My granny's picking up the full tab for my incarceration."

"Cool. Your parents must be even more devious than mine."

"Could be. They may be smarter than I gave them credit for."

* * *

Twenty-four anxious hours later, Cole picked me up in front of the supermarket. No, I hadn't informed Ruby of our liaison. Climbing into his toy-sized car I felt like a size 12 foot squeezing into a size 6 shoe. And this time I didn't have all those grocery bags to distract the eye. And how embarrassing when his anemic springs sagged under my weight. At least lumpy Dylan was thoughtful enough to drive a capacious and robust SUV. I fumbled with the seatbelt, which suddenly was several inches too short.

"Let me help you," Cole said, tugging on the belt and latching it after a monumental struggle.

"Thanks," I gasped, my breasts truncated by the confining belt.

"I don't know why my grandmother bought this car. She was also big like . . . uh."

"Yes?"

"Like my late grandfather."

I judged that dodge fairly tactful for a borderline A.S. case.

Pulling into his driveway, I marveled anew at his cloned street.

"You know, Cole, we live in a tract house in Hayward, but there was some variation in design and exterior colors. These houses are all *exactly* the same."

"Yes, the builder was striving for strict uniformity."

"You'd think after a few years the owners might at least have changed the paint colors."

"The siding is vinyl, Brenda. The color is molded in. You don't paint it, you just hose it off when it gets dirty."

"Oh. So you don't mind living in one of dozens of identical houses?"

"Not really. When I go in any neighbor's house, I always know where the bathroom is."

"That's an advantage, I suppose."

Cole had reached the age where his mother (thin, rabbitty) eyed his female guests and evaluated them as potential daughters-in-law. I got the feeling I wasn't rating very high on her mental maternal checklist. I felt like informing her that I likely wouldn't be marrying her son, just possibly having intercourse with him. Instead, I smiled and accepted her offer of a diet soda. We adjourned to the most remote bedroom, which housed a sewing machine, an ironing board, a tropical fish tank (no water, no fish), several tired recliners, and a music stand crowded with Cole's compositions. He dragged out Myron, his over-sexed micro dog, and returned with his dazzling instrument.

"Fast or slow?" he asked.

If he was referring to the pace of my seduction, my choice was full steam ahead.

He elaborated: "Shall we begin with a fast tune or a slow one?"

"Surprise me."

Cole squeezed off a lively number with a driving rock rhythm.

"Cool. What do you call that?"

"Composition Number 18."

"I think we could do better than that. That sounds like it could be a song about finding love in unexpected places."

"On a kayaking trip?"

"How about with someone who's been going out with your best friend? We could title it 'Best Friend Lover'."

"That might do."

"OK, I'll work on it. And now do you have something slower?"

Cole played a soft and dreamy number in waltz time.

"Very nice, Cole. You're a font of delicious melodies. That is such a rare gift."

"You really think so?"

"Definitely. That could be another love song–perhaps about two people who start out as friends, then suddenly feel a magical spark."

"On a kayaking trip?"

"Uh, could be. Or they could be collaborators in some creative endeavor. And the fellow could be on the rebound from a prior relationship."

Cole played through another half-dozen tunes–all fresh and original. And all suggesting to the lyricist a love song relating in a very personal way to the composer. Only he didn't seem to be getting it.

While I scribbled my notes, Cole sipped his soda and noodled around on his keyboard.

"Dylan's very excited about your date on Saturday," he remarked.

"That makes one of us. I suppose you've known him a long time."

"Since we were four. We both had the same accordion teacher, Mr. Gallagher."

"Any photos from back then?"

"I have one from our first recital."

"Let's see it."

Cole quickly returned with an album of snapshots. He flipped through it and held out a fading color photo of two smiling tykes burdened with outsized accordions.

One kid was devastatingly adorable. And one was a big lump.

* * *

More dorm room nudity this morning. This time from a new and shocking source: me. I decided if I'm to get naked tomorrow with Dylan (God

291

forbid), I should practice with my own kind. All previous mornings I had retreated modestly to the bathroom to get dressed. This a.m. I let my robe fall to the floor while I slipped on my bra and panties. Marie and Chloe pretended not to notice, but I'm sure they were wondering who shaved that hippo.

Should I be so crazed as to sleep with Dylan tomorrow, I won't be disrobing until darkness has been achieved. I'm not talking about dimming the lights. I'm talking about as dark as a pharaoh's tomb at midnight on a moonless night. I'm talking Helen-Keller-on-a-date darkness.

Naturally I'm somewhat curious about the act, though the whole thing sounds a bit improbable and icky. But I know about 12 seconds after docking has been achieved, Cole will find out. Which likely will render him even less inclined to give me a tumble.

Damn, what's a girl to do?

Speaking of sexual predators, Dylan called me at breakfast to say that the taping for the video went well last night. They'll be shooting the rest of the scenes today.

"I can't wait to see it," I said, trying to sound enthusiastic.

"I can't wait to see you," Dylan purred.

"See me how?"

"You know: stretched out before me in all your nubile glory."

"Oh that."

I expressed my need for total privacy and absolute darkness. Not to mention an industrial-strength condom."

"Your wish is my command. All will be as milady desires."

"You mean Brad Pitt will be there instead of you?"

He laughed. "Brenda, you set my soul on fire."

"I'd rather set your hair on fire. And most of your wardrobe."

Biggest news of the day: Ruby has another date. She has dug up another fellow who responded to her Craigslist ad. They are meeting downtown tomorrow for coffee. This one does not kayak or play the accordion. His name is Zane (I've already dubbed him Zane the Insane) and he's into magic and ventriloquism. His emailed photo was so blurry, we could only tell that he's white and male. He did not appear to be balding, so he's probably not 45.

Ruby's excited, but she says she's playing it cool this time. No sex unless it's Mutual Love, like with "you and Dylan" (her words).

I wonder if there's anyone in Stockton who doesn't know that I'm scheduled to have sex with Dylan tomorrow night.

Chapter 20

THE WEEKEND has arrived and all that that entails. I'm getting through the day by ignoring it and pretending it will go away. Not working so hot though.

I read my essays in Expressions class with even less enthusiasm than usual. My ghost story fell totally flat, and I don't think Mr. Ng appreciated the reference to incompetent teachers. For him, though, mere incompetence would be a vast improvement over his current status as laughably ineffectual.

Somehow the afternoon went by in a flash. Marie insisted on glamming my hair with her hot rollers. She also compelled me to don my best dress–a yellowish garment which the average person might rate as "sexy" if they were blind. I look semi-decent in it, but the armholes bind like crazy and the collar chafes. But no one ever said beauty was easy. The dress unzips down the back–assuming I haven't reflexively kneed anyone attempting such a liberty.

I knew Dylan was serious about our enterprise when I saw that he had washed his dad's SUV. Wax also may have been applied, as its bulging curves appeared unnaturally shiny. I climbed in anyway and kissed its heavily cologned driver.

"Wow, Brenda, you're a feast for the eyeballs! What color is that smokin' dress?"

"I believe they call this shade 'toddler spit-up.' What herbicide have you doused yourself in?"

"It's Wrambo Wrestler aftershave. Like it?"

"I may get used to it in 10,000 years. Where are we going for dinner?"

"Outback Steakhouse. I scored a two-for-one coupon on the Web."

Taking a cue from Mrs. Swengard, when we parked at the restaurant, I sat politely in my seat. Eventually, Dylan walked over and opened the car door. He reached in and juggled the handle.

"What's the matter, Brenda? Did the handle jam?"

"Thank you," I said, exiting. "You're such a gentleman."

I ordered the biggest steak on the menu. I was nervous, and when I get nervous, I need to eat.

I reached over and examined Dylan's tie, which featured a plethora of bikinied babes riding day-glo surfboards.

"Very tastefully done," I commented.

"Yeah, my mom and dad gave me grief about it too. I only wear ties ironically. I wore this one to my Aunt Jen's funeral and got some very nasty looks."

"Remind me not to die when you're around. Am I famous yet?"

"The video is 99 percent done. It's totally awesome. Wyatt's going to text me when it's posted. Should be like any minute now. I have my laptop in the car so we can watch it on the big screen."

Our steaks arrived and we dug in. I felt like one of those death-row inmates eating his last meal. Only the warden forgot my beer and my strawberry ice cream.

"So where are we going?" I inquired as Dylan sat back in the booth and picked his teeth with the tiny knife on his keychain.

"The Starlite Valley Motel. Out by route 99. It's all arranged, baby."

"How can a high school kid rent a motel room?"

"A buddy of mine is Indian. His family runs the joint. Don't worry, it's all set."

Right. And that's what worried me.

I felt something was amiss. "Shouldn't it be called the *Starlit* Valley Motel?"

"Sometimes it is. Its name varies depending on which of the neon letters have burned out. But the rooms are OK. And don't forget, it's the place where you will discover why God made you a woman."

I prayed He wasn't an angry and vengeful God.

* * *

Tonight the big red neon sign was proclaiming it the "Sta lite alley Motel." Just what I needed: a romantic venue making sarcastic allusions to my weight. It was a single-story L-shaped place that must having been hosting illicit rendezvous since the 1940s. A smaller sign flashed this beacon to the world: "LOW RATES. ADULT MOVIES. FREE WIFI." We parked in the last free spot by the rear wing. Somewhere nearby a woman was laughing and/or screaming hysterically.

"We're in Room 28," said Dylan, flashing the motel key.

"Did you get a non-smoking room?" I asked.

"Ramesh says they're all non-smoking."

Ramesh lied. The room bludgeoned your olfactory nerves with stale smoke aromas. The room had one queen-size bed, two end tables with tall ugly lamps, a scarred bureau holding a big-screen TV, one wooden armchair, and a naked closet pole with two metal hangers. A doorway in the rear led to an aqua-tiled bathroom.

"Not bad, huh?" said Dylan.

"We should put a lamp on the floor sideways. Then the Film Noir atmosphere will be complete."

"Would you like to freshen up, baby?"

"Freshen up what?"

"I don't know. Isn't that what guys usually ask?"

"I feel I'm adequately fresh at the moment."

Dylan set his laptop on the bureau, then switched on the TV.

"How do you feel about porn?"

"I'm totally for it as long as you measure up to the guys on the screen."

Dylan switched off the TV.

"How do you feel about brandy?"

"Is that what you've got?"

"Uh-huh."

"I'll take a swig."

The brandy burned all the way down. I continue to be amazed there are so many alcoholics considering how vile the stuff tastes.

I passed the bottle back to Dylan. He took a big swallow and shuddered.

"Damn, this is great, Brenda."

"What is?"

"You and me together like this. We'll remember this night for the rest of our lives."

"No doubt. Even if one of us is trying desperately to forget it."

"Well, I guess I better go empty my bladder."

I hoped he wasn't getting clinical on me. If he started tossing around terms like "vagina" and "fellatio," I'd be out the door in a flash.

"Right. I'll wait here."

Minutes went by and no tinkling was heard.

"What's going on in there?" I asked at last.

"I'm having trouble relaxing my sphincter. Would you mind stepping outside?"

"Outside in the parking lot?"

"Yeah."

"OK. No problem."

I went out and waited by the car. So much for his equipment never giving him a speck of trouble. Faint sounds of carousing could be heard from various rooms. Saturday night was probably the big night out here for hijinks and hanky-panky. A block away trucks roared by on Highway 99. How strange it felt to be standing there in the glare of the red neon outlining the roof.

Door 28 opened and Dylan beckoned me to return.

"Sorry about that, Brenda. My plumbing gets a little shy at times."

"No problem. I was hoping for a better offer, but nobody came along."

Dylan laughed and put his arms around me. "You really knock my socks off, baby. Shall we relax on the bed?"

The prospect didn't seem all that relaxing, but I assented. We kicked off our shoes, tugged down the spread, and got horizontal. The mattress encouraged togetherness by sagging in the center. We rolled together, embraced, and kissed.

"Does that dress unzip down the back?"

"It does, but there's too much light."

Dylan reached over and switched off the lamp. Red neon light streamed in through the flimsy curtains.

"Still too much light."

"It's not that bright, baby. And there's not much I can do about it."

"If you were a gentleman, you'd blind yourself right now."

"I would, darlin', but it's hard to play the accordion while reading music by Braille. It's pretty much a two-handed instrument."

Dylan rolled me over and pulled down the zipper of my dress. Next my bra was unsnapped and the top of my dress was gently pulled down over my shoulders. I wondered if this disrobing technique was taught in boys' health class. Suddenly, someone was sucking my bare nipple. That felt rather nice. It might be pleasant to nurse a baby–assuming you could skip the sex with men part. And didn't have to change its poopy diapers. And it wasn't burdened with your suspect DNA.

As Dylan was kicking off his trousers, his phone chirped. He reached over and checked the text on his screen.

"It's up, baby!" he announced.

"Your penis?" I asked, keeping it clinical.

"That and our song on Youtube. I say we watch it later."

I tugged up my dress. "I say we watch it now. Sex can wait."

"Not according to the bulge in my shorts."

I checked out his visible lump. Pretty impressive. Talk about squeezing size 12 items into size 6 places. I gave it a tentative poke. It felt decidedly stiff and tube-like.

"What do you think, baby?" he gasped.

"It's waited 16 years. It can wait another 10 minutes."

Dylan sighed and slunk over to his laptop. He powered it up and signed onto the motel's WiFi. He cruised to Youtube and located the newly loaded video.

"Damn, Brenda! We got 92 hits already!"

"Right. And all from your high school pals."

Dylan clicked on the start arrow and hopped back into bed. We leaned forward for the historic viewing.

Some busty blonde started singing my song.

It was my voice, but the other chick moving her lips.

She was slim and pretty.

Now she was swinging her flaxen locks, shaking her boobs, and pawing some stud.

It was the worst lipsyncing nightmare come true.

"What the fuck!" I exclaimed. "Who's the skinny bitch!!?"

"Uh, Brenda, what's the matter? That's Ryan Sinkay. She's very nice."

"Your goddam fake chick singer has a guy's name!?"

"Yeah, I guess. You don't like the lip-syncing?"

"Why should I!!? Everyone will think it's *her* singing!!!"

"So?"

"So I do the work and she gets the glory!!"

"Well, your song's about a girl and her sleazy boyfriends. So they needed to show a girl singing. But, see, the video mostly shows guys acting like scumbags."

But I'd seen and heard enough. I leaped up and started straightening my clothes.

"What, Brenda? You don't like it?"

"I'm done here, asshole. I suggest you phone Miss Big Tits Ryan and see if she's available for fucking you in some sleazy motel."

"But, Brenda, it was all out of my hands! The video part was entirely the Drama Club's doing. Ryan Sinkay wouldn't go out with me in a million years!"

"Yes. Well, that makes two of us. You will now put on your disgusting pants and take me home."

"But, but, honey, our date!"

"Your date with destiny is done, buddy. Get over it!"

Chapter 21

BY MORNING everyone and his uncle knew about my date fiasco. Mrs. Goldbline may be right; gossip is insidious and hateful. On the other hand, that was the medium through which I discovered how Ruby's coffee date with Zane turned out. The reason that guy was sending out such blurry photos was to obscure the fact that he was barely 14 years old.

Junior was hot to date her, but Ruby told him to back off and grow up. She wasn't dissuaded by his clever card tricks and ability to reel off tongue-twister sentences without moving his lips.

At breakfast The Arcadians watched the infamous video on Marie's iPhone.

"I don't see what the fuss is about," commented Ruby. "The credits at the end clearly state vocals by Brenda Blatt."

"Except everyone will assume the skinny blonde is me," I pointed out.

"So maybe you should feel flattered," she replied.

"She's not that skinny," added Elaine. "I'd kill to have her shape."

"Your video's got 412 hits," said Chloe. "That's quite a lot for being up less than a day."

"It's probably Ryan admiring herself every five minutes," I replied.

"Oh, look," said Marie. "Dylan has added a comment: Attention all viewers! The girl in the video is *not* the actual singer. The vocals are by the talented and charming Brenda Blatt, who also wrote the lyrics."

"How sweet," said Zoey. "He's trying to make amends, Brenda. You have to admit that."

"Too late," I replied. "The damage is done."

"Is he calling you?" asked Chloe.

"I wouldn't know. I switched off my phone."

"Well, at least you don't have to worry about being pregnant," said Zoey, looking on the bright side. "And if your song's a hit, you won't be mobbed by crazed autograph seekers."

As usual, Zoey was missing the point. The reason people write songs, sing in public, and generally show off is because they crave the spotlight. Yes, it's true: I want to be famous.

After breakfast I went back to my room and devoured four Heath bars. One thing was clear to me now: I'd rather stick tasty snacks into my body than Dylan's swollen anatomy. It must have been just curiosity that got me as far as that dreary motel. Sex without love really has no appeal. It seems so tawdry and icky and embarrassing.

Marie came in and gave me a skeptical look. I hope she realizes that the one thing I need most in this world is her unconditional love.

"I talked to Dylan," she announced.

"Oh?"

"He phoned me. He's quite distressed. He said to tell you he asked the Drama Club to reshoot Ryan's scenes with you in her place, but they refused."

"Bastards."

"Well, it seems that Ryan is the president of the club."

"That figures. What a bitch."

"It's not really fair to Dylan to make him suffer like this."

"I'm suffering more than he is."

"If you don't like him, you should tell him so."

"It's complicated. Cole's written some more great tunes. He wants us to write the lyrics. If we do more videos, I'll have to see Dylan."

"All the more reason to tell him you'd like to be friends. He'll understand."

"I do sort of like the big lug."

"Well, you can't string him along forever."

"I know. It's a disaster. Chloe's right. I should stick to puppies."

"You should listen to your heart."

"My heart's a big fat mess. Just like the rest of me."

* * *

As an experiment I switched on my phone. Two minutes later Dylan called. He apologized for everything except the federal deficit and global warming.

"That's OK," I said. "I'm not mad any more. I guess I wasn't ready to be with you last night."

"I understand, baby. I'd be touchy about people doing that to me too. It's a big step."

"Unless I'm mistaken, Dylan, sex doesn't usually involve people doing things like that to guys."

"No. We get a break on that. Well, I liked as much of you as I saw last night."

"You weren't supposed to see anything. That was our agreement."

"You could blindfold me the next time."

"I don't think there's going to be a next time."

"What are you saying?"

"I don't love you, Dylan. I like you a lot, but I don't love you."

"Is there someone else?"

"Uh, I don't know. I'm confused."

"Is it anyone I know?"

"Uh. I'd rather not say."

"If it's Cole, I got to tell you I don't think you're his type."

"And how would you know that?"

"I grew up with him, Brenda. He's like a brother to me. I know what he's thinking before it registers on his brain. He likes 'em light and delicate. I like girls with meat on their bones, not Cole."

"I didn't say it was Cole. There are lots of other guys in this town."

"Fine. Well, I'm still inviting you to my birthday party tomorrow night."

"It's your birthday?"

"Yeah. I'm turning the big 17."

"I'm sorry I've messed up your celebrations."

"Not a problem. How about I pick you up at six? No gifts or cards required."

"Will that girl Ryan be there?"

"No. I specifically did not invite her. How about it?"

"OK, if you really want me."

"I do, Brenda. A lot."

Later I found out that while chatting up Marie, Dylan also invited her to his party. I'm not sure how I feel about that. I love Marie, but I'd prefer that she remain cloistered here at all times like a nun.

I finished out this gala weekend with some clothes washing and ironing. Why are humans born to live such dismal lives? And why, when we're leading lives of quiet desperation, must our clothes be neatly pressed?

Sitting on the vibrating dryer I found myself thinking about Dylan's cotton-sheathed manhood. It was rather intriguing in a repulsive sort of way. I wonder what would have transpired had we opted to postpone viewing the video.

* * *

Good news on the Lumpster front. She's away in S.F. for three days at a workshop for oppressive educators. Everyone seems more cheerful, even the teachers.

Ruby was pissed that she wasn't invited to Dylan's party, apparently overlooking the fact that she had been ditched by Cole for general obnoxiousness.

"It's not fair," she complained. "You dumped Dylan, but you're still invited."

"I didn't dump him. I just said I didn't want to sleep with him."

"Right, Brenda. As if the one thing guys really crave is our friendship."

"You could be friends with Cole if you gave it a shot."

"After he trampled on my emotions? No way. Besides, I have many more Craigslist prospects to meet."

"Let's hope the next dozen are out of junior high."

"That kid Zane tried to feel me up—right there in a public coffee shop. I suspect a testosterone imbalance."

"All 14-year-old boys are horndogs, Ruby. It's a known fact."

Dylan specified no presents, but Marie and I left early for the supermarket to get a card and possibly a gift. Buying birthday cards never bothered me, but now I find it a real chore. Like what card is appropriate for a guy you just left in the lurch on a motel bed? I settled on a card with a cute Pekinese biting into a cupcake, and Marie bought one of those festive mylar balloons.

Dylan screeched into the parking lot a few minutes late. Like most males of our species he did a double-take when he saw Marie. OK, she's stunning. But it's not like Dylan has a chance with her. No way his genes will ever be uniting with hers. Guys should just face reality and get over it.

No kiss this time from Dylan; that was kind of unsettling. I smiled anyway and did the introductions.

"I understand you assisted with the lyrics for 'Riffraff'," said Dylan, trying to sound like an adult.

"I helped a little," replied Marie from the back seat. "But Brenda wrote most of it."

"All the good rhymes were Marie's," I said. "Dylan, it would be a shame to die on your birthday. You can't see the road ahead if your eyes are glued to the rear-view mirror."

"Oh, sorry."

Next time Marie rides out on the hood where Dylan can slobber over her without endangering human life.

There must be money in termites. Dylan's family lived in an imposing (as in grotesque) McMansion on a ritzy cul-de-sac. I found out later they bought it at a foreclosure sale for less than the price of the tiniest condo in San Francisco. When we entered their sprawling family room, about two-dozen partygoers stood up and cheered. I assumed they were clapping for the birthday boy, but it turned out the standing ovation was for me.

Sneaky Dylan had arranged the whole thing. Not only were they applauding, but they were demanding a song. So the boys grabbed their accordions, and we did an impromptu rendition of my one and only non-hit, "Riffraff."

After we finished, they clamored for more. Now I had always considered myself a future TV personality, rather than a singer, so I had no encores prepared. But several years back I had been deeply, deeply enmeshed in Norah Jones. Therefore, carried away by the unexpected acclaim, I made a spontaneous, unrehearsed stab at "Come Away With Me." Probably not in the right key and accompanied very raggedly by two accordions.

The applause at the conclusion was fairly thunderous, but I reminded myself this was suburban Stockton not "American Idol." Still, it was a welcome boost to my famished ego.

Someone handed me a soda and I got introduced to Dylan's friends, all of whose names I immediately forgot. Quite a few of the scumbags from the video were there. The bolder of them congregated around Marie and tried to get noticed by making provocative comments. She held her own like the master she is, chatting pleasantly but giving no one any encouragement. If you want an education in life skills, just stand next to Marie and watch.

I also met Dylan's parents, who were keeping a low profile in the distant living room. His mom was on the petite side, but his dad was your middle-aged big lump. Dylan's gut had a lot of ballooning to do if he was ever to rival his dad in that department. They seemed nice and not obviously appalled by their son's choice in ex-girlfriends.

I thought perhaps Cole was going to ignore me all night, but he walked over as I was stuffing my face with one of Dylan's mom's spicy cabbage rolls.

"Melinda says we just got our 2,000th hit," he announced.

Melinda's name I remembered. She was the goth chick who was boycotting shampoo and dressing from dumpsters. Girls who are naturally deficient in looks (like me) really can't fathom pretty girls who deliberately try to be unattractive. It just doesn't compute.

"That's nice," I chewed.

Cole observed my mastication process with interest.

I swallowed. "I suppose you heard about Saturday night."

Cole blushed in reply.

"What else did Dylan tell you?"

Deeper blushing.

Apparently Dylan had spilled the whole package.

I sighed. "I suppose he told you that I'm stuck on you?"

"That was, uh, sort of implied."

"Well I'm not," I lied. "That was just your pal leaping to conclusions."

"What is it about me that you dislike?" he asked.

Now there was a startling question.

"Not a thing, Cole. But I was given to understand that I'm not your type. For example, I'm considerably larger than Ruby."

"I never particularly liked Ruby. I found her extremely presumptuous."

"Yes, she's known for that. So what is your type?"

"I'm not sure I have one. Is it compulsory?"

"No, but most people have particular traits they find attractive. Now, take Marie over there."

"She's extraordinarily beautiful. And smart too, I think."

"Right. So would you say she was your type?"

Cole gave it some thought. "Probably not."

"Why not?"

"I think I would find her beauty disquieting on a daily basis. And I fear I would feel intimidated by her in bed."

"OK, so we've established that your type is not smart, super-attractive chicks. That narrows the field somewhat."

"Oh, I've thought of one thing, Brenda. I think I'm attracted to musical girls."

"Good. It's always nice to have interests in common. You mean like female accordion players?"

"Probably not. That might get too competitive."

"Singers?"

"Singers might work."

"Quite a few of the great singers are or were on the chunky side: Adele, Aretha, Ella Fitzgerald, Sarah Vaughn, Rosemary Clooney and Liza Minnelli in their non-dieting years. And then there's all those plus-sized sopranos in opera."

"Is Norah Jones big?"

"No, gorgeous Norah is one of the exceptions. She's a bit old for you, but you could send her an email with your photo. You might get lucky."

"I think a sense of humor is also an attractive trait," he smiled.

I worked on the guy relentlessly, but I never nailed down that he liked me. But he didn't give me a definite no either. So I may have some slight cause for hope.

Eventually the cake was carried out all aglow with 17 flaming candles, and I got nominated to sing the song. Dylan made a wish (perhaps involving my pants or more likely Marie's) and blew them all out in one go.

The cake was lemon coconut (one of my faves), and it was all I could do to limit myself to one piece. I did assist Marie in finishing hers, but that doesn't count. Helping a friend not waste food is just being planet-friendly.

Chapter 22

RUMOR HAS it that the Delphians are plotting something. No details yet.

At breakfast I suggested to the assembled Arcadians that we take advantage of the Lumpster's absence. "Madam Treasurer, how much do we have in the kitty?" I asked.

"Five big ones," replied Chloe.

"Good. Then here's a project for you. Tonight I want 30 extra-large pepperoni and mushroom pizzas delivered here at the dinner hour."

Chloe smiled. "That sounds great."

"It's a large order, so you might want to call around to get the best price."

"Will do," she replied.

"Tell them we want the pepperoni arranged on the pies in the shape of an "A." Tell them we insist on that."

"Good idea," said Elaine.

"Can I get mine with pineapple, spinach, and anchovies?" asked Ruby.

"Damn, girl, you're not pregnant are you?" exclaimed Zoey.

"Hardly," said Ruby. "I just like that combination."

"Chloe," I said, "explain to Ruby why I'm vetoing her request."

"Ruby, when The Arcadians are making a grand gesture, we need a compelling uniformity to have the greatest impact."

"Besides," I added. "Nobody would touch that combo except you and possibly me if I were desperate."

"But I don't like pepperoni," she complained.

"Nonsense," I replied, "everyone likes pepperoni, even confirmed vegetarians."

"You could pick it off," suggested Zoey.

"Who made Brenda queen of the world?" Ruby demanded.

"She's president of The Arcadians," Marie reminded her. "We all need to respect that."

"Let's put it to a vote," I said. "All in favor of my proposal?"

The motion carried by an overwhelming margin.

Odd development this afternoon. As we were headed toward Vistas class, Marie suddenly stopped.

"Uh, Brenda, you better go ahead without me," she said, looking distressed.

"What's the matter, Marie?"

"I, I have something I need to do."

"What should I tell Mr. Fulm?"

"Oh, I don't care. He probably won't notice I'm missing."

The absurdity of that statement was proven all too soon.

"Brenda, where's Marie?" he asked, putting me on the spot.

"Uh, she said she had something else to do."

Very stricken look on his face. The guy could barely speak. You could hear a pin drop in that room as 28 female hearts fluttered in commiseration.

"Oh, OK," he said. "Uh, let's make this a study time. Open your books and read chapter 12."

"But, Mr. Fulm," said a girl named Veronica, "we've already read that."

"Then read it again!" he snapped. "And no one leave their seats. I'll be right back."

But he wasn't right back; he was gone the rest of the period.

* * *

No sign of Marie after class, but she showed up as we were waiting for the cafeteria doors to be unlocked for dinner. She still looked unhappy, but she was her usual non-revealing self.

"I'm fine," she said. "I just needed to take a walk."

"Did you talk to Mr. Fulm?" I asked.

"Certainly not."

"Well, he didn't stay in class after he found out you weren't coming," I pointed out.

"He must have had something else to do."

"Yeah, there seems to be a lot of that going around."

"I checked your video," she said, changing the subject. "You're now over 2,800 views."

I wasn't sure whether that was good or bad. To be a hit weren't you supposed to go viral in about 20 minutes?

The pizzas arrived two minutes after the cafeteria doors were opened. Mrs. Castillo of the kitchen staff bustled over to see what was going on.

"Who ordered all these pizzas?" she demanded.

"Don't worry, Mrs. Castillo," I said. "The delivery dude says they've already been paid for. I bet Mrs. Lumpwapht ordered them as a surprise. Perhaps it was a student motivation tactic she learned at her workshop."

"Then take them behind the counter," she ordered. "We'll serve them along with the minced veal and broccoli."

Needless to say, the pizzas were a big hit–although the Delphians appeared to have some difficulty choking down their slices. I went back for thirds and possibly fourths. Quite a few diners smiled at us and waved their thanks. The minced veal and broccoli in a beige sauce proved less popular. Of course, it wasn't really veal; it was U.S. Government surplus turkey scraps. The broccoli appeared genuine, although it was boiled to death as usual.

Later, Cole phoned as I was trying to think of a word that rhymes with emotion besides devotion.

"Hi, Brenda. Any progress on the lyrics?"

"I feel fine, Cole. How are you?"

"That's not what I asked you."

"No, but friends usually begin conversations with some pleasantries before getting down to the nitty gritty."

"OK. And our songs?"

"I've been beavering away every spare minute. I have rough lyrics for the first two tunes you played for me, but I'm waiting for Marie's input."

"Is she working on them?"

305

"No, she seems to be in a state of emotional turmoil at the moment."

"Why?"

"Guy trouble would be my guess. It's a common malady around here."

"Is it over someone she met at Dylan's party?"

"No, Cole, I don't think you made that strong of an impression on her."

"I meant someone else, of course."

"No, it's none of your crowd. You Stockton guys don't even register on her radar. Now me, on the other hand, I'm not so particular."

"I think you should give Dylan another chance, Brenda. He really likes you and he's quite miserable."

"He seemed fine at his party."

"He was putting on a brave front for your sake."

"Dylan may not be my type, Cole."

"I think this type business is bogus, Brenda. I think if Dylan loves you, you should give him another chance."

"OK, your opinion has been registered. Anything else?"

"A deejay on a Modesto radio station might be willing to play our song."

"Really?"

"He's the uncle of a bassoonist I know. I emailed him a link to our video and he replied that he was impressed."

"Wow, Modesto could be our launch pad."

"That's how Elvis started."

"In Modesto?" I asked.

"No, in Memphis. A deejay there played his first little record and all the phone lines lit up."

"Wow, it could happen to us."

"You never know," said Cole. "Fame can strike like lightning."

"Better fame than electrocution," I replied.

It's all perfectly clear now. Considerate Cole is hesitating to ask me out because his best pal Dylan is still stuck on me. Damn, I should have had Marie entice the big lug into a bedroom for an extra-special birthday make-out session. That would have cured Dylan and freed up Cole to make his play for me.

* * *

I'm back to dressing in the restroom. I gave nudity a shot, but it's not for me. I'm way too self-conscious. It's very likely that I'll never have sex with anyone. Nuns seem to get along fine without it, and you don't hear much about them molesting the altar boys (or girls). Too bad I'm not religious. I imagine it's helpful to have some major distraction like Jesus to keep your mind occupied on those lonely Saturday nights.

Marie suggested two rhyme changes for "Rebound Baby" and said "Best Friend Lover" was perfect as written. Hardly the case because when I sing it, the lyrics strike my ear as clunky and lame. I wish she wasn't such a mess. It's very unsettling when the person you look up to as The World's Most Together Girl is suddenly losing it big time. And all over a guy who is Completely Off Limits.

Ruby has selected her next victim. This prospect is named Devin—not to be confused with Devon clotted cream (one of my favorites). He has red hair and freckles, and is alleged to be 19. For some reason he was wearing an eyepatch in his photo. Perhaps he's majoring in piracy at the J.C. He looked kind of portly, but hey I should talk. They are meeting downtown after class today for unspecified refreshments.

I phoned Cole at lunch time and told him I had two songs ready. He didn't sound very enthusiastic.

"What's the matter?" I asked.

"We only got five views since yesterday. Our song may have peaked."

"Well that sucks. Are they playing it on the radio in Modesto?"

"Not yet. The deejay says he has to get permission from the station manager to go off their playlist."

"No wonder nobody listens to radio any more."

"Yeah, I know. It's a dying medium."

"If radio stations had rules like that in Elvis's day, he'd still be driving a truck."

"Well, he'd probably be retired by now. He'd be pretty ancient."

"Are you doing anything tonight, Cole? We could get together and go over my lyrics."

"OK. I could pick you up at 6:30."

"Fine, but don't invite Dylan."

"He's busy anyway. He has a hot date with Ryan."

"Ryan the no-talent lip-syncer?"

"Yeah. She called him up and said she was very disappointed that she hadn't been invited to his party. Next thing he knows, he has a date with her."

So much for being in love with me. I didn't like the sound of that. Not one bit!

Latest Owen/Marie report: Both showed up for Vistas class today. Both were making a MAJOR SHOW of ignoring each other. The tension between them was enough to fry an egg. It all but crackled and smoked with an invisible flame. We're all wondering how much longer this can go on. Meanwhile, the Joads are taking forever to reach California. OK, they didn't have interstate highways back then. But, geez, they're driving a Hudson truck, not traveling in a covered wagon.

* * *

I must have gained weight (from stress?) since my last ride in Cole's shrimpmobile. This time I could barely breathe after we got the seatbelt latched.

"Do you want to go to my house?" he asked. "My parents are there."

"I hate parents. They're so fucking parental. Let's go get some ice cream."

Cole took me to a storefront place in a little plaza that sold donuts by day and ice cream at night. Being adventurous, I had to try their triple donut sundae: three scoops of ice cream (your choice of flavors), three syrups, and three toppings, all cascading over three donuts. It was a revelation. Cole had a single scoop of vanilla—no syrup, no toppings. It was boredom in a dish.

He read over my lyrics as I spooned, slurped, and chewed.

"These are quite good," he said. "But 'Best Friend Lover' is not quite there yet."

"I know. I'm sure Marie could fix it too. I may have to twist her delicate arm."

"Well, do whatever it takes. Gosh, I would get a severe headache if I ate that much sugar."

"Not to worry, Cole. I've built up a tolerance. How's your vanilla?"

"Very good."

"Do you ever order anything more, uh, exotic?"

"No. I like vanilla."

"So where's Dylan going on his hot date?"

"A movie and then Outback Steakhouse. He found another coupon on the Web."

The thought of that slut Ryan feeding her face in "our booth" at O.S. made my blood boil—not from jealousy mind you. I just can't stand a phony like her moving in on a sweet guy like Dylan.

"I hope she chokes on her steak," I muttered.

"Not very likely, Brenda. Ryan's also president of the Vegetarian Club."

I hate those high-school hotshots who pile on the dubious offices and activities to impress college admission committees.

"It's dark outside," I pointed out. "Want to go park somewhere and make out?"

Cole spooned in his melting vanilla and mulled it over. "OK," he replied. "Do you know a private spot?"

"Cole, all teenage boys are supposed to have such places scoped out in advance. It's a hormone thing."

"Oh, I didn't realize that."

"Well, the lane behind our school leading down to the slough is pretty deserted."

"I hope the road is passable, Brenda. I have a low ground clearance."

"No problem, Cole. If we get stuck, I'll get out and push. Or we can pick up your car and lug it back to the street."

"It's not that small," he protested.

My date embarrassed me two ways: He offered me his ice cream to finish. And he went dutch on the check. Over six dollars for my crummy sundae. What a ripoff.

* * *

We bounced and heaved down toward the slough, then parked in the romantic Stockton moonlight.

"I hope my shocks are OK," said Cole, unfastening his seatbelt. "I feel I should warn you right off, Brenda, that I don't have a condom."

"I thought all teenage boys carried a stash of condoms in their wallets. They learn that in the Boy Scouts."

"I wasn't into scouting. I was too busy with my music."

"But you had a condom that night with Ruby."

No reply from my date.

"What? You mean you were doing it bare? Wow, that's rather reckless."

No reply from my date.

"Cole, some conversation is expected on occasions such as this."

"Can you keep a secret, Brenda?"

"Sure. My lips are sealed–all of them as it turns out."

"We were faking it that night. It was Ruby's idea. I'm not sure what that deception was intended to accomplish. I haven't told a living soul– not even Dylan."

Ruby never made it with Cole! What a brazen liar that girl is. And so pathetic too.

"I don't see what's so funny," said Cole, sounding offended.

"I'm not laughing at you, Cole darling. I'm laughing at my friend Ruby. She's really too much."

"I thought so too. That's why I declined to continue our acquaintance."

It was much too chilly to step outside. And even if Cole had brought a condom, intercourse in his car was a virtual impossibility. So we leaned toward each other in the silvery moonlight, twisted uncomfortably in the confining seats, and locked lips.

It was rather nice in a contorted sort of way.

We went on like that for quite a while.

No further intimacies were attempted.

Chapter 23

MARIE CHECKED her iPhone first thing this morning. Only two more views since yesterday. The possibility of our song going viral seems to be fading fast.

"I don't understand it," sighed Marie. "'Riffraff' is a good song and you do such a great job on it. What do people want?"

"Apparently they want Justin Bieber. They want bubble-gum music with boyish haircuts."

We both sighed. Then I reminded her that Cole was demanding she apply her acute intellect to polishing "Best Friend Lover."

"Oh, OK, I'll give it another look. Or you could ask Chloe."

"I'm collaborating with you, Marie. And no one else. Besides, it might help take your mind off Owen."

"I am not fixated on Mr. Fulm, Brenda. He's just a teacher at our school."

Right. And the Vikings just visited England to see the tourist sights and eat fish and chips.

At breakfast Ruby filled us in on her date with Devin the Clotted. He's majoring in communications at the J.C. and hopes to transfer to U.C. Merced next fall. A comedian in training, he aspires someday to have his own late-night talk show like David Letterman or Jimmy Kimmel.

"He's already on TV," said Ruby. "He has a weekly show on the local community access channel where he tells jokes and interviews Stockton celebrities."

"They have celebrities in Stockton?" I asked, shocked.

"Of course. Last week he had on this old retired guy who made a model of the U.S. Capitol out of one million toothpicks. I think it's really rotten that our school is too cheap to spring for a TV."

"What's with the eyepatch?" said Chloe. "Does he have vision problems?"

"Not at all. He just wears that for his publicity photos. He says you got to have a gimmick to stand out from the crowd."

"He looks a little chubby in his photo," I pointed out.

"He's not fat, Brenda," Ruby replied. "He just has big jaws. I told him about your song. He says he may try to work you in some time as a guest on his show."

"Thanks. I hope I can compete with the crush of celebrities who must be clamoring for those prized guest slots."

"It's a very popular show, Brenda. He gets recognized all the time on the street."

"How come you missed dinner last night?" asked Zoey.

"Devin and I really hit it off," said Ruby. "He took me out for dinner."

"Oh? Where'd you go?" I asked.

"The Salvation Army soup kitchen. Devin says homeless people are a great inspiration for his humor."

"Well, don't let him think you're a cheap date," advised Chloe.

I decided to be nice and not reveal to Ruby that I'd found out about her deflowering deception. For her sake, I hope things turn out better this time with Devin.

Kaitlyn and some Delphians tittered as they sauntered by our end of the table.

"What's up with those creeps?" asked Elaine.

"They're cooking up something," said Chloe. "I can tell."

"So the witches are stirring their pot," I commented. "Big deal."

Dylan phoned a few minutes later to rave over "Rebound Baby" and perhaps rub it in about his date with Ryan.

"I'm hot to record it, Brenda. Let's do it on Saturday. We'll stick a camcorder on a tripod and shoot you singing and us playing. That can be our video."

"Are you sure I won't break your camera?"

"You'll be sensational, Brenda. This time the world will see you in all your glory."

I hoped that wasn't sarcasm.

"Speaking of sensational, Dylan, how was your date last night?"

"OK," he yawned. "We got back a little late."

"Why? Did you stop off at the motel?"

"Not this time."

"I thought you said Ryan wouldn't go out with you in a million years."

"I guess I'm hotter than I thought. She was all over me like fleas on a dog."

"Is she after your body?"

"I sincerely hope so. It's time somebody was."

"You're not particular who?"

"Well, my first choice chickened out."

Long silence on the phone.

"What time on Saturday?" I sighed.

"I'll pick you up after lunch. Say 2:00?"

"OK. See you then."

Hard to figure: If I don't care for Dylan, why am I so annoyed he's dating that b- - -h. I've never even met her, yet I feel like strangling her.

* * *

I was dragged out of Undercurrents class this morning and summoned to the Lumpster's office.

"Welcome back, Mrs. Lumpwapht," I said. "How was your workshop?"

"Never mind that, Blatt. What's this I hear about pizzas?"

"Pizzas?"

"Mrs. Castillo tells me you know something about them."

"Not me, Mrs. Lumpwapht. I merely volunteered the opinion that you might have ordered them."

"And why would I do that?"

"As an incentive to excellence. The pepperoni was arranged in the shape of an "A." We thought you were encouraging us to aspire to ever-greater academic heights."

"The day you get all A's, Blatt, is the day I drop dead from shock."

"Thank you for the vote of confidence, Mrs. Lumpwapht."

"Don't mention it. Now get back to class."

Titter torture? Every time I pass a Delphian in the halls, they look at me and titter like hyenas. What's that supposed to mean? I may have to practice my strangling technique on a few of them before I move on to Ryan.

Marie has wrought a vast improvement in "Best Friend Lover." I knew she had it in her if she just applied herself. She worked on our song all through Vistas class–pointedly ignoring Mr. Fulm and his discussion of the Joad family's dignity through rage. We kind of expected him to call on her anyway, but I guess he chickened out.

Perhaps inspired by my make-out session with Cole, I'm back to day-dreaming about sex. It may not be off the table for me after all. I'm thinking I may have to stock up on condoms, since Cole isn't taking the initiative in that department. If we find ourselves nude in a very, very dark place, I hope he's sized more modestly than Dylan. The act is likely to be traumatic enough without struggling to accommodate a jumbo specimen. Though I'm sure that super-slut Ryan could take on Dylan and have room left over for most of the football team.

Further thoughts: It is indisputably true that I have now kissed two boys. This is two more than at times I ever expected to kiss. Neither was vision impaired, so I must be attractive in some respects to males. Granted both of them are teens (hence likely horny in the extreme) and both are accordion players. It could be that I only appeal to a small subset of over-sexed musicians. Still, that's better than nothing. It may be that I'm destined to spend the rest of my life having sex with accordionists, and consequently listening to a great many polkas, schottisches, reels, jigs, etc. If this is what a girl in my looks category has to do to find love, so be it.

* * *

Friday morning. Only one solitary viewer deigned to watch our video in the last 24 hours. Just think: If the Internet had never been invented, I'd have no reason to feel this depressed.

In keeping with my mood, all my classes today were unrelievedly tedious–even Vistas class. Marie absented herself again, and Mr. Fulm was a semi-incoherent mess. Plus, I am thoroughly sick of the Joads and their many problems. I say pick those peas and get on with it. We were all much happier back reading about Elizabeth Bennet and her troublesome boyfriends. As Elizabeth says, "Follies and nonsense, whims and inconsistencies do divert me, I own, and I laugh at them whenever I can." Just try finding any such diversions in *The Grapes of Wrath*.

The Delphian Tittering Plague continues. I am one ragged thread away from committing unimaginable mayhem.

I thought Cole might check in, but no such luck. Effusive he's not. I'm trying not to wonder if Dylan is seeing you know who again tonight. You have to hate those resolutely slim girls who nevertheless get it together to grow large breasts. You'd think that would be a genetic impossibility. They serve no useful biological function except to trigger slobbering by boys.

I am reminding myself not to obsess about that.

Ruby sneaked out for a date with Devin. She is the only Arcadian entertaining a male this evening. I've been rehearsing our two new songs for the recording session tomorrow. "Rebound Baby" and "Best Friend Lover"–they do speak to my predicament.

* * *

Dylan was 15 minutes late in picking me up. I bet Lady Gaga doesn't have to cool her heels in some supermarket lot for a quarter of an hour waiting for her rides.

"Sorry, babe," he said. "I was running down a drummer."

"In the street? Are you rabidly opposed to percussionists?"

"No, I wanted a skin-banger for our session. We need more muscle behind our beat."

"Did you get one?"

"I hope so. We'll see if Jack shows up."

Jack was setting up his drums in the little room when we got there. He looked about 12, but Cole assured me he was 13. I got introduced, but today I wasn't getting more than a casual nod from anyone. So I dragged Cole into the hallway and made him kiss me properly.

"It feels weird kissing a girl in my high school," he remarked.

"After we finish up let's go ball on your principal's desk."

313

Cole looked thoroughly shocked.

"I was just kidding, guy. And how are people supposed to hear me with your baby drummer banging away?"

"I've already discussed that with Dylan. Jack is going to play softly, and Wyatt is going to watch the levels. We want your clever lyrics to be heard."

"Good. So kiss me again."

"Why?"

"Because singers are emotionally needy."

Dylan was fiddling with the camcorder when we returned. "OK, Brenda, we're going to video each take. And then move the camera to a new spot each time. That way we can inter-cut our shots in the final edit. You want to do something with your lips?"

"Like what? Have them waxed?"

"Your lipstick is a bit smeared."

"Oh, sorry."

I retreated to the ladies room to freshen my peachy coral. I also attempted a little emergency hair glamming. What I really needed was something like a giant corsage to conceal my bulk and distract the eye from my face. Or a big hat with a veil. Or better yet a burka like those oppressed chicks wear in Iran.

We got off to a ragged start. It didn't help that Wyatt banged one of those movie slates right in front of my face each time we started on a new take. It took six tries to get a decent version of "Rebound Baby." The last three we did without sheet music for a more "professional look."

We were midway through our fourth stab at "Best Friend Lover" when Ryan Sinkay strolled into the band room. She was even prettier in person. Not in Marie's class, but a "real looker" as my brother would say. She exuded a concentrated bitchassness that registered clear across the room.

"What's she doing here?" I hissed to Dylan, when we finished.

"We're running late. I'll go tell her to wait for me in the car."

"You do that."

Being annoyed apparently improves my singing. Our next take was by far our best of the day. Everyone seemed satisfied, so we decided we were done. While I was waiting for Wyatt to load the MP3s into my phone, I thanked Jack for donating his services.

"Thanks," he replied. "Want to get together some time?"

I was confused. "You mean like for playing music or what?"

"No, like on a date. You, me, and the moon in the sky like a big pizza pie."

He was pretty cute, but I recognized a junior greaseball on the make.

"Call me in about 10 years, dude. I may be down to your age bracket by then."

"I like the way you sing, Brenda. But you should ditch those accordions and get a real band."

"Thanks for the advice. You swing a nice beat, Jack, and you seem to know your way around a drum set."

"That's not all I know my way around," he winked.

More confirmation that my romantic destiny may lie with hormonal musicians.

* * *

Since Dylan the Rat was going off with Ryan the Slut, I invited Cole to ask me out to dinner. He checked the contents of his wallet and offered me a choice of tacos or burgers. I said let's go dutch and chose Chinese.

Cole was all for ordering one dish per person, but I said World Famine could wait and got my minimum five courses.

"Perhaps we should invite a homeless person to join us," he said, when all the food was laid out on the table.

"Sarcasm," I said, digging in. "That's a promising sign."

"Why is it promising?"

"Because it requires a certain subtlety of thought. You can be a bit literal at times, Cole honey."

"I am what I am. I think you should know, Brenda, I'm trying to save up for a new kayak."

"Better you should save up for a nice hotel room. How interested are you in getting laid?"

Cole gave it some thought. "Pretty interested, I guess. But I figured I would be going out with girls for a few years before it happened."

"Here's some news, Cole. It's not 1915. Father isn't lurking behind the parlor door with a shotgun any more. Seduction is way easier these days."

"Well, hotel rooms are out, Brenda. Too expensive and I doubt they'd rent one to us. I could phone you the next time my parents are away. My bed's only a twin size though."

"We'll manage. Or we could always do it in your parents' bed."

Another profound shock rippled across Cole's sweet face.

"I was just kidding, honey. Your bed will be fine. I'm looking forward to it."

"Right. Me too."

"But FYI: I expect and demand total darkness. So you may want to upgrade your drapes."

"How about we do it in my closet?"

"That might work. So why do you suppose Ryan is going out with Dylan?"

"I found out from Dylan about her weird name. Her parents pronounce her name ree-ann, but everyone else calls her Ryan like she's a guy."

"Well, obviously she's not a guy. And why is she chasing Dylan?"

Cole gave it some thought. "Maybe she likes him. He's a decent accordionist."

"Girls like her don't go out with guys like Dylan unless she's got some ulterior motive."

More cogitation by Cole. "He can be amusing. Lots of people laugh it up around Dylan. I think girls like that."

"Normal girls do, Cole. But not girls like Ryan. You know what I think?"

"What?"

"I think Ryan was impressed by our first song. I suspect she thinks 'Riffraff' is going to be a huge mega-hit. So she's glommed onto Dylan in case he turns out to be a Major Celebrity in the pop music world."

"Well, that's one theory."

"So what's wrong with it?"

"You forget, Brenda. Our song stalled on Youtube. It didn't go viral and Dylan's not famous. So why are they still together?"

"Because unlike us, Ryan has faith in our talent. She thinks we're destined for greatness. Dylan's little friend is just a groupie."

"A groupie, huh? Where do I sign up for some of those?"

"Forget it, buddy. You're already taken."

Chapter 24

VERY STRANGE development: Marie is missing.

She didn't sleep here last night and she hasn't turned up for breakfast.

"Hasn't anyone heard from her?" I asked, drowning my Sunday pancakes in fake maple goo.

"Not a peep," said Chloe. "And some of her clothes are missing."

"If she went away for the weekend, why didn't she tell us?" asked Elaine.

"Enough with Marie," said Ruby. "Let me tell you about Devin!"

"That can wait," I replied. "Has anyone tried phoning her?"

"Nobody has her number," said Chloe. "Do you?"

"I don't think so. She was always here, so I had no occasion to call her."

"I bet she's shacked up somewhere with Mr. Fulm," said Zoey.

"Don't be ridiculous," I replied. "She knows that's a certain jail sentence for him. She's way too responsible to give in to some mad crush on a teacher."

"Then where is she?" asked Chloe.

"Well, I for one don't care," sniffed Ruby. "So she went away for the day. What's the big deal?"

"The big deal is we're all supposed to be friends," I said. "We're supposed to look out for each other."

"Oh, really?" said Ruby. "Like you were so concerned when Brick disappeared?"

"Brick was different, Ruby. He told us in advance he was thinking about going south–which is just what he did."

"Should we inform the Matron?" asked Zoey.

"Nah, we'll handle this ourselves," I said. "We'll try to cover for her until she gets back. And, Chloe, how about trying to scrounge up a phone number for her?"

"I'll give it my best shot, Brenda."

I feel a little hurt that Marie didn't care enough to tell us where she was going. Or be here to listen to our two new song recordings. You'd think she'd show more interest, since she's the co-author of the lyrics. I mean we're serious about this song-writing enterprise even if she's not.

Ruby's big news: Devin took her last night to an abandoned Halloween corn maze on some outlying farm. They had "fun" darting among the dried stalks with their flashlights. They never did locate the center, and it took them nearly an hour to find their way back out. Ruby thinks it was a creative idea for a date, but I say the guy sounds cheap, cheap, cheap.

Later: Chloe reported there are no Malencottis listed in Ventura or Oxnard.

"That's weird," I said. "Because her dad is a big-time chef there. And her mother's a hotshot decorator."

"I checked Ojai too," she replied. "No listings anywhere in that area."

"Fuck."

"Shall I break into the Lumpster's office and check her file?"

"Let's wait on that. I'm sure she'll turn up soon."

* * *

Well, one mystery has been solved. We found out what the tittering Delphians have been up to.

Dylan phoned me with the news. Those bastards took some clandestine video shots of me stuffing my face with pizza and posted them on Youtube with the soundtrack from our "Riffraff" video. Their title: "Real

Riffraff Singer Is Real Hungry and Real Fat."

I watched the ugly mess on Zoey's Android phone, then phoned Dylan back.

"Can we sue?" I asked.

"I doubt it, Brenda."

"Can we get Youtube to remove it?"

"Probably, if we wanted to."

"What do you mean if we wanted to? It's a fucking insulting assault."

"It's catching on, Brenda. It's got over 38,000 views already. Cole says there's a big buzz about it on Twitter and Facebook."

"Great. The entire world is laughing at me."

"The world is hearing our song, Brenda. They're hearing you sing. Our version is starting to take off too."

"You mean you're not going to try to remove it?"

"It's not that bad, honey. And it's you on the screen–not Ryan lip-syncing."

"But I'm stuffing my face like a pig!"

"So you're enjoying pizza. Big deal. Who doesn't like pizza? You don't look that bad."

"Oh, I get it. You've been listening to Ryan. She's enjoying my humiliation."

"No such thing, Brenda. Really, it's good publicity for our song."

"Fantastic. You can play it at my funeral after I kill myself."

"You're not seeing the big picture, Brenda. They made that video to hurt you, but actually it's helping you. So the joke's really on them."

"You think?"

"It's true, Brenda. It's so fucking cool. Your enemies may make you famous."

Could be, but I doubt it. I know one thing for sure: Right now my enemies were making me sick. Big time.

I forced myself to watch it again. A smear of grease from the pepperoni glistened on my fat lips. I chewed like a fucking garbage disposal. And how about that glob of cheese dripping from my chin?

"We should have been more alert," I said. "How come nobody noticed them?"

"I saw Kaitlyn playing with her phone," said Zoey. "But she's always doing that."

I took a giant bite. I took a giant bite. I took a giant bite. The video repeated that horrid bite in time with the music.

"Kaitlyn may have sneaked the shots, but I know she doesn't have the smarts to do the editing," I said.

"It was probably Aubrey," said Chloe. "She was always good at stuff like that."

Aubrey was Chloe's former toady, who had rebelled (from neglect?) and gone over to the dark side.

"How soon will this be all over the school?" I asked.

"It's making the rounds now," said Chloe. "It's out there."

"Fuck!"

* * *

Having lost my appetite, I decided to skip lunch. Chloe thought that was a bad idea.

"If you don't come to lunch, Brenda, the Delphians will see it as a victory. You should at least show up—you know, to show the flag. To show you're not upset."

"But I am upset. Big time."

"But we can't let Kaitlyn and her crew know that."

"I'll come to dinner, Chloe. Marie should be back by then, and we can all walk in together. How's that?"

"OK. Want me bring you back something from lunch?"

"Nah, I'm not hungry."

I was hoping Cole would call to offer some comfort, but I didn't hear from him. Mr. Communicator he is not. It's just my luck to be attracted to boys you have to pry the words out of with a crowbar.

I spent a lonely afternoon in my room waiting for Marie to show up, but she didn't return or phone.

Where is that girl?!!

I had some cheese curls and a Heath bar or two, but they didn't ease my anxiety. It was getting dark outside when The Arcadians assembled in my room for the somber march down to dinner.

"Nobody's heard from Marie?" I asked.

"Not a peep," said Zoey.

"I bet she's having an interesting weekend," said Elaine. "I mean, doing whatever she'd doing."

"Yeah," I sighed.

"We need something," said Chloe. "We need something to show we're not defeated. Something to show our defiance."

"Mrs. Tiger Woods," I said.

"What?" asked Ruby.

I walked over to the closet, unburied my golf bag, and hauled it out. "Ladies, choose your club."

"Are we going to whack the Delphians?" asked Zoey.

"Only symbolically," I replied. "Unless they start something."

I distributed an iron to each girl, then selected the driver for myself. I liked the way the weave of the black graphite shaft glistened in the light. This was a club with authority.

We entered the cafeteria with the clubs resting casually on our shoulders. All heads swiveled toward us as we sauntered toward the serving line. We made a point of chatting among ourselves as if we didn't have a care in the world. Like we were five elite golfers strolling into the clubhouse after playing 18 holes.

Kaitlyn attempted a titter, but the other Delphians remained silent. We got our food and I led the way to our regular seats at the end of the first table. Sitting down–as prearranged–we all let our clubs clatter noisily to the floor.

"Darn," I said so all could hear. "I dropped my club."

A wave of laughter rippled across the room.

"So did I," said Chloe. "How clumsy of me."

More laughter.

"We should watch that," said Zoey. "Somebody could get hurt."

We then made a great show of unfolding our paper napkins and placing them delicately on our laps.

"How enchanting," exclaimed Chloe. "Pasta in a clam sauce!"

"Looks delightful!" I gushed. "I understand a prize is awarded to any girl who finds an actual clam."

"Oh, look," said Elaine. "I've discovered a tom-ah-to wedge in my salad!"

"Lucky you!" exclaimed Ruby. "Shall we commence dining?"

"Oh, let us do," said Zoey.

And so, with a show of refined manners that would make even Mrs. Swengard blanch, we commenced eating our Sunday night chow. We held our forks with pinkies elevated and nibbled tiny bites with restrained delicacy.

"I say, this is quite gourmet," commented Chloe.

"Isn't it just so?" I agreed. "Notice how the sand in the sauce suggests the environment of the absent clams."

"I feel like I'm practically at the beach," enthused Zoey.

We carried on like that for the rest of the meal to the delight of (most) of our fellow classmates.

As Kaitlyn and her deadbeat crew were leaving, they paused by our end of the table.

"Hi, Brenda," she said. "Heard from any riffraff lately?"

"Only in the last 30 seconds, Kaitlyn dear. I understand your video's proving very popular."

"It's got over 63,000 views as of two minutes ago."

"Well, I want to thank you for popularizing my song. You girls have been a great help."

Kaitlyn looked a bit confused. "Say what?"

"Yes, our song had stalled, but now it's on a roll again. Thanks to you!"

Her tiny mind scrambled for an appropriate comeback. "Uh, if you say so."

"Well, thanks again," I smiled. "I don't know what we would have done without you."

The Delphians scowled, looked questioningly at their leader, and stumbled away.

"They are in full retreat," observed Chloe. "It's a complete rout."

"So it seems," I said. "I only wish Marie had been here to see it."

Chapter 25

I WAS midway through a 300-word essay on the theme "What Thanksgiving Means to Me," when I was dragged out of class and sent to the Lumpster's office. As usual, she didn't seem very happy to see me.

"Good morning, Mrs. Lumpwapht," I said.

"Is it? Tell me, Blatt, do you have a phone number for Marie Malencotti's parents?"

"Why no. Don't you?"

"The number I have rings some place in Santa Barbara called Bing Bong Burgers. How long has she been gone?"

"Oh? Is she missing?"

"Don't lie to me, Blatt. Matron Beezle reports she hasn't been seen since Saturday. Why I'm the last to find out, I don't know."

"Do you know where she went?" I asked.

The Lumpster sneered and tossed a sheet of paper down on her desk in front of me. I sat down as I read its alarming contents:

> Dear Mrs. Lumpwapht,
>   I regret to inform you I must resign my position effective immediately. I hope the lack of appropriate notice does not inconvenience you unnecessarily. I am leav-

ing in order to marry Ms. Marie Malencotti, formerly a student at your school. As you can see from her driver's license photocopied below she is of legal age to wed.

Naturally, neither Marie nor I will be returning to your school. To be frank, we were not impressed with your school or your educational methods.

Sincerely yours,

Owen G. Fulm

I stared at the copy of Marie's driver's license in disbelief. According to her birth date, she was four years older than me. She's 20, not 16!

"They, they got married," I stammered.

"I doubt that," she replied. "I doubt that very much. No doubt the man is some kind of deviant. And driver's licenses can be faked. I've alerted the police. And now I'm trying to locate her parents. I expect they'll want to sue me. As if I should be held accountable for their failures as parents. And who said you could sit down?"

I stood up. "They love each other, Mrs. Lumpwapht. Everyone could see that."

She snorted. "Love! I very much doubt that!"

I tried to make sense of it all. "But if Marie is 20, why was she going to this school?" I asked.

"I suggest you ask your grandmother, Blatt."

"What?"

"I just checked with my accountant. According to our records, your grandmother paid for Marie's tuition."

Stunned, I sat down again.

"Get up, Blatt!" screamed the headmistress. "And get back to class!"

* * *

I didn't go back to class. I went up to my room and packed a bag. The rest of my stuff I figured could be sent for later. I took a city bus up to Lodi, then hitchhiked out in the direction of Iilivi's farm. The last two or three miles I hoofed it. The road went along the levee most of the way. I was beginning to wonder if I'd taken a wrong turn, when I spotted the big dog's head in the distance.

My brother, Iilivi, and two other men were just finishing lunch when I walked up the steps to his deck. It was chilly for dining outdoors, but I suppose the interior was cramped for big lunch parties.

"Hi, Brenda," said Buford, surprised. "How did you get here?"

"I walked part of the way. Can I stay with you for a few days?"

My brother nodded toward his boss. "Fine with me, but you better ask Iilivi."

"Of course you can stay," said Iilivi. "Can I fix you some lunch?"

"No thanks. I had a couple of candy bars along the way."

Iilivi introduced me to his other two workers, who were named Jaime and Flaco. The latter smiled at me and puffed on his cigarette. He was about my brother's age and was as beautiful as Marie. Very dark eyes, black hair, and a face straight from some ancient Aztec medallion.

Iilivi looked at his watch. "Make yourself at home, Brenda. It's time we were getting back to work."

"OK, thanks," I said. "Hey, Bu', is the trailer unlocked?"

"Sure, Brenda. It's just us out here. The burglars are all working in the city."

My brother is your slob's slob, but the trailer was in better condition than I expected. I found out later that Holly had spent the weekend and did some cleaning. No stains on the floor and no bad smells, so that was a relief. I found an empty drawer and unpacked my stuff. Since my brother had the bed in the back, I'd be bunking on the couch in the front. An accordion door could be folded out to close off the two rooms for privacy.

My phone was ringing steadily, but I didn't answer. I didn't call my grandmother either. The situation was clear. She had hired Marie to be my artificial friend. She must have been paying her plenty to put up with attending that crummy school and hanging out with me. All of Marie's interest in me and vows of affection were phony from day one. She was a total fake and I fell for it. What a fool I've been. She must be having a good laugh now. I wonder if Owen was in on the joke? I'll bet she was off with him during her so-called "long walks." The longest walk she probably took was straight to his bed.

Of course, Marie wasn't 16. I don't know how I ever imagined she was. She didn't look 16 and she didn't act like anyone my age. That must have been what Miss Porteau wanted to discuss. If only we'd had our chat before the Lumpster canned her.

I was stewing over this when Buford walked in and handed me his phone. "Mom wants to talk to you," he said.

"Hi, Mom," I muttered, gritting my teeth and nodding to Buford as he quickly exited.

Mother: Blah, blah, blah.

Daughter: "I'm taking a mental health break, Mother. It's either that or go insane."

Mother: Blah, blah, blah.

Daughter: "No, I'm not pregnant. I haven't even been with a guy."

Mother: Blah, blah, blah.

Daughter: "Yes, I realize you can get pregnant from heavy petting. I have not been within five miles of an erect penis. Is that clear enough for you?"

(OK, not technically true, but motherhood was NOT the issue here.)

Mother: Blah, blah, blah.

Daughter: "I found out about Grandma's little caper with the fake friend. You should tell her to stop sending the checks. Marie flew the coop. She ran off with one of our teachers."

Mother: Blah, blah, blah.

Daughter: "Oh, so you were in on it too. So that's how you were spying on me. I'm glad I got that cleared up."

Mother: Blah, blah, blah.

Daughter: "You were doing it for my own good? That is such a laugh. If I never have another friend in my life, you can blame yourself."

Mother: Blah, blah, blah.

Daughter: "I'm terminating this call, Mother. I'm not going back to that school. You can call them up and tell them that. I'm staying here with Buford for a few days. If you show up here before Friday, I'll throw you in the river."

Mother: Blah, blah, blah.

Daughter: "No, I'm not kidding. Drowning would be too good for you. Don't even think of coming here. Or Daddy either. I don't want to see the lying lot of you."

Mother: Blah, blah, blah.

Daughter: "Good-bye, Mother. I suggest you go wreck someone else's life."

On that note, I hung up.

* * *

My brother knocked off work at 5:30. He took a shower and dressed in the trailer bathroom, then grabbed a beer from the fridge and sprawled on the dinette.

"What are we doing for dinner?" I asked.

"I'm taking my meals at Iilivi's. He's a good cook and he hates eating alone. He says you're invited too."

"OK, that sounds good. Where does the shower water go?"

"Out a hose and down a gopher hole. Iilivi isn't too thrilled with that. So we can't use anything except non-detergent, biodegradable soap."

"I've been using the trailer toilet. Where does that go?"

"Into the holding tank. A guy comes once a week with a honey wagon and pumps it out. But don't go throwing a bunch of tampons in there."

"That won't be an issue."

My brother cocked an eyebrow. "You're not pregnant are you?"

"Why does everyone think that? Mom asked me the same question. I'm not pregnant! I'll let you know when I start fucking my brains out."

"Sorry. It's just you're looking kind of stressed."

"I'm major stressed. It's been a horrible week."

"Sorry. You want a beer?"

"No thanks. I'm not ready for alcoholism–yet. What's happening with your face?"

"It's indentations from the respirator I wear. They go away after a while."

"What does that fellow Flaco do?"

"He's kind of a carpenter, like I'm sort of a fiberglasser. He started last week. He was working for Lonny, but had to move on."

"Why was that?"

"A customer found a cigarette butt in their cake. It was Flaco's brand."

I know the feeling. Lovely Marie turned out to be the cigarette butt in my cake.

Buford sucked down the last of his beer. "Flaco's a good worker, but he only knows about 10 words of English. Jaime does the translating."

"Where does he live?"

"Who?"

"Flaco."

"He rents a room from Jaime in Lodi."

"Is he married?"

"I don't think so. Holly asked me that too. All the girls want to know about Flaco, but nobody asks me about Jaime. Why is that?"

"Well, Jaime doesn't look like an Aztec god."

Another idiot thing I did: being a snobette back in junior high, I signed up for French class instead of Spanish. As if I'll ever have a chance of meeting any cute French guys.

Dinner at Iilivi's was at seven. By then I was starving. A table folded down from a wall and sat three in intimate proximity. The fabulous meal was roast chicken with all the trimmings. Such a change from the swill served up at Ferncliffe Academy.

Iilivi was sympathetic and got me to spill about my life meltdown. I told him about the pizza video and Marie's treachery.

"It's unfortunate about Marie," he said, "I suppose your mother and grandmother meant well. But all those other girls who came here for the picnic–weren't they also your friends?"

"Ah, they just hung around me because I was buddies with Marie. She was always the attraction."

"And how do you know that?"

"I just know it."

"What about that guy you were going out with?" asked Buford. "What's up with him?"

"Oh, he dumped me for a skinny blonde."

Not totally accurate, but close enough.

Dessert was an incredible burnt-sugar cake with mocha-cream frosting. Truly an incentive to live on to taste it again.

"Iilivi, this cake is awesome," I said.

"Lonny brought it on Sunday. It's his latest creation. You don't think it's too sweet?"

"It's mouth ecstasy on wheels."

"He'll be happy to hear that, Brenda. You're one of his favorite people, since you brought us together."

"Well, only indirectly. And finding someone for Brick was all Ruby's idea."

"Isn't Ruby your friend?" he asked.

"Yeah. I guess. I'm sorry she sicced the cops on you."

"Well, her heart was in the right place, if not her judgment."

I assured him I'd be leaving on Friday, since I know I can put a big dent in people's grocery bills. He said I was welcome to stay as long as I liked. I offered to help earn my keep by washing windows or vacuuming, but I noticed that our neat-freak host's floors were spotless and his windows immaculate. He said I was welcome to push a broom in the barn if I felt a need for something to do. He also let me wash the dinner dishes in his tiny kitchen.

"Your house is very cozy," I commented, as I passed him the plates to dry.

"My house is ridiculous," he said. "But it suits my needs for now."

"If we all lived in houses this size, humans would have a much lighter impact on the planet."

"Very true, Brenda. And overpopulation would be kept in check by the increase in domestic shootings."

"You think people would get on each other's nerves?" I asked.

"Well, it hasn't happened yet with Lonny, but he's on the small side. And we're still in that initial glow phase."

"Have you met his parents?"

"Not yet. We're postponing that treat for the Christmas holidays. I'm hoping his father will be less inclined then to reach for his guns."

Chapter 26

THE TRAILER couch was fairly comfortable, but I didn't sleep much last night. Too upset. Beating Buford to the bathroom this morning, I took a shower and washed my hair with his funky, earth-friendly shampoo. And now I can't do a thing with it–or with my life.

Since we were on our own for breakfast, I had a bowl of cereal and ate 14 mini-donuts out of Buford's jumbo package. He blasted an egg in the microwave and ate it with a halved banana between two slices of raisin bread. Buford has always been into oddball breakfasts.

"Can you have Jaime tell Flaco that I'll be waiting for him in the trailer?" I asked.

"Seriously?" said Buford, startled.

"No, I'm just joking. I guess I'll take a walk. I don't suppose I can borrow your car?"

"Brenda, you don't know how to drive."

"I know, but a girl has to learn some way."

"Not with my car. There's some old *Playboys* in the closet if you need something to read."

"Right. Like I want to look at busty babes with their legs spread."

"You can probably borrow a book from Iilivi."

"Are there any little towns nearby?"

"Just Lodi. And it's a long hike."

"That's OK, Buford. I'll just sit here and go quietly insane."

"Suit yourself. Well, I got to go clock in. Have a nice day."

"You too, Bro'. Don't fiberglass yourself to anything."

The battery in my phone died, but I didn't bother to charge it. Who did I want to talk to in this world? No one.

I switched on Buford's laptop and checked the Youtube videos. The pizza gluttony had 544,617 views and Ryan's lip-syncing/boob-shaking had 126,834. In one form or another I was making my mark on the Web. I hoped the pizza video was not as bad as I'd remembered, but it was and then some. I may be off pizza for life.

At least the Indian summer weather was nice. The day was turning out to be warm and sunny. I took a long walk down the road, then got hungry, and walked back. By the clock in the trailer I had been gone for 45 minutes. It was promising to be a long day.

* * *

Today was the day for the truck to come and pump out the tank. I watched as the man connected his hose to the trailer's plumbing valve.

"Do you like your work?" I asked him.

"Sure. Why not?" he replied, a cigarette dangling from his lips.

"You don't mind having to deal with that, uh, material?"

"Not really. Most jobs aren't much different. You're always dealing with someone's shit."

"What do you do with it when your truck is full?"

"Haul it to the sewage plant in Stockton."

"Really? I used to go to a girls school near there."

"Yeah? I know that school. What's it called–Ferndale, Fernwood?"

"Ferncliffe Academy. We used to make fun of the name because the school has no ferns and is near no cliffs."

"Did you like that school?"

I gave it some thought. "In some respects I did, though it's hard to believe."

"Why's that?"

"The owner was a harridan. The teachers were mostly idiots. And the food was the pits."

"What's a harridan?"

"A total and complete bitch."

"Oh, yeah, that can make it bad. Well, I'm done here. You have yourself a sewage-free day, Miss."

"Thanks. I'm trying to."

Lunch was make-your-own-sandwich fixings on the deck. Jaime and Flaco drove off and brought back burritos for themselves. Perhaps they don't like Gringo food. Or perhaps Iilivi wasn't providing lunch for them. It was all speculation on my part, since I have virtually no experience with the World of Work.

Flaco, I noticed, was looking at me with interest. Not maniacally like Gianna, but he seemed to be studying me. Perhaps I was his first exposure to a fat American girl. I didn't dare look his way much because he was so acutely beautiful. I would like to know his story, but having no language in common made that prospect unlikely.

I had another piece of Lonny's heavenly cake. I was ready to marry Lonny–even if he was gay and I would soon weigh 900 pounds. Or Lonny could teach all his baking secrets to Flaco and I could marry him. Every day would be glorious, with only the occasional cigarette butt jolting the palate.

I napped through most of the afternoon, then woke up even sadder. I fought back the tears, but had a semi-monumental cry. I was crying over Marie, because in my heart I still loved her–which is really, really dumb.

* * *

Wednesday morning. I awoke to discover that during the night my life had not been magically repaired. It was still a mess. I'd had a disturbing dream that I was back at my high school in Hayward, and every boy in my class had seen the pizza video and made a pact to torture me about it daily. The scary thing is that's a nightmare that could very well come true.

After breakfast, for something to do, I watched the guys in the barn until the fiberglass fumes drove me out. My brother says he prefers this job to working in the brewery, but everything they were doing looked tedious and boring. As I was leaving, Flaco came out for a cigarette. He smiled and offered me one from his pack.

"No thanks," I said.

"Habla Español? he asked.

"No, sorry. Only English or French."

Fortunately, he didn't call my bluff by launching into fluent French. He shrugged and I shrugged back. He pointed up at the blue sky and smiled.

"Yes, it's a nice day," I agreed.

The weather was so nice I was almost persuaded not to throw myself in the river.

Flaco took a drag on his cigarette and looked me over. "Usted es una chica bonita."

It sounded like he was saying something about a bony chicken, but I didn't see how that applied to me.

"Well, I'm going for a walk," I said. "Don't work too hard."

I waved good-bye as I strolled away. He smiled and waved back.

Today I walked down the road in the other direction. Eventually, I came to a crossroads with a little country store. I went in and perused their abbreviated snacks aisle. I got two packages of mini donuts and eight Heath bars (their entire stash). When I was paying, I asked the Latina clerk if she knew what "chica bonita" meant.

"Yes, that means 'pretty girl'," she replied.

Wow, yet another reason to live.

At 11:30 Iilivi drove off in his vintage station wagon to get take-out Thai food for lunch. He returned nearly an hour later with two bulging bags and Chloe Ptucha.

"Hi, Brenda," she said. "Getting an early start on your Thanksgiving break?"

"Yeah, something like that," I said, giving her an enthusiastic hug.

"Lunch is in 10 minutes," called Iilivi.

"OK," I said.

"Iilivi tells me you're staying with your brother in a trailer," said Chloe. "Can I see it?"

"Sure. You're just in time for the tour."

We walked over to the trailer and I pointed out the first feature of interest. "See these pry marks on the door frame?" I said.

"Burglars?" she asked.

"Not hardly. It's where some firemen had to use a crowbar to get my mother unstuck from the entry."

"You lie."

"No way. It was a real highlight of our last vacation."

We stepped inside and Chloe looked around.

"Wow, this is pretty big," she commented. "And, gee, the bathroom has an actual tub."

"Which no Blatt has ever sat in, since we're all too big. I do take showers in there though."

"It's nice, Brenda. So what's with your phone? Everyone's been trying to call you."

"Uh, I think my battery died. Who's everyone?"

"Me, all The Arcadians, the Matron, the Lumpster, that Dylan fellow, and Marie."

"You heard from Marie?" I asked.

"Sure. She really wants to talk to you."

"Is she married?"

"Yep. All legally. They went to Las Vegas for a quickie. And they also got married."

I smiled at her jest. "Did you hear my grandmother was paying her to be my friend?"

"She told me some arrangements had been made. She wants to talk to you about that."

"Yeah, right. Did you know about it?"

"Me? Certainly not. I kind of doubted she was 16. I knew there was some mystery going on. For a while, I suspected she might be an undercover investigator for the state trying to get the goods on the Lumpster. But that didn't really fit with her falling in love with Mr. Fulm. I think she's sorry she deceived you."

"I doubt that."

"I hope you're coming back, Brenda. We can't lose you and Marie in the same week. That would be too much."

"I don't know. I don't know what I'm doing. I thought I'd stay here until Friday and then decide."

My brother poked his head in through the doorway. "Lunch!"

"Buford, this is Chloe," I said.

They exchanged polite hellos.

"Respirator marks," he added, pointing to his temporarily deformed face.

"Uh, OK," she replied.

My brother hurried off.

Chloe turned to me. "What was that about?"

"Male vanity."

"Oh."

* * *

The Gringos had Thai food on the deck while Jaime and Flaco joined us for enchiladas. Jaime and my brother stole glances at Chloe; Flaco looked mostly at me. Conversation seemed inhibited, but that's often the case when a pretty girl joins the group. Through some miracle, everyone declined to take the last piece of Lonny's fab cake–freeing me to prevent it from going to waste.

"Can you stay the rest of the afternoon?" I asked Chloe as we were helping clear the table.

"I better not, Brenda. I'm risking dishroom duty as it is. So what's the story on Flaco?"

"He's the apprentice carpenter. Cute, huh?"

"More like blazing eye candy. I noticed he was giving you the eye."

"He told me this morning I'm a chica bonita."

"So he's a flirt too. That guy could be dangerous."

"I've decided not to resist if he grabs me."

"No, I don't think I'd put up much of a struggle either. Oh, I almost forgot, Ruby's mad at you."

"What did I do now?"

"Her old boyfriend Cole showed up looking for you. I guess she hadn't quite grasped that you two are now an item."

"I was trying to be discreet about that."

"Well, now she knows and boy is she pissed."

"But she does have Mr. Eyepatch."

"Yes, for what that's worth. Their next scheduled outing is to an art show in the park."

"Devin's quite the big spender."

"That he is not. Oh, I have a message for you from Cole."

"What?"

Chloe cocked an eyebrow and leered. "He said his parents are going to be away next Saturday night."

I stifled a blush. "Oh. OK."

Possibly yet another reason to live. This day was turning out better than I expected.

* * *

After my shower the next morning, I daubed on some peachy coral. I interpreted this as a reassertion of the will to live.

My brother looked up from his shredded wheat mixed with canned crushed pineapple and said, "Wow, lipstick."

"Very observant. Someone ate all your donuts."

"I noticed. That lipstick looks good."

Possibly the first compliment ever from Buford on my appearance.

"Thanks. It was the best of the 5,000 shades we tested."

"I wish Holly would wear a little lipstick. Half the time she looks like she's playing tight end for the Chicago Bears."

Holly was a beefy gal with some lingering butch tendencies from her dabbling in Lesbianism 101.

"Just drag her to Macy's and offer to pick up the tab. This particular brand cost $85."

My brother's jaw dropped, exposing some unsightly cereal processing. "You're kidding!"

"Nope. Fortunately, a friend paid for mine. Well, a former friend."

It was another sunny morning. The trees across the river were wearing their fall colors. Birds were singing, pleasant country smells were wafting along on the mild breeze. Not a bad day for a walk. I was heading toward the road when a ten-year-old Honda Civic bounced along the rutted driveway. I recognized the driver and his passenger. The dusty car slowed to a stop. Marie got out and waved at me. I waved back.

Marriage agreed with her. She was so lovely she hurt your eyes. Mr. Fulm looked semi-radiant as well.

"Hi, Brenda," she said.

"Hi, Marie," I replied, feeling uncomfortable and shy. "Hi, Mr. Fulm."

"Good morning, Brenda," he replied. "You're looking well."

"Yeah, I'm sort of cutting school."

"So are we," he said.

"Brenda, can we have a talk?" asked Marie.

"Well, I was about to take a walk. There's a store a mile or so down the road."

"I could use a walk too. I've been riding in the car for ages. Where's Iilivi?"

"They're all in the barn working."

Marie put her hand on her husband's arm. "Owen, why don't you go introduce yourself to Mr. Ittiwangi? We won't be gone long."

"OK," he said, giving her a parting kiss on the lips.

The two of us headed off toward the road.

"Shouldn't you be on your honeymoon?" I asked.

"We're sort of making one up as we go along. So, Brenda, I think I owe you an explanation. And an apology."

"OK."

Marie said she had planned to start her junior year at U.C. Santa Barbara this fall, but she'd been struggling to pay the fees, which the Regents kept raising. She had resigned herself that she would have to drop out.

"I thought you said your parents were rich?"

"A lie, Brenda dear. One of many, alas. My father's the assistant manager of a burger joint in Santa Barbara. My mother sells recliners and mattresses in a furniture store. So I got a call from a guidance counselor at my old high school. A wealthy woman was looking for someone to mentor her granddaughter. She wanted a recent grad who had been popular in high school."

"So the counselor thought of you."

"I guess. Your grandmother said if I went to school with you for a year, she would pay for my final two years of college."

"And was she paying you as well?"

"No, but she did give me that credit card for expenses."

"So that's why you befriended me?"

"Well, your grandmother made you sound like this social basket case. I mean she painted a very bleak picture. So you can imagine my surprise when I got there, and you turned out to be this bright, lively, and together person. Really, a natural leader and so witty and fun to be with. So my job was easy. I mean all I did was give you a nudge or two."

"Like naming me president of The Arcadians."

"Well, informal sororities can be a good way for girls to meet and form friendships. Don't you think?"

"It worked for us. So you were reporting back to my grandmother?"

"She phoned me occasionally. Of course, I had to brag about you a bit. I kept it all in generalities though. I wasn't telling her everything that was going on."

"And then you fell in love with Mr. Fulm."

"Right. That was the big turn which nobody expected. We tried to keep it a secret."

"Well, you failed miserably. Everybody knew what was going on. Pretty much from day one."

"Really? And we thought we were doing so well hiding it."

"Hardly. Watching you guys was way more entertaining than discussing those boring Joads."

"Oh dear, that's distressing."

"So what are you going to do now, Marie?"

"Oh, it's all up in the air. It looks like we'll be living with my parents in Santa Barbara for the time being. We'll both have to find jobs of some sort. Owen has big college loans to pay back."

"You won't be returning to college?"

"Not for the foreseeable future, no."

"What was your major?"

"Psychology. I'd like to work someday with disturbed children."

"You mean like me?"

"No, dear. Kids with real problems. And you, Brenda, what are you going to do?"

"I don't know. Got any recommendations?"

"I think you should at least finish out the year at Ferncliffe. You've made good friends there, and you should continue with your song-writing and singing."

"Did you hear we're a hit on Youtube?"

"I'm sorry about that awful video that Kaitlyn did. I don't know what's wrong with that girl."

"I think she's jealous that she's not you—as are most of us."

"Well, I'm hardly perfect, Brenda. You can attest to that."

When we reached the little store, I had to restrain myself and buy only one package of mini-donuts. Marie got a cup of coffee and an apple. On the walk back I cleared up some other issues.

"So was Rodney made up too?"

"No, I did have a boyfriend in high school named Rodney. He dumped me for a cheerleader."

"Crazy guy. Did you sleep with him or did you really take a chastity pledge?"

"I slept with him I think three times. You have to recall that when I said that to you, I was trying to act like I was 16."

"Did Mr. Fulm start off thinking you were 16?"

Marie laughed. "He did! Because why else would I be a junior in high school? It scared him to death because he was so attracted to me."

"Right. And he was thinking you were jailbait."

"Exactly. Meanwhile, I didn't know what to do, because I was trying to pass for 16."

"A dilemma. So what happened?"

"We took a walk along the levee and I spilled the beans. He didn't believe me, of course. I had to show him my driver's license."

"He didn't wonder if it was fake?"

"No, I guess he really wanted to believe I was legally kissable."

"What happened that day you both disappeared from class?"

"We were kind of floundering about what to do. I broke up with him briefly. It was ugly."

"And had you been sleeping with him all those weeks?"

"No, we kind of did it the old-fashioned way. We held off until I had a ring on my finger and we were in a motel room in Las Vegas."

"Wasn't that kind of risky? What if you were sexually incompatible?"

"Well, what can I say? We dodged that bullet."

Marie's having fabulous sex with Mr. Fulm. Was I jealous? What Ferncliffe girl wouldn't be?

"What did your parents think of your getting married?" I asked.

"They were kind of shocked. It's been a surprising few months for them. They were amazed when I told them I was starting high school again in Stockton."

"I bet. Most people are glad to get out of high school."

"Oh, I had a good time at mine. It's college that's been a struggle. I gave them only a day's notice, but they managed to make it to our wedding."

"And do they like Mr. Fulm?"

"They do. But then, what's not to like?"

I asked if she was going to take his name.

"No, I think not," she replied.

"That's good. Malencotti is such a pretty name. Fulm sounds like you're clearing your throat."

"I know, Brenda. It's so dreadfully short. You hardly start saying it, when it's all over."

"Well, it's better than my name. Blatt sounds like a fart."

"Oh, I like your name, dear. It's nicely alliterative with Brenda."

"Right," I laughed, "I've got two names from hell."

When we got back, her husband came striding toward us. "Marie, darling, guess what? Your friend Mr. Ittiwangi offered me a job!"

Marie looked doubtful. "What sort of job?"

"Helping him build dog-shaped houses. He suggested we rent a cottage in Rio Vista. That's a scenic small town on the Sacramento River."

"It's a cute town," I commented. "I've been there."

"Sorry, darling," said Marie. "That idea doesn't have much appeal. I think we should stick with our plan and head back to Santa Barbara."

"Santa Barbara's nice too," I commented. "I've been there as well."

"Perhaps you're right," he said. "Come to think of it, I was pretty much all thumbs in my high-school shop class."

"Mr. Fulm, can I ask you a question?" I said.

"Certainly, Brenda."

"Now that you're a civilian, what is your honest opinion of *The Grapes of Wrath*?"

Mr. Fulm scratched his head. "Well, it's not my favorite novel, but Steinbeck certainly deserves a place in the canon. His book is a compelling portrait of its time and a forceful evocation of the economic dislocations of that era."

Once an English teacher always an English teacher.

We got a bit teary-eyed as we said our farewells. Marie gave me a hug and whispered, "Are we friends again, Brenda dear?"

"We're friends forever as far as I'm concerned," I replied.

She tried to give me her iPhone, but I refused.

"You should take it," she insisted. "Your grandmother paid for it."

"You keep it, Marie. Use it to call me sometime."

"That I shall certainly do."

I also got a hug from Mr. Fulm, who–though poor–I feel is just as good a catch as Mr. Darcy.

I waved and watched their car head down the driveway. I watched it all the way until it disappeared around a bend in the road.

Chapter 27

AFTER LUNCH I sat with Flaco on the deck and watched him smoke another cigarette. I wondered if he'd heard that cigarettes are bad for you. I imagined he smoked because he was lonely and far away from home. He was stuck in a foreign land with Gringos who were doing odd things like baking $1700 cakes, building dog-shaped houses, and hanging out in trailers with their brothers. He probably thinks we're all mucho loco.

You hear about people falling in love and marrying with no common language, but I think it would be tough. I mean how much smiling and pointing could you do before you both went insane? For example, Flaco pointed at my face and nodded approvingly. I think that meant he liked my peachy coral. So I smiled and said gracias. End of conversation. Then he got up, flashed me another smile, and went back to work.

I did the dishes in Iilivi's tiny kitchen, then snooped a bit. Up in the dog's head was a small bookcase. Among the books was a musty old hardback edition of *Pride and Prejudice* with this passage underlined: "There are few people whom I really love, and still fewer of whom I think well. The more I see of the world, the more am I dissatisfied with it; and every day confirms my belief of the inconsistency of all human characters, and of the little dependence that can be placed on the appearance of merit or sense."

Somebody was a more observant reader than me. That paragraph didn't register with me when I read the book, but how true it seems now. Finding a friend you can rely on is a rare thing, which is why I feel lucky to know Marie and Chloe. Do you suppose Iilivi marked that passage or some previous reader? I found a pencil and wrote "I agree" in tiny letters on the margin of the page, then returned the book to its place on the shelf.

After dinner, since it was a clear night, we looked at the sky through Iilivi's fancy telescope. Being far away from city lights made all the difference; the coal-black sky was ablaze with stars. I saw the crescent moon up close and the rings of Saturn (my first time for that). We looked for moons around Jupiter, but they had all taken the night off. Then I went to bed and slept like a log.

* * *

Friday dawned another nice day. Deciding that life was worth living after all, I plugged the charger into my phone.

My mother showed up around mid-morning. She had a surprise guest: my grandmother. They arrived in the gleaming black Chrysler Imperial with Manny driving.

"Hello, Brenda," said my grandmother. "How's your diet going?"

"Great, Grandma. I gained four pounds this week. Iilivi and his boyfriend make the most divine cakes."

Grandma frowned. "I don't like the sound of that, Brenda. You should show some restraint."

"I didn't get the gene for that, Grandma."

The big surprise was my mother. She was far from slim, but she had shed some weight. I asked her if she had been sick.

"Not at all, dear. I joined an exercise class and gave up sugar. The pounds are melting away. I've lost eight inches off my waist so far."

First my brother and now my mother. There could be hope for us Blatts after all.

"You've given up chocolate?" I asked, amazed. My mother was to chocolate as the Vikings were to rape.

"Yes, dear, and it's been a daily struggle. But I've found there are sources of pleasure in life other than chocolate."

Right, but is Brad Pitt accepting her calls?

"Good for you, Mom."

"She's setting a sterling example for you, Brenda," said Grandma, rubbing it in.

Grandma needed to go in the trailer to relieve her vintage bladder. Mom followed and had no trouble squeezing through the battle-scarred door. Manny headed off into the prune orchard, probably to locate a tree. Mom made a pot of tea and we three settled into the trailer dinette to thrash out My Future.

"I don't care what you say," I announced. "I'm not going back to that crummy school!"

"But, Brenda, you were doing so well there," said Grandma.

After about 20 minutes of vociferous arm-twisting, I began to show a slight inclination to yield.

"OK, I might consider returning to school, but I have some conditions."

"We're listening," said Grandma.

"That girl you hired to spy on me, I want you to pay for her college like you promised."

"But, Brenda," protested Grandma, "Marie was supposed to stay for the entire school year. And she barely lasted two months!"

"Nevertheless, she helped me a lot. So if you want me to go back to that school, you have to keep your side of the bargain."

"Well, I suppose I could, Brenda. But don't forget it's *your* inheritance I'm spending."

"That's fine by me. And Marie's new husband needs a job. He's a great English teacher. I need you to find him a job with a school district down in your area."

"I'm not a miracle worker, Brenda. Does the man have any qualifications?"

"He's fully certified. I checked with Marie. Isn't it true that you give a lot of money to the schools down there?"

"I am very generous," she admitted. "And I know several members of the Santa Barbara school board socially. I'll see what I can do."

"He needs some sort of job, Grandma. If not with the schools, then something else that pays well. Don't you need a manager for your estate?"

"I do very well managing my affairs myself," she retorted. "I'll interview the fellow and get a feel for his areas of expertise–assuming he has any."

"Good. Then I'm willing to go back to school."

"Fine," said my mother, with a sigh of relief. "How soon can you be ready? We'd like to beat the traffic back to the city."

"Not possible," I replied. "I'm willing to go back to school today, but only in time for dinner. And I need you to sign an excuse for my absence. Otherwise, I'll be stuck with dishroom duty forever."

"But, dear," said Mother. "What will we do all day?"

"We'll take Iilivi, Buford, and the workmen out to lunch. It's the least we can do for all the hospitality I've received. Then I'll show you around the place. It's very nice out here."

"I'm not going near that river!" exclaimed Mom. "You know, Enid, my very own daughter threatened to drown me in the river."

"What do you have to say for yourself, Brenda?" demanded Grandma.

"Desperate times call for desperate measures. Anyway, I was mostly joking."

* * *

We had lunch at a Chinese restaurant in Lodi that Iilivi likes. We sat at a big round table and had the deluxe banquet for eight. For once, Grandma didn't mind dining with the workmen. She spent most of the meal chatting up Flaco with her gardener-grade Spanish. She charged the tab on her elite triple-platinum rich person's credit card.

My mother may have given up sugar, but she was still packing in the other food groups. The two of us got somewhat competitive over the moo goo gai pan. As usual Buford was interrogated over his Life Plans, as if the guy has any. Nor was he willing to clarify whether his relationship with Holly was Progressing Toward Marriage. He did concede that he enjoyed fiberglassing.

After lunch Mom and Grandmother got a tour of Iilivi's little house. Grandma was so impressed, she ordered one for her Montecito estate.

"What on earth, Enid, are you going to do with it? asked Mom.

"I may need a caregiver in 20 or 30 years. They can live in the dog house. How soon can you deliver, Mr. Ittiwangi?"

Iilivi looked stressed. I'm sure that's a question he dreaded, considering his production facilities and crew.

"Probably not before summer next year," he admitted. "But we're giving your order the highest priority."

"Good. And tell Buford I don't want any screw-ups on my fiberglass. And I want it painted like a Boston terrier."

"Yes, I've noted that twice on your order form," Iilivi confirmed. "I usually request a $5,000 deposit."

"No problem," said Grandma, reaching for her checkbook.

Perhaps I'll give up my dream of N.Y.U. and think about applying to U.C. Santa Barbara. I could live in Grandma's dog house and hang out with Marie and Mr. Fulm. He could be a good resource if I decide to major in English.

While I was packing, Mom penned this note:

> Dear Mrs. Lumpwapht:
> Please excuse Brenda for being absent this week. There was a family emergancy and she was required at home.
> Thank you,
> Mrs. Broderick B. Blatt

I like that my mother misspelled "emergency." It shows how much I have to overcome to achieve academic excellence.

I was hoping to have a chance to say good-bye to Flaco before we left, but he was busy in the shop. Perhaps we'll run into each other some day on a deserted Mexican beach. Our eyes will lock and instantly our brief encounter in the past will be recalled. We'll frolic naked in the surf and make love on the beach—even though I've heard that sand can be quite abrasive to one's delicate tissues. More likely he'll be there with his wife, six children, and mother-in-law. He'll have a large gut and a severe cough from all those cigarettes.

* * *

I got dropped off in front of the school a bit past four—safely after my last class had ended. After so many days off, one needs to ease gradually back into academic life. Before I exited the car, I reminded Grandma of her promises to me.

"It will all be taken care of, Brenda," she said. "I rather enjoyed talking to that girl Marie. She seemed very level-headed and sweet. Perhaps I'll wind up adopting her and disinheriting you."

"Don't do anything rash, Grandma. And keep up the good work, Mom."

"I'll try," she replied.

"You might well emulate your mother," said Grandma. "I expect you to be significantly slimmer the next time I see you."

"OK, Grandma. I'll look into getting my butt amputated."

"Such a smart aleck!" she exclaimed. "She doesn't get that from *my* side of the family."

I said good-bye to Manny and exited the car before more damage was done. They drove off and I was back where I started from.

I got a warm welcome in my room from Chloe and Zoey. The latter has taken over Marie's vacated bed. My best friend was gone, but at least I'll have Zoey's impressive rack to look forward to should nudity be on the agenda.

"I think I should warn you," said Chloe, "the Delphians are gloating. Their video has over one million views."

"Oh, I'm beyond caring about that," I lied.

"You have two more videos on Youtube," said Zoey. "Have you seen them?"

So I watched "Rebound Baby" and "Best Friend Lover" on her Android phone. Each had over 200,000 views. There I was warbling away in the flesh. Well, at least I wasn't stuffing my face with cheesy carbs. And Cole and my peachy coral lips looked good. I peered closer at the screen.

"Jesus, Dylan's zipper is down," I said.

"Yeah," said Chloe. "Some people have left comments about his tighty whities."

"You sound great," said Zoey. "I wish I could sing like you."

"Give it a shot, girl," I replied. "I never knew I could until I tried."

At dinner I handed my note to the Lumpster.

"Even if it is an emergency, Blatt, you should check with me before you leave school. You had everyone in a panic."

"Sorry, Mrs. Lumpwapht. It won't happen again."

"See that it doesn't. And see Mr. Ng about the five essays you need to make up."

"OK," I sighed.

Like it would affect the course of world history if I skipped those.

Ruby was giving me the cold shoulder, but I'm used to that. As we were finishing our meager desserts, I suggested it was time for The Arcadians to think about new members.

"We need one to replace Marie and we're behind schedule on adding two new girls. Let's all have our nominations ready by Sunday."

"Can we retroactively blackball members?" asked Ruby.

"No, that's not permitted," I said. "So you're safe."

She gave me a very dark look.

Creepy Kaitlyn crept up creepily. "Brenda, you're back! I thought you had one million reasons to leave for good."

"No, Kaitlyn dear, you must have been thinking of yourself."

After dinner I checked in by phone with Cole. He said he had almost given up hope of ever hearing from me again.

"I was temporarily indisposed, honey. Any news on your end?"

"We're the toast of Modesto."

"Really?"

"My friend's uncle finally got permission to play our song. All the phone lines lit up."

"You're kidding."

"No, it's true. Of course, we had prearranged to have everyone in band class phone in. You can't leave these things to chance."

"No, I suppose not."

"He might play it again if the program director approves."

"Great. First Modesto and then the world. Are we having a date tomorrow night?"

"Do you want to, Brenda?"

"Sure. Let's get this thing over with."

Chapter 28

SATURDAY'S MAIL brought this warm note from Iilivi:

Dear Brenda,
Thank you for brightening our week with your presence. It was a pleasure having you visit and getting to know you better.
Now I owe you thanks both for introducing me to Lonny and for bringing me a cash customer.
My inner oracle informs me that you will soon have a joyous experience.
All the best to you,
Iilivi

I wonder if Iilivi's voice is referring to tonight's scheduled encounter. That would be nice. Frankly, like most girls, I'd settle for not being traumatized for life. Or not having to dial 9-1-1 due to a massive hemorrhage.

For a change Mr. Ng's Expressions class today was not entirely tedious. I had just finished reading my truncated, one-half essay on the meaninglessness of Thanksgiving, when two Stockton cops burst into the room. One of them was Tom, Zoey's crush, to whom they owe all those weeks of cookies.

For some reason I always assume cops are coming for me, but this time they targeted Gianna, dragging her screaming from the room. It turns out she'd been sending nasty notes to the Lumpster, threatening her with such vile acts as poisoning, tampering with her brakes, decapitation via meat cleaver, etc. She had disguised her handwriting, but for added menace had employed a glittering blood-red ink. The Matron conducted a discreet search of the rooms of likely suspects and found a full set of glitter pens in Gianna's desk. In a school full of maladjusted girls, my original roommate proved to be the wackiest nutcase of them all.

Not surprisingly, when I returned to my room I discovered that my things had been searched as well. Perhaps I should feel flattered that the Lumpster put me on her list of suspects. I must have left her with the impression that I'm not entirely harmless.

Lunch proved more pleasant than breakfast because Ruby the Resentful was away ogling art in the park with Devin. We discussed Gianna's arrest and wondered if she was gone for good. Yes, she was loony, but on the other hand our headmistress would be loathe to give up her tuition without a fight. We concluded that she'd probably be back. And how fitting that the culprit should be a Delphian. What a collection of losers.

Zoey regretted that she had missed seeing her cop. "How did he look?" she asked.

"Fine," I replied. "Very, uh, arresting."

"Was Gianna handcuffed to him?"

"Not that I saw."

"I could be his second wife," she speculated. "Cops often have troubled marriages because of the stresses of their job."

"I'll get you your own cop," said Chloe. "When you're older, I'll find you a nice single cop. A cute one."

"Really?" said Zoey, excited. "You promise?"

"Of course," she replied. "I always keep my promises."

I so need to get Chloe to promise to make me rich and famous.

Dylan phoned later as I was attempting to glam my hair without the benefit of Marie's hot rollers.

"Hey, Brenda, Cole tells me you're back at school."

"Yeah, I tried to break jail, but I got nailed by the FBI."

"Did you see our new videos?"

"I did. I noticed you were even flashier than usual."

"What can I say? I was checking the camera, the mikes, the music, the drummer, the sound levels, and all that stuff. But I forgot to check my fly. We considered reshooting everything, but you'd disappeared off the planet."

"I was taking a mental health break. Speaking of mental problems, how's your romance with Ryan going?"

"It's progressing. How are you and Cole doing?"

"Very well, thank you."

"Have you been reading the comments on Youtube?"

"I never read those."

"Why not? You've been getting some terrific raves."

"That's nice. But if 99 people said I was the greatest singer since Celine Dion, and one jerk said I was a fat, no-talent slob, I'd totally obsess over the negative comment."

"That's silly, Brenda. You know the Internet is full of creeps who like to put people down."

"I know. So I just avoid everyone's opinions. It works for me."

"I wish I worked for you, Brenda."

"We've been over this already, Dylan."

"Right. Well, I'll talk to you soon."

"OK. Thanks for checking in."

* * *

I was waiting in the supermarket parking lot when Cole drove up in his putt-putt car. Freshly purchased and stashed in my purse were six Heath bars and three condoms. I knew I could eat the six candy bars, but I wasn't so sure Cole could get it up three times. Nor was I positive I'd want him to. But three was the minimum number you could buy. No wonder sexual promiscuity was on the rise.

Like Dylan before him, Cole had gone in heavily on the cologne. Boys must assume there's a direct connection between the female nose and the muscles of her thighs. Perhaps they learn that in health class.

"What's that scent?" I asked, after I'd been buckled flat against the seat back like a frog in a dissection dish.

"Urban Guerilla," he replied. "I borrowed a splash from my brother."

"Oh? I thought perhaps you'd washed your car in it."

"Is it too strong, Brenda?"

"I'm coping. Where's your family this evening?"

"My parents are at an Elks lodge dance; my brother's spending the night at his girlfriend's."

"How old is your brother?"

"Nearly 20."

"Is he cute like you?"

"The girls seem to like him. He's kind of a frivolous person."

"Not musical?"

"Not much of anything, if you ask me. He likes cars and girls. Period."

"In that case, he probably wouldn't approve of your car or your date."

"I don't care what he thinks. I never have."

Cole wasn't much into decorating his bedroom. It was small and cramped. The furniture was Early American maple, the walls were largely bare. The only eye-worthy object in the room (besides me) was his gleaming accordion.

"Cole, your room lacks personality," I pointed out.

"Does it?" he replied. "I hadn't noticed."

Cole switched off the lamps, achieving a modicum of darkness. Not like London during the Blitz, but fairly dim. Lonely Myron (Cole's small horny dog) whimpered in the kitchen, where I insisted he be confined. I didn't need two males going at me simultaneously.

Cole's narrow bed would have crowded a monk. Nevertheless, we lay down on it and embraced. Our lips met and osculation commenced. It was, uh, it was . . . less than thrilling. Somehow in my arms he seemed a bit . . . well, unsubstantial. I broke off the kiss.

"Cole, honey, how committed are you to this enterprise?"

"I have an erection, if that's what you're wondering."

"Uh, I'm thinking this might be a mistake."

"Am I doing something wrong? Is it time for foreplay? I thought that happened after we stripped."

"No, you're doing everything fine. Couldn't be better. But I'm thinking now you may not be the, uh, right guy for me."

"What do you mean?"

"Would you mind terribly if I changed my mind?"

"About what?"

My date appeared to be as dim as the lighting. I decided to spell it out. "About having sex with you this evening right now here in this bed."

"Oh. Well, uh, no, I suppose not."

We disentangled and sat up on his bed.

"Cole, do you know where Dylan is tonight?"

"Believe me, Brenda, you don't want to know."

"No, I really do. Please tell me."

"All right, if you insist. He's at the Starlite Valley Motel with Ryan."

"Oh."

I was kind of afraid of that.

"Cole, is this their first trip or a repeat visit?"

"It's his first time there with Ryan. We were scheduled to make simultaneous history tonight. But I guess not in my case now."

"Cole, can I borrow your phone?"

"You're not going to call Dylan are you?"

"I thought I'd give it a shot. It's still fairly early."

"Why don't you use your phone?"

"He might not pick up if he knows I'm calling."

"You could text him."

"No, I want to speak with him in person."

"Oh, all right. He's on speed dial."

Cole pressed a couple of keys and handed me his phone. After two rings Dylan answered, sounding busy.

"Yes!"

"Hi, Dylan, it's Brenda."

"Hi, Brenda. What's up?"

"I'm here with Cole. What's up with you?"

"Not much."

"Where are you?"

"Oh, here and there."

"Are you at the motel with Ryan?"

"Yes, actually I am."

"Could I ask you a personal question?"

"OK."

"Have you done it yet?"

"Uh, what are you–phoning up for the play by play? No, we haven't done it yet. But we're about to."

"Where's Ryan?"

"She's in the bathroom freshening up."

"Are you on the bed?"

"That is pretty much the case."

"Is it room 28?"

"No, we're in 26 this time. It smells a little better, but the TV is smaller."

"Dylan, I made a terrible mistake. It turns out I do love you."

"Is this a joke?"

"No. I can see why you might think so. I thought I loved Cole, but it was only an infatuation. I just realized I love you. Quite a bit, in fact."

"Jesus, Brenda, that's great news. And I love you–more than ever. But you've left me in sort of an embarrassing situation."

"I know. I'm sorry for that. I just want you to know that if you have to go through with it, I won't understand. It will be totally over between us. I'm really lousy at sharing."

"So did you do it with Cole? Are you calling me because you were disappointed by his performance? Is that why you've seen the light?"

"Not at all, Dylan. We didn't do it. I couldn't go through with it."

"Fantastic, Brenda. You've made me very happy. Then I guess I'll call it quits here too."

"How far along were you? Are your pants off?"

"Yeah, but that's nothing new. I guess I'll make up some kind of excuse. I'll tell Ryan I'm impotent."

"How likely is she to believe that?"

"Not very likely at the moment, but I'll try concentrating on something boring. I'll think about Brahms' *German Requiem*. I hope she hasn't removed any more garments in the bathroom. Her amazingly sexy bra was dangling by one strap."

That was more information than I really wanted.

"I'm truly sorry I turned you down the first time, Dylan. I hope all this getting interrupted isn't too traumatic for you."

"Well, let's hope the next time is the charm. Oops, I just heard the toilet flush. I better go now, honey."

"I'm glad I caught you in time. Have a pleasant evening, Dylan. But not too pleasant."

"Yeah, you too. And give my regards to Cole. And tell him to lay off my girl."

"Will do, darling. Talk to you soon."

"Bye."

Beaming radiantly, I handed the phone back to Cole.

"That was the most ridiculous conversation I ever heard," he commented.

"A gentleman wouldn't have listened," I pointed out.

"Gee, Brenda, I hope Dylan thinks of a better excuse. I wouldn't want it to get around school that he has erection problems. If you can't get it up for Ryan, who can you get it up for?"

I didn't like the tone of that comment.

"Is Ryan likely to blab?" I asked.

"You tell me, Brenda. I find girls extraordinarily unpredictable."

"I'm sorry you've been left in the lurch, Cole. You're very attractive, and I'm sure lots of girls will want to go out with you."

"There is this girl Emily in my geometry class. I just found out she's really into kayaking."

"Good. You should ask her out."

"Really?"

"Why not? You've had lots of practice with me and Ruby."

"That's true. OK, maybe I'll do that. Well, sex is off the agenda. What should we do now?"

"What else? Let's go eat."

Made in the USA
Lexington, KY
22 December 2014